THE
THIRD
INSTINCT

THE
THIRD
INSTINCT

KENT LESTER

TOR PUBLISHING GROUP

NEW YORK

THE THIRD INSTINCT

A Forge Book
Published by Tom Doherty Associates/Tor Publishing Group
120 Broadway
New York, NY 10271

www.tor-forge.com

Forge® is a registered trademark of Macmillan Publishing Group, LLC.

Library of Congress Cataloging-in-Publication Data

Names: Lester, Kent, 1953- author.
Title: The third instinct : a Dan Clifford novel / Kent Lester.
Description: First Edition. | New York : Forge, 2022. | Series: Dan Clifford; 2 |
"A Tom Doherty Associates Book." | Identifiers: LCCN 2022034356 (print) |
LCCN 2022034357 (ebook) | ISBN 9780765382245 (hardcover) |
ISBN 9781466886582 (ebook)
Subjects: LCGFT: Novels.
Classification: LCC PS3612.E8196 T45 2022 (print) |
LCC PS3612.E8196 (ebook) | DDC 813/.6—dc23/eng/20220722
LC record available at https://lccn.loc.gov/2022034356
LC ebook record available at https://lccn.loc.gov/2022034357

Our books may be purchased in bulk for promotional, educational, or business use.
Please contact your local bookseller or the Macmillan Corporate and Premium Sales
Department at 1-800-221-7945, extension 5442, or by email at
MacmillanSpecialMarkets@macmillan.com.

First Edition: 2022

Printed in the United States of America

0 9 8 7 6 5 4 3 2 1

The Third Instinct is dedicated to the memory of Arnold Lester—
Air Force veteran, member of the greatest generation, and
beloved father, whose endless tales of flying adventures
helped to inspire this story.

THE
THIRD
INSTINCT

1

FROM HIS VANTAGE point behind a hedgerow of azaleas, Victor Moody peered out across a large expanse of freshly mowed lawn, the dew shimmering on the grass in the moonlight. The security door was on the side of the building standing silent and exposed, bathed in a pool of light, its security pad beckoning him forward like an actor to a stage.

Victor struggled to focus, the incessant drone of crickets roaring in his ears, driving him mad. He was still coming down from his last five Xanax, the dullness receding into the background as a fresh surge of adrenaline crawled its way up the base of his spine toward his brain like an insect skittering over raw synapses.

He jerked spasmodically, neurons firing in a rush.

Breaking out of the Xanax haze left him raw and jittery but his mind needed to be perfectly alert, hyperaware for this next task. His muscles seized again and he rubbed his shoulders for relief, noting the crisp sound of his Tyvek jumpsuit sliding against bare skin. The crickets grew louder, threatening to shatter his control, barely balancing on a knife's edge.

The quicker this ended, the sooner he could seek relief in a bottle of pills. Victor struggled to stop the trembling of his fingers, studying the smooth flesh of the featureless digits. No fake nails today, no danger of leaving behind an errant forensic clue. He rubbed his hands together vigorously, struggling to coax the circulation back into them. After another quick scan of the area, he unzipped the overalls and slipped out, naked save for a thin jockstrap. Then, padding silently across the lawn, he reached the door, taking care to avoid both security cameras along the way.

He hesitated. It took several glances at the numbers scrawled across the back of his hand to get the security code right but his efforts were soon rewarded by a satisfying click. Entering quickly, he left the door slightly ajar and the alarm system off. Inside the high-tech building, security cameras scanned the interior in a slow predictable pattern, which he had memorized. He counted out the cadence, waiting for the nearest camera to reach its zenith.

Then, Victor Moody began a long and graceful dance down the hallway, pausing, leaping, and scurrying with purpose at precisely timed intervals. His senses were hyperaware, his eyes dilated to the point where every shadow seemed vibrant and liquid.

He knelt at one intersection, counted out the cadence, turned right, and raced down the hall, past another intersection, then knelt for a brief moment. One final lunge placed him at the second security door.

The camera behind him began its lazy pirouette back in his direction. There was only time to punch in three numbers before leaping back against the opposite wall for another three seconds, then forward again for the final three numbers.

Another satisfying click echoed through his skull.

He slipped inside the inner sanctum, taped the door latch flush, and eased the door shut. He knew from previous visits that there were no cameras in this high-security area—too much to hide. Comfortable for the first time, Victor moved boldly and quickly. It took only a few minutes to find the precious vial.

A sudden spasm dislodged the glass container from his hand and he watched as it tumbled end over end in slow motion toward the floor. A movement quicker than his mind could register found his hand underneath the vial, an inch from the floor.

Victor sighed heavily and struggled to calm himself. He could not risk another unexpected spasm, so he wrapped the cold vial in gauze and stuffed it into his jockstrap. Even with the insulation, it was like walking around with a chunk of dry ice in his groin. Wasting no time, he returned to the laboratory door and counted the cadence.

The dance began again.

FIVE MINUTES LATER, he reached the exterior and raced across the damp grass to the bushes, heart pounding against his chest, nerves screaming under his skin, as if they would explode from his pores at any moment.

Once behind the cover of azaleas, Victor placed the sample, still icy cold, into a vacuum bottle, slipped back into his overalls, and raced back to his car, a scant flush of relief soothing his ragged nerves.

Once in the car, he greedily gulped down five Xanax and tried to catch his breath. He'd made it through the gauntlet of cameras. There would be no trace, no DNA, no fibers, no body hair.

No fingerprints.

A perfect heist, by a ghost.

It better pay off, he vowed to himself.

Cranking the car, Victor Moody backed out from behind the hedgerow and sped off into the languid Savannah night.

2

How DOES ONE relaunch a career that you destroyed while becoming an infamous national hero? How do you deal with a discovery that your new girlfriend is an adrenaline junkie with a death wish? Well, you *could* empty your 401(k) to finance a risky new startup, stubbornly refuse to leave your overpriced penthouse in the heart of downtown Atlanta, and propose to said adrenaline-fueled lover.

What could possibly go wrong?

Dan Clifford wasn't sure but he was smack in the middle of finding out. It seemed a viable plan at the time, only slightly insane. Besides, his only alternative would be to roll up into a ball and surrender to fate and he *hated* fate, much preferring the well-calculated odds of a long shot.

And so far, his insane plan seemed to be working. Dan's fledgling startup, SurMyz Consulting Group, had already garnered several consulting jobs with the FBI, thanks to his connections there. SurMyz specialized in the art of predicting the seemingly unpredictable, like future burglary targets in midtown Atlanta or likely embezzlement opportunities in state government, juicy targets for ambitious young special agents at the Federal Bureau of Investigation. A little data and a neural net processing server could go a long way.

As for the next phase of his plan? Dan hadn't a clue.

For all his training in prediction science, his ability to decipher the whims of Rachel Sullivan seemed hopelessly inadequate. Her firebrand personality required a light touch and her passions could change on a whim. Their relationship had hit the doldrums lately and Dan wanted to make a bold move, something to force Rachel out of her comfort zone. Otherwise, nothing would ever change or grow.

It was a risky strategy. It might drive Rachel away for good. She had a habit of disappearing on sojourns to "find herself" whenever their relationship heated up.

Dan had barely slept through the night, worrying about his next move. He stared at her dozing form sprawled across the sheets, her ginger hair framing an angelic face in the dim light. The first rays of dawn were creeping across the bed, gently curving their way around her breast, hips, and thighs, her chest rising and falling in a long steady rhythm, like a pendulum marking the measure of their brief time together.

Only an arm's length away, Rachel was pure and accessible in the moment, yet agonizingly out of reach, an enigma. She doled out intimacy in stingy doses, just enough to tease him with the promise of a future but lacking commitment.

He knew why. Rachel had spent much of her adult life with a genetic curse hanging over her future. Nature was cruel, damning her with a fifty-fifty shot at happiness, or misery. Her habit was to live for the *now*. To even consider a life with another person had become a verboten subject.

But she was still here, tangled in the sheets, with even odds at a future she refused to grasp. So he wanted to roll the dice, confront her head-on with the ultimate choice. It was a brash move that could shake things up or blow them apart.

The thought made him giddy and nervous, like a boy breathlessly sharing his first valentine.

As if reading his mind, Rachel sighed ruefully and moved toward him, planting a light kiss on his lips.

"Sleep well?"

"*Great* . . . you?" he lied.

Rachel yawned, stretched, pressed her breasts against his bare chest. "I slept pretty well but you were tossing and turning."

"My mind was active, I guess. SurMyz is reaching a critical juncture. Our existing contracts are running out and we'll need new ones soon—Hey, listen, I was thinking. How about dinner out tonight? I know a new place in midtown, great beer, good food, intimate."

"What?" She wrinkled her brow. "You don't like my Italian cooking anymore?"

"It's not the food." He laughed. "It's the cleanup. Are you Italian women all so messy?"

"Hey! That's sexist *and* racist. Besides, it's *Irish*-Italian," she corrected him with a playful poke at his ribs. "That means you get great food *and* wild times."

"Fine, let's give your wild cooking a break and relax in a nice romantic venue for a change. I need a break from work anyway, and you know I'll be there late tonight if I don't have an excuse—"

Bam, bam, bam!

The front door to the condo rattled on its hinges.

"Damn!" Rachel pulled the sheets over her head. "Is there something you haven't told me? Who's trying to break in—"

"Not a clue," Dan said. He jumped out of bed, staggered to the closet, fumbled for a seldom-used bathrobe.

Bam, bam, bam!

"Dan Clifford!" came a shout from the other side of the door.

He didn't like the sound of it, the authoritative bluster. "Hold on—coming!" he yelled, fumbling with the bathrobe.

At the front door, Dan intercepted his pet robot, Rover, and turned it off before it could answer the door. Judging from the tone of the voices outside, they would not appreciate the humor of a one-armed robot with a baseball hat greeting them. Dan collected himself and opened the door. He recognized the two men staring back at him intensely.

"Dan Clifford?"

"Of course." He registered his irritation. "Do you know what time it is?"

"FBI," the taller one said in a classic tone, as if they were perfect strangers. He flipped open his ID and brandished it. "You're wanted by Vince Peretti at FBI Headquarters, *now.*"

The man's emphasis on the word "now" actually relieved him. Vince was his contact at the Bureau for the SurMyz Consulting contracts, and urgency usually meant opportunity and a new contract, with higher fees.

During his work at the Bureau, Dan had learned that most FBI "special agents" had two distinct personalities, depending on the circumstances. In an informal setting, they came across as irreverent frat boys regardless of gender. You could tell they loved their jobs like a video gamer loves the thrill of the chase—lots of black humor and enthusiasm for the "game" of collaring the bad guys.

But when facing the public or "perps," special agents would transform into "all business" mode, adopting their official personas whenever the gravity of the situation demanded it.

Judging from the agents' demeanor, the gravity was high.

TEN MINUTES LATER, Dan was in the back seat of an agency car heading toward the FBI field office at a high rate of speed. The two special agents sat sternly in the front seat, staring out the front windshield with no acknowledgment of his presence.

He was missing his perfunctory two cups of morning coffee, surprised by the sudden visit, confused by the gruff attitude of the agents. It made him grumpy. They'd interrupted his big plans for a special evening with Rachel: lots of atmosphere, a quiet corner booth, and a diamond burning a hole in his pocket.

Agents in the FBI must all consider themselves "special," since every one of them bore that designation. No junior title, no ladder to climb for elite status, no just "agents." *Probably a contrived attempt to bolster the Bureau's image,* Dan thought. Why talk to an agent of the law when you can meet a "*special* agent of the FBI." The Bureau had always been image conscious.

His friend Vince Peretti had explained it this way: "When questioning a witness, you must establish trust and a willingness to talk. That goes more smoothly when the witness likes and trusts you."

That is, unless you were the "perp."

Then you became familiar with another alternate FBI personality: somber, businesslike, efficient, flat-faced, with about as much humor as an undertaker. Dan had been a perp before and it wasn't fun.

What the hell was going on?

Dan was reading "perp" all over the demeanor of his hosts and that worried him. It wouldn't be his first time in the back seat of a government-issue sedan, sweating. He remembered his agonizing ride to a congressional hearing in D.C., arrested by his friend Vince. He'd seen the business side of Vince's persona and he didn't like it one bit.

It had seemed like ages since he had taken part in a top-secret mission to intercept a bizarre organism emerging in Honduras. Stopped before it could spread, the dangers posed by the outbreak had been dire enough to earn the mission a top-secret classification. No one would ever know how close the world had come to a devastating fate.

But the public had a very short attention span. The events leading up to that near tragedy were soon forgotten when the Covid-19 pandemic took center stage. The pandemic had certainly been bad enough but would have paled in comparison to the devastation he and Rachel had prevented, an accomplishment he would never be allowed to discuss in public.

That left it to his hacking exploits to brand him with an infamous reputation. But then, everybody loves a maverick.

Dan had released a computer virus on national television, making him a news celebrity, a vigilante hacker, loved by nerds and hated by officials. If not for a presidential pardon for his illegal activities, he'd be rotting in some jail for cyberterrorism.

The act certainly hadn't helped him land a new job. Dan had struggled financially through the coronavirus pandemic just like everyone else. The conspiracy he had exposed led to the financial collapse of his former employer, NeuroSys, and he'd been unemployed ever since. Nobody wanted to touch a former hacker who had betrayed his own employer, regardless of the justification. He had little choice but to fund his own startup.

Since then, Dan Clifford had been squeaky clean, a virtual saint, a straight arrow . . . at least he thought so. This current situation had to be concerned with his SurMyz contract. What else could it be?

Dan had built SurMyz on the ashes of NeuroSys and GAPS, which he had invented while working there: a program designed to predict major climatic and geological events. Along with his prodigy programmer, Rudi Plimpton, Dan had cobbled together a neural network built from old NeuroSys servers left behind after the company assets had been sold off to a mysterious Latin American venture capitalist firm.

GAPS, the Global Assessment and Prediction System, had always been Dan's creation, so he felt no guilt in reusing much of its original code for his own company. NeuroSys may have stolen his job but not his skills.

While the "new" NeuroSys owned the patents to Dan's original GAPS program, they didn't control the real secret behind its success: Rudi Plimpton's genius. The forty-something programmer was a prodigy at designing deep-learning software. Rudi had been programming since childhood, trained during the infancy of the computer age. Computer language had probably altered the structure of

Rudi's brain about as much as Rudi had altered the computers themselves. And now, Rudi's programming skills had given SurMyz Consulting the reputation as a cutting-edge predictive consulting service.

Which was a good thing.

SurMyz paid the bills, which had become substantial, in part due
to his stubborn insistence on keeping his penthouse condo. The view
of the Atlanta skyline from there was just too perfect.

THE FBI FIELD office was located in the suburbs of Chamblee, not far
from Dan's condo in midtown Atlanta, so the trip there took only a
few minutes. He barely had enough time to gather his thoughts before
the car rolled to a stop in front of the gray concrete and brick building,
its only distinctive architectural feature being a row of four massive
columns that framed the front entrance.

The special agent in the passenger seat got out of the car, opened
the rear door, and gestured Dan toward the door. Inside, the security
check went quickly, due to his clearance level as a consultant. The two
special agents checked his pass one last time, then wordlessly led him
toward the elevator. A short ride later, the doors opened at the fourth
floor, where he was ushered down the right corridor toward one of the
building's many nondescript conference rooms.

Only, this room was anything but nondescript. Quite unlike the
typical "government-gray" rooms Dan was accustomed to on his prior
visits, this one was circular and dark, the walls lined with mahogany
paneling. It had the effect of drawing Dan's attention to the large oval
conference table commanding the center. Tall black leather recliners,
mostly occupied, were drawn closely around the table.

Vince Peretti was seated at the head of the oval, his dark hair
combed immaculately, his square Italian chin giving him a stately,
presidential look. That, along with his recent promotion to director
of Cyberterrorism for the Atlanta branch, gave Dan a clue about the
nature of the meeting. He felt a surge of relief, seeing his friend in a
position of influence. Most of the attendees were unfamiliar, except
for one glaring exception: Mark Odom, an epidemiologist from the
CDC.

What was he doing here?

Vince directed him toward an empty chair next to his own. "Glad
you could make it on short notice."

"Did I have a choice?" Dan fiddled with the executive chair, struggling to pull it close to the conference table as a ring of faces stared at him impatiently.

"Not really." Vince smiled weakly, barely glancing up from a stack of papers he was shuffling absently.

Once settled at the round table, Dan felt more like a peer but the demeanor in the room still projected "perp." No irreverent banter or casual conversation so typical of a classic FBI meeting; just grim faces and stale air. A couple of people at the table coughed gently behind cloth masks, remnants of the "Covid habit." Ever since the pandemic, the public's perception of style had changed. Masks had become habitual attire in many circles but a political statement in others, for reasons that made no sense to him.

Vince's shuffling stopped and he settled on a thin blue folder, spreading it open on the table. "I appreciate everyone's attendance at this hastily assembled joint task force. Dan, you're the last to join, so a few introductions. I believe you know Mark Odom, from the Centers for Disease Control and Prevention. You two were involved in the incident a few years back, I believe."

Odom responded with a curt nod. Dan remembered the tall, lanky Aussie as having a playful wit but today his expression was gray and sullen.

Vince continued around the table, reintroducing a couple of special agents Dan knew from the SurMyz contract and stopping at two young agents. "I don't believe you've met Special Agents Adam Pruitt and Lynn Holcomb," he said. "They're on loan from our domestic terror branch."

Dan nodded, shook their hands, making a mental note of the names. At the last person in the circle, Vince paused: "This is Barrett Hudlow, our liaison from Homeland Security's Counterterrorism unit."

Hudlow nodded curtly. He was somewhat portly, with pale sandpaper skin, tangled unibrow, and long locks of greasy silver hair that had been combed back from a prominent widow's peak. His ruddy cheeks hinted at a drinking problem and left him looking like a person in a perpetual state of agitation.

Dan took an instant dislike to the man. It was a common reaction he had developed toward career bureaucrats. Judging from the scowl on Hudlow's face, the feeling was mutual.

Dan glanced nervously at Vince. Joint task forces were seldom cordial, since agencies were often in competition with one another but Vince returned the glance with a look that hinted at some additional tension. The reason soon became clear.

"Let me say this for the record," Hudlow began, staring directly into Dan's eyes. "I do not approve of your involvement in this operation. I know your background, Mr. Clifford. You're nothing more than a common criminal."

Dan felt his face flush. "One man's criminal is another man's patriot, I suppose. Probably why I have a presidential pardon."

"Lucky you," Hudlow sneered. "I've seen your file. A sordid history, starting long before your recent exploits. Letters to congressmen, thinly veiled bomb threats. Seems your hacking exploits are part of a much more subversive trend. Why should anyone at this table trust your involvement?"

"Good question, frankly," Dan deadpanned. "Since I don't even know why I'm here." Hudlow's knowledge of his past history surprised him. As a young boy, he had lost his parents due, in part, to government oversight. His bitterness had lingered for years, prompting a letter-writing campaign to any politician who would listen. The prose may have lacked sophistication, he mused but . . . "Those letters you refer to were written by an adolescent. I was a bitter, young kid who just wanted the damn bureaucrats to do their jobs. You know, the reason why you're hired in the first place?"

Hudlow frowned. "Well, your adult behavior shows a great deal of recidivism, a lack of remorse, so I don't buy your excuses. If I had my way, you'd be undergoing enhanced interrogation at Guantanamo."

"Typical bureaucratic blather," Dan replied gruffly, unsure what else to say. Many of the activities leading up to his pardon were classified, which made any discussion of his actions difficult. Unable to mount a defense, he simply said: "Glad you're not in charge then," and turned his attention back to Vince. "So exactly why *am* I here? Doesn't seem like I'm a welcome member of this team."

Vince glared at Hudlow silently for several minutes. Finally, he turned his attention back to Dan. "Your role in this mission will become clear soon enough." He glanced around the table. "I know this task force was hastily assembled but I'd appreciate it if all members would refrain from schoolyard insults. We have much more serious issues to address." He glanced down at the case file on the table. "This is a domestic terror case, with a twist. For several years now, we've been tracking an ethereal group of hackers who call themselves the Firemen. Their leader goes by the avatar 'Chemerra.' Until recently, we knew almost nothing about their clandestine activities. They are extremely sophisticated and difficult to trace." Vince flipped through his stack of files and stopped at a red folder near the bottom. "We're not quite sure how they communicate. No emails, chat groups, cell phone calls. Most of our knowledge comes from peripheral sources, excited whispers from less sophisticated hackers, who have elevated the Firemen to mythical proportions. They are referred to in chat rooms as super-hackers. Recently, chatter on the dark web has intensified, enough to convince us that the Firemen are more reality than myth. There's talk of some big operation with world-changing consequences."

"Like what?" Dan squirmed in his seat, suddenly suspecting his role. He had acquired his own reputation as a superhacker, thanks to his past exploits, which had also reached mythical proportions.

Unfortunately for Dan, his hacking reputation *was* a myth.

"Can I finish?" Vince said. "In hacking circles, the Firemen are unique in two fundamental ways. First, they've managed to break into secure government servers, servers supposedly hardened against the most intense hacking attempts. We've identified Chemerra's digital signature and his technique is unique. He's not circumventing security with some work-around, social engineering, or zero-day exploit. Instead, Chemerra is *decrypting* the passwords, outright. That's supposed to be impossible, according to our crypto-analysts. These servers use the latest military encryption standards. It would take a million computers millions of years to crack these codes, yet Chemerra seems to decode them in days. Either that, or he is stealing the passwords somehow. If this method escapes to the general hacking population, the national security implications would be dire."

Dan's brow wrinkled. "Wait a minute, if this is a hacking issue, why is the CDC here?"

Vince shot Dan an irritated glance. "I'm getting to that. Which goes to the Firemen's other unique characteristic. They're not satis-fied with digital hacking. They've also gotten involved in *biohacking*."

The very mention of the term drew a hushed gasp from several members of the team.

Vince rubbed his fingers across his brow. "It's a trend we've been anticipating and fearing, for years now. The technology of genetic sequencing and manipulation has been moving ahead at light speed for the past decade. When the first human gene was sequenced, it took ten years and billions of dollars in investment. Today, anybody can send a sample off to a genealogy company and have their DNA sequenced in a couple of days. Even the lab equipment to do the sequencing has become cheap enough for any amateur biohacker to purchase it. Biohacking clubs have sprung up all over the country. Typically, their experimentation is simple and harmless, like creating a plant that glows in the dark. They sell them online. But there's always that potential for something more sinister. Ever since the Covid pandemic, every fringe group in the country has cooked up conspiracy theories for just about anything and everyone that they don't like. Every week the FBI gets wind of another crackpot group who wants to design the next worldwide pandemic, or thinks one has already been designed. This time, we're taking the threat very seriously. It's much easier to design a fatal pandemic than to get hold of a nuclear device or dirty bomb and unlike those threats, once released, a pandemic would quickly rage out of control. It's the favorite weapon of anarchists, because their end goal is chaos."

Mark Odom spoke for the first time. "Do you have any concrete evidence of an actual organism being engineered, or are we just talking about a lot of bluster?"

Vince said, "Well, we've traced a number of high-grade genetic-engineering machines that have been ordered on the dark web. Shipments have ended up in the Savannah, Georgia, area. We've intercepted chatter on the dark web with references to terms like"—Vince glanced down at the red file—"'final solution,' 'imminent,' 'kick ass,' 'enough for everyone,' and 'lethal.'" Vince looked back at Dan. "Your own Sur-Myz Phrase Tracking Software has escalated the threat level to high."

Dan knew about the increase in amateur biohacking. The CDC's rapid response team that he worked with in the past discussed it often, nicknaming it the "Prometheus Threshold," that moment in time when weapons of mass destruction would become available to ordinary citizens. The Covid pandemic had only made the threat more corporeal than ever. Wacky conspiracy theories inspired desperate measures by crazies. Theories of pizza shop Satan worshipers had already resulted in murders, and so-called secret cell phone conspiracies distributing the Covid virus via 5G towers had resulted in several communication employees being accosted. Who's to say a crazed hacking group might see DNA as the next great hacking domain? That thought propelled his mind back to memories of his own brush with a deadly microbe.

"So, is there an outbreak?" he asked. "Where? How bad?" Dan had a sudden urge to leave the room and call Rachel. As a microbiologist, she should be in this meeting, not him.

"No outbreaks," Vince said. "Not yet. We want to get on top of this early."

"So it's just internet chatter, right now?"

"Dan, if you'll let me finish." Vince's voice took on a hard edge. He looked like he'd been up all night, his suit uncharacteristically rumpled. "It's more than chatter. There's been a recent theft of biological material. Very dangerous material, from a pharmaceutical company in Savannah. We believe it's the work of Chemerra. He breached their high-level security using a password that is rotated once a week. Sound familiar? Dan, this is where you come in." Vince continued. "The organism was stolen from another person you've worked with before, a Dr. Esrom Nesson, I believe? In fact, it was Dr. Nesson who alerted us. He insisted that he would only talk with you."

"Dr. Nesson?" The mention of another name from Dan's past heightened his suspicions. A furtive glance from Mark Odom reinforced his fears.

"Nesson currently works for GenTropics Pharmaceuticals, one of the companies supplying Covid vaccines. The doctor was unwilling to share any details with me about the theft. Apparently, information on this stolen organism is classified and above my pay grade." Vince said it with a derisive smirk.

Dan felt a jolt of fear. There was only one organism that Dr. Nesson could be referring to, an organism that should have been left where it had been found. He looked down and found himself grasping his left hand to quell a tremor. "You say this . . . organism was stolen?"

"That's what Nesson says," Vince replied. "I need you to determine the threat level posed by this theft. If it's as serious as it sounds, we also need you to infiltrate the Firemen group. *That* is why you're here."

Dan's mind was racing. He'd suppressed memories of Honduras

for months, even as the Covid pandemic kept dragging the wretched images of sickness and death back to the surface. Honduras had been the worst and best thing that had ever happened to him. His relationship with Rachel had started there but it had also marked the discovery of an organism posing a danger far worse than any coronavirus. If biohackers had access to it . . .

"How am I supposed to find this *Chemerra* person? I might have an overblown hacker reputation but I don't travel in their circles."

"Chemerra will find you." Vince leaned back in his chair and stole a quick glance toward Barrett Hudlow. "Overblown or not, you have an almost mythical reputation in the hacking community and apparently Chemerra is a huge fan. We've spotted your name mentioned numerous times in chat rooms on the dark web."

"Oh." That was a problem. Dan wasn't sure how much to admit to the task force. He knew his way around a computer pretty well but he was no superhacker. Not even close. The Weatherman virus he unleashed had really been written by Rudi Plimpton, his genius partner. At the time, the stakes were high and he was under arrest. Taking responsibility for the hack was an attempt to protect Rudi and Rachel from incarceration. By the time his pardon had been issued, there was no reason to correct the deception. But now, if he rubbed shoulders with real hackers, he'd be exposed for sure.

Dan rubbed his chin in his hand, unsure how to proceed. "Look, I've been squeaky clean since that hack. I wouldn't know the dark web if I tripped over it."

"Bullshit." Barrett Hudlow huffed loudly. "How do we know Clifford isn't already a member of this terrorist group? He can't be trusted in a sensitive operation like this."

"I can vouch for Dan's integrity," Vince said. "I've known him for years. He earned that pardon. We have no alternatives; end of discussion." Vince quickly turned his attention back to Dan. "There's a convention in Savannah, starting tomorrow, called Nerdvana. It's a bunch of hackers, craftspeople, and makers who get together every year to share ideas. Perfect opportunity to show your face but first, this afternoon, we need to visit Dr. Nesson at GenTropics. It's only a few miles from downtown Savannah."

"This afternoon? In Savannah?" Dan said. "Sorry, I've got plans tonight."

"Cancel them," Vince said. "This can't wait."

Dan glanced around the table and saw a host of accusatory stares. *Crap.* "Well . . . then get me home to pack. Oh, and send someone to pick up Rudi Plimpton. I'll need him and Rachel to join us. They've both got security clearance and Rachel is a microbiologist."

"Absolutely not," Hudlow said. "No one else. We need a small and secure team."

Dan stared at Vince. "It's not a request. You want *me,* then Rudi's coming too."

Vince Peretti glanced at Hudlow, a faint grin curling the edges of his lips.

3

THE DRIVE TO Savannah took a little over four hours but to Dan, it had already seemed longer than that. Vince had insisted that the three of them travel together to debrief and prepare for the next day's events.

Dan struggled to concentrate on Vince's words. His mind was elsewhere, thinking about Rachel and the convenient lie he had told her back in his condo. On the way back from the FBI field office, he began having second thoughts about bringing her along. She had almost died from the organism in Honduras and the thought of seeing her go through that again was too much for him to bear. And if he told her the truth, she would insist on coming along despite the risk. So he conveniently left out the part about the stolen organism, mentioning only the hacking group.

He was a crappy liar and sensed Rachel's doubts but once committed to the lie, he just had to barrel through. He'd deal with the fallout later, assuming he made it back home in one piece. Better to have her angry than dead.

The three-car FBI caravan of black Chevy Suburbans began to slow as they reached the outskirts of Savannah. Dan wondered how Vince would handle their arrival at the Nerdvana convention. Talk about obvious. These government-issue vehicles were the opposite of understated and would advertise the FBI to any casual hacker. Thankfully, the route along Interstate 16 had been a long and lonely stretch of highway that connected Macon and Savannah. It meandered through pine forests and farmland and not much else.

Rudi was sitting next to him, snoring lightly, having been awakened by agents long before his usual morning rise. Dealing with authority figures was not Rudi's strong suit, so there had been some difficulty getting him in the car, requiring a call from Dan to smooth things over.

Vince Peretti sat in the front passenger seat, his ear glued to his cell phone, while Adam Pruitt drove. Dan stifled a grin, looking back and forth between Vince and Rudi. Two of his closest friends were computer geeks who could not be more different.

Vince Peretti was the epitome of a "G-man" with his tailored suit, dark hair, and square jaw. He approached his job in cyberterrorism with the cool efficiency of a CPA, which, he was. Vince had entered the bureau with a master's in accounting. Apparently that was the Bureau's favorite major, having transformed itself from an old-fashioned "gumshoe" agency into a more technically savvy, data-driven organization. Dan had heard that J. Edgar Hoover was an expert in the Dewey decimal system used by libraries, so the agency's systematic record keeping had started early.

Rudi Plimpton was a different character altogether. More "hippie bohemian" with long, dark locks of hair that swayed back and forth with every exaggerated movement. He sported a three-day-old beard that had come in scruffily. Rudi never bothered with fashion, as if the word had no meaning to him.

Unlike Vince, who had been schooled in data processing, Rudi had lived with computers most of his life. His father had been an engineer at Hewlett-Packard in the late eighties, which had given Rudi access to the latest in computing technology as a child. By the age of six, Rudi was tooling around the Arpanet, the early precursor to the internet. With little interest in school, girls, or sports, Rudi invested his formative years into learning low-level computer languages. Now, he was a forty-something man-child who happened to be the most brilliant programmer Dan had ever known.

Rudi had spent little time in Vince's presence and worked mainly behind the scenes. Dan was the "business end" of SurMyz Consulting Group and handled all their contracts with the FBI. It would be interesting to watch the two of them interact from opposite sides of the fence, so to speak.

After so many years working for other companies, Dan had found entrepreneurship foreign but exhilarating. The demise of his old employer NeuroSys had left a vacuum in the prediction analysis business, one that he happily filled with his new company. The FBI had been getting deeper and deeper into artificial intelligence and "big data" analysis, which had no doubt helped them pinpoint the threat posed by this Chemerra hacker.

"So what do we really know about this biohacking threat?" Dan said to Vince, who twisted awkwardly in the front seat to face him. "What's their motivation?"

"Not sure yet," Vince said. "Our intel is sparse, as you can see by the thinness of my file." Vince held it up as if to make the point.

Rudi stirred from his nap and yawned. "What's with the paper files anyway? I thought this was the *new* Bureau?" He snickered. "Didn't know 'Luddite' was your middle name."

Vince shrugged. "Paper files have their uses. Harder to hack or steal, for instance. Haven't heard of any Snowdens in the FBI yet, have you?"

"A point." Rudi gave Vince a grudging smirk and went back to his nap.

"How can you guys *not* know more about this hacker?" Dan said. "I thought the FBI was into everything nowadays, Stingray cell tower spoofing, internet traffic, video surveillance, facial recognition. Surely you've been able to collect a ton of traffic from hacker forums and stuff."

"No, and that's part of our concern. We don't know how they communicate but it's not through usual channels. Most of our intel comes from a flurry of recent posts, in dark web chat rooms, referring to *the Firemen* by name. We assume it's someone being sloppy or perhaps a disgruntled member. We know little else, except for the break-in and the security breaches. In each case, Chemerra obtained passwords ahead of time. Some of these biotech companies change their master passwords weekly. How's he getting them? An inside man?"

"Cracking," Rudi blurted, peering through one eye. "Gotta be cracking the passwords."

"How? These aren't ordinary people being socially engineered to give up their email passwords. These are secure organizations with military encryption and key cards."

"With enough horsepower . . ." Rudi trailed off.

"Unlikely," Vince said. "Cracking high-grade encryption would require millions of computers millions of . . ."

Rudi cackled derisively, drawing an irritated glance in return.

"We got millions of computers, all over the net, in people's homes, businesses, online stores—tons of horsepower, and then there's bitmining."

"You're talking about cryptocurrency?"

"Sure, Bitcoin, Kraken, Ripple, Ethereum, tons more. It takes thousands of math servers, millions actually, to do all that mining. Turn a few of the biggest mining houses into zombie servers and bam!" Rudi slapped his hands for effect, now fully awake. "And you've got a number-crunchin' Medusa that'll brute force the hell out of all the obvious passwords in a hundred different languages. Bound to turn up some winners eventually. Even white hats have dogs, girlfriends, and birthdays."

The look on Vince's face was a combination of irritation and doubt. "So, could *you* do it?"

Rudi shrugged, suppressed a grin, and pulled out his phone to stare at it. "Maybe, if I wrote it in assembler. Much faster that way."

Vince glanced at Dan questioningly.

"I wouldn't put it past him," Dan said. "Rudi's a guru with assembler language. It's low-level code one step above machine language. It's Rudi's primary language."

"Then Rudi, why not put together a test on what's possible, while Dan works the Firemen?" Vince said. "Figure out how long it would take. I'll give you a couple of hardened servers to bang against."

Rudi grinned. "Sure! Sounds like fun."

Vince turned back to Dan as Rudi zoned out on his phone. "Then there's the biological theft of your friend Nesson's classified organism. What can you tell me about it, without violating your security clearance? How are we supposed to fight something if we don't know anything about it?"

The mention of Esrom Nesson's name brought a new wave of concern. Dan and Rudi had been sworn to secrecy about the nature of their activities in Honduras. He could tell the lack of information irritated Vince but he didn't want to risk landing in jail. "Not much. Other than it's related to genetic manipulation." He paused to think. "What I don't get is this mixture of hacking and biohacking. Programmers love the clean and precise nature of computers—predictable, orderly— biology is wet and messy, imprecise. The two attributes don't seem to mesh."

Rudi looked up from his phone. "Makes total sense to me! It's all about bending the system to your will. DNA is just another computer—chemical algorithms—and RNA, that's where the action is." He became more animated. "DNA stores the program and RNA executes the code, like a function call. Mondo cool."

Dan and Vince both stared at Rudi like he was an alien.

"Since when have you become a biologist?" Dan said.

"Since, well, that operation we can't talk about . . ." Rudi cast a guilty glance toward Vince. "I got interested in RNA, when we worked with those, you know, computer chips . . ." Rudi jabbed Dan in the side with a wink, eyes darting back and forth between Dan and Vince. "Can we talk about them?"

"I think he remembers NeuroSys." Dan chuckled, turning back toward Vince. "What Rudi's talking about is the three-dimensional NeuroChip we helped design. They were the basis for the climate prediction system I sold to the government, before NeuroSys went belly up. Apparently NeuroSys repurposed them as gene chips, silicone detectors capable of deciphering genetic code in real time. It was a secret project. NeuroSys supplied Argonne National Laboratory with prototypes. They greatly enhanced our ability to decipher, the uh, thing we can't talk about."

Turning back to Rudi: "What have you been doing with RNA?"

Rudi giggled nervously. "I don't mean *live* RNA. Wetware is too icky for me. I'm talking about EteRNA." Rudi stared at them both, expecting recognition but receiving none.

"Eternal . . . what?"

"No, *EteRNA*. Play on words, you know? It's the coolest computer game around. RNA folding. Some guys at Stanford cooked it up. Turns out RNA protein folding is *really* tricky, with millions of possible combinations. Sort of like bio-origami. Fold the protein one way, you get a cat, fold it another and you get a giraffe. It's too difficult to figure out alone, so they turned the problem into a game. Hundreds of thousands of people play it, trying to figure out the best way to solve the folding puzzle. Turns out human intuition is better than computers. Stanford tries out the best solutions for real in the lab and virtual reality becomes actual reality. I've solved several protein folding challenges."

"You're not kidding . . ." Dan was amazed. "So, this game turned a bunch of amateur game-players into biologists?"

"Something like that. Only it's more complicated to actually do it in the real world, I'm sure." Rudi smiled innocently.

Dan and Vince stared at each other.

"Well, there's your connection," Dan said. "I guess it's not so far-fetched that amateur hackers would want to become amateur biohackers. Now we need to know *why*."

Vince said, "When we get to GenTropics Pharmaceuticals, you need to pump your friend Esrom for information. I need to know the risk, if not the details. Then I'm going to put in a request for security clearance. I don't have enough information to make heads or tails of this yet."

"So, then what? Am I supposed to walk up to this Chemerra fellow at the conference and say, 'Gee, I hear you're making a *mondo cool* pathogen to end the world as we know it. Why don't you tell me about it?' Something like that?"

"Come on," Vince said. "You'll think of something inventive. Weren't you the one who always wanted to be Sam Spade? Now's your chance to put your detective skills to good use."

"Yeah, I seem to remember you talking me out of amateur sleuthing. Whose side are you on?"

"The side that stops another pandemic."

"Who's Sam Spade?" Rudi asked.

Dan and Vince exchanged knowing smiles. "Rudi, don't you ever watch old movies?"

Rudi's brow wrinkled. "Old movies? Why would I?"

"Never mind," Dan said. "But if you ever get the urge to check out the golden age of talkies, check out *The Maltese Falcon*."

THE CARAVAN ROLLED up to the Westin Savannah River Golf Resort and Spa by midafternoon. They dropped Rudi and two of the cars off at the resort, due to its proximity to the Nerdvana convention, held at the nearby Savannah Convention Center.

Vince's car continued on, toward GenTropics Pharmaceuticals, a few miles down the Savannah River as it meandered toward Tybee Island. With every additional mile, Dan's anxiety level increased. He might have wanted to play Sam Spade but he could think of better inaugural cases than dredging up unpleasant memories from the worst/best year of his life.

Before long, a large GenTropics Pharmaceuticals sign popped into view on the right side of the road. They pulled off onto a long winding driveway that snaked its way through moss-covered oaks, ending at a bend in the river. The research facility itself was an indistinct beige structure sitting on a hump of land surrounded by low-lying marshes interspersed with fields of Spartina grass and flocks of white ibis.

The pharmaceutical building seemed out of place in this picturesque environment. Dan thought it an odd location for a high-tech structure due to the risk of flooding or hurricanes but he figured its high perch must give it some protection. Beyond the building, the marsh melted into the Savannah River as it ambled its way toward the Atlantic Ocean.

Dan stepped out of the vehicle and the full brunt of the Georgia late summer sun hit him in the face. The humidity draped over him like a steaming towel and instantly took the crispness out of his shirt. A patina of sweat erupted on his brow, bringing back memories of Honduras.

Near the front entrance, he and Vince were greeted by a man faintly resembling Dr. Esrom Nesson. Dan remembered Nesson as a light-skinned man with freckles, almost albino, with platinum-blond hair that hung loosely in sparse wisps. The mottled hair was still there but Nesson's complexion had grown much darker, almost to a normal tone. He wore a distraught expression that added to his unfamiliar countenance.

Dan approached and shook his hand. "Doc, you look . . . so different. Been spray tanning?"

Nesson managed a fleeting smile that drifted away as quickly as it came. "Alas, no, Mr. Clifford. What you're seeing is the wonder of genetic signaling." Nesson continued speaking as he led them through the front entrance. "We've been experimenting with an RNA molecule that stimulates the production of melanin in the skin, in the same way that excessive UV exposure triggers tanning. Basically, it's a free suntan, with no risk of skin cancer." He managed another weak smile. "Perks of the job."

"Well, you look great," Dan said. "More robust, I think."

"Thank you, my boy." Nesson picked up the pace, leading them down a long hallway to a lab protected by a security door. He punched in a code and ushered them in, glancing over his shoulder two or three times. "My apologies for the intrigue but hardly anyone knows about the break-in. I wanted to get you two out of sight as quickly as possible."

Finally, Nesson took the time to shake Vince's hand. "You must be from the FBI."

"That's right," Vince said.

Nesson gripped his hands behind his back and began pacing inside the large lab. "Dan, thank you for coming. I knew the confidential nature of this theft would make it difficult to discuss with the FBI. That's also why I haven't alerted company officials. The fewer people who know about this, the better. But long story short, this thief has stolen one of the most dangerous organisms known to man. If this falls into the wrong hands, I can't imagine—"

Vince interrupted: "Let's start at the beginning. What makes this organism so dangerous?"

Nesson's eyes darted between Dan and Vince. "I'm not really at liberty to discuss that. It's classified."

Vince pursed his lips, rubbed the side of his temple. "Yes, I'm all too aware of that. It seems the government doesn't want me to solve this case. I'm working to obtain the necessary clearance but in the meantime, I assume you can discuss the sensitive aspects with Dan, at least?"

"Yes, yes, of course."

"Good. Then I'm going to park my butt in that chair over there while you two talk. Then I need to hear about the robbery. I assume that's not classified?"

"Oh, certainly," Nesson replied. "My apologies for all the secrecy."

"I'm getting used to it," Vince said over his shoulder.

"Understanding guy," Nesson said.

"Vince is a good man," Dan said. "Tell me what happened. I'm assuming this is a pristine sample of you-know-what?"

Nesson nodded. "Yes. When we left Honduras, I was so excited by the organism's potential. It seemed like the perfect gene vector. Its ability to move genetic material in and out of cells with precision and ease was astonishing. If properly harnessed, it could advance genetic engineering by decades. You see, splicing genes is an imprecise process. A tool like CRISPR CAS-9 for instance, shows great promise but it's like a dumb scalpel, cutting and splicing small snippets of DNA but often placing them in the wrong position, or even repeating inserts. Many cures require a number of *related* genes to be spliced in all the right places. That was the organism's specialty. It seemed to understand the genome, to know exactly how and where to insert a chorus of genes, all in one fell swoop. With that ability, we could tackle tough challenges like regrowing amputated limbs."

"That's really possible?" Dan said, surprised.

"Theoretically, yes. Humans already possess the basic genetic ability to do so. Children can regrow fingers to their first joint until age nine. We would only need to tweak a few genes." Nesson held up his hand and scowled at it.

"But I was naive. In our first experiments, the splicing went well but the organism didn't know when to stop. It would seek out other genes, ones that weren't part of the protocol and reactivate them, as if trying to reanimate long dormant programming. Ever heard of junk DNA? They're mainly obsolete genes from our evolutionary past that are no longer needed. When it started reactivating them, I tried everything to restrict its actions, limit its abilities. I cut out entire swaths of its own DNA to cripple it but the damn thing would just reconstruct itself from the host cell's DNA, since all animals share a large portion of their DNA. Back and forth we went. Right when I thought I had it controlled, it would outsmart me, rebuild itself, and create some monstrous result.

Nesson continued: "So I gave it a new nickname—the Devil's Paradox—because it's completely and utterly baffling. Wondrous and uncontrollable, and evil, all at the same time. After numerous tries, I finally gave up, shelved the whole project . . . locked the whole Devil's Paradox in the back freezer . . . until the robbery. The thief knew what he wanted; didn't bother with anything else." Nesson ran his fingers through locks of thinning hair. "If the thief tries to tame this beast, he will fail. It could start a new pandemic, one that could make Covid-19 look like a morning cold. Uncontrollable, multiple pathogens, or worse!"

"Whoa, whoa, calm down." Dan grabbed Nesson's shoulders and held him firmly. This was not the bold, confident doctor Dan remembered from Honduras. Nesson was trembling. "Focus. Take a deep breath. I didn't understand half of what you just said."

"Yes, yes, you're right." Nesson raised his palms, appeared to steady himself. "I'm okay, it's just that . . . this was my responsibility and I blew it."

"You can't blame yourself; besides, we need you focused." As he spoke, Dan felt his own heart sink, suddenly realizing he had a unique perspective. No one else, except Rachel perhaps, could understand the horrific potential of this threat. Right now, Rachel was back in Atlanta and like it or not, the responsibility would fall on him to find the organism. He already knew enough about the Devil's Paradox to know that no time could be spared. "Let's get Vince back in the conversation, talk about the robbery, okay? Nothing classified about that."

Esrom nodded quietly. "Sure. Any way I can help."

Dan signaled Vince back over. "What can you tell us about the robbery?"

"Well, it should have been impossible, for one thing. We've got multiple security measures here. This lab requires a pass-code that is changed every week. I honestly don't know how the thief would obtain that."

"We have intel that the thief is a world-class hacker," Vince added in response. He took a long look around the lab. "Could it be an inside job?"

Dr. Nesson froze for a few seconds, thinking. "No, I don't see how. There's only one other person in the lab who knows about the organism's potential and has access to the storage fridge and that's my lab partner, Ada Kurz. But she was the one who discovered the theft. Besides, I trust her implicitly."

"Is she here now?"

"Of course." Esrom took out his phone and sent a text. "She's in the PCR lab next door."

Minutes later, a young woman in a motorized wheelchair glided into the room. As she approached, her chair magically rose up onto two perfectly balanced wheels, lifting Ada to the same height as the three men. Dan was struck by the woman's bright blue eyes and blond hair, cut medium length to frame an oval face.

She spoke with a subtle but distinct European accent. "Gentlemen, nice to meet you all." She shook everyone's hand, her uniquely balanced chair maintaining a rock-steady stance.

"Ada Kurz is our top molecular biologist," Esrom said. "She's the only other person I would trust with our most sensitive organisms."

"And you discovered the theft?" Vince said.

"Yes, that's right."

"And when did the theft occur, exactly? What night?"

Ada remained silent. Dan noticed her casting a wary glance toward Esrom.

After an awkward silence, Esrom broke in. "We uh, aren't sure exactly."

Vince frowned. "But you said Ms. Kurz discovered the theft."

"In a sense, that's correct." Esrom stole a second glance at Ada. "The problem is, we haven't touched that organism in over four months. It's tucked in a box at the back of the freezer. Ada only noticed it was missing when she went to retrieve it for some additional tests."

Vince let out a long, low breath, stretching it out for several seconds. "That's great. Let's summarize, shall we? Someone has stolen the most dangerous microbe on the planet, according to you, which we can't really talk about because it's classified and we have no idea when it was stolen or by whom, except that it happened sometime in the last four months. Have I got that about right?"

Dan had never seen Esrom so vulnerable, yet impenetrable. The man appeared to shrink several inches during the last few minutes. Before he could muster a reply, Ada Kurz spoke up.

"It's not Dr. Nesson's fault," she said. "It's common for dangerous microbes to sit undisturbed for months at a time. You obviously want to limit exposure to them. I had a new experiment designed to try and tame the beast. I assume you have a cherished photo of someone at home, Agent Peretti. Stored in a box somewhere? How do you know it's still there? When was the last time you checked?"

"Yeah but my dad's photo won't kill millions of people," he said. "What about security logs?"

"I personally checked them going back four months. Nothing seems out of the ordinary. We all work long hours. Only authorized personnel and security has logged in or out, that I can see."

"Who handles security?"

"We're serviced by a local firm, TaurusSec Systems."

Vince wrote something on his notepad. "Can you get me the name of the person in charge?"

"Certainly," Esrom croaked, his voice feeble.

BACK IN THE car, Vince turned to Dan. "Your friend in there has given me an almost impossible mission. There's no fresh evidence. I can't get the information I need to go forward. I'm afraid you've got your work cut out for you, Sam Spade."

Dan nodded quietly. If the Firemen were really planning something big, they could have as much as a four-month head start. He was more certain than ever that he had made the right decision to leave Rachel behind.

4

RACHEL SULLIVAN SAT on a bench at the Georgia Aquarium, studying the pale and corpulent bodies of three belugas as they danced for the crowd. Squealing children pressed their faces against the glass, casting ghostly shadows and waving toward the performers on the other side.

Who was entertaining whom? Rachel wondered what the belugas must think of their human counterparts. The two species shared completely different lives, separated by a mere six inches of acrylic and an eon of evolution.

The belugas led privileged lives, as far as belugas go. Two thousand miles from their birthplace in the Arctic, they were coddled in climate-controlled waters, cared for by a staff of cetacean experts equipped with the latest in medical technology, and fed scientifically optimized menus. Their days were filled with exercise and games and, of course, an endless procession of human visitors.

Rachel had worked part-time as one of those experts. Even at her distant perch, the belugas acknowledged her presence with looks of recognition in beluga speak. She loved working with them, even though the pay was meager. The work gave her the opportunity to hang out with Dan most of the time at his condo without worrying about missed salaries and job hunting. The rest of her time was spent in Savannah working part-time at the Skidaway Institute.

She laughed at the irony. This was her time to spend in Atlanta with Dan and instead, he was off traipsing around Savannah, without her, on some crazy FBI mission he refused to talk about. It wasn't like him to shut her out.

She was sailing the doldrums, alone, with nothing to fill her days except brooding thoughts. Not too long ago she was employed by NOAA, the National Oceanic and Atmospheric Administration, piloting her submersible, SeaZee, and working on real research, the kind that would keep her engaged and excited.

One rogue operation and the trashing of NOAA's prize submersible had led to her dismissal. If NOAA had known the true reasons for her actions, she was certain she'd still be employed there. But that damned confidentiality agreement the bureaucrats had made her sign had ruined everything—all to cover their ass.

What about hers?

No empathy or recompense, just silence. She had sacrificed her career to protect the public from the truth. Then, the coronavirus pandemic upset the world's apple cart, while she faced a future of menial jobs typically done by pubescent students.

Dan had saved her. He showered her with attention and loyalty. Their relationship had remained loose, relaxed, per her demands, but lately, she had noticed a change in his demeanor. He was putting more pressure on their relationship, letting it be known that he wanted a deeper commitment, the kind she refused to give. Why couldn't he just leave well enough alone? She was perfectly content to live for the day.

Rachel glanced back at the belugas. Inside their gilded cage, their lives had been fully ordained. In their reflection she saw her own: comfortable but never free. She took in several deep breaths as if preparing for a free dive. As long as she kept her future a mystery, there would always be an invisible wall separating her from a complete life. She let the air out of her lungs.

It was time to confront the future, head on.

She took one last breath, pulled out her cell phone, and made an oft-delayed call to her doctor.

AROUND NOON, MOLLY Daniels rolled over in bed and slid her hand beneath the sheets, hoping to get a rise out of her partner but he appeared dead to the world. She rolled back over, exasperated and quite hungover. What was his name again?

They had hooked up at a party near the docks, late in the evening. He had been a good bit further along the party train than she, but Molly had caught up quickly. The sex later that night, what little of it she remembered, had been dulled by an Ecstasy and tequila haze. Quite unsatisfactory.

After several more attempts at reviving her lethargic partner, Molly gave up and decided to take a shower. She slid out of bed and wandered through his apartment, finding a filthy bathroom that required some dexterity on her part to avoid touching anything significant while showering. Luckily, she discovered a few clean towels in the hallway closet and dried off. After getting dressed, she checked on her partner one last time: still snoring.

She considered leaving her name and phone number on the dresser but thought better of it. Another round in the sack would probably not be worth the trouble. Best to cut her losses and move on. The day was still young and the familiar ache was already growing inside her. It seemed she could never get satisfaction. She had a vague realization that her desires were excessive by most people's standards, yet it was the only thing that interested her of late. That, and her latest food obsession . . .

Her stomach growled. She was starving and had a bad case of cotton mouth. Another tryst would have to wait. She needed to fill the ol' piehole . . .

Molly checked what's-his-name's fridge, found a bottle of water, and took a long draw. Then she grabbed her purse and hurried toward the street, where she flagged down one of the pedicabs that prowled Savannah's Historic District. She directed her driver toward Starland.

Soon, he was huffing and puffing under the strain of the bicycle rickshaw as they rattled over pre–Civil War paving stones and pitted asphalt. Savannah was one of the few towns to escape the wrath of General Sherman during America's Civil War. The Union general had burned his way to the southern coast but spared Savannah from the inferno. Much of the original architecture and old-world ambiance remained, the oak-lined streets of old Savannah appearing much as they had one hundred and fifty years ago. Fingers of gray moss dangled from the tree limbs like pennants.

The pedicab driver paused to catch his breath before crossing over into more modern architecture. He grunted and heaved on the pedals and moved swiftly across Abercorn, into Starland.

Unlike old Savannah, the Starland District was more Molly's taste: seventies hippie kitsch. Her destination was a good distance away and the driver soon worked up a sweat. Once a thriving business center during the first half of the twentieth century, the area had become a ghost town in the fifties. But thanks to the influence of SCAD, the Savannah College of Art and Design, the area had been transformed into an artsy collection of design studios, shops, food trucks, and restaurants. It was now the domain of young, creative students with eclectic tastes and offbeat lifestyles.

Molly giggled as the pedicab rattled to a stop in front of her latest passion: Palm Frites. What a lovely idea! A little hole-in-the-wall eatery serving the best fries in town, slathered with one of ten different toppings, paired with a personal reading from the establishment's fortune-teller owner, Sister Simone Dumont.

Molly should have time to satisfy her hunger and still hook up with someone new before dark. When she entered the shop, Sister Simone was finishing up a tarot reading with some stranger. He was tall and slender, with dusky blond hair matted to one side of his head like a windblown shrub.

Sister Simone glanced up and smiled. "Ah, Miss Daniels, come meet Mr. William Detweiler, a wonderful young man with an exciting future. Destined for big things."

Will nodded at her and revealed a million-dollar smile. "Always nice to meet a fellow traveler."

Molly nodded back awkwardly, giggling to herself. He seemed pretty cute. Two for one deal, maybe?

Sister Simone rose. "Will, would you mind if I take care of Molly first? Then I'll get you both your favorite cones."

"Not at all, Miss Dumont," Will said. "I'll uh, just look through your astrology charts. Take your time." He smiled in a way that piqued Molly's interest and then ambled across the shop to a collection of charts on the far wall that held a collection of obscure star symbols.

Molly sat down and pulled the chair flush to the table. There were times when she wished she could just get her fries and go but Sister Simone was always insistent on a reading and Molly somehow felt obligated to play along, even though she really didn't believe in all that astrology stuff. The tarot cards were cool, though. Their artwork reminded her of Dungeons & Dragons, a game she'd spent much of her young life playing.

Sister Simone was decked out, as usual, in her full bohemian garb: peasant blouse and bright patterned skirt held together with a broad black sash. Her long curly black locks poked out from underneath a bright red cap that she loved to call her *bonnet rouge,* a symbol of freedom from the French Revolution, she claimed. Sister Simone had a tendency to talk with her hands in broad circular flourishes. Her ears, neck, and wrists were festooned with hoops, chains, and bracelets of all kinds, and her fingernails were so long that they had begun to curl under at the tips. With each broad flourish of her hands, Sister Simone jingled like a treasure chest. She would look outlandish in most places but here in bohemian Savannah, her style fit right in.

Sister Simone started the palm reading by donning a cloth mask and fresh pair of blue latex gloves. That had always struck Molly as odd. The pandemic was over.

She'd never met a fortune-teller so paranoid about germs but Simone had always insisted on good hygiene, to avoid spreading anything dangerous, she claimed. Sister Simone took Molly's hand and wiped it thoroughly with a fresh towelette, which she then placed into an empty glass jar that soon disappeared under the table.

Sister Simone smiled. "Let's see what's in store for you this week, shall we?" She stroked Molly's palm with her gloved hand and clucked. "Your heart line seems deeper, less broken or chained. It seems you are growing more determined but reserved. Holding your emotions in more lately?"

"I guess," Molly said. Truth was, she hadn't felt much of anything lately. Nothing seemed to bother her but nothing seemed *exciting* to her anymore either. "I do sorta feel bored, unsatisfied. I used to be so passionate about my art and stuff but I'm not getting much done lately. Sort of stuck, having a creative block, you know?"

"Ahh." Sister Simone nodded. "My dear, that can happen in times of transition. Perhaps a new period of your career is on the horizon."

Molly thought about that for a moment. "Maybe." *More like a new period of nothingness . . .*

Sister Simone continued to trace her finger across Molly's palm, her expression growing more intense. "My dear, your Venus Mount seems especially corpulent this morning. Here—" She pointed to the flesh poking up from the intersection between Molly's palm and thumb. "That would indicate a lot of sexual activity lately, am I right?" Sister Simone's eyes drifted up seductively.

Molly felt the blood rush to her face and glanced awkwardly toward Will. Thankfully, he had his back to them both, studying the charts on the wall, or pretending to . . .

Molly leaned forward and whispered, "Sister, I've really been horny a lot lately." She stifled a giggle with her hand. "Can't get enough."

Sister Simone's forehead wrinkled. "My dear, is that an unusual urge on your part?"

"Well, yeah. I just can't seem to turn anybody down. But then, afterward, I just feel . . . empty, you know? I used to have so many other things going on . . . but now . . ." Her voice trailed off.

Sister Simone wrote some notes on a legal pad. "Let's see if we can find some clarification in the cards." She removed her gloves and began deftly shuffling a thick deck of tarot cards. Her many bracelets and necklaces jingled with the movement, creating an almost hypnotic effect.

Once the cards were shuffled, she spread them across the table in a line from left to right. "Okay, let us examine your past, present, and future. This will lend us insight into the aspects influencing your destiny." She plucked three cards from the spread stack and placed them in a row in the center of the table, facing Molly. Sister Simone stared at the cards, her brow wrinkling. Molly's anxiety grew.

She picked up the first card with a flourish. "Ah, the Two of Cups. This signifies a union of souls. You've had a long-standing relationship, perhaps romantic, with someone who has anchored your spiritual life. The two of you have developed a deep mutual trust and understanding. But your relationship with this person has weakened over time, no? Your mind and soul were united but now, you are questioning those feelings."

She picked up the second card, hesitated for a moment before continuing. "The Eight of Swords. This is a test, my dear. A gauntlet. You are being challenged and must choose a new path. Your old life may be changing, new opportunities presenting themselves. Your future will be determined by the choices you make in the upcoming days. You must rise to the occasion; have confidence in your abilities to forge a new future. Understand?"

Molly sat there, confused. Sister Simone's sessions were always confusing but always felt relevant. "I guess so," she said. "I've got to make some tough decisions."

"That's right," Sister Simone said. "You must be brave, resilient." She returned the card to the table and picked up the final card, signifying the future, and hesitated. "This card, *the Hanged Man* . . . I wouldn't take this too seriously, my dear. You are facing a challenge beyond your control. You may be unable to help yourself through your own actions. You must be patient and let the challenge pass. You will have limited control over your destiny. Be pliant and accepting, for fate will carve a new future for you."

Molly nodded. She didn't like the prognosis Sister Simone gave her but it seemed appropriate somehow. She had been feeling passive lately, like she wasn't in control of her destiny, a passenger on a long trip, carried along by the winds of fate.

Sister Simone waited a few minutes for her session advice to sink in and then proceeded to question Molly more aggressively. "This former relationship, the one you have begun to doubt, can you tell me more about the person involved?"

Molly's gaze wandered as she considered the question. She felt a compulsion to answer the question but to do so would betray an oath she had made long ago. "It's just somebody I've known from the past. We haven't been in touch lately."

"And this great leader, who is he?"

Molly hesitated. "That's all I really want to say today. Can I just get a frites cone now?"

Sister Simone's eyes drilled into her, probing. "Of course." She smiled. "But don't let these doubts fester for too long without addressing them. I can help, if you share. Your future may depend on it." Sister Simone stood up and headed to the shop's kitchen. She retrieved a yellow bin from the freezer and scooped out a mass of potatoes, already cut into the shape of waffle fries. She placed them into a basket and lowered them into a fryer of hot oil. The fries sizzled and sputtered while Sister Simone fashioned two paper cones. She gazed at Molly and Will. "Shall I assume you both want your regular toppings?"

Will and Molly stared at each other as if looking for approval. "That's fine by me," Will said. Molly grinned and nodded. A few minutes later, Sister Simone removed the golden-brown fries from the fryer, placed them in the cones, and topped one with a bright green guacamole dip and the other with chili. "Here you go, my children. Enjoy."

Molly and Will left the shop together, their cones in hand. Molly smiled at Will, noticing that he seemed personable. Will didn't show any of the hesitance or awkwardness of most of the men she met. He seemed confident, bold, a keeper, she thought.

Will grinned back at her. "Sister Simone can be pretty aggressive, can't she?"

"Boy, I'll say." Molly giggled. "She's like a gypsy shrink."

"Well said. Hey, wanna drop by my apartment?"

Molly grinned. "I'd love to."

5

IN THE LATE afternoon, Dan and Rudi left the hotel and walked to the Savannah Convention Center: a waterfront complex with over 330,000 square feet of exhibit space. The sleek white building lay directly across from Savannah's historic riverfront area, where cotton had once been traded and shipped around the world. The center's modern lines were a stark contrast to the old brick buildings of historic Savannah but seemed appropriate for the high-tech Nerdvana convention.

The entrance fee was cash only, designed to ensure anonymity. Past the gate, two tunnels led toward the conference room floor, one marked with an icon of children led by their parents. Rudi chose the other one, a tunnel formed by two walls of large-screen monitors. According to Rudi, this was the "Wall of Sheep." Any newbies naive enough to enter the gateway with their unsecured phones would soon find their most intimate pictures and texts displayed on the walls. Dan noted a wide variety of images, shocked by the sheer number of "Nerdvana virgins" ignoring the warnings. The ease at which the hackers had breached their phones gave Dan a chill. He nervously stroked the burner phone Rudi had given him that afternoon. His real phone remained back in the hotel room.

"See what I mean?" Rudi said, giggling at a collection of nude photos. "Good thing you brought the burner. All your intimate pics of Ice Queen Rachel could be plastered here for all to see. Most people don't realize their phones are an open book."

"Gimme some credit, Rudi. I'm not dumb enough to take intimate photos with my phone."

"Not even in the heat of passion?"

"What and ruin the ambiance?" Dan smiled. "Whatever happened to good ol'-fashioned romance? Nowadays, nothing is left to the imagination."

"Don't know about that," Rudi said, as they reached the end of the tunnel. The convention floor opened out into a brightly lit expanse filled with an improbable mixture of high-tech gadgets, home crafts, lock-picking booths, and shop equipment; truly a nerd's delight. Dan considered himself "nerd-light," so even he was fascinated by the wide selection of technology.

The diversity of dress bordered on casual-goth, with a dash of hippie thrown in. Lots of tie-dyed T-shirts, cargo pants, jeans, and leather. Loads of people dressed in cosplay outfits representing their favorite video game heroes or movie characters. A surprising number of skinheads and bikers in leather jackets ambled through the booths catering to robotic arms, 3-D printers, jewelry, arts, and crafts. A surprising number of robots roamed the halls, although none of them appeared to reach the sophistication level of his own cloud-linked robot, Rover. Rover benefited from the sophisticated neural net processing chips left behind by his former employer NeuroSys.

Dan was only mildly familiar with the "maker community" that had established a strong presence at the show, showing off affordable fabrication machines of shocking sophistication: 3-D printers, CNC routers, laser cutters, circuit boards. The crafts made with them would have put machine shops to shame just a few years ago.

Rudi grabbed his arm and pointed toward a large registration board. "Hey, why don't you upgrade your appearance with a new T-shirt? Meanwhile, I'm gonna sign up for one of the capture the flag events."

"I thought you were allergic to exercise."

"Not that kind of capture the flag." Rudi shot him a derisive look. "Programming wars, to see who can hack into each other's data the quickest. You need to learn the vernacular." He glanced at the board. "Looks like a lot of phone hacks this year . . . let's see . . . hmmm: take over an android camera app and capture a screen grab of the opposing team." Rudi kept mumbling to himself as he read down the list.

"Sure you can keep up with these young hackers?" Dan said. "Aren't your programming skills old-school?"

Rudi looked insulted. "My *skillage* is up to date. Otherwise, my rep would be crap. Programming is semantics, knowing the soul of the

CPU, if you will. You never lose the edge. I bet I wipe the floor with these script-kiddies."

Dan laughed. "Good then. Show them how it's done. Keep an eye out for members of the Firemen. Meanwhile, I'll stroll the floor, look at the exhibits, see what kind of attention I can get."

Dan's gaze locked on a small group of men walking together whom he recognized as the FBI agents who had accompanied them from Atlanta. Even if he hadn't recognized them, it was painfully obvious that they were "feds." Their 5.11 tactical pants and polo shirts stuck out like sore thumbs. He suddenly worried about his own dress. Thankfully, he'd thought to wear an old pair of jeans but his University of Georgia T-shirt probably gave him away. Meanwhile, Rudi's "hippie chic" tie-dyed shirt and oversized cargo pants seemed oddly appropriate. It proved to anyone looking that Rudi cared not a whit about his appearance.

Thankfully, there were tons of booths selling T-shirts with provocative anti-establishment slogans. Dan rummaged through the pile, looking for something more "hacker-like." He settled on a shirt that said, HUMPTY DUMP, YOU'LL NEVER PUT YOUR DATA BACK TOGETHER AGAIN and pulled it on over his other shirt. The combo was a bit warm but he suddenly felt less conspicuous.

As he continued down the aisle, he sensed a set of eyes following him. He tried to relax and focus on the exhibits. A lock-picking booth caught his attention.

"Hey, wanna give our pick kit a try?" A guy stepped up wearing a T-shirt emblazoned with, ALL YOUR STUFF ARE BELONG TO ME. A set of what looked like blank keys on a chain dangled from his finger. "Bump keys, the lazy man's lock pick." The man slipped a sample into one of the demo locks at the booth and tapped the end with a small mallet. The lock obediently popped open. The man grinned. "Entry in five seconds flat."

"It's that easy?"

"Yeah, man, most of the time. Takes the art and skill out of it but when you're in a hurry . . ."

Dan eyed the chain suspiciously. "Those things legal?"

"As legal as any other key. These ten will cover about ninety percent of tumbler locks. Best deal at the show, fifty bucks for the set."

Dan decided they might come in handy one day and bought them.

The seller dropped them into a bag printed to look like a padlock and Dan continued down the show floor. After a while, he noticed an increase of lingering stares. Finally a young Asian girl walked up to him. She was petite but with an athletic build, wearing a tight pair of black pants and a dark blouse covered in faintly visible geometric shapes that reminded Dan vaguely of a Picasso painting.

"Hey, aren't you Dan Clifford?"

Dan shrugged. "That's me."

"Dude, you're my hero. Loved the way you kicked the *man* in the balls on national TV with the Weatherman virus. Would you sign my shirt?" She pointed to an area of empty fabric near her midriff and handed Dan a pen filled with a thick metallic ink.

Dan hesitated for a moment, captivated by the pictographs on her blouse. One abstract heart-shaped object in the middle of her chest glowed in a pulse-like rhythm. Leaning over, he signed in the blank box. The glow of the paint brightened immediately. "That's a pretty impressive shirt you've got there," he said. "How does it work?"

"Expressive textiles. I make them. The ink is fluorescent, powered via circuitry sewn into the fabric. I have a sensor embedded here"—she held up her arm, sporting a faint square under the skin—"that tracks my heart rate, skin conductivity, adrenaline, other stuff. The signals are picked up by the blouse and illuminates different designs based on my mood. My take on a mood ring." She gave him a thin smile.

"That's impressive. I assume that pulsating heart glowing on your chest means you're in a good mood?"

This time, the girl grinned broadly. "That's a pretty good guess. My name's Psue, with a *P*." She extended a hand.

Dan shook it. "Well, Psue, what's with the sensor under your skin? Didn't that hurt?"

"Nah, not with acupuncture. I'm into wetware, body hacking. The sensor updates my phone with health info too but with my line of expressive clothing, I can look in the mirror in the morning and see my health and mood instantly. So can others, sort of like full disclosure. You should drop by my booth," she said, handing him a card. "I'll show you some of my other designs. I have expressive menswear too."

"I'll try and do that," he said.

Sue looked at him demurely, then reached into her pocket for another card. "You should really attend our rave, later tonight. This card will get you in." She handed him a ticket emblazoned with a logo consisting of two crossed axes. "It's the hippest party in town, trust me."

Dan looked at the ticket, nodded, and walked away, amazed at the ease of blending in. This infiltration strategy just might work, if he could attract the attention of the right people. Psue, the textile designer, didn't fit that profile but he watched her as she headed through the crowd, stopping several times to show off Dan's autograph to admiring fans.

Psue's efforts attracted a small crowd that began to follow him down the exhibit hall like groupies, all clamoring for autographs. He stopped several times to sign a host of show items, palms, backs, T-shirts, and foreheads.

"You're my hero," one stranger in the crowd blurted. "That Weatherman virus was bitchin'. How'd you manage the breach into the National Weather Service?"

"Sorry," Dan said. "Can't divulge my trade secrets." Struggling to be as conversant and friendly as possible, he found the whole experience unsettling. It was difficult to imagine some of these nerdy kids as members of a secret cabal of hackers and terrorists, bent on destruction. They seemed harmless, until he reminded himself of the Devil's Paradox. The thought of anyone in this group experimenting with it sent shivers down his spine. Vince Peretti was right. He needed to know what the Firemen were planning.

As more people tried to strike up conversations, he became concerned about maintaining his cover. Dan Clifford was supposed to be the genius hacker but Rudi had been the real man behind the curtain. It was true Dan had cooked up the idea but it had required Rudi's former employment at the Weather Service and his back doors into their system to pull it off. He wondered if Rudi resented his misplaced fame. If so, he'd never mentioned it. Perhaps the avoidance of incarceration had been a fair trade. Dan knew that if any real hackers cornered him with technical questions, he'd be exposed in a heartbeat, so he decided to play the mysterious, tight-lipped hacker role.

His entourage continued to grow as he traversed the aisles. Their incessant questions were starting to irritate him. He was so distracted that he blindly stepped out onto a new aisle and almost collided with a gigantic mechanical ant lumbering its way across the showroom floor. Sitting atop the robotic beast was a diminutive man with a white beard dressed as Santa and wearing a red hat with two large antennas sticking out the top of it.

The mini-Santa spotted Dan and shouted. "Hey, I know you! Dan Clifford, the Weatherman. Here, catch!" He tossed over a small package wrapped with a bow. "Check out my product, compliments of the house. I call it Ant Mother. It's a complete computing platform with CPU, Wi-Fi, HDMI, Bluetooth, and USB-C, all on a motherboard barely larger than your thumbnail." He grinned broadly, his white beard sagging. "You can tie in tons of sensors, control wireless switching, give brains to any invention. The options are endless!"

Dan looked down at the tiny circuit board. Santa was right. It was the width of a thumbnail but twice as long. If true, the amount of processing power packed into the small package amazed even him.

He waved. "Thanks. I'll check it out."

Santa put the large mechanical machine back into gear. The mighty ant screeched and clanked, as the long legs slid forward ponderously. Santa waved and shouted over his shoulder. "If you like Ant Mother, give me a shout-out on the boards, okay?"

Dan sensed several pairs of eyeballs peering over his shoulders to stare at the gift. In an effort to lose his entourage, he cut through the crowd and slipped through one booth into the adjoining hallway. He weaved through the foot traffic and stopped at a large booth with a banner hanging over the top that said:

Generic YouGene, Anonymity for the Ages.

A row of masks covered the table, all facsimiles of the same face. On the left were simple printed cutouts with rubber bands but at the far end of the row sat several hauntingly realistic masks, supple and detailed, made with silicone. They looked realistic enough to pass as high-quality movie makeup. Behind them, a sophisticated 3-D printer rumbled, printing out another mask.

The man, whose face adorned the masks, walked up, held out a hand. "Generic YouGene, welcome to my booth. Hey, aren't you Dan Clifford, the Weatherman hacker? What an honor!" he said and shook Dan's hand enthusiastically.

Dan forced a smile and studied YouGene's face just to make sure it was the real thing. "Nice masks, by the way. If you don't mind me asking, why are you selling them?"

"Total anonymity, dude," YouGene said. "You can't go anywhere nowadays without security cameras and facial recognition tracking. A genuine Generic YouGene mask maintains your god given right to privacy! I take a scan of your face, overlay it with a 3-D model of my own face, and print out the difference in silicone. A little paint and artwork and you have a custom mask that fits perfectly. It passes all but the tightest scrutiny. You can wander in public without attracting attention. The *man*"—he held up a thumb—"will just see me."

"Yeah but what if someone commits a crime wearing your face? Aren't you worried about being blamed?"

"Nope." Generic YouGene grinned. "I maintain my anonymity through *You-biquity,* get it? My face is registered as open source, so no authority can use it to uniquely identify me. I can go anywhere now, just one of the crowd."

"And the paper masks?"

"Budget versions. They fool most recognition systems."

He eagerly pulled Dan down the table, showing off his wares as he talked. "This is Print-b-Gone," he said, picking up a small bottle. "Special clear latex. Dab it on your fingers and it'll totally obscure your fingerprints." He dropped the bottle into a sample bag.

"You'll also want some YouGene Cream." He picked up a larger bottle containing a white substance and cradled it in his palm like a snake-oil salesman. "Nowadays, you have to worry about leaving your DNA everywhere you go. Your unique identity is in your blood, your saliva, your hair follicles, even the dead skin you shed." He tapped the bottle for effect. "But YouGene Cream contains random DNA sequences collected from public gene registries. I sequenced the random bits and placed them in a colloidal suspension of preservatives. These molecules will last for ten years or more. Just rub this cream on your skin every day and you'll drive the feds wild!" YouGene swung his hands in an arc for effect. "Completely flummoxes their genetic sequencers with garbage molecules. I call it DNA steganography. Hides your own unique DNA in a haystack of chaos. Best of all"—he opened the bottle and smeared a small sample on Dan's hand—"YouGene Cream contains CBD oil and emollients that give your skin that youthful, healthy glow. Comes in lilac and sage. Here, smell."

Dan took a whiff. It did have a pleasant aroma. "Not bad."

YouGene dropped the bottle in the sample bag and thrust it into Dan's hands. "Here, take these free samples. Privacy insurance." Nearing the end of the table, YouGene picked up what looked like a full-face scuba mask. "Now, *this* is my crowning achievement, the Omni-Mask," he continued. "Made of optically clear silicone so you can see the wearer's expression. Has full HEPA-filtration and active ventilation that also covers the eyes. The HEPA filter contains carbon to neutralize tear gas. It's truly the universal mask. You can wear it every day during the next pandemic, or your next protest march. See here?" He picked up a sheet of printed emoticons. "The faint marks on the mask show where to place these round stickers, to obscure and stump the facial recognition software. Yet, your face is still identifiable to your friends." YouGene tilted the mask up. "I thought of everything. The mask comes with its own stainless steel straw, which you insert through this hole here." He demonstrated, sticking a tube through the bottom seal. "That way, you can keep hydrated while protesting."

Dan stared at the Omni-Mask and its implications. Anonymity, gene spoofing, fingerprint protection, and most importantly, protection against the *next pandemic*. It seemed that YouGene fit the profile of a Firemen member. He studied YouGene's face, trying to commit it to memory, then had a better idea. "Mind if I have one of your cheap masks?"

"Sure, no problem," YouGene said, dropping one in the bag.

"I get the impression privacy is a big issue for you and your friends." Dan said.

"Well of course!" Generic YouGene's eyes grew wide. "Everything we do is tracked, our phone messages, our purchases, what we eat, what we wear. Our location is tracked by the eye in the sky through our phones. It's all analyzed and accumulated in massive data warehouses. Before long, we'll all be a herd of mindless cattle, fattened up, entertained and manipulated by giant corporations, all in the service of the beast. Hell, the *man* knows what we plan to do before *we* do. We've got to fight back."

Dan felt a flush of heat on his face. The guy had sounded quirky at first but now Generic YouGene was beginning to lay out a conspiracy theory that could fuel a movement. In fact, his description of the "the man's" activities sounded a lot like Dan's own company, SurMyz Consulting Group. One of its specialties was tapping into the FBI's criminal database to collect the backgrounds and histories of convicted criminals. Then, using artificial intelligence, the program would predict the perp's future movements. Generic YouGene's concerns were not unreasonable or outlandish. Of course, SurMyz focused on criminals, not ordinary citizens. At least, that's what Dan told himself . . .

Generic YouGene was still talking. Dan had lost track of the conversation and struggled to catch up.

". . . before long, AI will predict everything we do, know our purchasing desires, steal our jobs. Then, we'll be totally dependent on the state, sucking at the teat of *Big Brother*. If we want to keep our privacy, remain as individuals, we'll have to fade into the woodwork. That's where my masks come in."

If Generic YouGene was any indication, Dan began to understand the motivations of the Firemen. The fear of no control leads to a fantasy of total control. What better way to express control than a pandemic? What was worse, the authoritarian state controlling our every movement, or the chaos of a mindless crowd, fueled by individual passions?

"Well, YouGene," Dan said, "you're certainly brave to sacrifice your individual identity to the cause. I wish you the best of luck."

"Strength in unity, right?" Generic YouGene pushed out his chest proudly. "The singularity is coming. If we don't prepare, we're doomed. Check around the show, you'll meet a lot of exhibitors who feel the same way."

"I'll do that," Dan said, choosing the opportunity to move on down the show floor. Generic YouGene's argument was compelling. Exactly the kind of rationale that could spark a revolution.

The next few hours passed by in a flurry of creative expression. The sheer breadth of imagination at the Nerdvana show was impressive, Dan thought, although he had doubts about the practical aspects of all that creativity. Computerized clothing, robotic ant vehicles, lock-picking contests, glowing cacti and jewelry made from circuit board parts seemed harmless at first but also a tremendous waste of time in his opinion. One thing they all had in common: they were creative expressions that required a high degree of technical sophistication. Brilliant minds were kept busy chasing frivolous pursuits, a chase that eventually ended at the "capture the flag" competition.

Rudi Plimpton was there, along with a large crowd of other programmers, all feverishly pounding on laptops cabled to cell phones. Apparently the goal was to gain control of the competing team's cell phone cameras. The contest had narrowed down to two surviving teams:

Rudi's team, made up of a bunch of collegiate types named the "Old Fogies," and a younger team of what looked like high school kids who called themselves the "Script Kittys." Unlike their younger adversaries, the Old Fogies were typing slowly and deliberately, conversing with one another often. The Script Kittys were more maniacal, fingers frantically racing across keyboards with astonishing speed.

Rudi almost looked sedate. Bored, even. Suddenly a loud alarm sounded and the Old Fogies raised their arms in triumph. Rudi held up his burner phone with a close-up portrait of one of the young programmers frozen in panicked surprise. The crowd roared in unison over what appeared to be a major upset by the Old Fogies.

After collecting his prize of circuit board kits and other electronic trinkets, Rudi spotted Dan in the crowd and ambled over. "That was a blast. Some of these prizes are pretty good actually."

"Looks like you put those youngsters in their place," Dan said.

"Yeah, pretty easy, really. None of them have a clue about low-level assembler. While they were wasting their time with upper-level scripting, we just slid in under the basement and pulled the rug out from under them."

Dan grinned. "Well, I guess your street cred is intact."

"How about you? Any progress with the Firemen?"

Dan wasn't sure how to answer that. He suspected that several people he had talked with were probably connected to the shadowy group but he had intentionally been subtle in his approach so as not to blow his cover. "No overt contacts yet."

"Well, there's a big shebang across town tonight that we should attend. If you don't hook up there, you might as well pack it in."

"Agreed." Dan stopped, fished around inside his padlock bag, and pitched Ant Mother toward Rudi. "Here. Add this to your collection of electronic trinkets."

Rudi looked down at the miniature computer and grinned, seemingly pleased with the gift.

RACHEL SQUIRMED IN her seat in the waiting room, sick of the stale air tinged with antiseptic and urine as children quietly sobbed in the background. She had hated doctor's offices ever since childhood. Why couldn't they make them more cheerful? Maybe with some bright paintings on the wall, a live garden, fish tank, *something*.

As a microbiologist, she was accustomed to the persistent odor of medicinal chemicals that permeated most laboratories but in this domain, she was not in control. Here, her destiny existed beyond her grasp, controlled by others.

It gave her the creeps.

She mindlessly flipped through her phone messages, while trying to ignore the whimpers of a four-year-old girl. This was a day she vowed would never come, a moment of decision. But the pull of Dan Clifford held greater sway over her actions than she wanted to admit. Having always been somewhat of a gypsy, she'd never needed the attentions of a man in her life, that is, until Dan showed up.

He made her happy. It was as simple as that.

She was doing this for him—no—for herself too. Their blossoming relationship had tempted her to fantasize about a normal life together, a life she'd never allowed into her thoughts, until now.

"Rachel Sullivan."

The pronouncement caused her to jump. She stood up and followed the nurse into a small exam room in the back office, where she sat in anticipatory silence. The minute hand on her watch crept ever so slowly across the dial—she squirmed, picked at her nails, paced the room, sat down again, yawned, coughed, stood up again, stretched— the time dragged on.

An agonizing ten minutes later, Dr. Anne Wilson entered the room and sat down some three feet away in a chair facing her. Dr. Wilson flipped through a stack of papers on her lap for several minutes, never making eye contact.

Finally, she raised her gaze to Rachel, her vision somewhat off center and distant. Her mouth opened to speak, then paused for an unbearable instant.The words spilled out awkwardly. "There is no good way to say this, Rachel," Dr. Wilson said, her brow sinking. "I'm so sorry to inform you that the tests were positive for Huntington's disease . . ."

The words hit her with a force that stole her breath. She gasped audibly, fell back into her seat.

So, that was it.

Schrödinger's cat was dead. Until that instant of finality, her future had been hers to live in blissful uncertainty, just like everyone else, but now, this doctor had stolen what remained of her bliss, simply by the act of looking into Pandora's box.

The finality of life had become palpable.

For a fleeting moment, Rachel's anger swelled, focused toward Dan. *He* had done this . . . *he* had tricked her into confronting her worst fear and in doing so, had solidified her fate from the ether.

". . . to be blunt."

Rachel struggled to refocus on Dr. Wilson's lips, which seemed to dance about wordlessly.

"You should begin to put your life in order. It is hard to say how long you have before . . . symptoms present themselves. A year . . . maybe even ten years. Who knows? It's hard to say but you'll need to plan for hospice care. If you have one, finish your bucket list. You may still have time left. Cherish it . . ."

Rachel barely comprehended the words. All she could think about was her father, suffering through the same fate, oblivious to his family and their sorrow that engulfed them. Through the darkening haze of shock, one thought formed with absolute clarity.

Dan Clifford would not suffer her fate and *she* would not suffer her father's.

Rachel rose to leave.

"I can put you in touch with a therapist . . ."

"What's the point?" Rachel said over her shoulder as she paused at the door. "I know the drill, I've lived it. Have you?"

Not waiting for an answer, she shut the door gently and strolled through the office, into the hallway, and out into the sweltering heat of an Atlanta summer afternoon. She paused, closed her eyes, and absorbed the weight of the sun.

6

THE RIDE FROM the Nerdvana convention to the "crave," as his guests called it, had been distinctly uncomfortable. Dan was sandwiched in the back seat of an SUV between Bob Sidian, a.k.a. Santa of the Ant Mother, and Rudi, who squirmed restlessly against the right door, threatening to spill out into the street at any moment. The smells of sweat and body odor from a day's worth of trudging around the convention center wafted through the small enclosure. This was about as close to Rudi as Dan ever wanted to get.

In the front passenger seat, Generic YouGene kept casting nervous glances over his shoulder as if he were afraid Dan and Rudi would vanish from the car. Dan felt vaguely like a trophy guest, someone who would be paraded around proudly by his hosts at the concert. The idea was repugnant to him but it needed to be done. He suspected that Generic YouGene had connections to the Firemen organization, which if true, could speed his meeting with the hacker Chemerra.

Their ride bounced roughly over the potholed road that paralleled the river, sending Dan's head into the vehicle's roof liner. "Where are we headed, exactly?" he asked, after the third head bump.

"The old Savannah docks," YouGene said. "There's lots of old brick warehouses out here, many have been abandoned or repurposed." He turned. "Which means more space for us to stretch out."

A long line of buildings passed by the car window, some modern and recently constructed, while others were crumbling into decay. Every few hundred yards, a large sandy field would interrupt the flow, filled with shipping containers that had been stacked precariously high. Dan wondered what would happen if someone ever needed a container from the bottom of the pile.

"Those containers empty or full?" he asked.

"Mostly empty," YouGene replied. "Thanks to tariffs and our trade deficit, they multiply like rabbits. They've become popular as tiny homes; I live in one. Cheap and built like tanks."

Eighteen wheelers roared past the SUV in quick succession, bound for the container fields where they would disgorge their contents into the ever growing pile. Near the end of one long container field, the SUV slowed, pulling into a lot next to a much older building, one built of red brick that stretched farther than a football field. Paint flaked from ten-foot-high letters on the building's eave, spelling the word COTTON.

Everyone piled out of the car and stretched their legs, grateful for the breeze blowing in off the Savannah River. A line had formed along the length of the warehouse, ending at a small entranceway. A group of volunteers wearing black T-shirts emblazoned with the word GOONS walked along the line, handing out what looked like chocolate coins imprinted with the familiar Bitcoin logo.

Another group of GOONS were gathering tickets. The entrance fee to the party appeared to be one of several different forms of currency: either a strange blue token from the Nerdvana convention, a printed card like the one Dan had received from Psue, or the whisper of a password Dan was unable to make out.

As they approached, Generic YouGene stopped and whispered into the ear of the nearest GOON, eliciting a wide stare in Dan's direction. The man nodded and shuffled all four of them through the door.

"Welcome to our home away from home," YouGene said proudly.

Unlike the aging exterior of the building, the interior of the warehouse had been recently transformed. It had an industrial feel, brimming with various manufacturing tools—CNC machines, saws, water cutters, tool cases, large work tables, drill presses, welding equipment— all shoved against the wall to clear a large area in the center of the warehouse floor. There was a second story, circumnavigating the interior walls, accessed by a busy steel catwalk that served to connect a series of small rooms that Dan guessed to be efficiency apartments.

A diverse crowd milled about, filling in the gaps between food booths, makeshift bars, and bandstands, some old, some young. Many wore cloth masks of varying designs, possibly a holdover from the Covid pandemic but there were also decorative masks, painted faces, and dazzling LED glasses.

YouGene eagerly led Dan and Rudi across the expanse toward the

rear of the building while Bob Sidian dissolved into the crowd. At
the far end of the warehouse, a temporary lounge area had been constructed out of shipping crates and lawn furniture. YouGene entered
the area and approached a barrel-chested man sitting on an overstuffed sofa.

"Dan, this is Craig Spivey. He's the proprietor of this place."

Spivey leaned forward and shook Dan's hand. "You can call me
Stoker," he said, exposing a row of luminescent teeth, surrounded by
a carefully coiffed brown beard. "Welcome to my little abode, I call it
Maker Haven."

Dan introduced Rudi and glanced around the large open expanse.
"I don't think I've ever seen a place quite this unique."

"It fills a need," Stoker said. "We have a strong maker community here in Savannah. Maker Haven provides them a space where
they can exercise their creativity, with access to the latest technology.
I provide them with low-cost housing so everyone can focus on their
primary passion without the need to spend money on expensive rent.
You'd be surprised how many unique products and businesses have
been cooked up here."

"How do you make money off the place?"

"Money's not the goal here," Stoker replied. "I made my fortune
in the gaming business. This is my humble attempt to give something
back to the community that supports my work."

"Well, consider me impressed," Dan said, hoping that he didn't
sound too artificially enthusiastic.

"Enjoy the festivities. Your token will buy you a special brew at our
bar over there." Stoker pointed in the direction of the band. "Walk
around, get to know everyone. You're most welcome here."

"I'll do that," Dan said. He turned to Rudi and whispered in his ear.
"Why don't we split up, cover more ground." Rudi didn't need any further encouragement. He nodded and took off for the nearest bar.

Dan ambled through the crowd, working his way toward the opposite end of the warehouse. He spotted several familiar people from
the Nerdvana convention, who had dressed up for the occasion. It
was obvious the warehouse "crave" was considered a premier hacker
destination for show attendees. Realizing that he had been on his feet
for hours without any food or drink, Dan headed toward the nearest
makeshift bar to cash in his complimentary drink token.

The sign hanging over the bar caught him by surprise: THE FINAL SOLUTION.

He wondered if these youngsters had any idea of its subtle reference to Nazi Germany. Perhaps they considered it a campy play on words. He leaned against the bar and presented his token, determined to find out. "So what is the final solution, exactly?"

A scrawny guy with a foot-long beard and a crimson skullcap reached into an icebox next to the bar and pulled out a plain brown bottle, popping the cap with a flourish. "Just the best damn brew in the world. Here," he said, beaming as he passed the bottle over. "We spent months working on this recipe. Must have gone through fifty unsuccessful batches of brew before we got this one right. It's the final solution, get it?"

"Ahhh," Dan said. He eyed the plain brown bottle. It had a small custom label depicting the caricature of a barefoot programmer, eyeballs bugging out. Underneath the picture was a line that said, IT'LL PUT A PEP IN YOUR STEP.

Dan cautiously took a swig and was pleasantly surprised by the full-bodied flavor: just the right balance of mouth feel and spicy hop notes. He could get attached to this beer. He suspected the Firemen were the brewmasters, along with their other talents. But so far, everyone he had met seemed harmless. He began to wonder if Vince Peretti's intel had been off the mark.

After a few more swigs, he turned and scanned the crowd. The open floor of the warehouse was rapidly filling up as a band began milling about on the small, ad hoc stage. If he was going to find Chemerra, he'd need to do it before the music started. He suddenly felt awkward and unqualified for the job. It wasn't like he had never schmoozed with nerds before. His industry was full of them. Heck, he considered himself an honorary nerd but when he had been the director of sales at NeuroSys, it had been easy to sell the benefits of neural net processing. This latest job required a unique form of guile and that was definitely *not* in his wheelhouse.

Reminding himself of the Devil's Paradox and the threat it posed was enough to stay motivated, so he scanned the crowd once more. How many of these young people could imagine the horror wrought by this rogue organism in Honduras? They'd skirted by almost unscathed during the coronavirus pandemic. Perhaps that cloak of protection had altered their judgment. Heck, most young people considered themselves invincible anyway.

Dan had seen the suffering up close and personal, unlike most Americans who remained sheltered behind a powerful medical establishment and the comfort of their delusions. As a young protester, the idea of unleashing some horrible new disease might seem "romantic" in some perverted sense, until your own face started to melt off.

Detached, delusional youngsters, drunk on their youthful adrenaline and the power of technology, naive to the end result of their actions. That sobering vision kept him focused on the severity of the threat, rather than the innocence and naiveté of the enemy.

He drifted through the crowd and introduced himself to anyone who seemed interested and he got a lot of interest. True to his reputation, Dan Clifford, the Weatherman hacker, attracted a small crowd of fans who pummeled him with autograph requests, handshakes, and questions. One notable couple stopped in front of him and gaped, their faces painted in a garish and varied geometric design.

"Hey, you're Dan Clifford, aren't you?" The person Dan guessed was the male of the couple held out his hand. "Hi, I'm Cauter Eyze and this is Flicker Girl. It's damn cool to meet you."

"Same here," Dan said with all the feigned enthusiasm he could muster, returning Cauter's handshake vigorously. "What's with the face painting? You two fans of modern art?" Dan grinned.

The couple seemed surprised by his question. "It's our dazzle anti-faces," the woman said. "Like it?" She tilted her head demurely to show off her accompanying hairdo, dyed in three bright colors and combed down in front of her eyes and nose. The whole spiky mess was held in place by copious amounts of hair gel. "We're art students at SCAD. Masks aren't our thing and the zombie heads are just too gross with their makeup. We prefer to style out. Besides, CV dazzle is just as unrecognizable as the other techniques."

The couple acted like Dan should know what they meant, so he went along. "Unrecognizable to whom? Who's tracking you?"

Cauter registered an expression of shock visible through his face paint. "Are you kidding? Everybody! I've spotted at least three feds since we got here, not to mention our equestrian adversaries."

"Say what?" Confused, Dam scanned the room and saw none of his compatriots, or horses, for that matter. This couple definitely had a paranoid streak. "I thought this was a closed party?"

"Our enemies find ways to sneak into our events. Your presence, I'm sure, attracted more than the normal share of feds."

"Probably so." Dan shrugged, straining to maintain a sincere expression, wondering what Cauter would think if he knew the "fed presence" was standing right in front of him. Maybe it was time to push the envelope. "With everyone poking their nose into your business all the time, how do you guys get anything accomplished? I mean, everything is monitored." He pulled out his burner phone and held it up.

Cauter's lips curled into a wry smile. "Burners are so old-school," he said with an air of pride. He pulled out a large smartphone and passed it over like a magical talisman. "This is what you need—one of our black phones."

"Really? What's so special about it?" Dan cradled the phone with what he hoped was the proper level of reverence. "You know every cell phone is traceable by its SIM card."

Cauter grinned. "Unless there's no SIM at all." He took the phone back and turned it on. "It's totally hardened, no SIM. All calls and messages go over public Wi-Fi, via VOIP. They're double encrypted and bounced around the globe via onion routers," Cauter said. "Defeats the whole cellular system. Totally untraceable, with spoofed IP addresses."

"And if there's no Wi-Fi?"

"Well, nothing's perfect but you'd be surprised. We've been wardriving the whole Savannah area, got it fully mapped, only a few dead spots." Cauter Eyze grinned again and hugged Flicker Girl as if to reinforce some point.

"How do I get one of these?" Dan said.

"Can't help you there," Cauter replied. "It's based on trust. But you could start with the proprietor." Cauter nodded toward the opposite end of the warehouse.

"You mean Stoker?" Dan took a final swig from his beer bottle.

"Stoker's the man, yeah." Cauter held out his own bottle of the Final Solution. "Want mine? Not a fan."

Dan hesitated, then took the fresh bottle. "Sure. No sense in wasting good beer."

Cauter grinned and patted Dan on the shoulder. "Just watch yourself. Truly an honor meeting you. Enjoy the party."

He and Flicker Girl dissolved into the crowd, leaving Dan alone again. He sipped on his new beer and chatted with a stream of admirers. Working his way across the dance floor, he was beginning to absorb the group's hidden language. The general audience was highly diverse but there seemed to be a core group of individuals who betrayed their identities through their body language and avatars, mostly patterned after incendiary themes. He suspected the Firemen were more restrained than the general crowd, familiar with one another, whispering in each other's ears, observing.

Recruiting.

Dan wondered if Chemerra was in the room, watching him. Despite several inquiries, no one seemed to know Chemerra's identity, even though many acknowledged the name. He had to hope that Chemerra would introduce himself at some point. Meanwhile, the crowd began loosening up in anticipation of the band.

Several musicians began to congregate onstage carrying their instruments. That's when Dan noticed something missing, something common to all public concerts: the requisite banks of huge loudspeakers. As if on cue, a musician began playing and Dan started to feel like he was living in an alternate universe. No sound emanated from the stage, yet the action of the musicians elicited a strong reaction from the crowd.

Everyone began donning headsets and earbuds, setting off a wave of frenzied dancing. Nearby, he could hear the muted sound of electronic music drifting out of the ears of the closest dancers.

Working his way through the gyrating crowd, he soon ended up where he began: near the back of the warehouse. Dan headed back to where Stoker reclined on a sofa and plopped down next to him.

"Interesting concert. It's a little disorienting to see all the movement without the cue of loud music."

Stoker smiled. "We started the tradition a few years back, after getting complaints from the neighbors about the noise. Now, everyone likes it, plus it has the benefit of making it so much easier to carry on a conversation."

Dan nodded and decided to risk another direct tactic. "So, is everyone at this party a member of the Firemen?"

Stoker's face went blank. "Firemen? I don't know what you're talking about."

"Really? Secret handshakes and passwords—avatar names like Bob Sidian, Flicker Girl, Cauter Eyze, Back Flash—come on, *Stoker*." Dan grinned knowingly. "If I remember my history, wasn't a stoker the guy minding the coal fires of steam engines? If you want to remain less obvious, you ought to consider more subtle avatars."

The slightest hint of a smile cracked Stoker's stone facade. "So, you think you've met these people?"

"Sure. Your group is well-known on the dark web. I've heard through channels that one of your members, Chemerra, has been talking about me. I was hoping we'd get the opportunity to meet."

Stoker's knowing smile dissolved. "Dan, your imagination's running away with you. Chemerra is a myth, the great hacker boogie man, if you will. Besides, if and I say *if* Chemerra happened to be a real person, which I doubt, it's unlikely he would just walk up and introduce himself to a total stranger. If you haven't noticed, most people here value their anonymity, something you definitely lack."

"That's true, I suppose. I'm probably the least anonymous hacker on the planet," Dan said, feigning sadness. "It's been difficult to, how do I say it, cultivate a meaningful dialogue with other hackers. I was hoping you could set me up with one of your black phones."

Stoker's right eyebrow twitched ever so slightly. "I see you've been getting along with the crowd quite well. To answer your earlier question, most of the attendees at these parties are casual acquaintances. I'd be very careful if I were you, striking up conversations with just anyone here. The hacker community is diverse—black hats, white hats, feds, goons—not everyone has the best intentions."

"I see your point. That's why identifying the right individuals, the *stokers* of the group, is so important." Dan smiled.

Stoker's gaze broke contact with him and fell on the crowd. Dan knew he had hit a nerve.

"Why not just relax and enjoy the party?" Stoker said, locking eyes with him again. "This is a low-key rave, simply for fun, a chance to network. Enjoy yourself but don't be pushy. That makes people nervous."

"Sage advice, I'm sure," he replied, sensing that he'd pushed a bit too far. Now, he sensed, was the time to back off and let things simmer for a while.

WHEN DAN STOOD up to head back into the growing crowd, a wave of dizziness almost landed him back in his seat. The beer had gone straight to his head. As he headed toward the nearest snack bar, he spotted Psue, the girl with the mood clothing, and headed in her direction. Before he could reach her, Generic YouGene intercepted him.

At least he *thought* it was Generic YouGene. There had been several other people on the dance floor wearing his silicone masks. They had fooled him before.

"Are you the real McCoy?"

"In the flesh." Generic YouGene rubbed his face briskly with both hands as if to prove it.

"That's just spooky," Dan said.

"Anonymity in ubiquity," YouGene replied, grinning.

"Right. What do you know about her?" Dan pointed at Psue.

"Who? Psue Dominus? That bitch is crazy."

"I don't know. She seemed pretty nice at the show earlier. Her expressive clothing line is pretty unique."

"Hah!" Generic YouGene shuddered. "You better hope to never meet her when the red lines on her sleeves are glowing. She's into martial arts, Krav Maga, Aikido, that kind of stuff. She's a grinder too, you know, body enhancement? She's got magnets in her fingertips, can sense electrical fields. I've heard she can lay you out on the floor with a simple touch."

"Really?" He had a hard time imagining the petite Asian girl as some ninja but he decided to take YouGene's word for it. After conversing a bit longer, the two of them split up.

At the nearest taco stand, Dan wolfed down two fully loaded creations, surprised by his appetite. The tacos had to be the best things that had ever passed his lips. The flavor was vivid and full and it made him thirsty. He headed back to the Final Solution beer stand but the bartender waved him off.

"Sorry, one beer per token."

"I can't buy one?"

"Nope. Limited release, hence the tokens."

A finger tapped him on the shoulder. Dan turned and was confronted by another fan. "Hey man, you can have mine." He held out his unopened beer like a hallowed prize. "Would you autograph my Nerdvana program?"

Dan signed the heavily creased booklet and took up the fan's offer. It seemed that every beer tasted better than the last and he relished the mouth feel of the heavy malt, flavored with just the right amount of hop finish. He took another long swig of the ambrosia and watched as the dance floor continued to fill.

The excitement of the crowd accelerated as an elite group of dancers dressed in white jumpsuits and featureless masks coalesced near the stage. Someone handed him a set of earbuds and pointed. "You're gonna want to hear this."

Dan placed the buds in his ears, his head instantly filling with the blast of electronic music. The dancing troupe milled about excitedly, waving their phones and tablets above their heads. Suddenly, their devices synchronized into a choreographed light show. A bright light spilled out across the stage and split into individual beams that seemed to lock onto each dancer like a magnet.

A grand image formed above them on a flat screen, containing the URL for a website. Gathering cues from the crowd, Dan pointed his burner phone's browser to the URL. Suddenly, his phone synchronized with the music and became part of the light show. Dan blinked, fascinated by what he was seeing: some type of massive networked performance. The observers had become part of the show. Lights of all colors flashed and flowed from one phone to the next, while the performing troupe danced onstage. He had no idea how the program could tell whose phone was lit up but all the devices seemed perfectly timed and coordinated, with the light show cascading through the digital screens like a stadium wave.

Suddenly, the bass beat of a powerful dubstep tune boomed through his earbuds, signaling the dance troupe to form a line, their magnetic beams of light clinging to the blank canvas of their jumpsuits, anticipating every twitch and movement. The music accelerated as the beams of light became animated, projecting images onto their partner dancers, transforming them into wild animals, mythological beings, Salvador Dalí paintings escaping their frames, robots, and superheroes. Each dancer in turn seemed to inherit the soul of their respective spirit creature.

Somewhere deep in his brain, Dan marveled at the technical sophistication needed to pull off the synchronized interplay between phones and dancers, but the effect seemed as much spiritual as technical. The unrestrained movement reminded him of trancelike performances he'd witnessed by the Puebloan peoples when performing kachina dances. The light beings he viewed onstage were the geeks' own spiritual kachinas, embodiments of their concepts and forces, amplified by the imaginations of the witnesses. The frenzied movement, the kaleidoscope lights rippling across the stage, the rhythm of the dance, all transformed the room into an audiovisual mind-trip.

The bass beat pounded, tickling the soles of his feet. The dancer's movements rose in intensity, culminating in an uninhibited display of raw emotion. The dance floor gyrated to the pulsing beat, phones bobbing and swaying overhead. The elite dancers onstage began a coordinated dance, moving as one.

Dan felt himself being carried along on the trough and crest of each beat-wave. A lone dancer took the center of the stage, her body gyrating madly, limbs swinging with robotic precision, as the spirit creatures closed in around her. The singular dancer's flesh fell away under the spell of the lights, revealing a dancing skeleton, twisting and whirling madly as the others pulsed in unison.

Dan squinted. Pinpoints of light expanded into blurry rings like exploding fireflies. The entire room seemed to morph into a multicellular creature—its individual cells coordinated and breathing as one.

Dan was overwhelmed with emotion and released himself to the will of the crowd. Ever tightening bodies swept him along a wave of humanity. The excitement and joy of the dance propelled him into a dimension of light, the boundaries of human form exceeded and unleashed.

He was sailing through a virtual world of imagination, thought, and creativity. The realization sent a sudden surge of fear through him as he sensed the collective power of the organism.

His thoughts struggled to organize themselves, neurons flickering, golden threads of causality enveloping the room, connecting everything to everything else. The electronic spirit beings continued their dance, while the child-geeks were given their kachinas, their spirit dolls, all teaching them how to act as one.

Dan tried to focus. What were the spirit beings telling him? His brain felt like a vise, the pressure intense . . . a sudden affection for these spirit beings filled his heart. His hands floated in front of him, disconnected, numb. Music pounded and writhed between his ears, driving ripples through the heart of his mind.

Where was his body? Was he a spirit dancer now? A kachina? His consciousness floated above the room. The spirit animals continued their glowing dance.

Uh-oh, a massive spasm hit his leg . . . threatening to steal his balance. The world spun around him like a carousel, horses circling like goons, his brain darting above the crowd on gossamer wings.

Where was his body?

A sudden and intense tugging pulled him partway back through the spirit world . . . and he watched himself staring at Rudi's face, who stared back at him quizzically, lips moving in unbearably slow motion, a muffled sound rolling out of bloated pink tongue matter.

"H e e e y m a a a n, y o u o k a a a y . . . z o o o m b b b i e ?"

What does a zombie look like, really? Rudi's face undulated . . . "This person, you s h o u l d m e e e e e e t . . ."

A young girl's face appeared in the circle of his consciousness. More muffled sounds . . .

He ripped the earbud from his right ear. Rudi was yelling . . . loudly.

". . . Molly Daniels here, knows Chemerra . . . She's his girlfriend." Rudi's screaming tore like daggers through his ears. "She can introduce . . ."

Suddenly, Molly's hand squeezed his and they were rushing across the room, pinballing off dancing bodies, ringing up points. A bell chimed . . . *ding* . . . *ding* . . . *ding.* Music pounded incessantly in his left ear. *Feet, don't trip* . . . They tucked and weaved across the floor like a ship adrift in a storm, tossed about by body waves, lost in a fury of confusion.

Steps.

Dan struggled to lift the stones attached to his feet, stumbling up and up, the hand of Molly dragging him ever higher, to a transcendent level. Suddenly the waves broke and he was drifting above the undulating mass of the body storm, slamming into wrought iron. One leap and he could float back into the fray . . . he could rejoin the spirit dancers . . .

Molly jerked him away from the darkness and into a blinding

light . . . bright colors and shapes assailed his sensitive eyes . . . a wall with no depth, a bizarre Picasso cubist dream. His body was struggling to keep up with his brain, which buzzed around the cubist room like a mad dragonfly.

Suddenly, two pink balloons drifted into his field of view and pushed him backward. He fell blindly into a field of cotton. The warmth of flesh wrapped his face, stole his breath . . . right as the lights went out . . .

7

THE CRASH OF thunder and lightning started a brush fire in one of his neurons, spreading rapidly, torching a flurry of thoughts that been arguing against thunder but rather, a storm inside his head. That's when his brain finally kicked into gear and Dan realized that the actual sound he'd registered was merely the rattle of keys hitting the top of a wooden dresser.

Eyes flicked open, letting in a stream of photons that scraped at sensitive tissues. He tried to sit up but felt like a bobble-head five times too large. It was difficult to balance. He tried to take stock of the situation, soon realizing his brain wasn't so much hungover as it was overstimulated.

Across the room, Molly Daniels stared quizzically at him as she gently lowered a brown purse onto the very same wooden dresser that had served as his morning Klaxon.

Head still spinning, Dan scanned the room. He was in a small apartment, tangled in sheets. Most of his clothes were piled at the foot of the bed. There was a vague recollection of dancing spirit animals, kachinas, and tits. A surge of panic shot through him as he remembered Rachel, alone, back in Atlanta. *Was he a two-timing asshole?*

"'Bout time you woke up," Molly said. "It's almost noon."

"I, uh . . . did we . . . ?" Dan oscillated his finger between the two of them.

"Hardly," she huffed. "You passed out the minute we got here, a real party pooper." With that, she left the room, her voice echoing down the hallway. "I headed back out for some fun."

Dan struggled out of the bed, feeling oddly disconnected from his body, his feet seemingly floating above the floor. Fitting legs into trousers threatened to become an exercise in futility. Like most people, he had suffered through epic hangovers before but nothing like this. It was more like being a passenger on a journey to another world. Fumbling to button his shirt, his fingers felt like sticks glued to the ends of his hands. His mind drifted back to the night before and the kachina dance, and a profound feeling that he had experienced something transcendental, almost religious, although he didn't fully understand the details.

Sounds of coffee being brewed soon drifted down the hall. He moved cautiously and spotted Molly pouring a stream of steaming water through a filter. Black water dripped like molasses into the glass container underneath. It was as if he could taste the coffee within the sound of the dripping, all in slow motion.

Thoughts drifted through caverns in his mind, bouncing from one hollow memory to another. They finally stopped on Chemerra and his official purpose.

Molly poured the thick, black substance into two glass mugs and offered him one. He took it eagerly, sensing the burnt aroma of roasted beans tickling the hairs of his nose. He took a sip. It triggered a cascade of thoughts that poured out of his brain like a waterfall. It was as if every swallow of coffee he had ever tasted drifted by his mind's eye in that moment. Tufts of steam wiggled and danced from the black pool of liquid like spirit beings. *Focus, dammit!* Reality was out there somewhere, he just had to reach out and grab it.

"So, where did you go last night, after I, uh, passed out?"

"To a friend's apartment," she said with a harrumph.

Dan was surprised he could remember anything from the night before but there were all the memories, lined up in his mind like a jury. "A friend like Chemerra, then?"

"No," she said curtly.

He pressed. "So, you two have an open relationship?"

"Of course," she replied, as if her answer was obvious.

Which it most certainly wasn't, in Dan's current mental state. "So when can we go meet him?"

Molly rolled her eyes and checked the messages on her phone— one of the black phones, he noticed. "I've left several messages but he hasn't replied."

"Can't we just drop in on him?"

"Of course not, silly," she said. "No one knows where Chemerra lives."

Reality was slipping out of his grasp again. "Wait a minute, I thought you were his girlfriend. How did you two meet, then?" It seemed like a reasonable question but Molly's expression made him feel childlike, moronic. A sudden burst of paranoia and insecurity flowed over him.

"We don't meet in person," she said. "I mean, like in the flesh. *Nobody* does, hence his name, dummy." Molly took a long draw from her mug. "We have an online relationship. Fact is, it's been awhile since we've talked. Chemerra has been really busy lately and I've been . . . distracted, I guess." She brightened for a moment. "But if Chemerra wants to talk with you, don't worry. He'll find *you*."

Enlightenment suddenly cut through Dan's haze of confusion. Whatever had happened last night, whoever had drugged him, all the hackers he had met—it was a total waste of time. Whoever Chemerra was, he wasn't about to show himself in a public forum, or be recognized, even by his fellow hackers. It was the kind of anonymity that had thwarted the FBI for months, a level of sophistication capable of hiding from federal surveillance, the FBI, Homeland Security, the NSA.

Did he really think he could waltz into some geek party and magically meet up with this notorious hacker?

Dan placed the mug on the kitchen counter. "Molly, thanks for the hospitality and the place to stay. Sorry if I was a party pooper but I've really got to be on my way. Here." He scribbled his burner number on a notepad anchored to the fridge. "If you talk to Chemerra, tell him to call me. I'd like to meet up."

Molly stared dubiously at the yellow piece of paper. "I wouldn't hold your breath," she said. "Chemerra's in one of his moods. *Very* private."

"Whatever," he said and bounced off the walls a couple of times on the way to the door.

Outside, he immediately recognized the location: the boardwalk overlooking Stoker's maker-space. Down below, Stoker and several others were cleaning up after the party, sliding machinery and tools back into their original positions. Stoker stopped and stared up at him with an amused expression.

Dan stumbled down the steps. The expanse of the warehouse floor seemed to take an eon to cross. It gave him the time he needed to return to some semblance of normalcy.

"I hope you enjoyed our festivities last night," Stoker said, grinning. "I see you met Coulee Babee."

"Who? Oh, you mean Molly." Dan's head was pounding. He spotted a plastic lawn chair, pulled it over, and plopped down in front of Stoker with relief. "I'm getting too old for this . . . I feel like I was rode hard and put up wet." He scanned the warehouse, now fully visible in its vastness. Rays of morning light streamed through the high windows, giving the space a brooding atmosphere. "Apparently, one of your guests had an issue with my presence. I was drugged last night."

Stoker leaned against a large table with a sincere look of concern. "Really? I can't imagine that. You're considered a hero by most of these kids. Who would want to harm you?"

"I don't know. Chemerra perhaps? All I can tell you is that someone drugged me with some mind-altering substance. I'm still struggling. Then Molly, or Coulee Babee, or whoever, rescued me, I suppose, although she doesn't seem too happy this morning."

Stoker's face turned red and puffed up into the shape of an overinflated balloon. "Tell me something Dan," he said, barely able to control his demeanor. "How many of those beers, the Final Solution, did you have last night?"

Dan struggled to remember. "Not sure. Four or five, I guess. People kept offering them to me."

Stoker's granite facade finally crumbled and he burst into hearty laughter. After a long, embarrassing guffaw, he continued: "There's your problem," he said. "Those brews are the penultimate creation of some of our, let's say, more creative biohackers. They used the latest genetic engineering technology, called CRISPR to alter the DNA of brewer's yeast. Their custom-designed yeast not only produces alcohol but the molecules THC, MDMA, and mescaline, you know . . . PEP . . . pot, ecstasy, and peyote. They've been working on that PEP formula for months. Hackers love the combination of creativity and transcendence, in reasonable doses, of course. Seems you overdid it and had your own, let's say, religious experience. Shall I call you shaman?" Stoker let out another hearty laugh.

"What?" The thought gave Dan a jolt. He had walked right into a biohacking incident like a fool. What else were the Firemen capable of? "So, your friends drugged me?"

"Not exactly. Guests were allotted one dose per token, remember? To liven up the group dance. Who knew you were such a glutton."

Dan suddenly remembered the server refusing to sell him an additional brew. That hadn't stopped random fans from offering up their allotment. "I don't suppose I need to point out the illegality of that, do I?"

Stoker shrugged. "Ever receive a speeding ticket? Common law is an interpretation. No harm intended. They're just kids enjoying life."

"Really? And what if these kids get angry and decide to brew up something more harmful? I'm not comfortable with the idea of these *harmless kids* having that much power to alter life."

"Says the Weatherman hacker."

"That's different," Dan said, his jaw set. "I was doing good. Who's monitoring them?"

"We monitor each other, obviously," Stoker said. "Like the rest of society. Who monitors the rich and powerful? The government? Their peers? Don't make me laugh."

Dan grew quiet. Just a few minutes ago, he had considered giving up, moving on, returning to Rachel. But he was reminded of the Devil's Paradox. These ordinary people, these innocent fools, held the power of evolution in their hands. But in nature, evolution plods along for billions of years, making small mistakes early and often, in fits and starts. In one age, evolution achieves great advancements, then renders life almost extinct the next. Five massive extinction events later, man barely hangs on.

But today, man has benefited and profited from those billions of years of mistakes, reboots, and achievements. Could a bunch of young computer hackers have the maturity or foresight to accelerate that evolution safely? As quickly as he had decided to leave this problem to someone else, he now realized he couldn't. There was too much at stake.

"I suppose you have a point," Dan said, changing his adamant tone and laughing at himself, hoping to put Stoker at ease. He recounted his bizarre evening with Molly, which elicited a sad smile from Stoker.

"I don't know what's gotten into that girl," Stoker said. "She used to be such a vibrant activist, involved in many causes and issues. But several months ago her passions just faded, that is, except for one, as you no doubt experienced. Now she just seems disinterested in school, the *cause*."

"What cause is that?"

Stoker gave Dan a knowing glance and smile. "Why, the one you seem so interested in. Your attendance at our party last night was no accident, although your introduction to some of our more, uh, creative customs was certainly unplanned." He chuckled again. "However, you should be more cautious with your probing questions. There are reasons for maintaining a certain level of, let us say, decorum and secrecy."

For the first time since he had arrived in Savannah, Dan felt as if he had made some progress in penetrating the many layers of secrecy around this strange group, the Firemen, all because of his own stupidity. *Might as well run with it.* "Well, my interest grew when I saw comments made about me by Chemerra on the dark web."

"Oh, that." Stoker looked away. "Names on the web are just names. Your actions built your reputation and identity as an activist, as someone concerned with the imbalance of power between the gatekeepers and the common folk. Let's just say that a person with your kind of passion attracts attention. But caution is warranted. There are many powerful forces aligned against us that can cause immense damage if we let our guard down."

Like my employer, Dan thought. In a way, he felt sleazy to be working undercover. Lying was not his strong suit and despite the risky nature of their activism, the Firemen, or at least the people he suspected to be Firemen, seemed sincere and friendly. *But serial killers seem nice on the surface too. Otherwise, how can they operate?* Dan wasn't sure what he expected when he met these people for the first time. Fire coming out of their ears maybe, or horns growing from their forehead? Vince Peretti had warned him about the tendency of undercover agents to identify with the criminals they infiltrate. While he thought about those issues, Dan noticed that Stoker was studying him intensely during their brief moment of silence.

"So, how do I arrange a meeting with Chemerra? I'm interested to learn more about him and your organization. How else will I know if I fit in, or agree with your agenda? And why haven't I heard of your secret society before?"

Stoker's face remained cold and unchanging. "What part of *secret society* do you not understand? Besides, I'm fairly confident you agree with our agenda. After all, it's also *your* agenda."

"What does that mean, exactly?"

Stoker smiled. "Everyone knows you exposed a conspiracy between politicians and Martin Orcus, the billionaire from Honduras. But we appreciate your unsung actions as well."

Dan felt a sudden surge of panic. This wasn't part of the original plan. The Firemen seemed to know far more about him than he had anticipated. "I don't understand what you mean."

"Come on, Dan. We know about your efforts in Honduras, so important that our own government has chosen to keep it all secret. We believe in the same threats, only older and more entrenched. Covid-19 should serve as a wake-up call, an eye opener."

A sudden fear overtook him. Had Chemerra hacked the CDC's secure databases that stored the details of their classified operation? Maybe that was why Chemerra stole the Devil's Paradox. He would know of its tremendous potential to cause havoc. The Firemen suddenly seemed more than simple misguided zealots but rather a group with a well-planned agenda. It was becoming frighteningly clear that the Firemen knew the dangers involved all too well.

"What threat exactly?"

"That, my friend," Stoker said, "will become clearer as you earn more trust." A catchlight seemed to twinkle in Stoker's eyes as he teared up. "A new age is dawning, my friend. Soon, the Firemen will unleash the greatest change in human history, ever. And you can be part of it, if you desire."

To Dan, that sounded like a frightening premonition of chaos forged by a cadre of zealots. Still, he needed to play along, burrow inside the organization, find the truth. He thought for a minute, struggling to find the proper attitude to convey. "Well, I would think my notoriety would afford me greater access. I have my own plans. I'd like to parlay with Chemerra sooner, rather than later. Otherwise we may head off in different directions."

"Patience, Dan," Stoker said. "We haven't maintained our secrecy this long without taking precautions. First, you'll need to register in our Minion program."

"What's that?" Dan asked.

"The Minion program is our way of building trust and seniority within the organization. Every time someone needs help with a project, they issue a 'Minion Call' using our custom phone app. You earn points and rank every time you volunteer. With a high enough rank you can begin making your own Minion Calls." Stoker held up his black phone and waggled it for effect. "When you reach Apprentice rank, you earn one of these."

Dan was starting to realize that infiltrating this group was going to take a lot more time than he'd thought. He needed to speed things up. "So, what? You expect me to do grunt work for other members? I would think my previous achievements would have earned me more credibility than that."

"Dan, you've got to prove your worth like everyone else. That's how it's done, no exceptions. In fact, we have a major event taking place which should earn you some serious Minion points, should you choose to participate."

Uh, oh, that sounded ominous. Dan decided he had little choice. "What event exactly?"

"Just show up here tomorrow and we'll get you started," Stoker said.

8

THE DRIVE SOUTH had given Rachel plenty of time to think. Her adventures with Dan had been cut short but contained everything that mattered. It had been a good life, she reasoned, short or not. There had been thrills, none more fulfilling than the last year. Now she owed him peace and a future. Not the future she had endured with her father, watching him become a shred of the man she had worshiped as a child. She could save Dan the pain of that familiar journey into nothingness.

The time she had left as herself, no one could know; the doctor had said as much. Despite their skills at treatment and disease diagnosis, Rachel found doctors to be poorly trained in the art of sharing bad news.

No problem.

She had prepared for this moment, having considered the inevitability for years. She had the power and freedom to write her own epitaph. She could either go out as the pitiful victim of fate, or as a heroic adventurer pushing the limits of flight. The latter was better and she knew the perfect way to accomplish that.

Her mood lifted as she turned off I-75 toward Moultrie, Georgia. She hadn't visited the area since she was a child but her memories were still bright and vivid: longleaf pines and sweeping fields of corn, cotton, and tobacco growing on the piedmont.

From what she could tell, things hadn't changed much in the ensuing years, except for a few conspicuous items looming over the crops like arched bridges: large center-pivot sprinkler systems rotating lazily across the fields. She'd never seen the huge structures from this perspective but knew the effect from the sky: row after row of green circles dotting the landscape like emeralds. When she was a kid, the fields were all square, oriented north, south, east, and west. You could navigate a plane by dead reckoning simply by following the property lines but no longer, unless you wanted to fly in circles.

A few miles north of town, Rachel turned her car east onto highway 130, past rows of dilapidated buildings, fields of corn and cotton. She kept her eye peeled for a distinctive pond bordering the highway and turned left past it.

She slowed to examine an old military checkpoint crumbling with age. A rusty sign had succumbed to the wind and weather, lying in a heap of bent steel, its letters barely visible: SPENCE AIR BASE.

According to the many tales her grandfather had told her as a child, Spence started out in World War Two as a military training base for young pilots earning their first wings. At the start of the Korean War, it was reactivated under commercial contract as Hawthorne Aviation, run by Bevo Howard, the famous aerobatic stunt pilot.

By the time Rachel arrived as a young girl, the base had been decommissioned but many of the old buildings still remained. Driving through the area, she was surprised to discover that a few modern structures had infiltrated the area, giving the aging air base a haunting atmosphere of old and new.

Her "Granda" had taught her how to fly here. By age eight, she had mastered the basic aerobatic maneuvers. Flying came as naturally to her as breathing.

Memories of those sultry summer days suddenly overwhelmed her with melancholy. Here, a thousand miles away from the family home in Chicago, her grandfather had been more of a mentor to her than her own father, who had often been absent, flying for Delta Airlines as a commercial pilot.

She followed the old road into Arnold Circle, near the center of the base and turned right onto a rough access road, cracked and rutted with age, that paralleled one of the old runways. She continued to the far end of the base and pulled up front of a familiar old hangar built in the forties.

The old tin-covered building still looked intact, surprisingly well preserved after so many years, its voluminous hangar door still secured by a rusted padlock. Rachel struggled for a moment to remember the combination, then rotated the old dial. A few hard pulls broke the rust loose and the padlock sprung open. Straining with great effort, she began lifting the door, its rollers squealing against pitted metal.

There it was, its colors still bright, even when viewed through the glittering dust cloud she had just kicked up: Granda's prize biplane, a Bücker Jungmann dual-seat trainer. Its twin wings looked almost birdlike with their alternating red and white stripes that had been painted at a diagonal.

Tears welled in her eyes as she stared at the venerable old plane. Granda had willed it to her, along with the old hangar, before his passing. Granda, more famously known as Finnegan Sullivan, had moved from Ireland to the states after the Second World War, looking for fresh adventures with his newlywed Italian wife, Rachel's grandmother. Many adventures later, he had retired to the sleepy town of Moultrie, adopting the old air base as his personal flying school.

Rachel had heard the stories countless times while sitting on Granda's knee as a young girl. Finnegan had been attracted to the area by Bevo Howard, one of the few other owners of a German Bücker in America. Bevo's plane was the single seat version, a Bücker Jungmeister. Bevo had developed quite a reputation for entertaining audiences with his famous aviation stunt, the snatching of a ribbon while flying the Bücker upside down a few feet above the ground. Bevo's stunt was so famous that when his plane was donated to the Smithsonian's National Air and Space Museum, it was displayed upside down.

When Rachel had started flying the stunt pilot circuit years ago in her Yak-55 stunt plane, she had wanted to incorporate Bevo's stunt into her routine but Granda had forbade her, since Bevo Howard had died performing the stunt.

Rachel circled the Bücker Jungmann tentatively, running her hands over the stiff textured cloth of the wings, the steel cabling, the old wooden prop. She smiled wistfully. Before she had met Dan, she had sold her Yak-55, but now she might have one last chance to fulfill a childhood dream.

She could do it in the Bücker. *Maybe.*

Looking at the aging condition of the thirties-era cloth plane, she knew some significant improvements would have to be made first. Her wistful smile curled into a devilish smirk. It just so happened that the perfect person to do those modifications worked right around the corner.

RACHEL STRUGGLED UNSUCCESSFULLY to crank the Bücker. The engine had always been kept well-oiled but the seventy-year-old radial was showing its age. It had been sitting too long in the musty old hangar without any tender loving care.

No matter. The plane was light enough to move manually. Rachel positioned herself behind the lower wing and started pushing. After ten minutes of huffing and puffing, she'd managed to move the biplane down the length of the old runway, past a set of new buildings, and left toward the far reaches of the old airbase and the headquarters of Maule Aircraft. She paused near the front entrance of the company's hangar to catch her breath and looked around the area. It seemed that little had changed since B.D. Maule relocated his company to Spence Airbase back in 1968 from its original location in Michigan. Rachel left the Bücker on the taxiway and headed inside in search of Brent Maule, B. D.'s grandson and current manager.

Maule Aircraft had been manufacturing bush planes since the forties. Known as a STOL or short takeoff and landing plane, the Maule Aircraft design had become famous for its ability to fly almost anywhere in the backwoods, in questionable conditions, and land in the tightest of spaces. It was a favorite plane of Alaskan and Australian bush pilots, who cherished its ability to land at speeds below thirty knots.

There was another unique feature of Maule Aircraft that made the factory a perfect fit for her plans. Maule was one of the few remaining manufacturers in the world that still worked with tubular framing and fabric coverings. While the wings of the planes were fashioned from aluminum sheet metal like most modern planes, the fuselage was still covered with a fabric made from a combination of Dacron and butyl acetate, the modern equivalent of the old cotton and cellulose nitrate coverings originally used on the Bücker.

Rachel found her man and approached him, beaming: "Hey Brent, long time, no see."

"Rachel Sullivan! As I live and breathe." He smiled broadly and gave her a good stiff hug. "I haven't seen you since your grandpa's funeral. How have you been?"

Rachel glanced away. "Oh fine, I guess. Look, I need a *huge* favor. I'm going to put the Bücker back in service and it needs refurbishing. Could you fit me into your schedule?"

Brent scratched his head. "Well, it depends. What do you need, exactly?"

She nervously glanced over her shoulder at the Bücker. "Well, the old girl is showing her age. I'm going to be pushing her pretty hard with some aerobatic stunts. That will require an all new skin, plus aircraft gauge steel cabling. I need the highest strength you've got."

Brent stared out the hangar door at the old plane and tapped lightly on his chin with an index finger. "Yeah, I can do that. Things have been a bit slow lately, what with the pandemic. I can probably fit her in. When do you need it?"

Rachel grinned sheepishly. "Well . . . I'm performing at the Atlanta Air Show this weekend. How about day after tomorrow?"

Before Brent could answer, she added: "Oh, and one more thing. That old radial engine is shot. I need something with more horsepower, anyway. How about one of those?" she said, pointing.

Brent's eyes followed Rachel's finger to her intended target, a 420-horsepower Allison turboprop engine that had been mounted on a custom float-plane. His eyes grew wide. "Are you serious?"

"As a heart attack," Rachel said. "Don't worry, I can pay cash. Granda's inheritance."

Brent's head drooped, wagged back and forth gently. "I'll have to do a new center-of-gravity calculation, probably extend the nose. That will require two all-nighters for several of my guys, plus myself." He stared out at the noble old Bücker Jungmann, squatting expectantly on the concrete on its fat rubber tires and tiny tail wheel.

"Dammit, Rachel. I had a fishing trip planned this weekend." He sighed. "Tickets for the show?"

"Absolutely," she said. "I promise. The stunt will be spectacular."

9

DURING THE RIDE back to the hotel, Dan's head was still spinning, literally and figuratively. The aftereffects of his drug overdose had left his brain scrambled. Right now, he needed to think clearly.

And he missed Rachel.

His embarrassing behavior the night before weighed heavily on his heart. He needed to hear Rachel's voice and know that he was forgiven. But first, he had to take care of business. As soon as he entered the hotel, he crossed the lobby and called Vince Peretti.

After three rings, Vince answered. "Who is this?"

"It's Dan. I'm on a burner, which is why you don't recognize the number. Rudi convinced me to leave my cell phone in the hotel room."

"Where have you been?" Vince's voice sounded strained, abrupt. "My agents lost track of you at the Firemen dance."

"Well, I, uh, was trying to infiltrate the group, which required flying by the seat of my pants a bit."

"Barrett Hudlow is going ballistic." Vince lowered his voice and mumbled. "I hate these joint task forces. Hudlow is convinced you've skipped town, or joined the movement."

Dan chuckled internally, relishing the idea of creating angst for the Homeland Security bureaucrat. He hated bureaucrats almost as much as politicians. "I've made some headway infiltrating the group but these kids are a conundrum. They seem friendly enough, even carefree, hardly the picture of a violent cult of zealots. I can't even determine how many members the group has. Certainly not the majority of people attending the party. No, I think the core group is small, elite, and very careful. I did see some things that concerned me, though. For instance, they've definitely experimented with genetic engineering. They're up to something big and I'm concerned it may happen soon."

"Did you meet Chemerra?"

"No, not even close. Not sure he was even there, frankly. They want me to participate in some rite of passage before they'll even admit to the hacker's existence."

"What's your next move?"

"Tomorrow, I'm heading back to participate in some big event they have planned."

Vince let out a low sigh. "Well, you need to keep in better touch. Our agents will be shadowing you but we can only get so close without arousing suspicion."

"Got it. I'll call or text on this burner, so note the number."

ON THE WAY back to his room, Dan knocked at Rudi's door.

The dark-haired programmer answered almost immediately. "What happened to you last night? Last time I looked, you were heading up the steps with Coulee Babee. Have you been a bad boy?" Rudi clicked his tongue three times. "Rachel's gonna be *pissed*." He wagged his finger to bolster the effect.

Dan brushed by him into the room, now littered with Rudi's signature pile of empty pizza boxes, candy wrappers, and half-empty bottles of RC Cola. "Nothing happened. But you could say I had a religious experience. Did you know that beer was laced with THC and peyote?"

"Yeah, cool brew. Definitely put a PEP in *my* step. Helped make the evening dance *intense,* man. Sorta reminded me of the old-fashioned raves."

"Well, I *didn't* know and people kept offering me their allotment. I basically passed out."

Rudi giggled. "Good for you, needed to rinse some starch out of that collar of yours anyway."

"Why does everybody think it's funny to get overdosed?" Dan was eager to change the subject. "Tell me you had some luck tracking down Chemerra."

That wiped the smirk off Rudi's face. "Sorry. That dude's harder to find than a three-dollar bill. Everybody acted like he was a ghost, maybe a bot, or a team of hackers. The guy's just too good, a super cracker, hacking legend. They say he's penetrated several military servers, righteous stuff, man. Nobody knows how he does it."

"Well, keep working on it here in the room, okay? Learn as much as you can from the dark web. Meanwhile, I'll try to make contact the old-fashioned way."

Dan left and headed toward his room. He was beginning to doubt the value of his undercover activities. Why would Chemerra be interested in him at all? It sounded like the Firemen knew enough to know that his hacking prowess was a fraud, that Rudi was the real prize. And yet, they kept treating him like royalty.

To what end?

Exhausted, he crashed on the bed, still suffering some disorientation from the drugs working their way out of his system. He missed Rachel, the sound of her voice, and needed to come clean about his behavior. He also needed to update her on Esrom Nesson's situation and bounce ideas off her. She'd be pissed for not being included but she'd get over it and no one had better insight into Esrom's background. Their relationship went years back when Dr. Nesson served as Rachel's academic adviser for her microbiology degree.

Dan reached over to the nightstand and retrieved his personal cell phone and made the call. Rachel's phone rang several times before voice mail picked up.

Odd.

She usually kept her phone with her at all times. Maybe she was in the bathroom or completing a dive in the fish tank at the Georgia Aquarium. No matter. He'd try again later and decided to rest his head on the pillow for a few minutes. His mistake was in closing his eyes.

He fell asleep almost instantly.

THE NEXT MORNING Dan woke with the sun, still dressed in yesterday's clothes but feeling more normal. After a long, hot shower, he dressed casually, not knowing quite what to expect from the day. He ordered a good old-fashioned Southern breakfast of scrambled eggs, bacon, and toast from room service and used the spare time to try Rachel's number again.

Still no answer.

He checked his messages, found nothing. That was unusual. Had she found out the details of his trip somehow? Was she pissed at missing the action? Or worse, had she gotten cold feet again and fled? It wouldn't be the first time she had gone rogue, when fear of commitment had settled in. He'd always been able to track her down but now, he was trapped in Savannah in the middle of a crisis and needed her support, not her consternation.

He tried again, only to get her voice mail again. He needed to wrap up this undercover operation and get back to Atlanta. It had been the catastrophe in Honduras that had brought them together in the first place and now he had to face the threat again, alone. If Chemerra unleashed the Devil's Paradox, all that sacrifice in Honduras would mean nothing. A feeling of dread washed over him.

After wolfing down his breakfast, he summoned another ride and arrived at Stoker's Maker Haven, just as the sultry summer heat began to move in. The place was humming with activity. A large crowd had congregated, all dressed in some sort of disguise, from Generic YouGene masks to ski masks, dazzle face painting, LED glasses, even the Guy Fawkes masks that had become popular from the movie *V for Vendetta*. Whatever the Firemen had planned for the day, it required anonymity and that only made him more nervous. Worse still, the masks prevented him from identifying anyone from the night before. There was bound to be a lot of overlap.

Inside the warehouse, he spotted Stoker in the far shadows and began winding his way through a maze of tables where volunteers were painting protest signs. He slowed in order to read the messages:

VACCINES ARE A RIGHT, GENTROPICS MONEY WHORES,
LIVES OVER PROFIT, GENTROPICS BELONGS TO EVERYONE,
BIG-PHARMA, SMALL MINDS

That meant a demonstration back at the site of the theft. It was too much of a coincidence to be accidental. Was he expected to participate? In front of Esrom? He'd be betraying his own allies.

The crowd was practicing protest chants as they painted. He could hear their anger building in the murmur of masked voices. Their words took on a strange rhythmic quality like a dirge or shanty. It was creepy. Sprawled across a large table was a sign painted with a rendition of the GenTropics distinctive logo: an eagle with wings outstretched, perched on a staff of interlocking snakes. Below the logo Stoker had painted a strange message: HERMES: GOD OF MERCHANTS AND THIEVES.

Dan's brow wrinkled. "I'm afraid the meaning of your sign escapes me."

Stoker looked up from his task and smiled. "Glad you could make it. It's one of our more esoteric protest signs, I admit. I assume you're familiar with this oft misused symbol, the caduceus?" He pointed at the dual snakes winding up the staff. "Lots of medical institutions confuse this with the rod of Asclepius, which is the true Greek symbol for medicine and has a single serpent wound on its staff. This caduceus," Stoker said as he painted a broad red slash across the pristine logo, "is the staff carried by the Greek god Hermes, the patron of merchants and thieves. The interlocking snakes represent the duality of commerce and crime. The addition of the Roman Aquila only adds to the insult. Quite the ironic Freudian slip, don't you think?" He grinned sardonically. "These assholes assume the public is ignorant of their ancient iconography but *we* understand. Medicine should be about caring for the sick, not lining the pockets of stockholders. Through their logo, GenTropics is advertising their true priorities."

"Is this my so-called rite of passage? Participating in a protest? Doesn't seem like the adventurous agenda of a secret hacking society to me." Dan faked a frown, hoping Stoker would reveal their true agenda. He suspected something far more dangerous than a protest.

"It is the mundane inequity of society that demands the attention of dedicated visionaries. Secrecy allows us to censor the gatekeepers." Stoker spoke with the eloquence of a statesman but as soon as he grinned, the illusion collapsed. "Besides, protests are opportunities for assessment and evaluation. How do you think we find new recruits?" He slapped Dan on the back. "I'm glad you showed up but if you're going to join us, you'll need to hide your identity from the cameras."

"Before we get into that, I need a men's room. Too much coffee this morning."

"No problem." Stoker pointed to a dark corner of the warehouse. "Over there."

DAN CHECKED TO make sure the other stalls were empty, then slipped into the one at the far end of the room and dialed Vince Peretti on his burner phone. He spoke in a whisper. "Hello, Vince? Dan."

Vince's voice sounded pinched, on edge. "I wondered when I'd hear from you. What's going on?"

"This event isn't exactly what I expected. It appears the Firemen are organizing a protest march to GenTropics. They're uh, dissatisfied with the company's exorbitant profits."

"That's it? A march?" Vince almost sounded disappointed.

"It could explain their rationale for stealing the Devil's Paradox. Who knows what they are planning *during* the protest? I doubt they have any idea what that organism is capable of, and that's what really scares me. They might be planning a release."

"How much time do we have?"

"An hour or two . . . Maybe. If they march the whole way there it might take them longer."

"Have you seen anything that could be used as a distribution device? Aerosol dispensers, pesticide sprayers, bombs, foggers, leaf blowers . . . anything like that?"

Dan thought about it for a minute. "Not yet but I haven't been here that long. I'll look around—"

Someone entered the bathroom.

Instinctively, Dan hung up in midsentence. He left the stall and moved to the sink to wash his hands. Standing in the middle of the room was a short muscular man wearing an old Richard Nixon Halloween mask.

The man raised both hands in a V for victory sign and exclaimed in a rather convincing impersonation: "I am not a crook."

Nixon stood there, staring right at him, as if waiting for a response but Dan just dried his hands, smiled briefly, and walked out the door.

Was that the guy from the Nerdvana show? Dan hated the disguises, all the masks and anonymity. Not knowing who he was dealing with increased his anxiety as he wandered through the maker floor, looking for any equipment that could be used to distribute pathogens.

After looking around the maker-space for thirty minutes, Dan found nothing suspicious and soon began to doubt his own fears. What could this secretive group possibly gain by releasing some infectious agent at a large public event? They'd be harming themselves. It didn't make sense.

But then, neither did the deniers of the coronavirus pandemic, who had stubbornly refused to wear masks, even though the science was clear that they could save many lives. It seemed that human logic had been one of the victims of the pandemic.

And yet, the Firemen, as deranged as their plan might be, seemed much more logical and calculating. There had to be something more complex going on. He just needed to figure it out, before something drastic happened.

AFTER RECEIVING DAN'S hurried phone call, Vince Peretti moved quickly, alerting the rest of the joint terrorism task force. Since the FBI didn't have a federal field office in Savannah, they had set up an ad hoc operations center at the state GBI's brand-new Coastal Regional Crime Laboratory.

The Georgia Bureau of Investigation was the state's version of the FBI and had recently opened a brand-new forensics center in nearby Pooler just a few miles from downtown Savannah. It was a posh venue, far from the sterile seventies facade of the Atlanta FBI field office. The CRCL or Circle, as it was called, was about as stylish as a government building was allowed to get: three stories of glass-clad metal and concrete, brimming with the latest in forensic technology, communications equipment, and a morgue the size of a small office building. Federal purse strings had become as tight as Vince could ever remember, yet somehow, the State of Georgia had money to burn.

Everything nowadays was about cooperation between agencies, so the joint task force had commandeered one of the many conference rooms. The room was bustling with activity. A wall of flat-screen monitors had been set up, providing live intelligence streams from local law enforcement, traffic cameras, the main FBI office, live video feeds from the field, and real-time internet data.

This was all thanks to the Atlanta Fusion Center, another attempt at developing cross agency cooperation. Fusion centers were developed as an answer to the chaos of 9/11. The secrecy, infighting, and competition between agencies had been exposed during the Twin Towers attack. The fusion centers were supposed to usher in a new age of cooperation and data access between multiple law enforcement agencies.

They worked, Vince mused, perhaps too well. Sponsored by Homeland Security but run by the states, they could collect an incredible volume of personal data, not only from federal sources but also from local law enforcement. Any agency could access the collective data.

Which was the problem.

No one took responsibility for the original information. It was like the Wild West, with data access loose and unmonitored. Being a former accountant prior to his term at the Agency, Vince would have preferred a more formal approach and accountability for what was essentially every citizen's private information.

Vince watched as Barrett Hudlow scampered from table to table, cell phone glued to one ear, sinking his talons of control into every agency. Since the task force was undercover, they had passed control of the Firemen's protest demonstration off to the local police department and sheriff's office. The locals would provide the task force with their eyes and ears in the field.

"And get your team on-site ASAP if you want to be in the fight." Clearly agitated, Barrett Hudlow slammed his cell phone on the table.

"Who was that?" Vince said.

"Huh?" Hudlow barely noticed Vince standing behind him. "Oh, that was the head of GenTropics' private security force. I was urging him to get their asses in gear if they wanted to protect their client's assets."

"Think that's a good idea?" Vince said. "Most private security firms are a bunch of hacks. Wouldn't it be better to let the local police take the front lines?"

Hudlow's scowl made it clear to Vince that he didn't like having his authority questioned. "They deserve the right to protect their client. And they're not hacks. Homeland Security works with private firms all the time."

"You mean like those guys playing an impersonation of your shadow?" Vince pointed at the two men Hudlow had never bothered to introduce. Hudlow's own private workforce was filled with hired contractors. Vince didn't like the way they were constantly lingering in the shadows, watching and listening to every conversation.

"True, we depend on hired help. There's plenty of well-trained security personnel back from the Gulf Wars. I trust them more than a bunch of south Georgia hayseeds in uniform."

Vince considered himself one of those Georgia hayseeds and didn't take kindly to the slight. "I think you'll find Savannah law enforcement quite capable. We hayseeds graduate from the same level of training as your Washington elites."

Hudlow released a derisive laugh. "Well, rounding up watermelon thieves is a far cry from the experience of meeting the enemy on the battlefield."

"So what branch of the armed services did you serve in?" Vince said, noting Hudlow's flaccid physique.

"Ha-ha, funny." Hudlow turned and walked off.

Vince suspected the only battlefield Hudlow had ever visited was near the coffee machine in the break room. Amazing how some government bureaucrats liked to live vicariously through troops or hired guns.

Perhaps jealousy played a role. Homeland Security's own Federal Protective Service, the police charged with guarding government buildings, consisted mainly of private security guards. Homeland Security had no field agents, which meant they had to rely on the U.S. Marshals Service and the FBI for local law enforcement. That, and the duplication of efforts between agencies had bred a natural animosity. Homeland Security had the authority but none of the teeth for getting things done.

It doesn't help that you're a jerk, Vince thought to himself. He watched Hudlow waddle away, his tiny squad of sycophants following close behind like lapdogs. The two men standing a few feet away smirked, turned, and followed the entourage.

Vince sighed as he scanned the hodgepodge of officers from ten or so federal and state agencies scrambling around the room trying to carve out their own turf. As the chief liaison officer for the task force, he was not only responsible for coordinating activities in Savannah but he had to report everything back to the Atlanta field office and endure the fusion center's feedback on every tactic and strategy. While the left hand might be aware of the right hand, the chances of them juggling anything of substance in this shit-storm of activity without dropping the ball seemed unlikely at best.

Vince took a deep breath, sat down, and called Atlanta.

IN THE TIME it had taken Vince to update the Atlanta Fusion Center, Barrett Hudlow had taken control of the entire operation. Perturbed by the man's attempted coup of his authority, Vince walked over and sat down next to Hudlow. "Give me a progress report."

Hudlow shot Vince a look of disdain. "I don't take orders from you."

"You can and you will," Vince said in a cold tone. "I'm the task force coordinator."

Hudlow stared quietly for several minutes, appearing to contemplate a confrontation. He obviously thought better of it. "I contacted the local sheriff's office and the Savannah police department," he said. "They're undermanned for this scale of operation, so I told them to let the GenTropics security force take the lead. They're mobilizing."

Vince knew he'd wasted valuable time on the phone, leaving a power vacuum that Hudlow was happy to fill. "As I said earlier, I disagree with that approach. Corporate security teams lack the training in crowd control. What's another option?"

Hudlow's vindictive stare ignored Vince's attempt at civility. "I've worked with this group before. This company, TaurusSec, is top notch; former Special Forces. They've got years of experience dealing with terrorists in the Middle East. I think they can handle a bunch of ragtag geeks."

"That's my point. These aren't foreign hostiles; they're American citizens."

"American terrorists," Hudlow clarified. "With biological weapons."

"Possibly. But we still have to follow protocol. This is not a foreign theater of operations."

"Might as well be," Hudlow huffed, looking back at his screen. "Have you seen the size of this crowd?" He pulled up a traffic cam video of the long caravan snaking its way toward the GenTropics lab.

Even Vince had to admit, the scale of the demonstration was impressive and it seemed to be growing at every turn.

"TaurusSec has a surveillance drone," Hudlow said. "We'll have a live feed any minute. If there's a biological event, we can move in real time. TaurusSec's intel will give us a strategic advantage."

Vince still didn't like it but in the interest of the task force, he decided to go along.

10

Lieutenant Holt "Maddawg" McAndrews had been dozing when the call came in from Barrett Hudlow. Receiving a communication from Homeland Security was a rare occurrence and the circumstance jolted Maddawg awake like a double shot of Red Bull.

After a couple of deployments in Afghanistan, or any war for that matter, boredom became a primary side effect of reentry into civilian life. Working for the security firm TaurusSec allowed him to put his former skills to good use but it still wasn't like the military.

Civilian companies were maddeningly slow at making decisions, which meant excruciating delays in getting anything done. But not today. Today, he had a clearly defined mission and a critical timeline. As was his habit, Maddawg scanned the large hangar at TaurusSec headquarters, assessing current conditions and available personnel. It was a skeleton crew, the weekend shift, but all of them had extensive service records and multiple tours of combat duty, either in Afghanistan or Iraq. McAndrews had worked with half of them on combat missions and knew the others, at least, by reputation.

Martino "Raptor" Ruiz was tearing down an AR-15, the parts lined up with meticulous care across the head of the conference table. Blayze "Moondog" Scott had his head buried in a copy of *Gun Digest*.

The other men in the room were all occupied by some pissant boring task or asleep, like himself only a few minutes before, until the call had put him on full alert.

"Listen up, people!" he shouted at sufficient volume to get the room's attention. "We've got a crowd control situation at GenTropics HQ this afternoon. A bunch of *terror-nerds* are staging a protest demonstration. Suit up. Full engagement gear, scramblers, tear gas, the works. We've got less than an hour, so let's get crack'n!" He clapped his hands together for effect.

The entire room snapped to attention immediately, their eyes bright with anticipation and purpose. He looked over at Jadon "Froggie" Pitts, who was still debugging the remote control software for their latest prototype of the Pegasus surveillance drone.

Maddawg approached. "Is that bird ready to deploy yet?"

Froggie pushed his thick Coke-bottle glasses back up the bridge of his nose. "What . . . now?"

"Why not?" Maddawg said. "Perfect time for a field test."

"Hell yes!" Froggie grinned broadly, his wide eyes magnified grotesquely by the thick lenses. "I'll get her fueled and launched. Then I can transfer control to the mobile remote."

Even though TaurusSec was a private security firm, their contract status with the Army had provided a lot of perks. They'd enrolled in the Defense Department's Excess Property Program—known as 1033—which gave equipment, including weapons, to local law enforcement agencies. Since most of Maddawg McAndrew's squad were former Special Forces operatives, they felt right at home with the gear.

With barely a word being spoken, duffel bags were stuffed with antipersonnel equipment, jammers, loudspeakers, noise-based crowd-control devices, shotguns, rubber bullets, body armor, helmets, shields, flash bangs, stingers, and tear gas grenades. Since becoming civilians, they had traded in their M4s and Heckler & Koch MP5s for the more conventional AR-15s but the basic function was the same.

Fifteen minutes later, the entire squad was loaded into their Lenco "BearCat," which stood for the Ballistic Engineered Armored Response Counter Attack Truck; a typical military moniker for an armored SWAT vehicle. "Granite Jack" Martin and his K-9 team would follow close behind.

Maddawg McAndrews finally felt legit, alive, for the first time in days. He had a righteous mission to complete and felt the familiar surge of adrenaline coursing through his veins.

AFTER AN HOUR of searching and observing the protest preparations, Dan was no closer to understanding the Firemen's motives, except to highlight what they viewed as excess greed on the part of GenTropics Pharmaceuticals. Judging from the group's indignation with authority figures, Dan began to wonder if the Firemen suffered from a severe messiah complex.

Stoker's prophetic words from the day before kept rattling around in Dan's mind: *A new age is dawning, my friend. Soon, the Firemen will unleash the greatest change in human history, ever. And you can be part of it.*

The gravity of those words prompted Dan to find Stoker and ask more questions, but before he could find him, a masked member of the crowd grabbed a bullhorn and signaled everyone outside. He had little choice but to follow the crowd out into the sunlight, where a long line of vehicles had amassed. Demonstrators started piling into the collection of public buses, trolley cars, pedal-powered mobile bars, and pedicabs. With a sudden cheer, the front of the convoy began snaking its way out of the parking lot and meandering down the street. It inched forward at a brisk walking pace, music blaring from boom boxes and cell phones, with demonstrators following along, piling into the free transportation wherever they could find space. Everyone seemed to be on their phones. Soon the entourage reached downtown Savannah where more demonstrators joined the procession. The protest had a festive air about it, not the ominous mood one would normally presume.

Volunteers were passing out disguises and Dan grabbed one of the paper YouGene masks and slipped it on, immediately feeling less conspicuous. By the time the head of the entourage had reached the grounds of the GenTropics facility, the crowd had swelled to several thousand protesters, thanks to social media and the ability to communicate instantly with others. The lead buses began unloading and soon, a tent city materialized, complete with booths, stereo systems, chairs, public address megaphones, water, gas masks, and other supplies, all being distributed free to the willing crowd.

Smack dab in the center of the Firemen's tent city stood Stoker's operations's center, a tent outfitted with computer terminals and a huge kanban board, tracking every activity. It was an impressive operation, using common agile programming methods to prioritize tasks. These kids weren't just a haphazard group of students; they were well organized and professional.

Organized enough to be dangerous.

Generic YouGene had brought his own van along, called the "Maskmobile," equipped with a state-of-the-art Wi-Fi system. YouGene's Omni-Masks were doing a brisk business out of the back of his van as another team of volunteers constructed more rudimentary versions from a combination of carbon filter masks and ski goggles.

Wearing his mask, Dan felt invisible as he walked the grounds, free to take in the details anonymously. There had to be dozens of Generic YouGenes in the crowd so he blended in seamlessly. Anonymity provided a powerful form of protest and it made him feel bolder.

Dan's earlier call to Vince had triggered the formation of another tent city adjacent to the protest. A strong contingent of local police and SWAT teams had gathered on-site, equipped with crowd-control barricades, assault vehicles, and riot gear. He recognized several FBI agents from the task force working undercover, wandering the perimeter, whispering into their sleeves and eyeing the crowd suspiciously.

A murmur rose from the crowd as a uniformed row of security guards suddenly filed out from the front door of the GenTropics building, equipped with their own assault rifles and riot gear. They formed a solid line across the front of the building, flanked on both sides by the local police force.

By noon, the preparations were complete. The protesters seemed energized and excited, the authorities wary. The battle lines had been drawn.

WILL DETWEILER LAY awake in bed next to Molly, his thoughts consumed by nightmares of his mother's death. He felt more pissed than usual, a step back in the wrong direction. He'd been making progress, especially since meeting Molly and Sister Simone. Their female influence had filled a void and kept him from feeling so alone. Today he had relapsed. Will considered himself to be a good person fundamentally but a bitter stew of anger and resentment seemed to be fermenting deep inside his gut. He felt like fate had doomed him to a life of despair . . .

A text notification on his phone stirred him out of his morose thoughts. It was a friend alerting him to an opportunity, one that just might relieve some of his angst. It was a protest march against the very forces that had made his life a living hell.

His mother had contracted Covid-19 while teaching her class of fourth graders. Who knew which one of those snot-nosed kids had been carrying the virus around like some invisible bomb? Her hospitalization had left Will's dad financially and emotionally devastated. He had lost his job early during the pandemic and with it, the family's health care. With no money coming in, their COBRA coverage didn't last either. Wasn't insurance supposed to provide relief for the unfortunate? During times of need? Instead, the insurance company abandoned his mother right when she needed it the most. Will spent sleepless nights in his bedroom, listening to his father sobbing, desperately searching for a solution, all the while struggling to support Will and his college education. He didn't even get to say goodbye to his mom, hold her hand, or kiss her forehead.

She just died. Another statistic unceremoniously stuffed into a pine box and dumped into the earth without even a funeral.

Will soon found himself out of college and out of work. He'd been working at a local restaurant, on the way to becoming a pretty good chef, but then the pandemic ended that budding career too. Just like his dad, Will was unemployed with plenty of time to stew over lost opportunities.

The demonstration scheduled for that day gave him a perfect opportunity to let off some steam. The rich assholes who owned Gen-Tropics Pharmaceuticals made obscene profits off their drugs, getting rich off the misfortunes of others. They had a wildly expensive monoclonal antibody treatment for Covid that might have saved his mom's life but only the rich and privileged could get ahold of it. William felt a rush of righteous anger that took on a life of its own. His mother had died for no cause, a waste. And nobody cared. He felt so alone, even while he made love to Molly Daniels. It was as if his heart had grown incapable of anything but anger.

GenTropics needed to pay . . .

Will turned toward Molly and nuzzled her ear. "Hey babe," he whispered. "Have you heard about this protest march? Why don't we join in?"

Molly rolled over, rubbed up against him. "Really? I'd prefer to spend the day with you. Let's order some pizza and spend the day in bed, being decadent."

"Aren't you interested in your old friends? They're making a stand, supporting what's righteous. I feel like kicking some ass today, don't you?"

Molly thought about it for an instant. *No, not really,* she concluded. A few months ago, she too would have been eager to get involved but now she only felt embarrassed and disinterested. Lately, she had become lethargic, needy. Rather than fighting the world's problems, she craved intimacy and Will offered her that. For the last week, she had been lost in him, obsessed with sexual satisfaction and Will's approval. She was certain he desired her too, even though he seldom showed it. Wandering about in a faceless crowd, in a protest that had little chance of succeeding, seemed like a waste of her time.

Her enthusiasm for the Firemen and their conflicts had waned.

She slipped her hand down the front of Will's sweatpants, searching for the locus of his desire. She smiled demurely and waited for the predictable response. Instead, she received a look of determined indifference. She knew the fight was over before it began.

Eager to satisfy him, she acquiesced, smiled sheepishly, and kissed him on the cheek. "Whatever you want, dear," she said and got up to take a shower.

11

CROWD-CONTROL BARRIERS AND armored vehicles had formed a demarcation line between the front facade of the GenTropics building and the daring demonstrators. A ten-foot strip of asphalt became no-man's-land, flanked on both sides by local police in riot gear. Behind the line, TaurusSec guards paced back and forth, dressed out in their own distinctive gray variant of assault gear, their faces obscured by balaclavas and goggles. Apparently, the Firemen weren't the only group obsessed with anonymity.

It was one faceless mob against another.

Dan noticed that the TaurusSec logo seemed closely aligned to the GenTropics logo, with the talons of its eagle gripping a quiver of arrows. The two organizations didn't seem to be hiding the fact either.

The most zealous demonstrators began gathering near the front of the crowd, chanting. Eventually, they grew tired and sat down in front of the barriers, forming social circles. A few guitars appeared and ragged melodies began floating through the din of the crowd.

Dan looked across the open area of the GenTropics campus, past the barricade and no-man's-land, to the large glass facade of the building. There, he spotted Esrom Nesson and his assistant Ada Kurz staring out from the other side of the glass. Even from this distance, Dan could see the look of distress on Esrom's face as he rubbed his hands together nervously.

Dan suddenly felt ashamed of his participation in this protest while his friend looked on, distraught. Thankfully, the Generic YouGene mask gave him a modicum of anonymity. Another stab of guilt caused him to turn away, back to the scene behind him, in hopes of identifying the purpose and goal of this gathering, before the Firemen could act.

One theme he noticed immediately: cell phones, everywhere.

Cell phones taking pictures, filming videos, capturing selfies tweeted in real time to friends and relatives. The activities unfolding on the outskirts of this idyllic Southern town were being recorded, processed, and projected around the world with the speed and efficiency of a sophisticated news organization, a nearly extinct service that society had abandoned for the gratuitous grapevine of social media.

The protest was the perfect venue for a public statement. But what did the Firemen want to say? Complain about the cost of drugs? The prevalence of masks made it difficult to identify them but he began to spot the Firemen by their behavior. They were organized, acting with a purpose, moving from group to group, inspiring and instructing. This protest seemed designed for an older crowd. What kids worry about health care? Even the coronavirus pandemic left them relatively unscathed, except perhaps for the loss of loved ones.

The vast majority of the demonstrators were young: in their late teens and early twenties. Decades older, Dan distinctly remembered that time of his life, the purgatory between parental dependence and autonomy that develops when faced with an uncertain future. Dan's step into adulthood had come at an early age when his parents died. Still, the process remained the same.

The recognition of injustice and hypocrisy comes far earlier in life than the wisdom to combat those same forces. These young soldiers had a disdain for authority but no viable solutions. It seemed the Firemen were attempting some kind of accelerated training or recruitment, a version of boot camp.

The Firemen who wandered the crowd, so visible and obvious to him now, weren't a band of overzealous nerds. Their deliberate actions impressed him and filled him with dread. The theft of the Devil's Paradox haunted him. Why steal something so powerful and destructive unless you planned to use it?

He spotted Psue Dominus, wearing her trademark expressive clothing, glowing and undulating in the harsh daylight. She was moving through the crowd, wearing a traditional white Kabuki mask bearing the angry visage of an old woman with long, flowing locks of black hair and ceremonial horns affixed to her forehead. The mask's bright red mouth and glaring yellow teeth had an intimidating effect, much like the frightening visages of ancient Samurai soldiers with their exaggerated clothing and decoration. Psue moved in catlike motions ever closer to the barricade, using a weird combination of martial arts movements and theatrical Kabuki dance movements. She was practically inviting the TaurusSec guards to engage with her. The bizarre behavior seemed to have the requisite effect, unnerving the security forces and causing them to move back defensively.

Inspired by the theatrical display, the younger protesters stood up from their seated positions and marched back and forth along the barricade, brandishing their signs and chanting slogans. All the while, other protesters roamed the crowd with cell phones and video cameras, documenting the activities.

This precarious standoff between the protesters and law enforcement went on for the better part of an hour and likely generated several terabytes of video footage. Local law enforcement seemed confused and intimidated by the bizarre behavior, designed to be provocative yet nonviolent.

Meanwhile, back at the Firemen's operations center, Dan spotted the barrel-chested profile of Stoker, who seemed to be overseeing the operations of YouGene's ad hoc Wi-Fi network, set up to handle the tremendous volume of social media content and perhaps to power the Firemen's black phones, which depended on Wi-Fi to bypass traditional cell phone networks.

Dan could see the local authorities checking their cell phones, watching the coverage filmed by the crowd. The real-time video strategy had an immediate effect on them. It became clear that the local police force was losing the battle for the hearts and minds of the public. Dan sensed that the standoff was reaching a tipping point.

A sudden whine of propellers distracted his attention. Surveillance drones from both sides of the barricade swarmed into the air and circled each another like predators testing their opponent's resolve. Higher up, he spotted several local news helicopters that had finally converged on the scene. Farther in the distance, above the maelstrom of news copters and drones, Dan recognized a few other indistinct shapes, barely visible from the ground. One was a familiar Cessna 182 that Dan recognized, fairly certain it was a Stingray. Rarely acknowledged officially, Stingrays were devices the FBI used for covert operations: electronic jammers that could imitate cell phone towers and intercept cell phone calls and text messages. He imagined Vince listening in on the conversations below but knew that the truly strategic conversations, the ones among the Firemen on their black phones would continue in private.

There was another vehicle Dan spotted, far above the Cessna, a black speck that moved much more quickly. He strained his vision and felt certain the black speck was a delta wing–shaped craft he did not recognize.

MADDAWG MCANDREWS PACED restlessly behind the barricades, co-ordinating the TaurusSec team via digital radio. When he had first been contacted by Barrett Hudlow, Maddawg envisioned a handful of nerds with signs but the long line of vehicles that had disgorged protesters like a swarm of bees had his adrenaline pumping in full battle mode.

His pulse rate picked up considerably as the terror-nerds started gathering near the ragged barricade, prompting local enforcement to call in more supplies and SWAT teams.

The enemy had assembled a formidable force with well-organized pockets of resistance.

McAndrews thought back to the Capitol insurrection and reminded himself of how quickly things could go south. They would need to be ready for anything.

He clicked the transmit button three times to alert his troops.

MADDAWG: "Everybody check in." Over the next several minutes, every member of his team announced their presence and current location. He needed intel before the enemy had a chance to act. "Froggie, is Pegasus operational?"

FROGGIE: "Yes sir. Got the keyhole-15 lens at five centimeters."

MADDAWG: "I need intel." In modern warfare, McAndrews knew that strategic advantage came from superior battlefield awareness. The Pegasus drone gave them that in spades. Based on modern sat-ellite technology, it sported the latest in high-resolution optics but unlike its bigger brethren that operated from the borders of space, the jet-powered drone provided perfect low-altitude imagery. Its resolving power was incredible compared to the peasant opposi-tion they typically encountered. But they were in America now and these terror-nerds had their own advanced technologies.

FROGGIE: "Sending a live video stream from their operations center. I can almost read the text on their computer screens."

MADDAWG: "What would it take to establish clarity?"

FROGGIE: "I'd have to drop altitude by at least fifty percent."

MADDAWG: "Then do it."

FROGGIE: "Yes, sir. Just know that our presence will be detected."

MADDAWG: "Anyone with eyes to the sky is gonna see news copters and planes landing at Savannah International. We're just another random speck."

FROGGIE: "Gotcha. Descending."

Maddawg walked over to his own operations center for an update. "Raptor, do we have Wi-Fi intercept?"

Martino Ruiz was staring at his own wall of monitors. He looked back over his shoulder. "Not much, sir. Most of the Wi-Fi is encrypted. It appears they've got their own virtual private network. A few amateurs are sending videos and Instagram pics through the GenTropics public Wi-Fi but the majority of the traffic is locked up tighter than a witch's ass."

MADDAWG: "If we can't break the encryption, can we break the Wi-Fi?"

RAPTOR: "I can try."

MADDAWG: "Then do it." McAndrews took the opportunity to contact Barrett Hudlow at the fusion center. It was standard protocol for the two groups to coordinate their activities and he knew the FBI was flying a Stingray. Between their two technologies, they could shut down all communications, Wi-Fi and cell. He placed the call, received a positive response from Barrett, and waited.

It took only a few minutes for him to notice a change in the crowd's demeanor. They became agitated as their cell phones died. Like addicts deprived of their drug of choice, the youngsters became disorganized, confused, and distraught.

Maddawg grinned in triumph. *Let's see what these terror-nerds do without their precious phones,* he thought.

DAN WATCHED WITH great interest as Stoker reacted to the sudden loss of Wi-Fi signal. It seemed that he had been expecting the move and signaled Bob Sidian from Ant Mother. With a cursory nod, Bob flipped a switch on a circuit board filled with a bank of hundreds of the tiny Ant Mother computers, which lit up like a bank of Christmas lights.

Stoker stuck his thumbs up. "Let's see if the gatekeepers can jam *this,*" he said.

Dan looked down at his burner phone and saw a strong signal. A cheer coursed through the crowd. He walked over and whispered in Stoker's ear. "How'd you do that?"

"Heck, they're always trying to jam our signals but Bob's Ant Motherboards use old 'Wi-Fi A' chips. They're old-fashioned but when you have a bank of hundreds of them it amplifies the signal tenfold."

MUCH TO COLONEL McAndrew's dismay, the apparent confusion of the terror-nerds was short lived. Within a few minutes, the organized behavior returned. He knew that within every seemingly disorganized mob, there were always a few clandestine organizers, pulling the strings, like bell cows to a herd of cattle.

He wondered when to expect a decisive move but activities on the other side of the barricade remained sedate, almost party-like. The unique behavior reminded him of an old Sun Tzu quotation from *The Art of War*: "Let your plans be dark and impenetrable as night and when you move, fall like a thunderbolt."

That thought put him on heightened alert as he scanned the crowd. *The calm before the storm.*

WILL DETWEILER AND Molly Daniels had been late in arriving but finally managed to make it through the snaillike pace of traffic. Their Uber driver dropped them off at the far edge of the GenTropics parking lot. Excited, Will moved forward at a rapid pace, barely aware of Molly struggling to keep up behind him.

He immediately sensed that the demonstration had dissolved into a party atmosphere, with his young peers congregating into dance groups and conversation circles. A burst of frustration and anger welled up inside him like a shot of adrenaline. This wasn't a party. This was supposed to be a serious event to protest the injustice of needless deaths. The ambivalence gnawed at his gut.

Where was the indignation? The activism?

Will wanted to lash out, to *do* something that would express the depths of his loss. His mother was gone, her life wasted, their family devastated. Where was justice? Will Detweiler collapsed to his knees and began sobbing like a child, even as he felt Molly's hand squeezing tightly on his shoulder.

12

Vince Peretti continued to monitor the calls intercepted through the FBI's Stingray. So far, the cell traffic had been uneventful, even pedestrian. The sheer lack of serious intent or actionable intel left him feeling confused and increasingly nervous about the true plans of this group of biohackers.

What was their endgame? Vince eyed Barrett Hudlow across the room. He distrusted this bureaucratic operative, who seemed willing to share their intel with practically anyone.

It had been his experience that private security firms could be loose cannons, more eager to please their customers than to follow the rule of law. Even the FBI had fallen prey to an overzealous attitude in the past. During the seventies, the FBI had developed a notorious reputation for their COINTELPRO programs. FBI operatives had used the most despicable techniques to infiltrate and compromise any political group that they deemed to be an enemy of the state. In reality, many of those groups had simply been disadvantaged people using the rights given to them by the Constitution to express their frustrations. When the debacle became public, it damaged the FBI's reputation for decades.

Vince wasn't about to let Barrett Hudlow put their rehabilitated reputation in danger. He wandered over to Hudlow's computer station, which contained an impressive video feed coming from the TaurusSec drone. It was a clear aerial view of the entire protest area. As he watched, it zoomed in to the action taking place right at the boundary between the protesters and the security personnel.

As Will Detweiler sobbed, he felt a swell of anger overtaking the sadness in his heart. He wanted to make a statement, not like these kids who seemed more interested in checking their emails than participating in righteous protest. He jumped up and started moving forward through the crowd, barely aware of Molly tugging at his arm. She kept pulling him back from the action but in a furious thrust of anger, he jerked his arm away from her grasp. Near the barricade, Will found a group of protesters painting signs with broad strokes of red paint. To him, the bloodlike paint symbolized GenTropic's complicity in the death of his mother. Will decided to make his own unique statement. He grabbed a can of red paint and rushed forward, intent on spilling the guilt of red across the face of the sterile GenTropics building.

As he rushed forward, he sensed a flurry of activity to his left. Two soldiers, clothed in gray suits of armor and balaclavas, moved to cut him off. Will picked up the pace, reached the barricade, and flung his can of red paint toward the GenTropics corporate sign. The crowd cheered as the can sailed in a broad arc through the air. It collided with the sign, spilling its contents across the lettering in rivulets of red. For the first time in ages, Will Detweiler felt a sudden sense of release and justification for his mother's death. The feeling of elation was quickly replaced with a burst of heat and pain that ripped through the middle of his chest.

McANDREWS FELT UNSURE of the situation as the Wi-Fi network seemed to defy all attempts at jamming. The return of communications seemed to embolden the young terror-nerds and they began inching forward, threatening the integrity of the barricade.

Suddenly, an aggressive movement caught his eye in the middle of the throng. One man raced forward through the crowd with decisive intent, a mysterious container of some substance in his hand. Hudlow had warned him earlier in the day to be on the lookout for any unknown substances.

Maddawg's reaction was sudden and instinctual, honed through years of combat in the Gulf. He glided forward in an arc to intercept the interloper, fell to one knee and brought his AR-15 to his shoulder. A split second later, the solid thump against his shoulder signaled that a .223 round had left the barrel and was racing toward its target with ruthless efficiency.

DAN WAS STILL focused on Stoker's attempts to thwart the jamming operation when he heard a crisp *crack* echoing through the air. His gaze followed the sound to a surreal scene taking place right up front, like a drama from a movie.

A uniformed man moved forward, dropped to one knee, and fired his weapon. A mere twenty feet away, Dan watched in horror as a young man slumped to the ground, a red mist exiting his back.

It took a split second for him to realize what had happened. The man fell forward and slumped to the ground, the red mist settling into a round stain that spread across the back of his T-shirt.

Screams ripped the air as the man lay motionless on the ground. The crowd surrounding him parted instantly, fanning out in all directions. Dan felt himself being propelled forward. A split second later, he was kneeling on the slick bloodstained asphalt, ripping the paper mask away from his face. The man's chest heaved up and down in exaggerated motions. He was in obvious distress, his breathing rough and labored. Red foam bubbled out of a ragged hole.

Dan's EMT training from his scuba diving days kicked in and he recognized the pulsating foam as evidence of a sucking chest wound. Instinctively, he reached into his back pocket and fished out his wallet, fumbling for a credit card, pressing it against the bubbling fountain of blood, hoping to seal the hole before the man's lungs collapsed.

"Call 911!" he screamed at the top of his lungs. "Call 911!" A wall of young terror-stricken eyes stared back at him from the crowd. Still, Dan forced himself to focus on the victim, desperately struggling to survive, gasping for air.

Dan rolled him over, careful to keep pressure on the wound. The man stared up at him with pleading eyes, straining to breathe, heaving desperately against dead air. He grabbed Dan's arm, squeezed.

Dan redoubled his efforts, pressing the feeble piece of plastic against the man's back, hoping for time. At the periphery of his vision, Dan saw the agonized face of Molly Daniels, punching madly at her phone with trembling hands . . .

SISTER SIMONE HAD decided to close her Palm Frites shop early, as all her customers had been lured away by the protest march. Now, she stared at her TV screen in horror.

She recognized the young man she had mentored and now he was dead.

Could her own actions have contributed to his fate? She paused to calm her racing heart and took stock of the situation. Hadn't Will Detweiler made his own choices? And that security guard. Why did he have to act so violently to a simple act of vandalism? What could she have possibly done to prevent it?

The question lingered in her mind as she struggled to determine the next move. She sat for a while, her eyes closed, hoping for some divine guidance. After what seemed like an eternity, nothing came. Just a shallow sense of emptiness and doubt. She opened her eyes to the stark reality that she'd have to fulfill her obligations. Otherwise, it'd be her own neck on the chopping block.

Her hands trembled as she lifted the phone, uncertain what to say or how. She just had to flow with it, give the facts. With difficulty, she dialed the exclusive number and waited breathlessly.

"Why are you calling on my private number?" the voice answered.

Sister Simone took a deep breath. "We have . . . an issue . . . in Savannah. Have you been watching the American news? One of our subjects is dead; I won't go into details on the phone." Sister Simone paused, gasped for breath. She had never been put in this situation before. Nothing this obvious.

A long moment of desperate silence ensued. Sister Simone struggled to stop her uncontrollable shaking.

Finally . . .

"I see from the news that a protest got out of hand." The voice on the other end paused for several agonizing minutes. "What does this have to do with us?"

Sister Simone struggled to remain calm. "The man who got shot was one of our subjects. I really don't know if we contributed to this situation, sir," she said with great humility. "But Mr. Detweiler's behavior at the protest aligns with what I have observed: increasing anger and unpredictability as the regimen continued. The effect was quite different from the female subject."

"How so?"

"Well, the female subject exhibited a lack of presence and individuality. She seemed more concerned with her sexual needs and abandoned most other interests in the real world." She shivered at that revelation, concerned that her honesty would be misinterpreted as disloyalty. "I tried everything to help them, sir, but the effects were unpredictable."

There was an agonizingly long pause. Finally, a response. "I understand . . . roll everything up and get the hell out of there. Make sure you erase all evidence of our activities. Is that clear?"

Sister Simone fought to keep from stumbling over her own words. "Oh, yes, sir. Where should I go, exactly?"

Another pause that seemed longer and more intolerable than the other.

"Back home," the voice said. "Ship everything first; carry nothing on the plane. Is that clear?"

"Oh, *yes, sir.* I'll be gone in a few hours, sir." Sister Simone hung up the phone and exhaled deeply. She was beginning to wonder why she had ever gotten involved in the first place . . .

VICTOR MOODY ROSE suddenly and restlessly from a catatonic sleep, as copious amounts of Ambien wore off. The high doses he now needed spawned a number of vicious hallucinatory nightmares, so it usually took him several shaky minutes every morning to calm his racing heart.

Once stabilized, he rose quietly, padded to the kitchen, and began preparing a breakfast of shrimp and grits. He just didn't have the appetite for eggs or bacon anymore. A shuddering tremor forced him to steady against the fridge door. He bowed over, his entire frame shaking violently. A few agonizing minutes later, he wrested control and willed himself forward.

You are in control. You are the master of your fate. He repeated the mantra several times until his psyche calmed, then dropped several pats of butter into a pan and threw in some peeled shrimp, letting them sizzle there, until they turned bright red. He spooned in a large dollop of cooked grits and stirred, finishing the dish off a few minutes later with a generous sprinkling of cheese.

Shimp and gits. He remembered the play on words from his early childhood, several lifetimes ago, when he was innocent and optimistic, barely able to form the *R* sound. The memory hung like a tiny thread to his former life, a gossamer link that could disintegrate at any moment.

Victor took his plate to the table and dug into the warm meal, relishing the flavor. He sat in silence, eating his fill. A harsh ringing suddenly threatened to destroy the peace of the moment. Victor sunk his face into his hands and squeezed as the ringing continued to assail his senses. Fed up, he lunged across the room and answered the phone.

"How are you doing?" the man said.

Victor suppressed a cry, determined to appear strong. "Tell me what progress you've made. Are we any closer?"

"Yes, of course," the man said. "We're only a few days away from a cure. But we have an issue, one you must resolve for us."

Victor sagged in his chair. "What about the cure?" he repeated.

"As I said, we are making great progress. It's hard to rush these things, you know. Biology is so unpredictable but soon we will have a solution for you. You'll be traveling here, a new man. In the meantime, we have a complication that could endanger our efforts, something that might delay your cure. You don't want that, do you?"

"Of course not," Victor said. He knew the inevitable cost that would be exacted for his desperation. "Go ahead, tell me."

The man paused, then started slowly. "One of our experiments, working on your cure, I might add, may have been compromised. We can't afford for it to be exposed. It would be far better . . . if one of our test subjects were to disappear."

A long moment of silence ensued. Victor had no stomach for the details, yet the man wanted him to agree verbally. But he vowed internally to wait, to make the man say it himself, to accept responsibility. He was sick of the subtlety, the cowardice.

Another silent moment passed, slowly, excruciatingly.

Finally, the man acquiesced. "Look, I promise this will be your last job, until your cure, but it's critically important. Should be easy for you. She's a loose woman. You could easily win her favor, then take care of the situation. Her name's Molly Daniels. You know her, right? She visits the bar scene regularly in search of, well, companions. We're tracking her, we'll send you location information. Just make sure she disappears . . . quietly. Don't leave any evidence behind. That shouldn't be hard for you, right?" The man laughed nervously.

Victor could hear the guilt in the man's voice and hated him for it. "Okay," he said finally. "One last time, then the cure, right?"

"Yes, exactly."

"When?"

"Tonight, most likely. Be ready."

Victor hung up, livid over the absurdity of his task. How was he going to seduce this woman? He was a freak, a monster. She would be repulsed by him now.

He held his hands up, slender and trembling, the monstrousness clear in the starkness of his gaze. Had his gamble been worth it?

Victor thought about the task. He'd be forced into heavy makeup: false nails, penned-in eyebrows, a wig, to hide the naked, hairless flesh. He'd noticed another change in recent days, a progression. His smooth, hairless skin had grown rougher, like eternal goose bumps that seemed to wax and wane with mottled textures. Molly Daniels would have to be desperate to see anything attractive in his contrived appearance. It made more sense to just kidnap her outside the bar. No pretense of humanity or normalcy.

He possessed none anyway. He would simply add it to another long line of monstrous deeds born of desperation.

13

DAN STUDIED THE haggard face staring back at him from the bathroom mirror of the hotel. His eyes were drawn and tired as if he were carrying the burden of decades in their glassy orbits. He could still smell the metallic tang of blood drifting up from the bright red stain on his shirt as the drying edges began to turn brown.

The smell of death was something he'd hoped was behind him but the passing of the anonymous protestor had shaken him to his core. Whatever the Firemen had planned for the day, the unforeseen actions of the young man and the trigger-happy TaurusSec guard had thrown everything into disarray. The party mood of the demonstration had erupted into chaos, along with his anonymity. Dan Clifford's face was plastered across the news, a reminder of the Weatherman virus revisited by the press in yet another senseless act of violence and sorrow.

Dan's shoulders sagged as he peeled the sticky shirt away from his skin. As he stumbled into the shower and felt the hot water rinsing away the evidence of death, he felt a surge of restless anger.

Where the hell was Rachel? Why didn't she answer her phone? Surely she had seen the news by now. He regretted his offer to help in this FBI fubar.

So far, the Firemen looked at him as a misguided savior, a man interfering with a group of youngsters searching for a cause. The local police and TaurusSec seemed to be itching for a chance to turn anyone and everyone into enemies. Had Americans gotten so bored that they had to manufacture homeland enemies? Our enemies used to lie in faraway places. Now, we just fought each other. It was a horrible waste.

Dan stepped out of the shower, dried off. His burner phone rang.

Only two people had that number. He snatched it up eagerly and was greeted by the voice of Stoker.

"Are you okay?"

"What do you think?"

"That was pretty heroic work you did out there."

"Who was that guy?"

"Didn't know him personally but Molly Daniels told me his name was Will Detweiler. He was one of her, uh, friends with benefits but she seemed pretty upset, so I suspect he was more than just a casual acquaintance."

"So, what was the whole point of that damned protest?" Dan could hear the anger in his own voice. He fought to adopt a more conciliatory tone. "What was your goal, before everything blew up?"

There was a pregnant pause on the line. "What do you mean? Wasn't it obvious? We needed to hold the money grubbers accountable, before the next phase. And despite the shit-storm that occurred, your actions drew more attention to the cause, exposed the violence of those TaurusSec assholes. It was more news coverage than we could have hoped for on a normal day."

While Stoker talked, Dan slipped into a hotel robe and sat down on the edge of the bed, contemplating a raid of the minibar. "What's the next phase?"

"That's need to know," Stoker said. "And right now, you don't."

"Maybe I do." Dan hated the idea of being used as some perverted promotional tool for an unknown agenda. He'd seen enough death to understand the stark harshness of the real world. "Life is not a game," he finally said.

Stoker paused his monologue. "You're right. It's not but what do you call corporate sales meetings where marketing executives cheer their sales graphs and schemes to squeeze more profits out of sick people?"

Dan could think of nothing to say, other than that he had grown sick of this whole charade. He just wanted to see Rachel and enjoy a few simple pleasures.

But . . . duty called.

He needed to speed things up. "Look, when I dropped by after the Nerdvana convention, I wasn't expecting to get politically involved and now I'm involved. I'm heading home tomorrow. If Chemerra wants to meet, it needs to be sooner rather than later."

Judging by the long silence on the line, he had hit a nerve.

Finally, Stoker spoke. "Well, we appreciate your help today. Have a nice trip home."

Crap. He'd overplayed his hand. Dan's mind struggled for a way back into the conversation, when Stoker spoke again.

"Of course, if you're still interested, drop by tomorrow on your way out of town and I'll see if I can make some arrangements. Maybe we can find some answers for you."

Dan held the phone away from his mouth for a moment to muffle the sound of relief. "I'll see if I can swing by tomorrow around ten, assuming Chemerra will be around."

"Chemerra's available for the right cause," Stoker said cheerfully and hung up.

Dan exhaled. Perhaps a raid of the minibar was justified.

THE NEXT MORNING, Dan booked a ride over to Stoker's maker-space and knocked on the outer door. A disinterested-looking young girl with pink hair and gothic dress slid the large door to one side, metal screeching on metal. A moment of recognition passed across her face and she wordlessly pointed toward Stoker, sitting at his usual position near the cocktail bar at the far reaches of the dimly lit warehouse.

Dan's footsteps echoed in the large space. It had been completely transformed since the party and the protest. All the machinery had been returned to their original positions. Young people shuffled back and forth between the drills, band saws, CNC routers, and laser cutters, consumed by their own private projects. They barely noticed his passing.

Dan reached the bar, rubbed his hands together. "So, where's Chemerra?"

Stoker gave Dan an incredulous look. "You didn't expect him to be here in person, did you?"

"I thought that was the definition of *meet*."

Stoker's expression softened. "Chemerra doesn't appear in person for just anyone. You're still a pledge, a stranger. If you want to understand our world, you must first be reborn . . . from the womb of Echidna."

"What?" Dan's patience was wearing thin with all the distorted symbols and allegories that the Firemen had pummeled him with during the last few days. Whatever their agenda, they had an irritating way of obfuscation. He took a deep breath and reminded himself of the goal: identify the ephemeral Chemerra for the FBI. For that, he might need a different approach.

"Okay, what's next then?" he said.

Stoker stood up. "Follow me." He led the two of them along a circuitous path through the machines, across the warehouse, and toward the far wall.

As they approached, the thin outline of a heavy metal door appeared from the shadows. Stoker reached the door and punched in a long series of codes into a keypad. The unit's light turned green and Stoker glanced back expectantly. "Ready?"

"Ready for what?"

"To see the world through different eyes."

Dan shrugged. "Bring it on."

Stoker pushed the door open, its metal hinges protesting loudly.

In the center of the cavernous room sat two large black spherical cages about ten feet in diameter, resting on a platform of rollers.

"What the hell?" Dan said.

Stoker grinned. "Echidna, our Virtusphere technology, only better. The cages are carbon fiber, with power assist. They allow for unrestricted movement in a virtual-reality environment. The powered rollers overcome the globe's inertia, making it virtually invisible to the user." Stoker walked across the expanse toward a wall of shelves. "This system is our own design, the most responsive virtual-reality environment on the market, powered by a massive bank of graphic servers."

Dan studied the two large globes. "So . . . *what*? We're supposed to climb into these hamster balls? Whatever happened to face-to-face meetings?"

"As I said, Chemerra does not meet *anyone* in person. Anonymity is sacrosanct."

Stoker began pulling bundles of material from a nearby shelf. "Here, put this on. It'll allow Echidna to track your movements and provide some, uh, very realistic tactile feedback." He handed Dan a black suit festooned with white dots.

Dan took the bundle and stared back at the cage, suddenly flashing back to misadventures he had endured in another human-sized globe, while diving in Honduras. The prospect of entering another constrictive globe triggered an involuntary shiver. He stared at the setup, as his phobia clawed its way to the surface. This seemed safer, an open cage with ventilation. What could go wrong? Shaking off his brief panic, he shrugged and slipped into the black body suit.

"How the hell am I supposed to know how to operate this thing?"

Stoker was struggling into his own generously sized suit. "Don't worry. I'll be your guide, your squire. In five minutes, you'll be prancing around in our alternative world, like you've been there forever." He helped Dan slip on a small backpack filled with electronics that connected to the suit. An antenna projected out of its back, hinting at some type of wireless communication to another device.

Stoker handed Dan an Oculus Rift headset and a pair of hand controllers. "These controllers are agnostic. Depending on the story context, they will serve multiple purposes, implements, and weapons."

"Weapons?" Dan had played his share of video games but today he was not in the mood. The very real death of Will Detweiler still weighed heavily on his mind. "Look, I don't have a lot of time here. Can't I just skip all the theatrics?"

"No," Stoker said bluntly. "This is not a game. It's a test. If you want access to the Firemen, you must prove yourself worthy." Stoker guided Dan over to one of the cages and helped him enter through a small hatch. Once inside, Stoker latched a circular cover over the hole, locking Dan inside. He continued: "This will be as real as anything you have ever experienced. At times you will feel an electric impulse emanating from parts of your suit. These will provide you with tactile simulation."

"You mean like shocks?"

"Mmm, similar but don't worry. They're harmless but intense. Once the simulation begins, do NOT attempt to leave until your quest is complete. Otherwise, you will be banned. Understand?"

Dan huffed. He watched Stoker climb into the other globe, worrying that this virtual-reality exercise might hold some unwelcome surprises.

Stoker's voice echoed through Dan's headphones, transmogrifying from its familiar tone and timbre into a foreign voice and accent. "Are you ready to meet Chemerra?"

"Yes." Dan slid the Oculus Rift headset over his eyes and felt the world expand from the small room into a large virtual landscape. He was standing in a large field, bathed in sunlight. Birds chirped in the distance and wind rustled through the trees. The full acuity and resolution of the graphics and the aural imagery was breathtaking, tickling his senses with its stereoscopic brilliance. The effect left him disoriented and overwhelmed.

He stumbled around in awe, circling to take in the full expanse. This was far from the simplistic graphics he had experienced in previous video games. Instead, this virtual world exploded with detail and intensity. He could only imagine the amount of graphic processing needed to power this real-time simulation.

Dan walked forward cautiously, feeling his way through the bizarre, high-definition world. At an intellectual level, he knew his steps were powering the globe while he stood in place, that the globe was rotating underneath his feet. Yet, the combination of visual and tactile feedback fooled his senses in a way that seemed frightening, hypnotic.

A few fleeting moments passed when he could still sense the presence of his virtual suit, the pressure of the headset against his face, the slight tingle of electric signals traversing his body, the sensation of a large globe spinning underneath his gait. But soon after, even that connection to reality disappeared.

He had transcended into another world.

The field opened up into a verdant green landscape, dappled with streams of sunlight peeking out through clouds far above. He walked across a broad, flat plain, taking in the sights and sounds. In the far distance, he could see the indistinct shapes of a city, skyscrapers poking above the horizon. A movement to his right caught his attention.

A diminutive creature, elf-like, with large pointed ears and a protruding nose, walked alongside him. The creature was wearing a set of comical medieval clothes.

The creature grinned. "Welcome to your new life. I'm Elyon, your guide through this world, understand?"

Dan nodded, or at least he thought he had. It was hard to know for sure. He seemed to feel a stiff wind blowing from the left, judging by the motions of the virtual trees and an indistinct tingle he felt on the left side of his face. He adjusted his posture instinctively, leaning into the wind. Taking a few more halting steps forward, he shivered and reminded himself that this was all fake, an illusion. But that knowledge did little to convince his senses. They told him a different story: that this world was real and could affect him in real ways.

He continued forward, experiencing the world viscerally.

Elyon, his elf-like guide, was obviously manned by Stoker, who he knew was standing only a few feet away in the other globe, joining him in virtual space. The resulting cognitive dissonance was exhausting and Dan's brain soon surrendered to the virtual world. The full richness of Echidna's world had consumed him.

"Follow me," Stoker's voice said. Elyon waddled forward on short legs. Despite his cartoonish appearance, the elf moved naturally and expressed himself through an amazing level of facial detail, all presumably controlled by his virtual suit's strategically placed sensor arrays.

They walked on for what seemed like a long time, covering a mile or so of perceived distance.

Elyon directed him toward a pyramidal structure protruding from the center of the green field. As they approached, Dan could make out the outline of a door centered on an angled wall. Elyon thrust an ancient key into the door's keyhole and twisted it decisively. The door creaked open, the sound echoing through the dark expanse below. He stood to one side and motioned Dan to enter.

Dan stared into the abyss and balked. His long-held fear of small, dark places reared its ugly head.

Then, reminding himself that this was not real, he took a deep breath and moved forward. Adjusting his gait inside the globe into the downward motion of a long flight of stairs felt awkward at first but his legs soon adapted to the strange squatting motion and he picked up speed. Traveling farther down into the stifling darkness, he could feel the familiar tightening of his throat and quickening of his pulse. Despite repeating the mantra *this is all fake,* his phobias roared back. He suddenly wanted no part of this simulation and considered ripping the headset off but resisted the urge. He continued forward until his downward gait leveled out into a long, dark tunnel, dimly lit by flickering torches. The crackle of their dancing flames echoed in the narrow chamber.

Dan stopped, hands to his legs, breathing heavily. The physical exertion of moving forward endlessly inside the rotating globe had caught up to him.

Elyon was several paces behind in virtual space and struggled to keep up on his short, elfin legs. It suddenly dawned on Dan that Stoker might be in questionable physical condition. He had to cover the same physical distance as Dan inside his own dome.

Elyon fell to his knees, giggling, gasping for breath. "Your eagerness betrays you, my friend." He paused, taking in huge gulps of air, struggling to find enough breath to continue. "First, you must endure a test of will to prove your worth, understand?" He rose shakily from the ground, took a ceremonial bow, and swept his arm forward. "I am Elyon, your huckleberry friend," he said, giggling. "Wherever you go, I go, like two drifters off to see the world." Elyon giggled again, then grew more serious. "Your rainbow is waiting 'round the bend. Follow the clues and you will find Chemerra's inner sanctum, by its end."

Taking that as a directive to move forward, Dan surrendered to the rules of the game and continued into the dim labyrinth of the cave. Every few feet the tunnel split, prompting him to take several exploratory diversions. Not knowing how to traverse the complex layout, he continued down the main path. Several minutes later, a large framed gate appeared in the distance.

Behind him, Elyon's voice echoed through the hollow expanse. "Your first test lies ahead. Solve the challenge. Look to your weapons."

The voice had barely faded when brightly colored spiders the size of basketballs began to drop from the ceiling on gossamer threads of silk.

Their sudden appearance caught him by surprise, triggering a rush of panic. Chemerra knew his phobias. He had long suffered from two basic fears: dark, constricted spaces . . . and spiders. Before he could process the threat, the horde of multicolored spiders had covered the space between them.

Their speed was incredible. Dan screamed reflexively, desperate to fend off the grotesque creatures as they crawled over his body. Rays of light streamed from his hands as his panic peaked. He suddenly realized that the controllers in his hands had transformed into pistols. Acting instinctively, he pulled the triggers and felt a satisfying jolt as beams shot forward. The spiders scrambled away, offering him a momentary instant of reflection. Taking control of his emotions, he began aiming and firing. The spiders scrambled away but a few stragglers made it past the weapon fire and pounced. A series of blinding shocks tore through Dan's virtual suit. He slung his arms wildly, throwing the spiders into the tunnel. He fired again and again, desperate to keep the creatures away from him.

Before Dan could catch his breath, another barrage dropped from the ceiling. More focused now, he tried to control his breathing, firing between breaths. The beams that found their targets elicited an explosion of brightly colored mist. His rate of fire could barely keep up as the spiders descended relentlessly. With each barrage, a few spiders would make it past his laser and deliver a devastating shock that seemed to vary depending on the spider's color.

He was running out of energy and desperately needed to stop the onslaught.

Beyond his panic, Dan began to recognize a pattern. The spiders' rate of descent and their pain levels varied according to their color, giving them a ranking.

He could prioritize his shots.

The cyan spiders dropped most rapidly, the green ones far more slowly, the orange ones somewhere in between. By firing according to color, he began to make progress against the onslaught. After what seemed like hours, he managed to match the onslaught's pace, atomizing the creatures before they could reach the floor of the tunnel. Once a rhythm developed, his panic lifted, allowing him to focus on each target calmly and precisely.

The onslaught finally ended with a perfect kill rate. Dan bent over, gasping for breath.

Elyon cheered from the sidelines, jumping up and down with glee. "That's the way! You did it! Good job!"

A hint of reality poked into Dan's consciousness as he stood straight. He could feel the globe oscillating under his feet. The moment passed quickly. He was back in this virtual world, standing defiantly in the dimly lit tunnel, viewing the open gate before him.

"What next?" he said, feeling a genuine sense of accomplishment.

Elyon smiled grimly. "Now we move forward, into the abyss. There are many new challenges ahead."

"Bring 'em on." Bolstered by his victory, Dan moved forward more confidently. The tunnel continued straight ahead.

They walked for what felt like several miles, minutes, or paces . . . Dan wasn't sure. Distance was something he could only judge by the measure of effort exerted by his legs.

He suddenly came upon an ornate gate that had been carved into the right side of the tunnel.

Deep within its hollows a loud bellow sounded, shaking the walls: a low, resonant sound, filled with threat.

The bellow thundered again.

"What the hell was that?" Dan glanced back at Elyon.

The little elf seemed visibly shaken by the sound. "The Minotaur, ruler of the labyrinth," he said. "We must avoid his wrath. Move on!"

Needing no motivation, Dan picked up the pace, scrambling along the dimly lit tunnel. The bellow of the Minotaur followed him as he moved forward. A split in the tunnel suddenly appeared.

Dan looked back at Elyon. "Now what?"

Elyon shrugged. "You must make your own choice."

The Minotaur's bellow grew nearer, the sound appearing to originate from the left, prompting Dan to head right. The path contained numerous pathways left and right, creating a confusing jumble of choices. He'd lost all sense of place and time, moving forward on instinct rather than logic. There was no time to stop and think, to reflect. He scrambled down the tunnel until an ethereal vision stopped him in his tracks.

The profile of a woman stood in the tunnel bathed in gossamer light.

"Who are you?"

The apparition spoke, her voice deep and mellow. "I am Ariadne, daughter of Minos," she said. "My brother, the Minotaur, poses a great risk to you." She held out a glowing ball of thread.

"Take this," she said. "And use it to trace your movements forward. The labyrinth is long and confusing. If you can negotiate its turns and folds, you can conquer the Minotaur."

"Thank you," Dan said, taking the glowing ball. When he looked back up, Ariadne had vanished.

Dan unspooled the yarn as he progressed. After several dead ends and backtracks, the ball of thread had shrunk to the size of a golf ball but Dan had memorized a distinct path. Taking the last path available, Dan was confident he had found the way out. But at the tunnel's end, he encountered a door barring his way. Several iconic shapes adorned its facade. He tested each symbol, twisting and turning the shapes, hoping to find some movable piece that would unlock the barrier.

He didn't like being caught at this dead end and glanced back down the tunnel, his gaze following the glowing thread as it wound its way into the fading distance. He must either decipher the puzzle at this door, or backtrack a long distance to the previous junction.

The puzzle on the door seemed random, holding no perceptible pattern. Several of the icons rotated but the puzzle made no sense. His concentration was interrupted by a loud bellow echoing through the darkness.

At the far end of the tunnel stood the profile of the Minotaur, outlined by flickering torches. The creature was huge, organic, and frighteningly realistic. Clouds of mist pumped from his nostrils as he huffed, his mighty chest heaving in rhythm with the sound. His hoofed legs were bent, draped in oily fur. Above the legs, the hairy torso of a man supported a horned bull's head.

This is not real. Dan had to repeat the mantra several times, because the horrific visage of this monster betrayed every logical sense that he could muster. The musk of the creature seemed palpable as it wafted down the tunnel. The stimulation of senses sent a surge of panic through his body, as real as anything he had ever experienced. He stared at the creature, frozen in place, his body trembling.

He mustered enough will to turn back toward the door, desperate to find a means of escape. In a dark niche on one side of the tunnel he spotted the outline of a small shaft, barely large enough for a human to crawl through. Its destination disappeared into darkness.

In a moment of clarity, he realized the true purpose of this perverted test. Chemerra had forged an emotional trial for him to traverse. Either solve the complex puzzle at the door, or confront a weakness he had spent a lifetime struggling to conquer: taphephobia, the fear of being buried alive. Memories of his childhood, the death of his parents, his trials in the darkness—all suddenly consumed him.

Dan hated this mysterious person, this Chemerra, for invading his privacy and stripping his emotions raw. He wanted out of this fucking simulation and all its discomfort. He wanted to rip the headset off and find relief in the real world. But he paused, cursing under his breath. If he did that, Chemerra and the Firemen would win. He would fail. Strangely, he found his thoughts drifting to Rachel. What would she want him to do? He felt a sudden jolt of shame over his weakness.

The Minotaur's bellow shook the walls of the tunnel. The clatter of hooves against stone signaled the approach of the mighty creature as it raced toward him. Dan had but a split second to react. The horror of the narrow tunnel beckoned, its maw swallowing his resolve.

Screaming a loud curse, Dan flung himself into the dark hole and crawled into oblivion.

He squirmed and struggled through the suffocating path, crawling on his hands and knees, feeling the oppressive weight of the tunnel as it grew tighter and more constricting, its weight smothering him in panic.

Far behind, the Minotaur's frustrated bellow reverberated down the tunnel. Dan closed his eyes and crawled forward, fearing the future, confronting the past. Memories flashed across his mind's eye. Light shimmering across a table, porcelain dishes stuttering across a hutch, falling to the floor, his mother's hand reaching out like the petals of a sagging rose, the world collapsing around him with a suffocating weight. Darkness. Screams of pain. Loss. Terror. Helplessness.

The memories tore at his soul, yet Dan continued to crawl forward, the moans of the Minotaur receding.

The floor of the tunnel suddenly gave way and Dan felt himself falling, against all logic. The simulation had fooled his senses. He felt himself lying across the slick floor of a large cavern, the oppressive walls of the tunnel, a memory.

He stood up, regained his balance, and took in the new location. The expansive space was filled with stalactites poking from the ceiling, grasping toward stalagmites rising from the cavern floor. The cavern's ceiling receded into darkness but the rock formations were illuminated by thin, bright tendrils of light draping the rocks.

Dan approached one of the strange glowing structures. The light appeared to emanate from strange wormlike creatures dangling from sinuous threads attached to the stone ceiling. His presence seemed to excite the creatures, intensifying their light. The bioluminescence was sufficient enough for him to make out the faint outlines of the cavern.

The cavern floor was strewn with bones, broken pottery, and remnants of human refuse. He shuddered, certain that he could smell the fetid stench of rotting flesh. Moving forward through the cavern, he used the glowworms as signposts. The journey grew more repressive with each step. He could feel sweat trickling down the backside of his virtual suit.

How had Chemerra known about his phobias? The experience had been supremely unpleasant so far, challenging his desire to continue. He wanted to quit the whole charade, abandon the mission, walk back into the bright light of reality, if not for the threat posed by the Devil's Paradox.

The voice of Elyon interrupted his thoughts.

"Praise for conquering the Minotaur!" Elyon seemed to appear from nowhere. "Congratulations! Do not dally, for you are now in the domain of Argus Panoptes, the creature with a hundred eyes. His vision is great but he is deaf."

"Yeah, well, I'm tired of all this virtual crap. I'm ready to call it quits and head back to the real world."

Elyon's reaction was stark. "Oh, no! Don't do that, you are so close. Beyond Argus lies the lair of Chemerra, in the flesh!"

"So, what now?"

"You must traverse the cavern to the exit while avoiding the gaze of the many-eyed one. At the far end of the cavern you will find the exit. Stealth is paramount."

"Okay then." Dan studied the layout of the cavern, charting a path through the towering stone structures. He could use the dim light from the glowworms to illuminate his path. He moved forward cautiously and immediately heard the faint sound of footsteps nearby. He stood still, straining to place the origin of the sound. Thirty yards ahead, the outline of a nude form stepped out from the shadows, the body covered with hundreds of blinking eyes. They darted from side to side, taking in everything, until they all seemed to focus on Dan's location.

A piercing jolt of electricity traveled through Dan's suit, dropping him to his knees.

"Run!" Elyon screamed. "Do not let Argus rest his gaze on you!"

Another jolt of pain prompted Dan into action. He raced through the columns, dodging and weaving, to put as much distance as he could between himself and the many-eyed creature. Argus Panoptes seemed to anticipate his every move, drawing closer every minute, the echo of his approaching footsteps pushing Dan farther away from the exit.

He was not escaping Argus so much as being herded by him. A glance back at his former path revealed a clue. His motion through the stone structures had excited the glowworms, leaving an illuminated path for Argus to follow, like a path of glowing breadcrumbs. If he wanted to escape this creature, he would need to find a diversion.

Dan suddenly changed course, reversing his track back toward the many-eyed creature, garnering another debilitating stab of pain from his virtual suit, before darting into the shadows. He crawled around on the cavern floor until he found a sizable stone. He picked it up and flung it across the expanse. It hit one of the distant stalactites, the sound echoing through the stones. The glowworms inhabiting the stones lit up with bright intensity. Dan peeked out from his hiding place and spotted Argus Panoptes moving toward the bright glow.

Taking advantage of the opportunity, he raced through the stone obstacle course, bobbing and weaving, away from the stalactites and the glowworms, toward a black area obscured in darkness. Without enough light to see, he tripped several times on the uneven floor, falling to his hands and knees. The surface of the hard carbon fiber globe felt just as unforgiving and painful to his joints as the rocky surface of this simulated world. Dan's frenetic pace had drained his stamina as he reached the exit. In the far distance, he could hear the frustrated screams of Argus as he passed through a large stone archway into a new cavern.

On the other side, a black lagoon encircled a rocky island. In its center, a huge stone ledge jutted out over the opening of a large cave. The entire area was disorienting, the ceiling of the cavern draped with stars and a surprisingly bright orb of light. A full moon. It didn't make much sense in this underground simulation but Dan supposed Chemerra could build whatever fake world he wanted.

"Good job!" Elyon's voice shouted from the shadows. "You have eluded Argus. As your squire," he puffed, "I have fulfilled my mission. Meet Chemerra on your own terms. I bid you goodbye."

"So where is he?"

"Where else?" Elyon pointed in the direction of the island cave. "You must first cross the lagoon."

Another challenge, Dan thought. What was he supposed to do? Figure out how to simulate swimming on the bottom of his globe? Thankfully, he spotted a small circular object resting on the shore that looked like an ancient boat made of animal skin. He looked up to ask Elyon about it but the virtual elf had vanished.

Dan picked up a long stick next to the boat and stepped into its

center. The craft was highly unstable and he could feel the floor swaying back and forth under his feet. He thought about sitting down in
the small craft but decided to stand, carefully pushing the boat across
the water with the pole. With patience and concentration, he managed
to make it to the other side, glad that he would not find out what the
simulator would do to him if he fell overboard.

He scrambled up the rocky shore and approached the cave entrance. The simulation should have hardened him somewhat by now.
He'd gotten accustomed to the high-definition imagery and realistic
movement in the globe but the deafening roar that emanated from the
cave entrance sent a shiver down his spine and left his knees shaking.
It was as if he could *feel* the sound vibrating his body and wondered if
the suit was sending out minuscule electric pulses to simulate the feeling. Regardless, the monstrous sound triggered a primal fear inside
his gut telling him to run. It was all he could do to muster the will to
stay, so strong was this basic instinct.

The creature that slinked out of the cave only reinforced his reaction.

A giant lion glided toward him with a smooth grace that belied its
monstrous size. Its tongue licked a row of glistening teeth. Behind the
creature's mane, the dark profile of horns appeared, until the head of
a goatlike creature rose into full view and moved forward on a long
neck that appeared to be attached to the shoulders of the lion. The
mythical apparition poked its goatlike features to within a few feet of
Dan and began to speak in a deep voice.

"Welcome to my lair."

As the multiheaded creature spoke, Dan could feel the fetid breath
of the lion's head washing over him. He dropped to his knees and for
a fleeting moment, the texture of the cage under his hands broke the
spell and he could sense the tingling of tiny electrical shocks tickling
his face. The reality was soon overwhelmed again by the illusion.

Embarrassed by his timidity, Dan stood back up and cautiously
approached the mythological chimera, reminding himself of ancient
images of the being, part lion, part goat, part snake. Where was the
snake? His mind searched for the right introduction.

What does one say to a monster?

"Nice place you've got here," he stammered, instantly regretting
such a stupid introduction.

The Chimera laughed heartily. "Yes, a tremendous feat of pro-gramming, wouldn't you say? One's mind can get lost in here forever."

Dan's pride returned and he reminded himself why he was here, to learn more about this mysterious hacker and save the world from a horrific pandemic. But first, he needed to establish a peer dialogue with this person, who was likely just some pimple-faced kid ensconced in his mother's basement. At least that's what he told himself to regain the psychological high ground.

Dan said, "I'll admit, it's a quite impressive virtual-reality simula-tion but I fail to understand the need to meet like this. What's wrong with real-world relationships?"

The Chimeric creature laughed again. "And what makes you think this world is less real than the one up there?" The goat's head ex-tended his gaze toward the cavern's ceiling.

"Well, for one thing, the world above is where we live, suffer, and die. There, we feel things for real, with real consequences for our ac-tions. We're vulnerable to the laws of physics. This simulation is just fantasy."

"Really?" The goat's head tilted to one side. "You feel nothing here? Right now, your pulse is racing at a hundred forty beats per minute, yet you are standing still. You were cowering in fear only a moment ago. You're sweating profusely. Moments ago, you confronted your false fears that haunt you in the so-called *real* world and overcame them. *Here. Now.* It that not real?"

Chemerra had a point. He had conquered his two most debilitating phobias in virtual space. And yet, in the *real* world, he was forced to remind himself constantly that his fears were imaginary, irrational, out of touch with reality.

"You make a good argument," he said. "But there are things you do not know. My fears, while imaginary, were born from real-life trag-edies."

"You mean the death of your parents in an earthquake?" Chemerra replied. "Your being buried alive? It must have been terrible, knowing that you were trapped and helpless as spiders crawled all over your body in the stifling darkness."

Dan stared at this grotesque creature, mad and worried. How did he know all of that about his past? Chemerra seemed to have tapped directly into his mind.

"I, uh . . ." He struggled to find something to say.

Chemerra continued: "This world serves a great purpose, one that all our disciples must learn. Our brains conceive reality but our hearts cannot discern the difference between fantasy and reality. To our emotions, this world is just as real as the one above, but here, you can fail, learn, and begin anew. Up there, your mistakes will get you killed."

Dan's vision of some pimple-faced kid in a basement was rapidly vanishing. This person, whoever he was, had the wisdom of a much older person, someone who had a basic understanding of how the world really worked. He wasn't sure if that encouraged him or frightened him.

"Look, Chemerra, may I call you Chemerra?"

"That is my name."

"Good," Dan said. "Here's what I think. I've noticed you and your Firemen spend a lot of time playing games, cosplaying, imagining yourselves as superhuman heroes and animals as you dance the night away in drug-addled states. But what's *really* going on?"

Dan resisted his revulsion of the creature and stared directly into the goat's eyes as he spoke, ignoring the lion's breath as it washed over him. "What's your real game? You care about the truth. Why else organize a protest at GenTropics? And what about the death of Will Detweiler? I felt his life leave his body."

The lion roared, driving Dan back reflexively. Chemerra spoke again. "Your confidence in the *real* world is greatly misplaced, my friend. Do you really think the public has any grasp of *truth*? We are bombarded daily with hundreds of advertisements, promising us happiness for a price that can never be paid. Our leaders fill our heads with false claims, pitting our emotions against our own best interests. Social media stirs our anger and fills our minds with false facts. Media and entertainment cajoles us with false dreams, all while selling us more products through crafty product placement."

Chemerra grew more animated, stepping forward. "How is that world any truer than this one? Yes, many of our young disciples and pledges are victims to that false narrative. We must harden ourselves to . . ."

Chemerra's attention suddenly diverted and the creature froze in place. Minutes passed.

Dan wondered if the simulation had encountered a glitch. He was about to speak when Chemerra let out a tortured roar that shook him to his bones.

"What have you done? Traitor!"

The tail of the beast whipped forward and a viper's head sunk its virtual fangs deep into Dan's arm. A paralyzing jolt of electricity shot through Dan's virtual suit. The last thing he heard was a loud ringing, then blackness.

14

DAN FOUND HIMSELF lying at the bottom of his globe, the concerned face of Stoker staring down at him.

"Are you all right?"

As Dan struggled to sit up, his muscles trembled from the powerful shock he had received. "I . . . I think so. What happened?"

"You tell me!" Stoker said. "I've never seen Chemerra that pissed before. You must leave and never come back."

Without saying another word, Stoker helped Dan out of his virtual suit, finally adding: "I've ordered you a ride back to the hotel. Whatever you did or said, it got you banned." Stoker led Dan out of the simulation room and ushered him across the warehouse floor into the bright sunlight of the real world.

Dan wasn't quite sure he wanted to return to it, after all.

As his ride pulled away from Stoker's warehouse, Dan felt disoriented and unbalanced. His senses were still attuned to the virtual simulation inside Echidna and struggled with the juxtaposition of the two worlds. Which one felt more real?

He fought to regain a grip on the present moment, his eyes slowly adjusting to the bright sunlight of midday as he watched the coastal architecture of Savannah stream past the car window. The experience inside Echidna still haunted him. Its emotional effect lingered, influencing his thoughts.

What the hell just happened? He had no idea what had pissed off Chemerra. Then, a thought came to mind and he dialed Vince Peretti's number. After three rings, Vince answered.

"What the hell did you do?" Dan said flatly.

There was a long pause before Vince replied. "We were tracking your virtual fingerprint online. The other night at the party, our agents spliced a gateway into the warehouse network. We've been trying to track Chemerra's IP address back to its source. You know we've got pretty good tracking software. We thought we had it traced to an old building on River Street, so we breached. Unfortunately, all we found was a remote Wi-Fi repeater. We obviously set off some alarm because Chemerra's signal went dark."

"Well, what did you expect?" Dan said, his anger growing. "The guy's a world-class hacker! And why didn't you warn me? I *told* you I was developing trust. Now, I'm blown. This whole thing is a shit storm, all because you didn't trust me to get the job done. Why the hell did I waste my time on this mission?"

"Look, I'm sorry," Vince said. "It was a strategic mistake. I take full responsibility but it was Barrett Hudlow who insisted on tracking Chemerra's virtual signature. I shouldn't have listened to him in the first place but that's the current situation I have to deal with, all this interagency cooperation. Lots of bureaucratic bullshit."

Vince's apologies meant little to him. Dan had interrupted his own plans, put his relationship with Rachel on hold, risked his health, all for nothing. "Well, I'm persona non grata, so I expect you'll provide me and Rudi transportation back to Atlanta, the sooner the better."

All Vince could muster was, "I understand." He hung up.

Dan's anger grew but most of all, he felt like a failure. The impending threat was still out there and he was powerless to do anything about it. The FBI would have to figure it out on their own. At least now, he could focus his attention on Rachel and her whereabouts.

A sudden wail of sirens interrupted his thoughts and he turned to see a local Savannah police car approaching at high speed, lights flashing. Dan expected the vehicle to pass them but instead, it settled into the tight space behind his ride. A second vehicle appeared from behind and rolled forward, past his ride. It forced the driver off the road onto the shoulder. A moment later, officers had surrounded the car, guns drawn. A loudspeaker in the vehicle directly behind them squawked to life. "Attention! Dan Clifford! Exit the vehicle with your hands above your head. Do it *now!*"

What? Dan glanced back at the vehicle directly behind them. Two officers were kneeling on the grass, weapons drawn and pointed in his direction. This didn't make any sense. He sat frozen, unsure what to do.

"Dan Clifford! Exit the vehicle with your hands above your head! *Now!*"

Dan could tell by the officer's tone that he was deadly serious. Moving slowly toward the left passenger door, he popped it open gently, taking care to push his hands out in advance of his body.

"Exit the vehicle now!" the officer commanded.

Hands raised above his body, Dan slid awkwardly out of the door and stood shakily.

"Facedown on the ground, now!" the voice commanded.

He knelt on the hard asphalt, his hands raised stalwartly above his head and then awkwardly dropped to the pavement. Within seconds, the officers rushed forward and pulled his hands behind his back. He could feel the cold steel of handcuffs clamping down on his wrists.

"What's going on?" he pleaded. "I'm working with the FBI. Contact Vince Peretti at the Atlanta field office."

"Shut up!" the officer yelled. "Dan Clifford, you're under arrest for armed robbery. You have the right to remain silent, do you understand?"

"What? No!" Dan screamed back. "I'm a liaison with the FBI! Check with FBI headquarters, Vince Peretti!"

"Yeah, right," the officer replied. "And I'm Tom Sawyer. Shut the fuck up!"

His hands bound tightly behind him, Dan felt the officer jerk him up from the pavement and drag him to the nearest police vehicle. They shoved him into the back seat of the squad car and wordlessly departed. As the vehicle passed the scene, Dan watched as officers cuffed the distraught driver and stuffed him into the second vehicle.

IN THE SAVANNAH police department, Dan was fingerprinted and photographed, all without a word being passed between him and the arresting officers. Then they unceremoniously ushered him to a cell at the back of the jail. As the officer walked away, Dan shouted, "Don't I get a phone call?"

The officer failed to look back, waving his arm dismissively.

He settled into the smelly confines of the cell and stewed. A few hours ago, he was working undercover for the FBI trying to stop a madman with a dangerous pathogen. Now, he sat in jail, accused of some unknown crime. There was no choice but to settle into his cot and try to catch some fitful sleep.

A few hours later, a different officer visited his cell. "You got a lawyer you'd like to contact?"

"Finally! Why wasn't I offered my call hours ago?"

The officer smirked. "Look, buddy, we can retain you for twelve hours without cause. You're lucky I bothered to check in this soon. Shut your piehole or I'll let you sit here for another eight hours. Think about *that* the next time you break the law."

"I haven't broken any law," he said. "I don't even know what I'm charged with but if you contact Vince Peretti at the FBI, you'll find out I'm an undercover agent. I haven't done anything wrong."

The officer laughed. "Yeah, I'm sure. And I'm a movie star. Get your head out of your ass and show some respect or I'll let you stew here overnight."

Dan struggled to regain his composure. "Look, I'm sorry if I come across as disrespectful, Officer, but I really am working with the FBI. If you'll allow my phone call, I can clear this whole mess up." He put on the most disarming expression he could muster.

The officer chuckled but unlocked the cell door and ushered him down the hall to a small room with a phone. "It's one call, so make it count. Otherwise, no amount of drama is gonna save your ass."

"What exactly was I arrested for?"

"Let your lawyer fill you in," he said and slammed the door.

Dan stared at the phone, feeling totally violated. Once these Savannah officers perceived him as a bad guy, all civility disappeared. Dan Clifford was the enemy, undeserving of rights. Only problem was, he had no idea why and no one seemed willing to tell him. He checked his watch. It had been three hours since his abduction and he wondered what Vince Peretti must be thinking at this point. He dialed the number and waited, tapping his finger on the table impatiently. Several tentative rings later, Vince answered.

"Thank god!" Dan blurted. "I thought I was going to rot in jail." He explained the situation and waited for an apology that never came. Vince told him to be patient and he'd straighten things out.

After another hour in the stinky cell, Dan heard the voices of Vince and Barrett Hudlow echoing from the adjacent room. A lively discussion seemed to be taking place. Finally, the two men arrived at his cell, accompanied by the officer who had arrested him earlier, now wearing a more conciliatory expression. The officer unlocked the cell door and stood to one side, refusing to make eye contact or acknowledge his presence.

Dan couldn't resist. He leaned close to the officer's ear and whispered, "Told you so."

The officer stared at the floor. "I, uh . . . my apologies. It appears our computer system was hacked. Special Agent Peretti explained the situation to me. We would like to apologize on behalf of the department. I hope you will accept our apology."

Dan stared at the man, then back at Vince, who gave him a pleading look of contrition. As pissed as he was, he decided to let things pass, just in case he needed their cooperation later. "Sure, no problem. Although, you might want to wash your mattresses. They're *filthy*. And in the future, double-check your sources before pulling your gun on innocent citizens, okay? Otherwise I might have to sue your ass for false imprisonment."

"Got it," the officer said, straining to accept his dressing down silently.

As they walked out of the station, Dan felt a certain degree of satisfaction at wiping the smug expression off the guy's face but he realized Chemerra had just proven how dangerous he could be. When they reached the FBI vehicle, his frustration boiled over. "What the hell happened?"

Barret Hudlow said, "It appears Chemerra hacked into the police database and planted a fake APB report, stating that a man matching your description had robbed the local bank at gunpoint. These officers were just doing their job. As I warned you, Chemerra is dangerous on many levels."

"This whole mess could have been avoided if you guys had warned me of your trace ahead of time. And look where it got you. Nowhere. We've both been made fools of by this guy."

Hudlow huffed. "How do we know you didn't warn Chemerra yourself? Seems you're awful chummy with these terrorists."

"Warn him, how? I had no idea you were tracing him, remember? Besides, wasn't that my job? To gain their trust? Something you couldn't even give me."

"As a civilian, you're on a need-to-know basis and frankly, I *don't* trust you."

"Well, the feeling's mutual. Only I have a valid reason; you don't." Dan could feel the blood rush to his face. He stepped forward into Hudlow's personal space.

"Enough bickering." Vince said, stepping between them. "We'll just have to find another way. Dan, there's no reason for you to stick around any longer. I'll arrange transport back to Atlanta tomorrow. I appreciated your help, regardless."

Dan nodded, both relieved and frustrated with failure. He certainly wouldn't miss a bureaucratic idiot like Hudlow. Still, he didn't like to lose and worried about the aftermath. Would Chemerra release the Devil's Paradox just to spite them all?

"What other leads do you have?" he asked.

Vince simply shook his head.

ON THE RIDE back to the hotel, Dan was eager to see Rachel again soon. Still, the past few days bugged him, having gotten so tantalizingly close.

Before everything went to hell.

Why did Chemerra gave a crap about him in the first place? And what was the Firemen's endgame? Their activities seemed bizarre and conflicting.

His mind was still restless as he reached the room. He wanted to take a long, hot shower to wash away his failure and the prison stink. But first, he needed to check in with Rudi and tell him they were headed home. On the fifth knock, Rudi answered, distracted as usual. The mound of junk food wrappers, clothing, and equipment had grown larger since his last visit.

After a cursory nod, Rudi headed back to a small table in the corner of the room stacked with servers, a monitor, and a vintage mechanical keyboard. He resumed typing and Dan could hear the faint traces of a familiar tune leaking out of Rudi's high-fidelity headphones. It was a song Dan had just heard playing a few minutes ago in the elevator.

Dan lifted one ear cup and spoke loudly. "Thought you liked seventies rock? What's with the vintage music? Andy Williams, right?"

Rudi removed his headphones and ran his fingers through an errant strand of black hair, propping it back up on the top of his ear.

"Yep, 'Moon River,' Andy's signature song," he said, grinning, as he often did when sharing something he considered prophetic. "Audrey Hepburn sang it first though, in the movie *Breakfast at Tiffany's* but then Andy adopted it as his theme song."

Dan couldn't help but laugh. "I thought you didn't like vintage movies, much less vintage music."

"Never thought about it, frankly. Why watch something old when there's new movies all the time? But your Sam Spade reference got me thinking about the past, so I watched *The Maltese Falcon*."

"And?"

"Being in black and white sucked but the story was actually retro cool."

"And how did that lead you to *Breakfast at Tiffany's*, exactly?"

Rudi grinned again. "Crazy coincidence, that," he said. "Every time I went to buy food, 'Moon River' was playing in the elevator on the Muzak. Drove me crazy. Got the tune stuck in my head. Hummed a few bars to Google and it brought up *Breakfast at Tiffany's*. Audrey Hepburn was *hot,* so I did a little more research. Did you know the guy who wrote 'Moon River' lived right here in Savannah?"

Dan marveled at the circuitous design of Rudi's brain, capable of connecting disparate threads of thought together in strange and unexpected ways. Dan called it "thinking globally" and it probably explained Rudi's programming brilliance.

Another random thought seemed to interrupt Rudi's train of thought. "Hey! Where the hell have you been? I was starting to worry."

"Yeah, you look worried." Dan laughed, enjoying the relief of a little lighthearted distraction by his quirky friend. "What else have you been doing?"

"Tracking the dark web and posts from the Firemen, like you asked. What the hell did you do? You're public enemy number one with them right now. I thought the idea was to sidle up to 'em?"

"It's a long story."

Dan knew the explanation would require far more time than he wanted to share but Rudi needed the update. He swept away some pizza boxes and settled into the one other chair in the room to recount the last twenty-four hours. When he finished, Rudi stared at him, aghast.

"You mean the G-men screwed it up? After asking us down here?

I've met some of their white hats at conferences, thought they were better than that. Sounds like they need to go back two or three grades in hacker school. Even I know better than to fall into a honeypot!" Rudi shook his head.

Dan shrugged. "Regardless, my cover's blown. Might as well pack up. We'll head home tomorrow."

"Sorry, my friend," Rudi said. "Least you'll find out what Rachel's been up to. We also need to bolster our security at SurMyz Consulting. The Firemen will be after our ass. Meanwhile, I'll keep following the phreaker buzz on the dark web . . ."

"Thanks." Dan turned to leave when a couple of recent memories flitted across his mind's eye like a butterfly. He remembered the image of a moon shimmering on the dark waters of Chemerra's underground cavern. Then, Andy Williams in the elevator.

Dan turned back to Rudi. "Who did you say wrote the song, 'Moon River'?"

Rudi pulled his headphones off. "Say what?"

"'Moon River.' You said the writer was from Savannah?"

"Yeah, Johnny Mercer. He was a famous Tin Pan Alley songwriter from the thirties, born right on Moon River by the way, hence the song title."

Rudi's fingers danced across his keyboard, the mechanical keys clacking loudly. An image popped up on Wikipedia. "Tin Pan Alley lyricist. Wrote 'Moon River' for *Breakfast at Tiffany's,* staring Audrey Hepburn."

Another faint memory tickled Dan's brain. "Can you pull up the lyrics?"

"Sure." Rudi's fingers flitted across the keyboard.

Dan read through them, his jaw dropping at several lines: *Two drifters, off to see the world . . . My huckleberry friend . . .*

The words of Elyon's strange rhyme.

Dan's mind was a jumble. He felt manipulated, steered. Atlanta beckoned but something about the contrived nature of his challenge in Echidna bothered him. Why go to so much trouble in the first place? And why him? He might have been considered a celebrity among hackers but he was far from the kind of talented programmer who could hang with a superhacker like Chemerra, or Rudi Plimpton, for that matter.

He revisited an earlier thought that Rudi might be the final prize. It made more sense. But then, why not reach out to Rudi directly? And why the bread crumb trail to Moon River? Now, even the false APB report seemed contrived. Chemerra, if truly angry with him, could have exacted far more damage than sending him to jail for a few hours. Like emptying his bank account, for instance.

"So Moon River is in Savannah? Where, exactly?"

Google Maps popped up on Rudi's screen. "Just a few miles south of here."

Rachel could wait one more day, he decided. "Rudi, see if you can find a boat rental shop near Moon River; something with a skiff."

15

WHEN DAN'S RIDE pulled up alongside the river and stopped, he did a double take at the scene in front of him and immediately questioned Rudi's choice of venue. "You sure they rent boats here?" he asked.

"That's what the map says," the driver replied.

Pinky's Bait an' Beer was a collection of shacks perched alongside the Skidaway River, ensconced behind a maze of cypress pilings that lined the shore. The old pilings were encrusted in barnacles, split from years of sun and decay, held together by a boardwalk that snaked along the riverside. A smattering of trawlers were anchored along the boardwalk's length, varying in size from simple two-man fishing boats to monstrous commercial vessels all festooned with an illogical array of flags and colorful decorations, for what purpose Dan could only guess. Trawling nets swayed in the breeze, clanging against their masts, the remnants of their last catch stubbornly clinging to the fibers. The thick odor of rotting fish and salt spray wafted in the breeze like a fog.

Above the trawlers, a colony of seagulls circled in expectation of a free meal but most of the boats were idle. In the distance Dan could see a few stragglers drifting in, the last hauls of the day, their winged scavengers hovering with rapt anticipation. One trawler in particular caught his eye. A huge net swayed from a framework of cranes, filled with gelatinous masses, teasing the gulls with every swing. The name on the boat's bow was printed in large bold letters: JELLY BALL EXPRESS. He couldn't imagine eating the bizarre masses of protoplasm about the size and shape of a basketball but from what he had heard, jelly balls or cannonball jellyfish were serious commercial merchandise in Asian markets, considered a delicacy there.

He refocused on finding a skiff and headed toward the warren of shacks that lay in the shade of cypress and pine. Hanging from the main building, a large, rotting sign read: PINKY'S BAIT AN' BEER, LIQUOR IN THE FRONT, POKER IN THE REAR.

The bar seemed barely capable of standing upright, with large gaps showing between the aging wood siding. By some miracle it managed to survive the numerous storms that visited Savannah. To the left of the decrepit structure loomed a mound of oyster shells.

Dan had seen similar dive bars before but none this disheveled. It was basically a tin roof and a few open-air structures tied together with makeshift boarding. There was certainly no way to lock the place up after closing time. Dan assumed the owner, Pinky, depended on the disinterest of thieves, considering its state of disrepair.

The bar was noisy, filled with the squawks of gulls, constant din of crickets, and the mumble of conversations shared by trawler captains. Dan could barely hear himself think. He approached a crusty old bartender who was wiping down the worm-etched wood with a rag.

The din of crickets grew louder. He traced the sound to a stack of paper cartons filled with the noisy insects, alongside a line of empty beer bottles, depicting all the brews currently available.

He sat down on a stool and addressed the old man. "Would you happen to be Pinky?"

"That'd be me." He meandered over and propped his elbows on the old cypress bar, made of a trunk sawed in half. His face was a map of time spent in the sun, with canyons of aging skin and forests of graying beard stubble. A pack of cigarettes poked out of the rolled left sleeve of his T-shirt. The letters on the front spelled, WHAT THE F**K U LOOKIN' AT?

Dan glanced around the tables at a sparse crowd and tried to act nonchalant. "I'm looking for a boat to rent for the day. Your website says you have some. What have you got available?"

Pinky chuckled. "You saw my website? First time for everything, I suppose. Least I didn't totally waste my money. You want a boat?"

"Yep, for the rest of the day. A small fishing boat or skiff will do. Anything, really."

"Nope."

The curt answer caught him by surprise. Dan stared, waiting for a follow-up. "Pardon?"

"Normally, I got lots of boats, skiffs, flat-bottoms, dinghies, fishin' boats . . . but not this weekend." Pinky poured himself a shot out of a bottle of Jack Daniel's and downed it unceremoniously. "Blessin' of the Fleet, down in Darien, you know," he said, as if Dan would understand.

Seeing Dan's blank expression, Pinky continued. "The Blessin' of the Fleet, the annual festival, goin' on this weekend, thirty miles south 'a here. Every local and his uncle's down there. Cleaned me out. That's why it's so damn quiet here." Pinky gave his head a dismissive roll around the room, ending with a scowl of disapproval. He spit a brown stream of tobacco juice into a bucket under the bar. "Can't sell my bait, even to the tourists. Most of it'll go bad by next week." He spat again, just to put a point on his comment. Then, Pinky let loose a gap-toothed grin. "'Bout that boat . . . there's always *Mossy Lynn*. She's a pontoon."

Dan shrugged. "If it floats and has a motor, I'll take her."

Pinky's grin broadened, his sun-dried eyes disappearing into folds of skin. "Well, she handles like the floating turd she is. Don't 'spect to get nowhere fast. This late in the day, best not to get lost out there in the channels." Pinky cackled. "Of course, if you have to spend the night, you can sleep in her. Quite comfy actually. Thirty bucks for the day. She's out back, next to the cement elephant."

"The what?"

"Cement elephant, can't miss it." Pinky flicked his head toward the docks. "No keys in her. Just give the motor a stiff pull. Should crank right up."

"Thanks." Dan handed Pinky two twenties. "Keep the change." He figured it wouldn't hurt to get on Pinky's good side.

After buying a map of the waterway, Dan headed around back. Sure enough, a few hundred yards farther down the docks, a baby elephant cast from concrete was perched on a small rise above the river. It appeared to be sitting inside a small fenced-in cemetery, the elephant's purpose a mystery. Maybe the gravestone of a circus performer?

Dan spotted *Mossy Lynn* tied at the docks. It was an old pontoon boat missing its awning and seats, with a full-sized casket mounted on the deck. The casket's viewing door had been propped open and a rail attached, so the person manning the "boat" could stand inside and steer using a long tiller attached to an outboard that had seen better days. A sign above the contraption read, DON'T WAIT A LIFETIME, USE

IT NOW. Dan laughed. Pinky had a sense of humor. The thought of piloting this floating monstrosity felt ridiculous but beggars couldn't be choosers.

After one pull on the starter rope, the antique motor roared to life, thumping, coughing, and vibrating. There would be no sneaking up on anyone. He pulled out, snaked a path around a number of large trawlers, and headed down the Skidaway River. Unfolding the map, Dan began tracing his movement. A few miles downstream, the river arced toward starboard and joined with what he assumed was Moon River. According to the map, Moon River was less of a river and more of a collection of snaking tributaries, small channels, and estuaries.

He felt exposed, piloting this monstrosity down the river. Thankfully, Darien's Blessing of the Fleet had emptied the river of traffic. It was dead calm. *Mossy Lynn* wasn't exactly the garbage boat Pinky had made it out to be. Her twin pontoons cut through the water efficiently but the vibration from the ancient motor rattled through his arm and torso, adding to a feeling of unease that grew as he scanned the river. The coffin worked quite comfortably as a chair, if one ignored the ludicrous nature of sitting upright in a box meant for the dead. Dan eased the throttle back, bringing some welcome relief from the noise and continued down the confusing labyrinth of channels, scanning both shorelines, unsure exactly what he was looking for . . .

OPERATIVE ONE WATCHED from his government-issue vehicle as Dan Clifford maneuvered the bizarre craft into the river. This scenario was unexpected and he decided to check in for further instruction. He pulled out his phone and hit speed-dial.

"This is One. Suspect is on the move, traveling via the river, in a, uh, distinctive watercraft. No idea as to destination but we'll have to abandon the car and follow by boat."

The voice on the other end paused, then spoke definitively. "Keep on Clifford at all costs. Do whatever is necessary."

Operative Two heard the conversation and shrugged his shoulders, grinning. "Looks like we're taking a cruise."

"True." Operative One winked. He entered Pinky's bar and approached the man he judged to be the one in charge. "You Pinky?"

The man leaned forward on the bar with an attitude. It was something Operative One had grown accustomed to.

"Who's askin'?" the man said.

Operative One flipped out his Homeland Security badge and waited for the deferential response that usually accompanied the display of his official credentials.

Pinky stared at the badge for a moment, then spit a huge ball of stale tobacco into a pail under the bar. "Am I supposed to be impressed?"

"We need a boat to rent."

"Ain't got any." Pinky picked at the skin on his nose and looked away into the distance.

"I don't think you understand the situation," Operative One replied. He shoved his badge back in Pinky's face for effect. "There's a big cigar boat docked out front. Who owns that?"

Pinky's eyes darted between Operative One and the badge, his eyes squinting in disdain. "That boat's named *Shyla*. She's a vintage Donzi 43 ZR and my private craft. Totally off-limits. Touch her and you'll be talking two octaves higher."

Operative One waved his credentials again. "Well, do whatever you plan to do, because we're taking her, one way or another." He leaned forward into Pinky's zone of comfort, a classic intimidation move, speaking calmly and definitively. "Listen carefully, old man. We are Homeland Security and the Patriot Act gives us the power to do whatever the fuck we want. We can make your life a living hell, with no rule of law, no legal recourse. We can stash you in a jail cell for a month without a lawyer. Is *Shyla* worth the trouble? How about your bar? You wanna keep it?"

That was the stick. Now the carrot.

Operative One leaned backward in a gesture of conciliation. "Look, I promise we'll take good care of *Shyla,* even fill her massive tanks for you, have her back by the end of the day, which shouldn't be long. No scratches, I promise."

Pinky stared at the man with an expression that was impossible to interpret. After a long pause, he pitched a set of keys in the direction of Operative One. "Knock yourself out," he said and spit the remaining dregs of his chaw toward the man's shoe.

Five minutes later, the two operatives pulled out of the dock in Pinky's sleek cigar boat, her massive engines quaking under the thin hull. Operative One rubbed incessantly at his boot, grumbling. "Should have iced that asshole."

"Just shut up and focus," Operative Two said.

Operative One nudged the boat's throttles forward. It rewarded him with a throaty growl. Aware of the boat's massive horsepower, he gingerly steered the craft out into the channel and toward Dan Clifford's last location, keeping a respectful distance. *Shyla* was not the ideal surveillance craft, with her massive motors, so Operative One kept a greater separation perimeter than protocol would normally warrant.

Back at the bar, Pinky repacked his mouth with a fresh wad of chaw, placed deftly between cheek and gum. He reached down below the bar, pulled out a black phone, and dialed a number.

A voice answered.

"Incoming," Pinky said and hung up.

BARRETT HUDLOW HUNCHED over his computer in his private office, an earbud jammed into his left ear. Dan Clifford had proven himself to be the predictable foil he had imagined. Once a terrorist, always a terrorist. He leaned back in his chair and contemplated his next move. If his assumptions were true, it would be bold, tricky, and highly profitable.

16

As Dan continued down Moon River, he noticed a distinct change along the shoreline. The suburban houses with their private docks thinned out and eventually disappeared, giving way to trees and estuaries. He wasn't sure how he would find Chemerra's hideout but had a hunch it would be remote and distinctive. He also felt Chemerra posed no real threat to him. If he'd really wanted to hurt Dan, he could have done far worse than sending him to jail. It seemed more like a warning than a punishment.

Chemerra's subtle clues about Moon River had been premeditated, designed for Dan's eyes only and hidden from the FBI, so he had made the decision to keep his current activities to himself. Vince and Hudlow had already proven to be untrustworthy.

He motored on as the sun dropped lower in the sky. Now touching the tops of the trees, the receding light altered the appearance of the estuary dramatically, casting dark shadows over the swamp. At this point most solid land had given way to small islands and hammocks. There were no roads, only travel by boat.

A perfect location for a perfectly private person.

The tributaries narrowed and the overhanging cypress canopy seemed to lean in, its mossy tendrils reaching down toward him. An occasional cabin, perched on stilts, would appear in the private bends of the swamp, each subsequent one spaced farther apart. Somehow, Dan expected to recognize Chemerra's lair when he saw it. He tried to visualize the shape of Chemerra's cave from Echidna.

The channel made an abrupt bend to the right and Dan pressed the rudder to the stops. The twin pontoons carved a broad arc, barely managing to avoid the shore. He leaned over to avoid a wall of moss hanging over the water. Then, straightening out at the end of the curve, a long straight expanse of water opened up and Dan knew instantly that he had found Chemerra's lair.

Nestled in the backwaters of the swamp, a gray cypress cabin hovered above the water on stilts. In the very center of the building, a large picture window stared back at him like the eye of a Cyclops. The entire building had a surreal look about it, almost cartoonish. The wall containing the picture window angled downward, as if on the verge of collapsing into the water. A large overhang jutted out above the window. It was, in fact, this unique shape that reminded him of the jutting rock over Chemerra's cave in Echidna, the picture window echoing the yawning maw of the opening. A dim white light glowed from inside the structure.

Dan cut the engine and steered the drifting boat toward a small dock at the base of the stilts and pulled alongside a powerful-looking speedboat that was missing the pilot's chair.

The left pontoon of *Mossy Lynn* rubbed against the edge of the dock, making a subtle squeaking noise. He jumped off and tied up the craft, then followed a winding footpath to an elevator. He paused there, assessing the situation. From a distance, the cypress cabin looked like any other rustic structure hiding in the swamp, but up close, he could see technology bristling everywhere.

Yep. Gotta be the place. Taking a deep breath, he entered the elevator and pushed the button. It rose silently and swiftly, coming to a stop directly across from a heavily fortified steel door.

The glassy eyes of several video cameras peered down at him as he pressed the doorbell. Dan had a sudden twitch of anxiety, wondering if this was truly a good idea. Suddenly, the door swung open and a face appeared.

"You!" Dan said. "What the hell?"

"Who did you expect? Some pimply-faced kid living in his mother's basement?"

OPERATIVE ONE HAD been following Dan from a respectable distance, until the coffin boat vanished around a sharp bend in the river. He eased back on *Shyla*'s throttle and drifted silently toward the left shoreline, leaning out to catch a glimpse down a long, straight sight line toward a bizarre structure at the far end of the channel. Concerned about being spotted, he immediately reversed course, backing up just far enough to avoid detection from the building's large picture window.

"Time to check in, don't you think?" Operative Two said.

Operative One nodded and made the call. "This is One. Suspect has stopped on the river and entered a weird building. Damn thing looks like Salvador Dalí's house, pitching forward like it's going to fall into the water. My bet is it's the perp's hideaway, far enough out in the sticks for privacy. We're about five hundred yards out. Will have to cover the rest of the distance on foot if we want to remain undetected."

The radio crackled in response. Even with the poor reception, Operative One could hear the tenseness in Hudlow's voice. "Approach carefully. The element of surprise is paramount if we want to obtain the prize. When you confirm the perp's identity, breach the building. Then we've got the son of a bitch."

"Affirmative." Operative One signaled his partner and they scrambled up onto the shoreline, keeping to the shadows of the forest.

17

DAN'S PRECONCEIVED NOTIONS of Chemerra as either a hulking beast or some nerdy programmer were shattered by the person staring across the threshold at him. It took him a minute to find his voice. "You're *Chemerra?*"

The woman in the wheelchair frowned at him. "Is it such a stretch? Don't be so presumptuous as to think that a hacker can't be female."

"That's not what I meant," he replied. "You're Esrom Nesson's assistant, Ada Kurz, right? I don't understand. I thought you were a geneticist, one of the good guys."

"I can't be more than one thing?" With the barely perceptible movement of her hand, Chemerra, or Ada, or whoever she truly was, turned her motorized wheelchair around and beckoned him into the room. "Shut the door behind you," she said over her shoulder.

They entered a narrow white alcove. To the left was the large picture window Dan had seen from outside.

"Does anyone else know you're here?" she said.

"Maybe not," Dan said, feeling challenged by her question. "But maybe."

She turned the chair around. "Well, you left your personal phone back in the hotel, so I'm guessing not."

"How do you know where my phone is?"

Ada Kurz remained silent but shot him a condescending stare as if to say, *Are you serious?* "Anyone follow you?"

He decided candor would score more points. "Not to my knowledge."

Ada turned again and continued into the middle of the room facing the window. Her choice of decor was stark, modern, and featureless. Everything was white: tile floor, walls, ceiling, furniture, cabinets. Only the occasional bric-a-brac item offered a splash of accent color. The monochromatic shapes had no edges or contrast and that messed with Dan's depth perception.

In contrast to the colorless decor, the large picture window glowed like a giant TV screen, the colors of dusk painting a sultry mood. The window pointed east, toward sunrise and the Atlantic Ocean. At this time of day, the eastern sky was tinged with slate and green. The window itself angled down steeply, holding no reflections from the sky, appearing to disappear into the outside scenery.

"Interesting home," Dan said. "What's with the bizarre architecture?"

"Eyes in the sky," Ada replied. "Latest spy satellites can read a restaurant menu from a thousand miles up. The angled glass gives me privacy from above while still offering a view."

"You're pretty paranoid."

"With good reason. There are a bunch of people looking for me."

"Point taken. Is that why you left me clues?"

Ada allowed the hint of a smile. "In part, yes. I had to lure you here alone, without the prying eyes of your FBI friend. But it was also a test of your perception. You did well."

Dan scanned the open floor plan. It appeared Ada had a thing. The white decor extended into every room, giving the entire home a sterile laboratory vibe. He wondered about all the monotony.

On the other hand, Ada's motorized wheelchair was anything but featureless. It bristled with computing equipment, electronics, and motors: a practical server on wheels. Yet, he noticed the absence of a monitor or traditional keyboard and realized the reason for the decor. As Ada glided across the room, her attention was drawn to some invisible object, hidden from view behind a pair of augmented reality glasses that she wore. She stopped, the fingers of her left hand darting across a strange keypad strapped to the chair's armrest.

Suddenly, images from several security cameras appeared on one wall. The source of the light seemed to come from a digital projector mounted on the wheelchair's outer frame. No matter where Ada moved, her white walls and surfaces offered a projection opportunity.

The entire house was a computer monitor.

She quickly scanned the images, punched the keypad again, and the images disappeared. Her attention returned to him. "I'm sure you've got questions, so fire away."

He hardly knew where to begin. "Well, I understand how you stole the Devil's Paradox. You just walked out of the lab with it. My question is: why?"

"Really?" Ada's expression reflected genuine shock at the question. "You still don't get it, do you? I'm not the thief. I thought you'd understand the truth by now but it appears you know nothing."

"So, you're not working on a biological weapon?"

She hesitated, cocked her head to one side. "That answer is complicated."

"If you didn't steal the Devil's Paradox, who did?"

"I've got my suspicions but first things first. You and your FBI friends are wrong about me. I'm not some evil hacker. I am one of the good guys."

It had been Dan's experience that every criminal considered him- or herself a *good guy,* finding justification for even the most heinous of acts. "If you're a good guy, why hack into secure computers? Steal data? Hide behind black phones? Live in a fantasy world of virtual reality? Organize demonstrations that get people killed? Support bio-hacking? What are you trying to accomplish that's so *good*?"

Ada smiled woefully. "I fight for the faceless masses; that's what Firemen do. We battle *gatekeepers,* rich assholes who want to charge us for the right to a free and happy life." As she spoke, her movements became more animated. "The American dream of a free world is a sham. Instead, we live as ignorant slaves, brainwashed into doing the bidding of our overlords. The rules in *this* world are created by the whims of our masters."

Dan could see the passion in her eyes but he didn't buy Ada's argument. "Your young, impressionable Firemen friends? I can understand them buying into these conspiracy theories, but you? You seem mature enough to know better. How old are you? Mid-fifties?"

"Age is irrelevant. Why are you so willfully ignorant? With your background, I would expect more from you. If you look carefully, you'll see the truth, lingering like an invisible shadow. The evidence is so pervasive and obvious that it disappears like the edges of a shadow on a cloudy day. It's still there but hidden in the glare of light."

Dan stared at her. Ada spoke to him as if she knew every detail of his life. It left him feeling violated. "How do you know so much about me?"

"Let me cast a bright light on your ignorance," she replied. "Your life is an open book, like most citizens. I know every product you've bought, every ad you've viewed, every email you've sent, every love text you've sent to your girlfriend, Rachel. I know all your friends and contacts, your business emails. I can map your every move over the last year, thanks to your phone's GPS. Since I have that information, you can bet your overlords possess it too. They are master manipulators of the mind, praying on your blindness to the invisible forces that enslave us all."

"Wait a minute." Dan held up his hand, disturbed by Ada's intimate knowledge of his life. "It seems you're the manipulator, and who are these overlords you speak of? Sounds like something out of a bad fiction novel."

Ada grew quiet for several moments, appearing to ponder how to continue. "Since you mentioned novels, allow me to tell you a story from the past, a history lesson of sorts. Just open your mind."

Ada twiddled on her hacker keypad. A slide show of images appeared on the wall, depicting a series of archaeological ruins. She began talking, glancing up and to the left, as one would do when recalling a story from memory.

"Three thousand years ago, several ragtag tribes along the Tiber River came together to form the world's first republic, called Rome. Its senators ruled for centuries and were chosen by the people, creating the first representative democracy.

"Then, at the turn of the millennium, Julius Caesar crossed the Rubicon and declared himself grand emperor. From that moment on, the Republic of Rome ceased to exist. All subsequent rulers declared themselves emperors endowed with absolute power. Since they had not earned the right to rule through achievement, their reigns were often disastrous, self-serving, and incompetent.

"Still, Rome managed to grow in power and influence over the ensuing centuries. Why? Because another group stepped in, ruling from the shadows, collecting great wealth and power, while the emperors were maintained to hold the attention of the citizenry. Rome's true rulers became the Praetorian Guards, the emperors' version of the Secret Service, elite soldiers drawn from many legions. The Praetorians often came from the equestrian class, so we'll call this shadowy group the Horsemen. Meeting in secret

underground caves, they schemed to rob Rome's wealth and control its population. As their power grew over the centuries, the Horsemen began to feel invincible; entitled to their legacy. Meanwhile, their figurehead emperors reigned, perished, and were replaced, often chosen by the Horsemen themselves."

As Ada spoke, a stream of historic images scrolled across the white wall of the cabin.

Dan sighed aloud. "Hate to tell you but I've heard this story before."

Ada raised her hand. "Patience. I'm getting to the interesting part."

This was not at all what he'd expected to find when arriving at Chemerra's door.

Ada continued.

"Rulers cannot survive without the cooperation of the people, so a citizen army was formed, a group of watchmen to enforce the laws. In 6 A.D., Emperor Augustus formed the Vigiles Urbani, the watchmen of the city, consisting mainly of freed slaves who served as the policemen and firemen of Rome."

A thought popped into Dan's head. "And that's where your group got its name, the Firemen."

Judging from the frown on Ada's face, his interjections were not appreciated.

"May I finish?" Ada twiddled on her keypad, bringing up a new image on the wall: an artist's rendering of the burning of Rome during the rule of Nero.

"For three centuries, the Vigiles protected the city from random fires, established order and the rule of law in the streets, all directed by the Praefectus Vigilum, a member of the equestrian class appointed by the senators. But the hubris and greed of the Horsemen proved insatiable. By three hundred A.D., the Praetorian Guard had wrested control of the Vigiles from the emperor and the senate and placed their own Praetorian Prefect in charge. By this time, the Praetorians had stolen most of Rome's wealth, gutted the military, and appointed mercenaries with little loyalty to Rome to defend its borders. Rome became a shell of its former self, leaving it vulnerable to

attack. The citizens of Rome suffered, their wealth and property stolen. Confidence in the Republic fell. In 300 A.D. Barbarians attacked, breaching the walls of Rome for the first time. The Horsemen abandoned the city as the attacks intensified, taking most of Rome's wealth with them. Over the next century, they dissolved into the countrysides of Gaul and Britain, changed their names and identities, used their wealth to establish themselves as local chieftains, nobles, and lords. They built castles and continued to exploit local populations by using their time-honored tactics of bread and circuses. The Horsemen left the Firemen to clean up their mess. Unfortunately, it was too late to save the empire. All was lost."

"Bread and circuses," Dan said. "I know the term but how did the Horsemen use it for exploitation?"

Ada smiled grimly, finally acquiescing to his constant interruptions. She seemed satisfied that Dan was at least curious. "The phrase 'bread and circuses' was coined by the Roman poet Juvenal. He realized that Rome's endless tributes, the gladiatorial games, the races in the Circus Maximus, and free bread for citizens were all based on a singular strategy designed to keep the general population in line. When you're entertained and well fed, you'll ignore all kinds of atrocities.

"The Horsemen had tapped into a basic human flaw. We think first with our hearts, not our brains. Why? Because *speed* of decision-making is favored over *accuracy* when surviving in a predator-prey world. Over the eons, humans evolved emotions as the great tiebreakers, forcing us to move without thinking. Fear is more important than truth. We're not the logical beings we imagine. Instead, our emotional *lizard brains* drive our logic, cause us to jump to conclusions, to *think fast* and act faster."

The intensity of Ada's eyes grew as she continued: "Our brains evolved during that old predator-prey world, where thinking fast was essential to survival. But now, we live in a modern society with complex problems that demand reason and foresight. But *still*, our lizard brains hold sway, trumping our intellectual potential. We are prisoners of our basic emotional instinct. The Horsemen realized this quirk of human nature and exploited it.

"They think of themselves as the world's only true thinkers," she continued, "distinct from us emotional plebeians. They're cold and calculating. They use ruthless logic. They are not swayed by morals. Their methods are timeless. If a populace gets disgruntled, they start a war, cut taxes, create a common enemy to stir the heart. An inflamed populace will ignore all the bullshit going on around them. It works just as well today as it did then, better actually, since we live in an interconnected world."

Dan had always considered himself the ultimate pragmatist, logical and aloof, so he imagined his expression betrayed his skepticism. "True, people do stupid things based on emotions. Anyone who's been in love knows that. But using emotions to build an empire? Not convinced."

Ada frowned. "What would you sacrifice for the ones you love? Your own life? Your reputation? It's illogical to sacrifice for others, if you're not going to be around to enjoy the fruits of your sacrifice. Yet people do it every day. The powerful need only to tap into your emotions to pull at your heartstrings, like puppet masters." Ada moved her wheelchair closer. "The Horsemen have used these tactics for two thousand years, because they *work*. Why else would corporations continue to spend billions on advertising to sway our emotions?"

"It's a compelling story but you talk as if this secret society of Horsemen still exists."

"They do," Ada said with no hint of sarcasm.

"So how come I've never heard of them before?"

Ada's expression twisted into a sardonic smile. "What part of 'secret society' do you *still* not understand? Besides, the name 'Horsemen' is only what *we* call them. We have no idea what they call themselves. Their identities are secret."

"You *do* understand," Dan said, "that it's pretty hard to take this seriously. Ancient societies still fighting a two-thousand-year-old war? Sounds like a good premise for a video game, though."

"Don't be smug. It's not as ludicrous as it sounds." Ada rolled her wheelchair over to a bookcase filled with dusty old tomes. "Greek and Roman society still has a large influence on our modern world." She pulled a book from the shelf entitled *The Satires of Juvenal* and stroked the cover reverently. "Our entire legal system, corporate laws, architecture, all originated during the Roman Age. The tradition of naming animals, plants, chemicals, and drugs by their Latin names began with the Romans. Look around Savannah at the neoclassical architecture. The design for Washington, D.C., came directly from the Roman forum. Is it so hard to imagine that the ruling families of Rome survived? I'm sure you've heard of old money, just not *how old*, perhaps."

Dan shrugged. "Hadn't thought about it. But if they're so secretive, how do you know they exist? Where's your proof?"

Ada paused, her expression caught in a moment of uncertainty. Finally, breaking free, she continued.

"*Me*. I'm your proof." She removed the shawl covering the bottom half of her wheelchair. Ada had no legs, only withered, flipper-like stumps. "I'm one of the Horsemen's monsters, a product of their tactics and my father's emotional frailty."

Dan was shocked by the sudden reveal, instantly self-conscious. "I'm, uh, so sorry."

"Don't be, I'm used to the stares," she said and replaced the shawl, smoothing it out unceremoniously. "I've always been the freak. When you grow up with no legs, there's plenty of time to play around with lab equipment and computers. As a child, they were my toys, my playground friends. My classmates wanted nothing to do with me."

Ada's face reflected defiant satisfaction. "The Horsemen have always invested heavily in potions, drugs, pharmaceuticals. So much better to breed a dependent population. As a boy, my father grew up in a close-knit German community which had immigrated to Argentina as refugees of war. Father became friends with the son of another German family with centuries of accumulated wealth. The family promised him a wonderful opportunity when he graduated from college. Father began working for the family's company as a research scientist. He was told that he was being groomed for their secret organization. His research focused on a drug called thalidomide that was marketed aggressively in Europe during the fifties and sixties as a cure for morning sickness. One problem . . . it caused massive birth defects."

Ada straightened her shawl again. "My father soon became the perfect example of emotional thinking. When it became clear that his research had led to thousands of deaths and deformities in newborn children, he refused to believe it. His ego wouldn't allow him to accept his culpability, so he convinced himself that the drug was harmless, that the birth defects had come from radiation poisoning from atomic weapons testing, which was common during that time. Of course, there was no evidence at all but he doubled down, grew more intractable. My father became so convinced of his fantasy that he chose to prove the drug's safety by feeding thalidomide to his own pregnant wife."

Ada sat up straight and defiant in her chair. "I'm it, the embodiment of my father's chemical error, the legacy of his own betrayal of reason."

Dan stared, stupefied. The thought of a father intentionally risking his child's life through some false belief repulsed him. "Ada, sincerely, that's horrible. How did he explain his actions to you when you grew older?"

Ada shrugged. "I never knew my father. Once he was forced to confront the undeniable truth at the hospital, once he saw the *monster* he had created, my father went home and hung himself. My mother made sure to tell me the story, so that I would learn a hard and painful lesson. Anyone can become a victim of their own misguided emotions. Mother fought for years to obtain compensation from the original investors, the family who had promised us a place in their bright and hopeful future, but they abandoned us. Suddenly, we were too imperfect for their pristine world. When I attended college, one of my professors introduced me to the Firemen and I learned a new reality."

The air between them grew awkward and still. Dan looked away, finding eye contact too uncomfortable in the heavy moment. He struggled to absorb Ada's tale, unsure if he believed it. But as the saying goes: *just because you're paranoid, doesn't mean they're not after you.*

Chemerra, the *chemical error.*

Dan wondered why Ada would share such a deep and personal secret with him. Then, a horrible thought occurred to him. "Is that what you're doing?" he said. "Creating some lethal organism to strike back at the Horsemen?"

Ada frowned, placed Juvenal's book back on the shelf. "Aren't you listening? I would *never* make the same emotional mistakes as my father! Follow me." She moved quietly and quickly through the room and down a long hallway toward a white door, barely visible in the featureless wall. Dan followed. She stopped at the door, opened it, and motioned Dan inside.

18

OPERATIVE ONE STRUGGLED to make progress toward the crooked house. He looked back at Operative Two, who was stumbling and cursing.

Operative Two let out a stifled moan. "This sucks! Look at my suit." He pointed down at his legs, which had disappeared up to mid-calf in thick mud. "I'm gonna write this suit off on your expense account. My elephant-skin loafers are ruined."

"Fine," Operative One replied, as he inched forward through the brambles. "If we get the boss what he wants, I'll buy you a new suit, shoes included."

After the sun dipped below the trees, the light quickly waned, making it virtually impossible to avoid the incessant potholes and mud bogs. In the twilight, the forest had become a dim adversary, its tree limbs and Spanish moss waiting to grasp and cling at them. He was starting to regret his decision. It had seemed prudent to stick to the forest rather than the shoreline, in order to avoid the line of sight through the building's massive picture window.

But the forest had turned into a squishy raft of putrid leaf litter, mixed with the occasional mound of solid earth that tripped them up at every turn. He cursed under his breath and swatted a gnarled branch away that stuck to his jacket.

A few seconds later, a yelp from behind echoed through the pines. "Son of a bitch! You hit me in the face! Watch what you're doing."

"Shut your mouth," he whispered back. "You're going to give away our position." Operative One turned back around and flailed at a cloud of hovering mosquitoes. Every few feet, he was forced to stop and brush the horde of insects off his clothes. He realized now that it had been a mistake to come this way but it was too late to turn back. Barrett Hudlow had made it abundantly clear to the both of them that the element of surprise was paramount for obtaining the prize. Otherwise, Chemerra might have time to hide it, or formulate an escape strategy, or worst of all, demand a lawyer.

"Next time, I'm in charge of tactics," Operative Two whispered from behind.

"Shut up and keep moving."

DAN STEPPED INTO the doorway and stopped, his mouth agape. Ada had outfitted her spare room with the type of technology found in the most sophisticated laboratories. "You must have thousands of dollars invested in this room."

"Tens of thousands," Ada said proudly. "You're right about one thing. I *am* working on a microbe, one that will change the world." She rolled past him into the center of the room and spun in a complete circle. "Right here, in my own personal lab, I have the freedom to work without limits. But I would *never* work with the Devil's Paradox, not after a serious accident that occurred at GenTropics. No, I'm working on something completely different." Her eyes gleamed. "I'm developing a universal vaccine, one that will end pandemics once and for all. It will protect the world from all flu viruses, past, present, *and* future."

The bold statement caught Dan completely by surprise. "A universal vaccine? That's possible? If so, then how come no one's developed one before?"

"For one thing, it's hard as hell," she said. "But the main reason is because there's nothing in it for the pharmaceutical companies. They make huge profits from existing vaccines: Ebola, measles, Covid-19, childhood diseases. What's more profitable than a medicine that everyone needs to take, whether they're sick or not? And then there's the seasonal flu vaccines, which require fresh formulations year after year. It's a billion-dollar industry."

Ada's expression darkened. "Why stop the gravy train by developing a single universal vaccine that could grant immunity to most viruses in one simple dose?"

"But that's crazy," Dan said. "Thousands die each year from viruses. Millions to Covid-19 alone. To purposely avoid inventing a treatment that could save millions of lives? That would be unconscionable."

"And that surprises you?" she asked. "Corporate charters are written to make money for their stockholders, not to save lives or serve humanity. When I took my idea for a universal flu vaccine to Gen-Tropics, they dropped the project like a hot rock. I've been forced to develop it on my own, here, in this lab."

"Then how do you explain smallpox? Didn't a vaccine eradicate it from the planet? Doesn't sound like a profit-driven venture to me."

"Yeah, but that was just one virus," she replied. "And it was a coordinated effort by the World Health Organization. Since then, vaccines have become big business. Flu viruses, in particular, mutate all the time. There's always some new threat right around the corner to stir fear in the populace; and nothing loosens wallets faster than fear. The gatekeepers love products that get their customers hooked—alcohol, cigarettes, painkillers. What's more addictive than a vaccine that saves your life?" She rubbed two fingers together. "Money. It's the universal mammon, the only thing they worship."

Dan shook his head, laughing at the absurdity of her claim. According to Ada Kurz, the FBI had everything backward. She and the Firemen were trying to *stop* the next pandemic, not start one. Either that, or Ada was a great liar . . . he wasn't quite sure what to believe. "So how does this universal vaccine work, exactly?"

"It's highly technical, obviously," she replied, hesitating for a moment. "I like to use a flower analogy to explain it. Do you remember all the depictions of Covid-19 in the news, of a round ball with purple buds sticking out all around it? That's the 'corona' of a coronavirus. Viruses aren't really alive. They need a living cell to make copies of themselves. So, those buds are the keys used by the virus to unlock human cells. They match a specific receptor on the cell wall that will open the door. Then the virus enters and forces the cell to do its bidding."

Dan interrupted her. "I understand how a virus works. Tell me about the universal vaccine."

"I'm getting to that," she said, frowning. "Those buds on the virus are big, visible targets, what we call antigens, because they activate the body's defenses. Eventually, the immune system will design a custom antibody that neutralizes the antigen, rendering it and the virus harmless. Antibodies are very precise though, made for one specific antigen and they take time to manufacture. Most vaccines work by presenting the target antigens to the immune system before an infection can occur, so that the body has time to make antibodies. To do that, early vaccines used live viruses that had been weakened so they couldn't infect the patient but would still stimulate the immune system. That's how polio was defeated. Modern vaccines just use the antigens themselves, manufactured snippets of DNA or RNA, without the virus." She smiled. "Those buds on the outside of the coronavirus? I like to think of them like flowers to a bee, bright and easy to recognize.

"There's a problem though," she continued. "Viruses mutate all the time because those surface antigens are complex and because they want to hide from the immune system. It's called antigenic drift. So, think of those flowerlike buds changing constantly. A red rose might become a yellow rose, or a daisy. Suddenly, the immune system doesn't recognize the antigen anymore. Antigenic drift is why vaccines must be targeted to each new virus. That's why we have new flu vaccines every year."

Dan held up his hand to stop her. "Okay, let me see if I'm following you. In order for a universal vaccine to work, it's got to ignore those changes in the antigens, right?"

"Yes, exactly," she said, her eyes sparkling with excitement. "Or, you can train the immune system to target a different antigen altogether, one that never changes, something universal in viruses. This is where you come in," she added, smiling. "I read your complexity professor's papers on Syncrenomics and got stuck on complex fractals and how they can be derived from very simple formulas. Always self-similar but never exactly the same. What a vaccine needs is a simple, unchanging target, the starting formula. Going back to the flower analogy, what is something that all flowers have in common?"

Dan thought about it for a minute. "I don't know, leaves, stems."

"Bingo!" Ada seemed pleased by his comprehension. "For flowers, a stem is a stem, more or less. Stems support the flowers and send them food and water. Their basic design remains the same, even while the flowers vary. In the case of a coronavirus, a protein stem links the outer buds to the body of the virus, much like the stem of a rose. The proteins of a viral stem are simple. Stems don't drift. My universal vaccine targets the universal stem, not the ever-changing buds, so the immune system learns how to target thousands of different viruses, all with common 'stem' proteins. Once the immune system makes antibodies for that common factor, you're protected against all viruses that use similar ways to invade a cell, which is mostly everything."

Dan's thoughts returned to Rachel as he listened to Ada's descriptions. As a marine microbiologist, Rachel also used similar analogies to "dumb down" her explanations to him. He felt like he actually understood the basic principles Ada described. "So, instead of targeting your vaccine to the unique and visible attributes of individual viruses, you've identified something mundane and unchanging, that all viruses share and you've targeted that, what we call in complexity a crux factor, the simple rule that underlies complex functions."

Ada grinned broadly. "Yes! You've got it. When I studied your background and read your papers on crux factors, it inspired me to think more simply, rather than getting mired in the complexity of the immune system."

The two of them grew silent for several minutes.

Dan finally broke the silence. "In theory, this all sounds great but you're right back where you started, aren't you? This universal vaccine is still going to need some big pharmaceutical firm to put up the billions of dollars necessary to test and manufacture it. But if they're not interested . . ."

"Don't worry, I have a solution for that too." Ada grinned. "Who needs big drug factories, sub-zero fridges, distribution systems, and testing when a human body can manufacture the vaccine at no charge? I've attached the vaccine to a contagious retrovirus. No expensive shots, no control by gatekeepers. Free for everyone, rich and poor. Just catch something like a mild cold and be vaccinated against other viruses, forever. It's a simple distribution system that nature has used for billions of years. In fact, the world's first natural vaccine was a contagious pathogen. Doctors noticed that milkmaids were immune to smallpox, because they had been previously infected with a cowpox common to their trade but harmless to humans. Simple and efficient."

She rolled her chair over to a large incubation oven and stared at it reverently. "Somewhere in this tray is the world's first 'self-replicating universal vaccine.'"

To Dan, the sheer boldness of Ada's idea sounded magical and horribly reckless at the same time. "Wait, you're going to infect the world with a new, untested, artificial virus? What if it mutates, becomes virulent, killing rather than helping? What if it doesn't work the same way for all people? If you've been reading about Syncrenomics, then you must know about the unexpected trickster. You'd be playing god, letting serendipity and chance decide who lives and who dies."

"Drug companies do that every day," Ada replied, shrugging. "Who passes judgment on them? Besides, I've thought of that possibility and have a way to make the risks vanishingly small. My contagious virus doesn't infect human cells, only simple organisms that hide in the body like vagrant passengers."

"Huh?" Dan was instantly confused. "How does *that* work?"

"My communicable vector is a phage, a virus that only infects bacteria, prokaryotes. Human cells, eukaryotes, are much different. The phages I use only infect lactobacillus, the common bacteria found in milk, yogurt, and the human bloodstream. Our bodies are filled with billions of them. The phages infect the lactobacillus and are programmed to produce the universal flu antigens that will educate the human immune system. If the phage mutates, it will only affect its bacterial host, not the human host. That's about as safe as it gets."

"You're pretty sure of yourself." He hesitated, wondering how much information to share. "As you probably know, the Devil's Paradox mutates unpredictably. I've seen the results . . . how do you know your phage won't jump to humans?"

"Because phages are fundamentally different from the viruses that infect human cells. It's like trying to cross a mouse with an elephant. Esrom and I abandoned the Devil's Paradox months ago precisely because of its complexity and ability to alter genes from any type of living cell—plants, animals, fungus, bacteria, you name it. We tried altering its DNA to make it safe but the strategy failed. I've seen its unpredictability up close. That's exactly why I chose a phage for my vector. Much simpler and easier to work with. Oh, and by the way, I know everything about your time in Honduras, perhaps more than you do. No need to hold back."

"How?" he asked. "It's obvious you've broken into military servers but in my experience, that should be impossible. How do you do it?"

Ada smiled. "I'm *Chemerra,* the superhacker, remember? I know everything about you. I know you're not the Weatherman hacker but that friend of yours, Rudi? We'd be very interested in welcoming him into the fold."

"You're not answering my question. How do you brute force a

password that's supposed to take thousands of years with current computers?"

That mischievous smile again. Ada hesitated, studying him with her piercing blue eyes. She finally seemed to conclude that she could trust him. "Who says I use current computers?"

"Computers gifted by aliens, then?"

"In a sense, yes." She motored silently down the row of lab tables to a grid of tiny sample tubes, thousands of them laid out like a checkerboard, sorted and maintained by a set of automated robotic arms. "This is what I call my 'wetware' computer. You know, DNA is a very versatile molecule. In fact, you can use it to break the toughest encryption codes in the world."

Another fantastical claim. "Uh, how do you make DNA compute?"

Ada laughed. "DNA *is* a computer. Think about it. A single complex molecule, wound into a double helix, containing all the logic necessary to create an entire human being, a being empowered with a brain powerful enough to comprehend the miracle of his or her own existence. If one DNA molecule can do all of that, it can certainly decrypt a simple hash code."

Dan's thoughts circled back to Rachel again. Ada possessed the same passion, recklessness, and knowledge of biology. "How does that work exactly? The short version, please."

"Not sure there is a short version," Ada said. "But I'll give it a try. Most computer systems are secured by password hashes: one-way mathematical algorithms, impossible to decrypt. But you can guess at the password and match it to the hashed result. Military-level systems use long passwords that are changed weekly or monthly. As you said, it would take a conventional computer thousands of years to guess all the combinations." Ada pointed to the grid of tubes on the table. "But RNA and DNA molecules are vanishingly small. There's enough DNA in this one tray to store over a zettabyte of information. That's *one trillion* gigabytes. These vials contain a DNA computing device, genetically engineered to solve encryption hashes."

Ada clearly enjoyed the opportunity to share her accomplishments with another person. She had to be lonely, being so anonymous and secretive. "Unlike an electronic CPU, a DNA computer is highly specialized. I have to sequence a different DNA molecule for each password hash, then I unzip the two halves of the helix. A 'guessing machine' is then added to the mix, basically a string of random RNA molecules bombarded by X-rays. The RNA mutates into random combinations. A zettabyte of guesses is so large that the correct answer to the hash is usually in the mix somewhere. The random RNA strings find their matching hash DNA and hook up. Given enough time and enough mutations, the entire hash will be solved. When that happens, a release of enzymes alerts me that a solution has been found. It usually takes less than twenty-four hours. Since RNA is so small and numerous, the guesses run several orders of magnitude faster than any supercomputer ever created. That's about as simple as I can make it."

Dan scratched his head. "I'll have to take your word for it but the real question is: *why?* Why break into all these official sites? It seems you've got plenty of legitimate work to be doing instead."

"To level the playing field."

"What playing field?" Dan said.

"Between the Horsemen and Firemen, of course. Dan, I know your background, your studies in complexity. You, of all people, should understand the necessity for balance of opposition. Without balance, the system runs out of control, destroys itself. For centuries, the Horsemen have been gathering power, subjugating the masses. The invention of the printing press and the Age of Enlightenment allowed us to regain some of our freedom and influence. Then, during the Industrial Revolution and the Gilded Age, the Horsemen regained their power, amassing huge fortunes. The internet and modern technology have allowed us to bounce back but the battle has never been so fierce. The Horsemen are getting desperate. They're developing a newer, more aggressive strategy to supplement their tactics of bread and circus. They too are weaponizing . . . to subjugate the masses once and for all."

"How?"

"That will take more explaining." Ada turned her chair and headed back toward the door. "How about some coffee first?"

It was a rhetorical question, so Dan followed, wondering what would come next.

INSIDE TAURUSSEC HEADQUARTERS, Froggie Pitts sat at the control panel of the Pegasus surveillance drone, twitching with anticipation at testing his new toy for a second time. The call from the "big boss" had caught him unprepared and he had scrambled to get the autonomous jet fueled, prepped, and launched.

He transmitted a new command to the Pegasus, instructing it to complete yet another holding pattern over southern Savannah. Freed from the controls, he used the moment to wipe the grime off his Coke-bottle glasses. Now, stateside, he had the option to go back to contact lenses but habits were hard to break. During his tour of duty, the alkali dust of the Middle East had wreaked havoc on his military-issue contacts, plus the risk of losing one during a mission was unacceptable. So he had adapted to the heavy lenses, learning how to sight down a barrel with them on. Wearing anything else now seemed . . . unnatural.

Thanks to the drone's autonomous mode, piloting was a cinch. He only had to transmit a broad command and let the vehicle's neural brain control all the detailed maneuvers. It was powerful, yet disconcerting. He still preferred full piloting mode but the autonomy had its advantages. It allowed him more time to focus on the surveillance footage being sent by the drone's keyhole camera.

He watched as the two Homeland Security operatives left their boat and stumbled up the riverbank, disappearing into the tree cover of the surrounding forest. Occasional breaks in the canopy allowed him to track their progress, which had slowed to a crawl.

He pointed the keyhole camera toward the strange structure farther down the river. The house's actual shape was hard to determine from this altitude, as the walls of the structure were not plumb. In fact, their angle had the effect of making the walls disappear, giving the building a strange two-dimensional outline from above, like a decal that had been pasted on the swamp below. That is, if you could see the outline at all. The metal roof of the building had been painted with a camouflage pattern that blended into the surrounding forest almost perfectly. He never would have spotted the structure from the air if Dan Clifford's bizarre coffin boat had not approached it a few minutes earlier.

Froggie gave his glasses another perfunctory wipe, slipped them back on, and waited for the big boss to reconnect.

A crackle of static, and the secure line came to life. "Mr. Pitts, what's happening now?"

During his tour of duty, Froggie had become accustomed to gravel-voiced commanders with their gruff, direct styles but this new civilian boss . . . gave him the creeps. In the military, the commander's way was the only way. No hesitation. Civilian service was more complicated. His new boss had a smarmy attitude and weak voice, yet demanded more than the harshest drill sergeant.

"Target is established. The two government operatives are in pursuit. Clifford has entered a residence, deep in the backwoods."

"Can you see inside the house? Identify the target?"

"Uh, not currently. The building is not conducive to surveillance."

"What the hell does that mean?"

Froggie rubbed a patina of sweat off his neck. He could hear the frustration in the man's voice. "Sir, the structure is designed to obscure aerial reconnaissance. The walls are not plumb. At this angle of incidence, I cannot establish a view through the windows. That would require a much lower angle of incidence."

Long pause. "So get one! I need to confirm the target's identity."

Froggie swallowed hard. "Sir, I'd have to drop below operational altitude, which would expose Pegasus to detection by locals. Our military contract specifically requires stealth."

"Yes and this is not a sanctioned military mission," the big boss stated. "Until the contract is signed, this is *my* drone, understand? And right now I have a critical need to identify the enemy."

"Yes, sir, but . . . just to be clear . . . you want me to violate our rules of engagement, correct? Even though it may threaten exposure of the Pegasus Project?"

"Yes, yes. Let me worry with the details," he said. "I'm giving you an order. Get me an image of the target and transmit it to me."

"Yes, sir." It was unlike Froggie to question orders but in the past, they had always come from commanders who went by the book, knew the rules of engagement, were qualified. The big boss? Not so much. Anyway, he'd done his best to cover his own ass, so Froggie did what every soldier was trained to do: follow orders without hesitation.

He sent a command for a descent spiral, choosing to drop altitude over the ocean. At least that would provide some protection from detection. They were only a few miles off the end of the runway at Hunter Army Airfield, so with any luck, the locals would see the low-flying Pegasus as just another jet coming in on landing approach.

ADA'S KITCHEN'S DECOR maintained the same monotony as the rest of her house: the cabinets, floor, and countertops were all stark white. As she moved about the kitchen, images flickered across the white surfaces from her chair's video projector. Every few minutes, Ada's attention would be diverted by an image and her hands would twitch suddenly across the twiddler keyboard. She would type madly for a few moments, then return to her prior task. Ada, a.k.a. Chemerra, multitasked, very much like her mythical multiheaded avatar, the Chimera.

Whenever she needed something from an upper shelf, the four-wheeled chair would rise up to balance on two wheels, lifting her to eye level. The motion was always abrupt and happened without any interaction on Ada's part. How she controlled the chair remained a mystery but the act of three hundred pounds of metal and human balancing against the pull of gravity seemed jarring and counterintuitive.

Woman and machine had become one, a cyborg constantly connected to the web, even while going through the mundane task of brewing coffee.

Dan considered himself something of a coffee connoisseur, so he studied her brewing technique, executed with the precision of a laboratory geneticist, grinding the coffee with a burr grinder, creating particles of uniform size and structure. She measured the coffee by weight, not volume, then used the penultimate drip brewer, a Technivorm Moccamaster, to bring it all together.

Soon, a satisfying hiss accompanied a dark stream of liquid flowing into the Moccamaster's carafe. Ada pulled the pot out prematurely and poured two cups of the brew, presenting one to Dan. He inhaled deeply, took a careful sip from the rim, and closed his eyes, savoring the rich, tart brew. Ada Kurz was as talented a barista as she was a biologist and hacker.

They both sipped quietly for a moment, staring out through the large picture window as the afternoon light waned. A great shadow from a stand of trees behind the cabin crept across the river, blotting out all detail and leaving only a faint outline of its banks. Soon, a dark wall of impenetrable forest was all that remained.

It was Dan who finally broke the silence. "So if you're really developing a universal vaccine, why the discussion about a new pandemic on the dark web? I've seen the posts."

"Because we didn't post those threads. The Horsemen did, impersonating me. They wanted to alert the FBI to our activities."

"If that's true, then why did you lead me here with clues? Why share your secrets with me, especially after you discovered I was working with the FBI?"

Ada huffed. "Don't fool yourself. I've known of your involvement with the FBI since the beginning. I know everything about you, Dan, remember? Your company SurMyz Consulting Group, your friend at the FBI, what's his name? Vince Peretti? I know about your adventures in Honduras, NeuroSys, your weather prediction system, your complexity science professor, even your favorite brand of coffee. I hacked your cell account, computer, and credit card accounts. You're predictable but you *did* surprise me in one regard. I thought you'd at least hear me out in Echidna before betraying me. *That* I didn't expect, not from your psychological profile." She stared out the window as she spoke, unwilling to look him in the eye.

"For what it's worth," Dan said, "I didn't know the FBI was tracking me at the time. In fact, I'm getting pretty damned tired of being left in the dark by everyone."

"Well, I'm not doing that, not any longer." Ada turned her chair to face him. "It's time for you to wake up. You've seen firsthand evidence of the Horsemen, hiding in plain sight in positions of power and influence. They've got their hands so far up politicians' asses they could tickle their Adam's apples. And I guarantee, they know as much about you as I do."

"How would you know that?"

"Because I used the same cellular system to track you that they would, Signal System No. 7. SS7, for short. It's the global cellular network that coordinates all cell phone traffic. I had to hack into it using my DNA computer but the Horsemen? They *own* SS7, or at least a part of it. For access, all you need is ownership of a mobile phone network somewhere in a small, third world country, like Honduras, for example. Their cell business has the keys to the entire system. Simple as that, totally legal. That's why we always disable the SIM cards in our black phones. We communicate through Wi-Fi only, with several layers of encryption and onion routing. There's no privacy on a commercial cellular network. It's a joke. The posts about a pandemic were part of the Horsemen's coordinated misinformation campaign.

They planted those messages precisely to get the FBI and Homeland Security to do their dirty work for them. You just got caught up in the scam."

"Again, why am I here? What makes me so important to you that you would risk your anonymity?"

"If the Horsemen were going to send the feds after us, I wanted a double-double agent working with them, someone who might listen to reason."

"And you think I'm that person? I'm not even sure I believe your story," Dan said. "That might not have been a smart move."

"I think you're coming around, more than you want to admit. You're a better choice than a total stranger. Besides." She laughed. "You took down one of the Horsemen's own, interfered with one of their biggest operations in Honduras. Next to me, you're probably top on the Horsemen's hit list, definitely persona non grata."

"Who?" He thought for a moment. "You mean Martin Orcus, the billionaire? He was part of this Horsemen group?"

"That's what I've been trying to tell you, they've been under your nose the whole time."

Dan's head was spinning. He remembered when the stock offering for his former employer, NeuroSys, had collapsed, due to his exposure of Martin Orcus on television. Then the assets of the company were mysteriously transferred to Honduras. Did the Horsemen own NeuroSys now? What were they doing with a multibillion-dollar computer chip factory?

"I'm not gonna lie," he said. "This two-thousand-year-old battle you talk about is still pretty hard for me to swallow. Most secret societies get exposed eventually. How else can you recruit new members?"

"Look, the Horsemen aren't like the Moose Lodge, Freemasons, or Shriners, which are just quasi social fraternities. The invisible organizations are the ones you should worry about. Ever since the fall of Rome, the Horsemen have hidden in the shadows. That's how they protected their wealth. They've adopted new names, new identities. They meet in underground temples, their principles never written down. They pass their wealth and knowledge along through inheritance, to their family members or most trusted associates. And they want to destroy the Firemen, because our mission is to weaken their influence and power. If the public had any idea how entrenched and powerful they were . . ."

"And yet you willingly shared the Firemen's secrets with me, a total stranger," Dan said.

"Dan, you're no stranger to me but you're partially right. We have to keep our identities secret to avoid our enemies, but total secrecy is harder for the Firemen. We must constantly recruit new members. We are unified by a principle, rather than wealth and family ties. The Horsemen survive through their genes; we survive through *memes*. But only the members at the highest levels know the depth of the Firemen's cause, our entire history. You ask why we organize these social events, demonstrations, play around with virtual reality; it's about recruiting, filtering, training and initiation. We're constantly rebuilding our army."

Ada rose up in her chair so she could stand face-to-face with him. "I'm trusting you with this information, Dan, because I believe in you. Recently, the Horsemen have become more aggressive. They're trying to infiltrate our ranks. They're scared of the power we've accumulated through the internet. They're changing the game."

"How, exactly?"

"You met Molly Daniels recently, right?"

Dan remembered his awkward encounter with Molly and cringed. "Yeah, she was hanging out with Will Detweiler, the man who was shot and killed by *your* security force."

"Not mine. TaurusSec works for GenTropics Pharmaceuticals. No one, not even Esrom, knows my true identity. Molly used to be one of our top lieutenants: smart, enthusiastic. Then something changed. She lost all interest in the cause. We think the Horsemen drugged her somehow, altered her personality."

"How do you know that?"

"I've broken into some of the Horsemen's secure messaging systems, which they use sparingly. They often talk in code but I've heard references to behavior modification experiments and 'pharming.'"

"Wait a minute, I thought 'pharming' was a hacking technique." Dan remembered discussing the technique with Vince Peretti and Rudi at a prior meeting at the FBI. "Isn't it similar to 'phishing'? Except that you route the victim to a fake website?"

Ada grinned. "Good for you, Dan. That is a strange coincidence, I'll admit. But in this case, I'm talking about a genetic engineering technique. The term is a portmanteau, a combination of two words, in this case, 'farming' and 'pharmaceuticals.'" Ada made two quote marks with her fingers. "'Pharming,' as in pharmacy with plants."

She typed on her twiddler keyboard and an industry article appeared on the kitchen wall. The article was titled in bold letters:

Pharming's Success Story: Insulin for Pennies

"Pharming is already used to produce artificial insulin. Transgenic genes were transplanted into yeast cells, which produce insulin, instead of alcohol, as a byproduct. Much cheaper than harvesting from the traditional animal sources. There's also been work inserting transgenic spider genes into goats. They produce spider silk protein in their milk, which can be easily extracted for superstrong fibers. The technique is sort of similar to the one we used in our party beer, the one you overindulged in." She smiled. "It's pretty good stuff, don't you think? It's a way for us to learn the techniques, to understand the Horsemen's true goal."

It was the first time Dan had seen Ada smile. "And that goal is . . . ?"

"Massive behavior modification." Ada's expression grew serious again. "Imagine if you could control an entire population by making them more docile. That would be the Horsemen's dream tactic for subduing an increasingly empowered public. In fact, nature's already accomplished it, though behavior modification. Ever heard of toxoplasmosis? It's a parasite passed through cats that can infect humans. It may have already altered the personalities of thirty percent of the world's population. The parasite attacks the brain, altering the behavior of men and women differently. Men become more impulsive, risk takers. Women become more compliant and sexually oriented. Sound familiar?"

Dan thought back to Molly's advances and her eagerness to help him, of Will Detweiler's impulsive behavior at GenTropics. "How?" he blurted, his mind swimming with possibilities.

"I'm not sure but I think that's why they stole the Devil's Paradox. Pharming takes sophisticated, multigene engineering, something the Devil's Paradox is particularly good at but as you know, it's too powerful and unpredictable. *They* don't know that. The Horsemen are businessmen, manipulators, and lobbyists, not scientists. Putting such a powerful gene-editing tool into their hands is like giving a high school kid an atomic bomb along with the blueprints."

"Isn't that the pot calling the kettle black? Your own biohackers are doing the same thing. You don't see the irony?"

"Of course I do," she said. "Which amateurs are more dangerous? Kids experimenting to learn? Or powerful individuals with an agenda of domination? I'll take the kids any day. Truth is, technology is an untamed beast. We can avoid it, give the Horsemen all the power, or we can harness it for good, learn to coexist with the technology. We've got to understand the technology if we hope to stop those who choose to use it against us."

Dan shook his head, feeling disoriented, somehow disconnected from the familiar world he had grown accustomed to. So much deception, lying, misdirection, crazy theories.

He didn't know where to find *truth* anymore.

But he knew one truth: the Devil's Paradox was real. He had seen its terrible potential firsthand. Will Detweiler's death was real. He had felt the man's life leaving his body. There *had* to be some way to separate the truth from all the lies, because reality is an unbiased taskmaster. It doesn't care what people think or believe. It does what it does, and the ignorant suffer. No amount of faith would change that. Ada's heart-wrenching tale about her father proved that point powerfully.

19

FROGGIE PLACED THE drone into a shallow descending arc, high enough to look over the treetops but low enough to see through the cabin's picture window. The drone's keyhole camera used the latest technology designed to work from high altitudes, so at this low level, it would be like using binoculars to stare across a room. He aimed the camera at the cabin and locked into anti-shake mode.

"What do you see?" came the insistent voice of the big boss. "Patch me in!"

"One moment." Froggie linked the video to the boss's encrypted feed. "How's that?"

"Very clear, thank you."

The drone continued its inexorable journey toward the cabin. Froggie kept resetting the camera's zoom level to keep the view centered on the cabin's main area. From his angle, he could see into the structure, past the picture window, through the building, and into the kitchen. Two people were facing one another, their bodies framed by kitchen cabinets. They seemed deeply involved in conversation, oblivious to the action taking place outside their limited world. One of them sat in a wheelchair and it took Froggie only a split second to recognize its occupant, someone he had seen numerous times at work. "Sir, it appears Clifford is meeting with Ada Kurz, the lab assistant at GenTropics."

"There's no one else there? Just the two of them?"

"Sir, I don't see anyone else," Froggie said, noting the level of distress rising in the boss's voice. He moaned silently, expecting a dressing down or series of unreasonable demands. "It appears to be a false alarm, not the meeting with the terrorist we expected. He's probably interviewing her about the theft of the microbe."

The drone continued forward, drawing perilously close to the target. Froggie was about to pull up to make another circular pass when an image popped up on the back wall of the kitchen, containing a news article.

FROM ITS VANTAGE point, the camera's resolving power could clearly make out the title:

Pharming's Success Story: Insulin for Pennies

A moment passed, then the boss yelled: "That's it! That has to be Chemerra!"

"What? Are you sure? Ada Kurz?" He'd known her for over a year. Cute. Unassuming. The idea that she could be this dangerous super-terrorist they had been warned about made no sense at all.

"I'm sure! That article is the giveaway. She works for GenTropics? Right under our noses?" The boss's voice reached a fever pitch.

Right under their noses indeed. It suddenly made sense to Froggie. He wasn't exactly sure what the boss had against her but it was a brilliant piece of clandestine spycraft, infiltrating the enemy's main operation. He almost admired her stealth and gumption. Then he realized that the plane had gotten perilously close to the cabin. He quickly initiated a pull-up maneuver.

"What are you doing?" the boss man screamed.

"I have to circle around, sir, obtain some more distance. We were coming close to buzzing the cabin, which I'm sure would alert the principals."

"Reacquire the target as quick as you can," the boss said, his voice trembling with excitement. "Is the drone armed?"

"Uh, yes, sir. Full complement. Why?"

"Just get that camera back on the two of them."

"Yes, sir." Froggie found himself hesitating. It would require ten minutes to circle back around, at least. He wondered what could possibly be accomplished by another pass. They had already identified the main operatives. Regardless, he initiated the command and the drone reacted obediently.

ADA KURZ STARED at Dan, her eyes exploring his. "Do you understand now? Why I wanted you involved? Why you were *already* involved but didn't realize it? Soon, you're going to have to make a choice of whom to believe . . ."

Dan struggled to find some sharp edge of reason or logic that he could use to make sense of all the deception and betrayal. For the last few years, it seemed like his life had become one lie after another.

"I understand that *you* believe what you're saying but I'm still not sure I can trust you or the Firemen. How do I know this isn't your own misinformation campaign? How do I know *you* didn't poison Will Detweiler? You locked me up in jail. You organized a demonstration at your own place of business. You're the one with full access to the Devil's Paradox. You see my conundrum? Your story sounds convincing." He turned his palms up. "But how do I know who's telling the truth?"

"How can you ask that, after all the vulnerable information I've shared with you?" Ada seemed crestfallen, her eyes glistening. "Don't you see yet? Truth hides in *tragedy*. When all the world is crushed and hope is lost, truth confronts us with all its terrible ugliness and ferocity. Only then does the truth show itself." A tear traced a crooked path down her cheek. "But it doesn't have to be that way. You don't have to wait till it's too late. Still don't trust me? There's something you should know about Rachel. Discover it, then tell me I'm lying."

"What?" Dan felt as if he had been hit in the chest with a bat. "What do you know about Rachel?"

"It's not for me to say, Dan. Look to your penthouse, your webcam. Then go to Esrom. Ask him about the accident and about a treatment. That's where you will find the rest of the truth . . ."

"What the hell does that mean?" Dan screamed. He began to panic. "Tell me! What about Rachel?"

"It's something you must find for yourself . . ." Ada's attention was suddenly drawn to the wall, as a series of surveillance videos popped up, showing two men approaching the building's elevator. Ada turned back to him. "You said you weren't followed . . ."

"Not that I was aware . . ." Dan stared at the security camera image, unbelieving. That asshole Hudlow had tracked him, even after he left his phone back in the room.

The hum of the elevator signaled their approach. Soon, a polite knock sounded at the cabin door. Ada hesitated for a split second then swung the door open.

The two men were covered in mud, their suits disheveled, yet they carried themselves with an air of authority. The one who appeared to be in charge thrust his arm forward, holding an unfolded ID. "We're with the Department of Homeland Security. May we enter?"

Ada stared at the two comical figures with their muddy suits. She seemed to make a decision and backed her wheelchair into the hallway. "Sure."

The two men entered the space and began examining everything. The four of them stared at each other expectantly, unsure how to proceed.

Dan just wanted them to go away, so he could debrief Ada about Rachel. He stepped forward. "What do you want?"

The two men looked at each other, ignoring Dan's advance and focusing on Ada.

"We want to know if you're the terrorist, Chemerra," said the first operative, matter-of-factly.

Ada looked genuinely surprised. "Who?"

The first agent grinned, aimed his phone at her face, and took a picture. He stood silently for a few minutes then looked up, apparently surprised at what the phone told him. "According to my facial recognition program, you're Ada Kurz, correct? Employed at GenTropics Pharmaceuticals?"

Ada's expression maintained a stoic image of neutrality. She smiled pleasantly. "Yes. What can I do for you?"

"Let's cut to the chase, Ms. Kurz," he said, a smirk growing across his face. "We know who you are. You're the terrorist Chemerra."

"Oh?" Ada tilted her head to one side in genuine surprise. "Why would you think that? I work for GenTropics, after all. We're the victims here. This terrorist, Chemerra, has cost the company an incalculable amount of money."

A hint of doubt fluttered across the first man's face and he glanced around the room nervously.

Dan watched the scene from the periphery, amazed at Ada's ability to lie convincingly. He recognized the two operatives as members of the joint task force. They were Hudlow's shadow men. Despite Ada's guilt, he once again felt used, lied to, tracked, and betrayed by the very men he was supposed to be working with. In an instant of clarity, he made a fateful decision. "Ms. Kurz is correct," he said. "I'm here to discuss the very serious ramifications of this theft with her. You guys should know that. I work for your boss, after all." He took a defiant step forward, letting his feelings of genuine anger show through.

The two men glanced at each other, betraying a sense of insecurity as they processed the situation. Finally, the first operative spoke. "Well, if that's true, then you shouldn't mind if we have a look around, right?" He nodded to his colleague, who responded by heading across the room toward the hallway, his head on a swivel.

"Do you have a warrant?" Ada said. "Last time I checked, I still had rights."

The first operative grinned. "Madam, if you're innocent, you shouldn't care if we look around. Besides, the Patriot Act says we can do whatever we want in the case of an imminent terrorist threat. If I want to, I can throw both of you in the brig, with no trial, no lawyer."

Dan couldn't believe what he was hearing. Vince Peretti had always followed the letter of the law but these yahoos from Homeland Security were a different breed. It pissed him off. Whether Ada was innocent or guilty, she deserved her day in court. Dan blocked the second operative's path. "I think you need to check with your superiors before you start violating this woman's rights. Call Vince Peretti at the FBI."

The first operative took a step forward. "We don't work for the FBI and you need to step aside if you want to remain a free man," he said, jutting out his jaw.

Dan stood his ground, glaring back intensely. At that moment, he didn't care about Ada's guilt. These men were acting like vigilantes.

The first operative glanced back at Ada. "Of course, you could make things much easier on yourself if only you would provide us with your codebreaker software. It's your bargaining chip." He grinned and shrugged his shoulders. "However, if my partner finds anything damning, you'll spend the rest of your life behind bars. We consider your codebreaker to be an invaluable weapon against our nation's enemies. All you need to do is agree to cooperate with my boss and we might be able to ignore some of your other activities, assuming you're really as harmless as you claim. Wouldn't you prefer to work with the good guys?"

Ada smirked at him. "So you want me to break into secure systems for your boss? You're not the good guys, just penny ante crooks. You have no idea the true forces operating right under your nose."

Ada's brashness caught the man off guard and his expression

hardened. "Well, I have one idea. You're about to be in a shit-pile of trouble." He nodded at his partner and pulled a firearm out from underneath his soiled jacket. "Tear this place apart while I babysit our two guests here."

THE PEGASUS DRONE had completed its circular track, acquiring its target for a second time. Five miles out, the drone's keyhole camera locked onto the cabin's picture window, its sophisticated tracking and anti-shake mechanisms providing a rock-steady image of the cabin's interior.

Froggie was surprised to see the addition of two more people in the room. Apparently, the two Homeland Security operatives had arrived. Even from this distance, Froggie could see the tension between the four people. The two Homeland Security agents were engaged in a heated discussion with Dan Clifford and Ada Kurz.

A burst of static signaled the presence of the big boss. "What's happening? Where's my feed?"

"Acquiring." Froggie typed madly. "It appears Homeland Security is in the process of arresting the terrorist," he said.

The big boss's voice suddenly rose an octave. "That cannot happen! We must prevent Chemerra from revealing what she knows!"

Froggie was confused. "What do you mean, sir? She's your enemy. Why wouldn't you want Homeland Security to arrest her? Isn't that the goal? Get her out of your hair?"

The boss growled, "You don't understand anything! I've been looking for this person for twenty years, if she shares her knowledge with the authorities . . ." The transmission went silent.

When it returned, Froggie was shocked by the steely resolve of the voice on the other end. "Terminate the target, now."

"What?" He froze. "Can you be more specific?"

"You heard me," the big boss repeated. "I need you to terminate the target, in fact, terminate them all, before they have a chance to share information with one another."

Froggie had heard such a definitive command before, when his fellow soldiers were at risk. He'd obeyed without hesitation. After all, the command had come from his military superior. But now? "Sir, these are civilians and government operatives."

"This has to be done."

"I, uh . . . You know it would be traced right back to us. A drone firing on a residence, even this far out in the boonies, would be detected by neighbors. We'd be on the national news in hours." He felt a surge of sweat streaming down his back. There was a long pause giving him hope that he'd talked some sense into the man.

"Let me worry about the press coverage. We'll figure something out. We've been waiting for years for this opportunity. What if Chemerra starts talking to the feds? We'll be exposed." The big boss's voice suddenly took on that dead-calm tone Froggie knew all too well. "This has to be done . . . now.

"Fire!"

He wavered, his thumb trembling over the drone's fire button. Flashbacks to Afghanistan flooded his mind. Chaos. Violence. Innocents. This was the enemy, right? Bad guys. Civilians . . . Americans. For the first time in his military career, Froggie contemplated insubordination.

"Mr. Pitts, did you hear me? I said *fire*. Now!"

20

"Run!" Ada Kurz yelled, acting in such a bizarre fashion that Dan froze in his tracks.

One minute, Ada was sitting in her wheelchair, looking up at the agent from Homeland Security, an accused criminal overshadowed by a federal official. The next instant, she was screaming like a banshee, driving up and forward on the two wheels of her motorized chair, pinning Operative One to a kitchen cabinet. The full weight and energy of the wheelchair's steel-and-chrome structure pressed against his body, as Ada's forearm slid up under his chin and against his neck. Her elbows pinned his arms back. The agent had been so surprised by the move that he had fallen backward without resistance, the gun in his right hand falling to the floor.

"Get out!" she screamed in Dan's direction. "They'll kill you!"

Far from energized, Dan stared in a stupor, enraptured by the slow-motion scene that was suddenly playing out. Seconds seemed like minutes. He stared as the agent struggled against the weight of Ada's chair, while Ada continued screaming, her words lost in the chaos.

The second agent, frozen in place and gaping at the inexplicable scene, began to stir, his prior training in self-defense kicking in instinctively. He lunged toward Ada, intent on pulling her away from the other agent.

Dan was a spectator, watching surreal events play out before his eyes like a virtual-reality game on a computer screen. The next instant, he became a player, lunging forward, defending Ada's rear position. His instinctual training in tai chi began to kick in but a few milliseconds behind the second agent. He intercepted the man's forward motion and redirected it toward the back of the kitchen, giving Ada a few precious seconds to do . . . *something*. He could imagine no endgame for this maneuver but soon realized he had acted before his core had found balance.

Dan's body twisted, absorbing all the agent's forward motion. He fell to the floor, the breath knocked out of him, the agent's fists pummeling his face. He reached up and grabbed the man's throat, splaying out his elbows to draw the man's face closer and shield the energy of his fists.

The two of them stared at each other for a brief moment, struggling to think in order to plan their next action, when a mighty roar shook the cabin.

A SHOWER OF splintered glass and metal engulfed the room like a waterfall, filling the floor with debris. The agent hovering above him suddenly released his grip as his face exploded in a red mist. It rained down onto Dan's face, stinging his eyes and filling his open mouth with the taste of rust and copper. He gasped and coughed, his arms struggling against the limp weight of the man who had taken on the characteristics of a sack of potatoes.

The roar continued for what seemed like ages, filling Dan's mind with terror.

Then, all went still.

The rattling drone of crickets and tree frogs accompanied the smell of sour swamp air as it quickly filled the room. Dan gasped, rolled the lifeless body of the agent to one side, and staggered to an upright position.

A gurgling noise came from the two lumps of flesh lying in front of him. Dan rushed forward. The other agent was also dead, his body riddled with bloody holes.

Sprawled next to him was Ada's torso, writhing and struggling. He rushed to her side and immediately saw a bullet wound piercing her neck. She was still alive, struggling to breathe, bloody foam bubbling from a hole in her trachea.

He searched the debris for something to stem the blood loss and found a dish towel. He pressed it against the wound. "Shh, relax. Slow your breathing. Hang on. I'll call for help." Dan ransacked his pockets, suddenly remembering that his phone was still sitting back in the hotel on his dresser. Ada's hand thrust her black phone forward.

Dan started to call 911 but she slapped his hand away, wordlessly mouthing something unintelligible. The expression on her face told him everything he needed to know. She shook her head, then grabbed her phone, swiped to a login page, and pressed his finger against the screen.

He stared down at the bloody fingerprint that stained the phone's glass, written in Ada's blood. Her eyes pleaded at him. She nodded and mouthed two words that he recognized.

You're it.

As if putting a final point on her message, she poked her finger into his chest, heaved with one last bubbling gasp, and went limp. Dan stared at her, uncomprehending.

What the hell had just happened?

He scanned the room. The large panoramic window was now a gaping hole into darkness, allowing the dank night air to encroach into the formally pristine room. A thick layer of shattered glass covered the floor and furniture. Bullet holes were everywhere, staining the pristine white decor with blood, dirt, and splinters. The holes traced a wobbly line across the kitchen and down the hall, about a foot above the floor. They continued down the hallway and across Ada's laboratory door like a huge scar. Dan realized that had he not been lying supine on the floor, he'd be dead too.

He stared through the open window into the gloom, searching for an assailant. That much firepower had to still be out there somewhere. He stared at the dark shapes, straining to spot any movement but the forest had grown still. The crickets were chirping as if nothing had happened.

He was a sitting duck, the last remaining target bathed in light, poised for another kill shot.

A stream of thick smoke billowed out from underneath Ada's laboratory door. Then the lights went out.

DAN CRAWLED ACROSS the floor, waiting for his night vision to adjust. He reached the elevator, now inoperable. He stumbled down a set of stairs adjacent to the elevator that led to ground level. As he scrambled out into the humid night, a few flickers of light played across the trees. He looked back to see flames licking the front of the house. Outside, dusk had given way to the suffocating darkness of a moonless night, one that he hoped would afford him shelter from attack. He half ran and half slipped down the bank toward *Mossy Lynn* and escape.

At the shore, he regained his footing and froze, straining to detect any foreign sound against the backdrop of droning crickets, any rustle or cracking of twigs that might betray a sniper or more likely, a small army, judging from the torrent of bullets that had assailed the cabin. His senses honed by adrenaline, Dan heard a faint sound in the far distance.

The whine of a jet engine.

The sound grew louder and more distinct, revealing the source of the onslaught. He had few options. Escape via boat would be impossible. He'd be a sitting duck, so he turned and ran back toward the woods, hoping to keep the cabin between him and the approaching jet.

FROGGIE HAD WAITED until the absolute last minute to fire but his instincts drove him forward. A career of training following orders was not easily broken. As his thumb met fate on the trigger, he watched with detached horror as the drone's twin chain guns unleashed their fury on the unsuspecting occupants of the cabin. The flurry of rounds had barely met their target when he was forced to pull up at a steep angle to avoid hitting the target head-on. The drone's momentum and power drove it into a steep ascent that would have torn apart a lesser plane. But because Pegasus did not have to make adjustments for human cargo, its structure had been reinforced to survive g-forces well in excess of human capability.

The screen's display went black as the drone's camera stared into a moonless sky. At this point, Froggie released manual control of the drone and ordered it into another circling maneuver. In the background, he could hear the excited voice of the big boss screaming over the com.

"Yes! Got 'em! Good job, Mr. Pitts! Now, circle around and let's make sure the targets are terminated."

Froggie wiped his forehead and leaned back into his chair to catch his breath. He had already anticipated the boss's order. The maneuver would give him a few minutes to contemplate the aftermath of what they had just done. His career might be over. In fact, he might be spending the rest of his days rotting in some jail cell. Firing on civilians? How the hell did the big boss think he could cover that up? The chances seemed remote, bordering on impossible. He knew that the sound signature of a low-flying jet was relatively small. You don't normally hear an approaching jet until the very last minute but on a quiet night in the woods? If anybody in the vicinity was sitting outside on a deck, surely they would have heard something. He decided that after a battle damage assessment, he'd urge the boss to get the hell out of there pronto.

Pegasus finished its circular route and locked on the cabin again. Froggie winced at the horrific damage done by a hailstorm of jacketed bullets. He could see the long line of destruction that had traveled across the structure with the devastating precision of the drone's tracking and anti-shake mechanisms. Just as he was sure no one could have survived, he spotted a brief movement in the kitchen.

Then the screen went blank.

"What the hell happened?" the boss said.

"Power outage, I think, sir. Switching to infrared."

Just as he feared.

Froggie swallowed hard as a ghostlike figure crawled across the floor and disappeared through a side door. "Someone's alive, sir."

"Well, what are you waiting for? Fire!"

DAN HAD BARELY reached the edge of the woods when the growl of machine guns started plowing up the earth beneath his feet. He dove behind a sprawling cypress trunk, remnants of a once majestic tree that had since disappeared. The hollow rattle of bullets sunk into the trunk's far side but didn't make it through. It appeared that the plane had shot blind, right through the cabin, anticipating his position as he had run up the hill. Now the plane's speed worked to his advantage. It would have to circle around for another strafing run. He needed to be anywhere but there.

He took off at a 90-degree angle from the trunk, stumbling and fighting against overhanging branches and Spanish moss. Stopping for a moment to catch his breath, Dan glanced back at the cabin. Flames were poking out the shattered windows and creeping up the sides. In a matter of a few more minutes, Ada's cabin would go up like a brushfire, urged on by the abundance of air being sucked in from below the stilted structure.

Gasping for air. Dan traced the jet's sound as it receded then circled back around. They had seen him almost immediately after he left the cabin, despite the cloudless night. That meant they had night vision. He'd stick out like a beacon no matter where he went. He had no choice but to struggle on but he would try to keep the flaming building between him and the jet, hoping it would blind the night-vision camera. He altered his path to parallel the jet's approach and lit out again. He could barely see, tripping over roots and fallen branches, cursing the whole way. Thankfully, the flames from the cabin began to provide moderate illumination. He heard the jet approach, jumped behind another tree, and waited.

It screamed by directly overhead but no gunfire. He was invisible, for the moment at least. Unfortunately, in order to keep the cabin between him and the jet, Dan was being driven farther into the woods.

The solid earth began to tremble and waver. That meant swamp ahead. He'd have to risk another left-hand turn, back toward the river. There was no telling where he'd end up on his current path.

He stepped over a log and immediately fell forward into a dark mass of unimaginable muck. A powerful rotten stench erupted from the morass and assaulted his nostrils. He sank up to his waist in pluff mud, a demonic mix of rotting plant matter, dead fish, brackish water, and every other kind of estuary detritus one could imagine.

Dan held still and tried not to panic. More movement would only drive him deeper. He took several deep breaths, tried to relax, take in his surroundings. In the distance, he could hear a lone owl, singing a soulful tune: *whoo, who, who, who, w-whoo, whoo. Who are you in my domain?*

Thankfully, no sound of a jet. Had they given up? Or turned things over to a ground-based hunter?

To his left, the faintest of sounds, something brushing against leaves. A scuffling noise, like a raccoon or fox. He held perfectly still, as quiet as a stone and listened. There was a long moment of silence, broken only by the soulful cries of owls. A hint of woodsmoke drifted across the marsh.

Despite the sultry evening, his body warmth was being sucked away by the pluff mud. He could not stay here much longer. Slowly, he began to move, hoping to find solid ground or something to lift himself out of the muck. He tried to go horizontal, to spread out his weight but no matter how slowly he moved, the sucking mud held onto his legs tenaciously. Some sound was inevitable and as he lifted one leg, a juicy slurp overwhelmed the night sounds.

Suddenly, he heard deliberate movement, one of aggression, not stealth. A blinding light engulfed him. "Gotcha! You son-of-a-bitch!" The shape slid forward, an indistinguishable blob behind a brilliant light.

Dan could do nothing but raise his hands. "I'm an innocent by-stander," he pleaded.

"You almost led me into the swamp. Then we'd both be trapped." The man stepped forward into the halo of his own light, just enough for Dan to see the gray barrel of a rifle aimed directly at his head.

21

"HERE," THE DARK voice said. "Grab this."

"Don't worry, it's not loaded." The shadowed man poked the barrel of the rifle toward Dan's head for effect.

He reluctantly grabbed the end of the rifle and held on. After a mighty struggle and another loud slurp, his legs popped out of the pluff mud and he felt hard ground under his feet again.

"Whooo! You stink!" the man said. "Follow me." With that, he pointed a dim red flashlight into the distance and headed off, snapping an ammunition magazine back into his rifle.

Dan had no alternative but to follow, wondering if he had left the pan for the fire. They threaded their way through a dense canopy of cypress trees until a riverbank suddenly appeared from nowhere.

The man hopped in the back of a jon boat, rummaged around under his seat, and threw a wrinkled tarp in Dan's direction. "Sit on that. I know the boat's not much but I'd prefer to keep the mud off the seats."

Dan did as instructed and the boat took off at a slow clip, powered by a small electric trolling motor sitting adjacent to a large outboard. Thanks to the choice of engine, the flat-bottomed boat cut through water silently. He scanned the skies for jets but could see little in the moonless sky.

"They're gone," the man said, as if anticipating Dan's next question. "I watched the drone break formation and head out a few minutes ago." The man seemed to know the area by memory, winding around several bends in the ever shrinking river without a single mishap on what had become a dark and starless light. Suddenly, he turned the boat to starboard, cut the motor, and drifted straight toward a large cypress tree that had fallen across the water. As the boat grew nearer, the cypress tree magically floated to one side and allowed them passage. The tiny trolling motor revved up again and they continued up a narrow winding channel. Dan looked back to see the tree magically float back into place.

"That your security gate?" Dan said.

The man chuckled. "I value my privacy." A few minutes later, he turned off the trolling motor and the boat drifted to a silent stop alongside a cluster of giant rotting tree trunks.

As Dan's eyes adjusted to the dark, a ramshackle shanty boat seemed to materialize from the trunks. He stared at the dark cluster and realized that the boat's exterior had been covered with long vertical strips of tree bark, each one cut to a random length, which had the effect of breaking up the linear lines of the square structure. Long strands of Spanish moss were draped over the ragged edge, further hiding its true design. The contraption blended into the woods almost perfectly, its disguise betrayed only by a shallow deck that ran around the outer wall and the occasional hint of light peeking out from behind cypress shutters. From twenty feet away, the whole structure would be invisible to the casual observer.

After hopping onto the deck, the man grabbed a hose from a barrel on the boat's porch and aimed the business end at Dan.

"Strip," he said.

Dan did as he was told and was immediately hit with a stiff spray of tepid water. After a good rinse, the stranger pitched a pair of sweats in his direction.

"They're probably too small for you but they should get by until I can get your clothes through the washer." He grabbed Dan's discarded clothes and entered the houseboat.

"There's a washing machine on this thing?" Dan said to the man's backside as he disappeared through a doorway that seemed to materialize from a blank wall. Light suddenly spilled out from the interior.

He pulled on the snug sweats and followed the man inside. The stranger was short, around five foot seven but wiry and muscular and well-tanned, like boiled peanuts left in the pot for too long. It was as if the heat had reduced the stranger to his bitter essence. He definitely kept fit. After deftly removing the ammunition magazine from his rifle, the man cleared the chamber and propped it up in one corner of the room. His fluidity of motion hinted at someone with a strong military background.

The interior of the houseboat had the opposite vibe of its outer appearance: warm and inviting, with square walls and sturdy construction. It was small but meticulously neat, decorated in an eclectic collection of antiques, Ikea furniture, and reclaimed salvage. Electronic equipment lined one bookshelf, looking out of place among the "salvage chic" decor.

On another wall hung a variety of firearms.

One nearby shelf overflowed with a collection of picture frames, their contents giving Dan an instant snapshot of the mystery man's past: Marine veteran, probably from the Gulf War.

Dan could hear the sound of a washing machine running in the room at the far end of the houseboat. A few minutes later, the mystery man reappeared and smiled for the first time.

"Your houseboat is far more inviting on the inside," Dan said. "Why all the camouflage outside?"

"Privacy is underappreciated," the man said. "This boat gives me peace and quiet, control over when and where I interact with the so-called normal world. Been working on the old girl since I returned from the Gulf. I call her *Gillie*," he said, grinning.

The man held out a hand. "I'm Dakota Pell. You can call me Dak." He motioned toward the singular couch lining one wall. "Why don't you sit down and tell me what the hell happened back there?"

As THE SUN began to set, Rachel Sullivan studied the large wooden structure for the last time. After repeatedly measuring the distance between the poles and their heights, she'd gone through the complete banner-raising procedure with her two volunteers until they were sick of her demands. Tomorrow, five minutes before the stunt, they would raise the gossamer banner between the two poles and quickly run for safety. With any luck, her plane would hook the banner on cue and she'd make it into the record books.

Regardless, she held no fantasies of success. The ribbon-cutting stunt by itself was dangerous enough, but she had decided to up the ante by combining it with another one of aviation's most difficult stunts, the outside loop. To her knowledge, no one had ever combined the two together. Most likely, she'd drive straight into the ground. *But hey.* She shrugged. *That's why they called it a death-defying stunt, after all.*

Rachel swallowed away a lump in her throat. It would be an honorable way to go, quick and painless. At least that's what she kept telling herself as her thoughts circled back to Dan Clifford and the adventures they had shared together.

Adventures they *could* have continued to share, if only for a few chains of proteins that had repeated themselves one time too many in her DNA. So much loss, from a father dying of the same affliction, to her half-brother, murdered senselessly. Dan had been her one bright light in a life filled with heartache.

The sound of movement from behind prompted her to wipe away an unfamiliar wetness from her cheek. A strong hand gripped her shoulder and she turned, forcing a smile, wondering if her eyes would betray her. "Hi, John. Coming to the show tomorrow?"

"Wouldn't miss it for the world," he said.

John Martin the Third was an old friend from the stunt-flying circuit, who along with his father and grandfather, made up what she considered the ultimate family of superfans. Together, they represented three generations of Air Force brats, their legacy going back all the way to the original Army Air Corps, before it became a separate branch of the military service, the United States Air Force.

John studied Rachel's ribbon-holding contraption with jaded eyes. "I gotta say, you've got bigger cajones than me, to attempt such a stunt. Ribbon cutting from an outside loop? Together? How'd you pull that off in a thirties-era biplane?"

Rachel forced another smile, deciding to keep the truth to herself, that she hadn't actually attempted the stunt yet. This was gonna be a one-off deal.

She acknowledged the rest of the family, shaking John Martin, Jr.'s hand and bending down to hug "Big John" Senior, the original John Martin, who at ninety-nine had chosen to use a motorized wheelchair to negotiate the massive grounds of the Atlanta Air Show.

She turned back to John the Third. "You'd be surprised by this old biplane. The Bückers are still considered one of the best acrobatic planes ever built. That's why the Germans were still using them as trainers in World War Two, that is, until my granda stole this one."

"What? This is your granddaddy's plane? I don't remember any vintage biplanes ever sporting turboprop engines."

Rachel allowed herself a laugh. "Well, I had to make a few enhancements for this stunt, the engine being one of them. She's still got a lot of life in her."

Big John Senior poked his grandson in the side with his cane. "Sonny boy, haven't I told you the story of Finnegan Sullivan, the Mighty Sparrow? Rachel's granddad? He was a famous Irish ace, the scourge of Mussolini." Big John's movements became more animated as he turned back to Rachel. "Educate my grandson on how we used to do it back in the day, before all them fancy jets and missiles," he said, chuckling.

"Well, why not," she replied. "I haven't told that story in a while." Truth was, the thought of reliving Granda's old story, recounted to her numerous times as a child while sitting on his knee, flooded her with relief. She needed something to keep her mind off tomorrow. "Um, where to begin." She rubbed her chin and began the recitation from memory.

"My granda, Finnegan Sullivan, was one of 'the Few,' who flew for the British during the Battle of Britain. He established a reputation as an ace pilot flying a Spitfire, earning him the early nickname, 'Spitting Finny.'

"Finnegan racked up an impressive number of kills, becoming an ace within days of his first flight. He continued to rack up kills, until his boss, Keith Park, was relocated to Malta. Finnegan followed him there to take on the Italian and German forces. One day in 1943, Finnegan's Irish luck finally gave out and he was shot down over Sicily in his Spitfire.

"Finnegan managed to bail out but broke his leg on the landing. It was late afternoon and he was being chased by the local Italian militia. Luckily, a young maiden from a nearby farm stumbled upon him, as he was crawling through the grape fields. She took him back to her farm and nursed him back to health. The Italian maiden was Emma Giordano, who later became Finnegan's wife, my grandmother.

"For months, the Italian militia searched for Finnegan but Emma and her family kept him hidden away in the loft of their barn. After months of recovery, Spitting Finny began to feel the tug of the war calling him home and he decided to return to Britain to rejoin the war effort.

"But how? He was hundreds of miles from the nearest Allied outpost, behind enemy lines.

"Finnegan decided on a bold move. A few miles from the Giordano farm, a Luftwaffe training school had been built to instruct Italian pilots. Early one morning, Finnegan arrived at the school to find the grounds silent and abandoned. The night before, a squadron of German pilots had

left for a midnight raid against Malta forces. Finnegan seized the opportunity and calmly walked across the training grounds in a set of clothes dyed to approximate the jumpsuit of a German pilot. He climbed into the one remaining plane at the school, a Bücker Jungmann biplane. Before anyone could react, Finnegan cranked the engine, taxied to the runway, and departed, leaving the shocked Italian students behind. It appeared that he had gotten away scot-free, when a lone German pilot returning from his midnight run took pursuit. The pilot was low on fuel and ammunition from the prior mission and wanted to end the dogfight quickly.

"Finnegan soon realized the gravity of his predicament. He was being pursued by a far superior aircraft, a Messerschmitt Bf 109 F, the backbone of the Luftwaffe's modern fighter force. It had a top speed of three hundred and fifty miles per hour, a full two hundred and forty mph faster than the Bücker. However, Finnegan's plane had one trait the Messerschmitt lacked—mobility.

"Craning his neck around, Finnegan watched as the Bf 109 closed the distance between them quickly. He waited until the first barrage of twenty mm cannon rounds flew past. Several of the explosive-tipped rounds passed harmlessly through the Bücker's fabric fuselage, its resistance insufficient to trigger the round's fuse.

"Then, Finnegan whipped the Bücker into a steep turn, using its two stubby wings to outmaneuver the Bf 109. Constrained by momentum and speed, the Messerschmitt raced past his position. The German pilot was forced to make a wide Immelmann maneuver to reestablish contact with Finnegan's slow but nimble Bücker.

"Finnegan knew he had to stay close to the ground, using the twisted topography of the local farmland to his advantage. Otherwise, the Messerschmitt would soon overtake him. He dipped low, the Bücker barely skimming the ground, and entered a stand of fruit trees. Finnegan glanced back and spotted the Messerschmitt diving at high speed. He heard the sudden buzz of the MG 17 machine gun and watched in horror as rounds tore up the ground around him. He whipped left, barely a foot or two above the ground, the overhanging branches tearing at the plane's dainty wings. The Messerschmitt roared past, turned, and lined up for another strafing pass but Finnegan had spotted his escape. Timing his movement precisely, he suddenly shot up through a gap in the trees and aimed his Bücker Jungmann directly at the Messerschmitt.

"Surprised by this sudden aggressive move, the German pilot flinched.

He hesitated as the Bücker bore down on the fast-moving plane. Then, at the last possible movement, Finnegan reversed course as a shower of 7.92 mm rounds whizzed by, tearing a few new holes in the fabric fuselage. The German pilot was determined to follow the Bücker's latest path, to end the fight once and for all. He locked his plane onto the Bücker's tail. The g-forces of the high-speed turns pushed the German to the edge of consciousness. For Finnegan in the slower Bücker, the turns were much more benign and he wiggled the plane back and forth, up and down, darting in and out of trees, hay bales, and barns, using any movement to present a difficult target.

"Low on ammo, the German had to pick his opportunities carefully. He slowed his plane and tried to stay on Finnegan's wake but suddenly, Finnegan took a right turn, too sharp for the Messerschmitt to follow. Finnegan looked back to see the German pilot's terror at realizing his mistake. Looming straight ahead of the Messerschmitt were the bright red walls of a barn. The German tried desperately to pull up but the Messerschmitt's momentum carried it relentlessly forward.

"The overpowered Messerschmitt collided with the barn and erupted into a ball of flame."

Rachel stared at the three men's enraptured expressions as she finished the story with great satisfaction. "And that's how my granda Finnegan got his new nickname, the 'Mighty Sparrow.' He proved that in aerial dogfighting, mobility beats speed and power." She grinned and felt a swell of love and melancholy as she watched the three veterans revel in the same dogfighting tale that had hypnotized her so many times as a child. Finnegan's favorite lesson of conquest over limitations had been burned into her memory.

"So this is the very plane?" said John Martin, Jr., staring at the Bücker reverently.

"The same," Rachel said. "Granda flew back home low to the ground to save fuel and managed to make it to Malta before sundown without any further encounters. Believe me, he had a tough time landing on the island while piloting an enemy craft but luckily, the local controller recognized Granda's signature wing waggle as he approached for landing. The plane was soon surrounded by security, until Granda was identified."

"That's what I'm talking about!" John Martin Senior said, waving his cane for effect. "When your life's on the line, forget all those fancy electronics. A dogfight comes down to you and your courage. The pilot with the greater resolve wins."

Rachel hugged the three men and headed back to her hotel room, filled with pensive reflection. Her granda had lived such a full life and now, she was destined to bring her own short life to an end. Thoughts of Dan played through her mind as she let the tears flow, unrestrained for the first time since the two of them met in Dan's apartment years ago. She missed him horribly but knew that this would be the best way to end their relationship. Short and sweet. Dan could get on with his life without her and she would be spared the long journey into madness and death.

BRADLEY GRUBER LEANED over the back of the programmer's chair for a better view and stroked the Patek Philippe watch on his arm, a habit that had become barely noticeable to him after years of routine. Still, the repetitive motion had a calming effect, one he needed at the moment. He *hated* his stints in La Ceiba at the factory, much preferring the back rooms of Washington, D.C., to the backwaters of Honduras.

As a self-proclaimed influencer par excellence, Gruber felt his considerable skills were being wasted at this facility. His talents were better utilized in Washington, where he could rub shoulders with elite idiots and power brokers, instead of wasting time on the front lines berating the hired help. The thought elicited a wave of resentment that eroded his outwardly calm demeanor.

But Bradley Gruber also considered himself a loyal soldier, dedicated to the cause and sometimes that demanded sacrifice. So he'd force himself into the role of mentor as requested, regardless of the humiliation. He'd need a new approach though, since his patience with this lackey had run out. Breathing rhythmically, he refocused and tried to parse the young man's mood and mental state. The guy was fidgety, scratching at his scalp and arms. Gruber's instincts told him that the mannerisms reflected nervousness more than deception.

"Okay, Bob," Gruber said in the silkiest voice he could muster. "Tell me again, the key issue that's holding you up."

Bob, the programmer, continued to fidget. "Honestly, I'm trying to stay on schedule but this chip software is totally bonkers. I'm used to modern object-oriented programming languages but the guy who wrote this code was a dinosaur. It's written mainly in assembler language, super-low level. No one uses it anymore, except maybe for device drivers."

Bob wiggled in his seat, jabbed at the computer screen with his index finger as if to emphasize the point. "I'll grant this guy one thing: he was a mad genius. I've never seen low-level code like this written at such a high abstraction level, which only makes it harder to decipher. It's cryptic. Trying to interpret his design and meaning is practically impossible."

"So, rewrite it in some other language," Gruber said with a shrug.

"I've *tried* that," Bob said pleadingly. "But I can't get anywhere near the performance. I guess that's why he wrote it in assembler in the first place. Modern OOP languages are high-level, multilayered. His bastardized assembler code has OOP-like qualities but at a lower level, and thousands of times faster. I honestly can't figure out the logic. It's like translating a book without understanding the language or the culture."

Gruber crossed his arms, trying to hide his frustration. He had little technical expertise in this area. After all, he specialized in the egotistical minds of powerful men, not scientific minds. Scientists were logical, working at their craft for years. To understand their psychology, he needed to understand their science.

Not his bailiwick.

He hated excuses made by lackeys but especially when he was unsure of their validity. These DNA chips had been inherited from the assets of NeuroSys, a company the cartel had acquired through chance. They were supposed to have infinite promise but only if their potential could be tapped. But like most acquired assets, they were only as good as the creative minds who had invented them and unfortunately, those minds hadn't come with the purchase package.

According to the technicians, DNA chips could decode genetic information far faster than traditional PCR machines, whatever those were . . . even the corporate prospectus said so. One thing he did understand though: fast genetic decoding would mean fast genetic engineering. That was the hot button.

Gruber placed a reassuring hand on the programmer's shoulder.

"We both know this project is months behind schedule. Somehow we've got to find a way to get these DNA chips working. Without them, our geneticists are flying blind. They're depending on *you* for their tools. They have deadlines. We're all cogs in a large and complex machine. Do you really want to face the wrath of our boss? I certainly don't. He's not a man you want to cross."

Bob's stature seemed to shrink. He looked as if he were about to cry. Waving his arms helplessly, Bob pleaded: "I don't know what to do! Maybe we could get the original programmer back here? At least then, I could get him to explain his spaghetti code to me. Maybe then, I could make some progress."

Bradley shook his head. He could ramp up the psychological pressure but his years in the influence trade told him that additional pressure would only make things worse. This programmer didn't lack motivation. It was a talent gap, an unfortunate choice of personnel.

He sighed. "I'm afraid the original programmer is unavailable."

Bob's face went slack.

That's when Gruber had a brilliant thought.

He might be able to solve the problem and return to the States at the same time. It would be the perfect excuse to abandon this godforsaken place. The logistics would be complicated but taming complexity was his talent, after all.

Gruber left the programmer's office and when he was out of earshot, dialed the Pater's number. "Sir, I'm afraid the DNA chip project has stalled. We'll need help from the outside."

There was a long pause on the line. "Help from where?"

"I believe we need to connect with some old adversaries in the States who might possess the knowledge we seek."

Another long pause left Gruber feeling anxious. Finally the Pater replied, "Do whatever is necessary. We must get this project back on track." Another pause, then: "Your trip to the States may prove fortuitous. We've managed to eliminate our greatest enemy but in doing so, we have exposed ourselves to scrutiny from federal authorities. We used our automated drone for the operation and I fear there may be witnesses to some foul play. You're the expert at embarrassing situations, correct?"

"That is my forte, yes," Bradley replied.

The Pater then proceeded to recount to him the entire drone attack in Savannah and their use of firepower.

Bradley listened carefully, not believing his fantastic luck. When the Pater was finished, he smiled. He knew just the way to obfuscate the evidence, assuming certain factors were present. "These guns on the drone, can you provide me with a technical contact at TaurusSec? Someone with expertise in the drone's capabilities?"

The Pater gave Gruber the contact information for Froggie Pitts. "So, can you solve this conundrum?"

"Yes, sir, that is my specialty, after all. Let me talk with your operator first and I'll be able to provide more information."

"Whatever you need. Just get it done," the Pater said. "This is your chance for redemption, Bradley. Don't fail me again."

Again? Gruber resented the inference. In his many years of dedicated service, he'd never failed the cause . . . except for one embarrassing debacle with an American senator and the collapse of the NeuroSys IPA. But that wasn't his fault. Randomness was often unavoidable . . .

"I won't, sir, I promise," he said with feigned humility. The Pater was demanding but predictable. He was, after all, a power-hungry narcissist, just his type . . .

Bradley decided to take a stroll outside the factory, to clear his head. During the late evening, the heat and humidity of Honduras was as least bearable. He stepped out onto the gangway that circumscribed the dome of the chip factory and paused to listen to the incessant mooing of livestock wandering the dark spaces below. The night air smelled like a damned barnyard.

After considering his options, he dialed the number for Froggie Pitts.

"Yeah, who's this?" Froggie answered.

"Mr. Pitts, I work for your boss and I need some technical information about your Pegasus drone. I understand you had a breach of security recently."

Froggie remained silent for several minutes. Gruber could imagine the man's mind running through its options, trying to decide the best response.

"Mr. Pitts, let me alleviate your concern. I'm not here to place blame. I am a fixer. My goal is to help, uh, *lubricate* the situation for our mutual benefit. Can you give me some technical information about the drone?" He could detect an audible sigh of relief at the other end.

"Sure, anything I can do," Froggie said.

"Good. Now that we're on friendly terms, can you describe the armaments on this drone?"

"Uh, sure, I guess," Froggie said. "Pegasus is equipped with chain guns, for defensive purposes, mind you. I did not approve of their use."

"Yes, yes," Gruber replied. "I really don't care. I just want to know the specifications."

"Oh, okay. They're modified SAWS, equipped with extra-long chains."

"Saws? Can you translate?"

"They're a pair of heavily modified M249 Squad Automatic Weapons . . . *saws*. Belt-fed light machine guns. Their lightness and compact size made them a good fit for the drone."

"And the ammunition they use?" Bradley asked.

"Uh, well, standard 5.56mm NATO rounds. Same as the M4 and M16. That way, a squad can use all the same ammo. Common sense, really."

"And are any of these rounds used in civilian weapons?" Bradley asked.

Froggie grew silent for a few minutes. "Uh, not exactly. They're similar to the .223, though."

Bradley sensed an opening. "Similar in what ways? And what civilian firearm?"

"Well, same caliber round but less power. The .223 is fired from an AR-15."

Bradley grinned. "So you're saying once they leave the gun, the bullets are interchangeable."

"Uh, rifle, sir, not gun," Froggie said, unable to prevent himself from correcting the semantic faux pas. "Rifles are for fighting, guns are for fun. But, yeah. The round is more or less the same."

"Excellent, Mr. Pitts," Bradley replied, his grin broadening. "You've been most helpful. I wouldn't worry about your exposure at this point. I should have this situation under wraps quickly. Relax."

"If you say so, sir," Froggie said and hung up.

Bradley was excited, confident that he had a plan that would wash the cartel's hands clean, while gaining him freedom from the backwaters of Honduras.

"Time to plant a flag," he said gleefully.

22

"WELL?" DAKOTA PELL repeated.

Sitting in Dakota's camouflaged houseboat, Dan struggled to make sense of the last few hours. He felt numb, disconnected from reality, as thousands of thoughts raced through his mind all at once.

Pell just stood there, staring at him with an expectant look on his face.

A germ of defiance forced itself to the surface. "Why don't *you* start first?" Dan said. "Who the hell are you exactly and why should I trust you? Since I almost died out there, I'm not exactly in a trusting mood."

"Ada asked me to keep an eye on you," Dakota said, as if his side of the story needed no further explanation. "I've been trailing you for days, ever since Nerdvana." He crossed the room and pulled a seltzer from the fridge, took a deep swig. "I followed you to her cabin, watched the feds approach. I was about to intervene when all hell broke loose. That drone caught me by surprise." Dak's brow furrowed. "I assume she passed quickly."

"Ada? Yes," Dan said, his voice cracking. The scene at the cabin kept replaying in his mind's eye. "The only reason I'm still alive is because I fell to the floor when the assault came. I was below the line of fire. Where did the drone come from? The Horsemen?"

A grim smile tweaked the corners of Dak's mouth. "So Ada told you about them, did she? It was my job to protect you. In that regard, I failed. I suspect the drone was an experimental prototype being hyped to the military by the Horsemen. They're into robotics, among other things. And the Army is looking for a semiautonomous aircraft that can provide close-air support and reconnaissance to soldiers in the field. The drone's base of operations is probably near Hunter Army

Airfield. TaurusSec has a facility there, near the far end of the base. Their former military connections give them unique access to command channels."

Dan could barely focus on what the man said, because one word, "autonomous," triggered a storm of questions in his mind. Ada had claimed that Martin Orcus, the secret financier of Dan's former company NeuroSys, had been a member of the Horsemen. NeuroSys manufactured neural net processors, perfect for artificial intelligence and "autonomous" robotics. It was the same neural net processor that powered Dan's household robot, Rover. The same processor that he and Rudi had helped develop for the company and that had powered the autonomous underwater vehicles Dan had sold to NOAA for their global analysis and prediction system. But when he exposed a conspiracy involving Martin Orcus using his infamous Weatherman virus, Dan had lost his job and the company had moved to Honduras, permanently.

And now, the bitter irony hit him. Ada Kurz may have been murdered by the very technology he helped develop . . . he couldn't erase the horrible memory of Ada's life fading away in his arms . . . and her warning about Rachel:

There's something you should know about Rachel. Look to your penthouse, your webcam. Then go to Esrom. That's where you will find your truth . . .

Dan buried his head in his hands and sobbed, allowing a release of emotion unfamiliar to him.

"You're in shock," Dak said, staring at him uncomfortably. "I know what you're experiencing but you've got to focus. Your life depends on it."

Dan regained his composure and the room grew quiet, the lull appropriate somehow, a memorial to Ada's passing, perhaps. Outside the houseboat, the crickets chirped a mournful dirge.

Dan's adrenaline was on the ebb and the weight of exhaustion bore down on him. He stared at this strange man, Dakota Pell, trying to determine if he was truly trustworthy. There had been times, back at Nerdvana, when he had felt a creepy feeling, a tingling in his neck as if someone was watching. On several occasions he'd spotted the short-statured man weaving his way through the crowd at a distance. "So, you're one of them, the Firemen."

Dak stared quietly, his expression completely unreadable. He pointed toward the fridge. "Beer?"

Dan rubbed his forehead, felt a deep throbbing between his eyes. "Why not?"

Dak brought him a can and Dan took a grateful and generous swig. The two men stared at each other for several more minutes.

Dan broke the silence. "So again, who *are* you exactly? You're older than most of those kids in Chemerra's army. You don't strike me as the typical member of a band of nerds."

"What's typical?" Dak said, smiling.

"I'm guessing you're a veteran, too old to be joining a group of misfits, wouldn't you say?"

Dakota chuckled. "You think the Firemen are the misfits? Yeah, I'm a Marine, born and bred, now and forever. Let's just say the Firemen have developed their own unique brand of dissent and I respect that. But they're not misfits."

Dan thought about Ada's universal vaccine and how groundbreaking it might have been, now in a heap of ashes. That led his thoughts back to Rachel. "Do you have Wi-Fi in this houseboat?"

"Sure," Dak said. "I'm hooked into a neighbor's server about three miles from here, via a Yagi antenna and amplifier."

"And, you're sure I can make secure calls on these black phones and browse the internet too, right?"

"Yep, guaranteed secure."

"Can you bring me my phone? I need to check something, make a couple of calls."

Dak stared at him with a look of concern. "Be careful who you call and what you say. You're still a fugitive."

"Understood."

Dak left and returned with Dan's personal effects. He stared curiously at the black phone, noting the bloody fingerprint lingering on the dark screen. "Whose black phone is this? Surely not yours."

"It's Chemerra's," Dan said. "The last thing she did before dying was to register it to me. Why, I do not know."

Dak stared reverently at the phone, holding it at a distance like a bomb. "She 'registered' it to you?"

"Yeah, I tried to get her to focus on her wound but all she could think about was giving me her bloody phone."

A strange expression came over Dak's face, a new intensity replacing the confusion that had lingered there. "Then it looks like you're it." He gently handed the phone to Dan like a hallowed prize.

"What?"

"The beneficiary of Chemerra's work," Dak said. "With that phone, you possess all of her records, passwords, notes, files, and the top ranking in the Minion app. That means you can gather the troops with the full weight and authority of the top hierarchy."

Dan cradled the phone dubiously and unlocked the screen with his fingerprint. A message flashed momentarily: "Successful Facial Recognition."

The message just as quickly disappeared, leaving behind a cell phone screen that looked like any other, with icons representing the most popular social media apps. Dan swiped through a couple of screens but saw nothing unusual, not even the Minion app. He did notice two unique icons labeled SECURE PHONE and SECURE NET. He looked up at Dak one more time. "Untraceable, right?"

"Absolutely. The origin of the source is completely untraceable, at least according to two Firemen members who work for the NSA."

"The web browser too?"

Dak nodded.

There's something you should know about Rachel. Look to your penthouse, your webcam. Then go to Esrom. That's where you will find your truth . . .

The webcam Ada spoke of had recently been installed on his pet robot, Rover. It disturbed him to think that Ada had been using it to spy on him. He typed the IP address of the webcam, logged in, and activated Rover's autonomous mode through a set of commands. An image of the penthouse's interior popped up. He used a set of navigational controls to move Rover through the condo, fearful that he might encounter Rachel's lifeless body at any moment.

But instead, nothing.

The robot rumbled through every room, turning left and right to scan every nook and cranny but after several passes through the entire floorplan . . . nothing. No Rachel, nothing out of place. The condo was as still and somber as a tomb. Dan felt a momentary flush of relief, then confusion. He was about to give up, when he spotted a slip of paper perched at the foot of the bed. Rover maneuvered to the location until the letter filled the webcam's screen.

Dan recognized Rachel's hand:

Dear Dan,

I will never forget the love and support you have given me. Although our time together has been short, I feel as if we have lived a lifetime together. But now, I must ask you to set me free, both for your sake and mine. You see, I finally decided to get tested, in hopes that we might be able to develop a true life together. Alas, I am sad to say, the tests came back positive.

I have Huntington's.

I endured the long and painful death of my father from this disease and I do not want you to see me in that state. I want you to remember me as I was, when we laughed, cried, loved, and shared adventures together. You are a good man. I want only the best for you. Freedom from suffering is the one last gift I have left to give.

Please accept my gift and allow me to go out on my own terms. Do not attempt to find me.

I love you. Always did, and always will, so long as I am able to function on this earth. You deserve so much more.

Yours forever and always,
Rachel

The black phone trembled in Dan's hand as tears fell to the screen, meandered down its face, and mingled with Ada's bloody fingerprint. Dan absently wiped the watery mixture away with his thumb, as echoes of his childhood flitted across his mind's eye, nightmarish images from his parents' deaths . . . and now this.

What more could fate steal from him? How much more loss? He felt a heavy, smothering cloak of sadness pressing against his shoulders.

Dak Pell watched neutrally from across the room. "Bad news?"

Dan nodded silently. Knowing Rachel, she would not hang around long enough for the full effects of the Huntington's to show. She'd find some spectacular way out. He had assumed she was simply off on one of her sojourns, that he'd have plenty of time to hunt her down, but now he knew the horrible truth.

Their life together was over.

Despite her request, Dan couldn't just abandon Rachel, not while they still had time left. "I've got to get out of here . . . *Right now.*"

"Bad idea," Dakota said. "Not if you want to remain a free man."

"I don't have a choice!" he screamed. "This has been a disaster. I've been shot at, lied to, abandoned, and now I find out that Rachel . . . I've got to find her." Dan jumped to his feet, circled the room restlessly, feeling the full weight of despair sinking into his bones.

"Stop." Dakota grabbed his arm firmly, held him in place, his expression dispassionate. "You want sympathy? You can find the definition in the dictionary, between 'shit' and 'syphilis.' Self-pity is for losers. I don't care what your day's been like. You're in the shit now; focus or die. Plenty of time for mourning later."

Dak's expression grew more intense and he invaded Dan's zone of comfort. "Know this. The Horsemen will never stop looking for you, until you are dead. The feds are probably on your trail too, so *think.* What can you do to honor your comrades, your loved ones? Figure it out, then *do* it."

Dan stared back, unnerved by Dak's bluntness. His felt his heart literally aching, mourning for Rachel's presence.

The truth hides in tragedy.

Dak was right. As a child, when the pain of his parents' deaths became unbearable, Dan found relief in only one proactive instinct: *anger.* It had always been more tolerable than grief, and certainly more productive.

At that moment, Dan could feel the heat of anger simmering in his gut like a flame.

Dakota studied Dan's mood carefully, turned, and walked toward a staircase at one end of the room. "Why don't we step outside for some fresh air and talk." He tilted his head, signaling Dan to follow. Reluctantly, Dan mustered the energy to rise from the overstuffed couch.

They headed up the staircase. On the second level of *Gillie* sat a modest bunk, its sheets and blankets drawn perfectly straight and wrinkle free, so that one could bounce a quarter off its surface. The second floor was constructed from steel grating, so that any dust or dirt would simply fall to the floor below.

Dak turned and opened a small hatch that led out to a deck on the houseboat's roof. A wall of humid air enveloped them as they stepped out onto the platform. Overhead, the moonless sky had cleared, revealing a dusting of stars spanning the narrow opening in the cypress canopy. The din of crickets grew louder, joined in symphony by the bellows of frogs, occasionally interrupted by the screech of an egret or the crunch of a rotten tree branch falling into the black water.

It was the type of remote location that he and Rachel would have relished together but on this night he simply felt the oppressive humidity weighing him down. They sat down in two teak Adirondack chairs, their heads barely higher than the houseboat's fencing. Camouflage netting rimmed the top of the fence, breaking up its profile, while allowing them to peek out through the holes in the netting.

Through the dense cypress forest, the beams of searchlights played across the night sky, signaling that the authorities had reached the ruins of Ada's cabin.

Dan realized that Dakota Pell was right. He needed to shake off his grief and formulate a plan, determine the depth of his troubles and get his pursuers off his back. Pulling Ada's black phone out again, he dialed Vince Peretti's private mobile number.

Vince answered on the fifth ring. "Who is this?"

Judging from the background noise, Vince was already at the crime scene. "This is Dan."

"*Dan?* What the hell have you done?"

"Just wait before you say anything more. Is Hudlow with you?"

"He's on scene. Why the hell can't you follow simple instructions?"

A jolt of anger coursed through Dan's body. "Just shut the hell up and listen! I'm in no mood to be dressed down, not after the night I just endured. First off, keep this conversation to yourself. I don't know what Hudlow's told you but he's a friggin' liar."

Vince paused before answering. "Hudlow said his men followed you to this private residence and when they knocked on the door, you opened fire. Hudlow claims he heard the whole thing on his secure line."

"That's a damn lie, Vince, and you know it. Does that sound like me? There were hundreds of rounds fired. How did I do that? The four of us were attacked by a drone. We were all inside the building together. I'm lucky to be alive."

"A drone?"

The tone of sarcasm tinged with anger in Vince's voice told Dan all he needed to know. "Look, check the trajectories of the rounds. They all came from the direction of the river. Check the position of the bodies."

"That's gonna be difficult since you burned down the entire structure. We're sifting through the rubble now."

"I didn't start the fire," Dan shot back. "Hudlow's men were there to steal Chemerra's codebreaking software. They had no intention of arresting her. Then, some drone shot up the place, started the fire. I know it sounds crazy but you *know* me, Vince. I'm telling the truth. Follow the evidence. You'll see."

There was another long pause before Vince spoke again. This time, his voice was lower and calmer, more measured. "Frankly, I don't know what to think anymore. This whole operation has been a disaster from the beginning. I know one thing, though. You've got to come in and explain why you were out there in the first place, because right now, you're prime suspect number one. You said the person at the cabin was Chemerra? Our records show the home was owned by Ada Kurz, an employee at GenTropics Pharmaceuticals. We interviewed her at the facility, remember?"

It was Dan's turn to pause. Maybe he had said too much already. While he trusted Vince's intentions, he wasn't so sure which side of the argument his friend would fall on, in the end. Vince was a G-man through and through. Until he knew more, Dan decided to keep some things to himself. "Well, then Hudlow's men made a mistake. They thought she was the terrorist and tried to bargain for the code-breaking software. Then all hell broke loose. I'm telling you, *do not* trust Barrett Hudlow."

"So, come in and let's straighten all this out."

"How? After the Weatherman virus last year, do you really think I'll be treated fairly, especially with Hudlow's fabricated story? Several of his men on your joint task force are dirty."

"You have to come in, tell your side of the story. I'll do my best to protect you but if you don't, you'll become a fugitive."

Dan's head was swimming. Was Hudlow in league with the Horsemen? No, his men were killed too. Who could he trust? Dak? The Firemen? He needed time for his heart and mind to settle.

"Vince, just follow the evidence. Keep your eyes on Hudlow every minute and do not allow him to walk away with any evidence. But sorry . . . this time, I'm fixing things myself."

Before Vince could reply, Dan ended the call. At that moment, an alert popped up on Ada's black phone stating, "Identity reconfirmed." Then it disappeared again.

"See? Told you," Dakota said. He rose from his chair to pick up an errant pine cone that had fallen to the deck, then straightened and peered out through the darkness toward Ada's cabin. "If what you just said is true, this Hudlow character will have you framed for this whole mess by morning."

Prime suspect number one. Dan couldn't believe it. First, he'd been lied to and then made the scapegoat. "Surely, somebody had to notice that drone flying overhead. It's going to be impossible to hide that, right?"

"I wouldn't be so sure," Dak said. "That's the thing about low-flying aircraft. You can barely hear them until they're right on top of you. This swamp isn't heavily populated, planes fly in and out of Hunter Army Airfield all the time."

"But the gunfire, surely . . ."

"The burst of automatic weapons fire didn't last long, a few seconds at most. No one except a former military soldier would recognize that sound."

"So, if you're right and the drone is managed by TaurusSec, then the Horsemen must have ordered the hit."

"Most likely."

"So TaurusSec is just a bunch of mercenaries."

"More or less." Dak absently rotated the pine cone in his hands. "Look, a lot of veterans find jobs working for these independent security firms as soldiers of fortune. It's a natural fit for their skill set. Corporations love the high degree of skill exhibited by these quasi-military organizations. TaurusSec just happens to be one of the more unconventional firms."

"So why aren't you working with them?"

"Believe me, I've thought about it," Dakota said. "But once you've served as the tip of the spear for a while, the poor judgments of the 'spear throwers' become a source of disillusionment. I have serious concerns about the direction this country is taking. There's no balance of power between leadership and the populace. I don't approve but I *do* understand the draw these mercenary groups pose to veterans. A great Marine once said, *'The rifle is only a tool. It is the hard heart that kills.'*

"You know, the military spends billions of dollars every year investing in that hard heart. They train it, challenge it, pick at it until the callous grows a mile thick; all, so that we can face the enemy with deadly intent. How do you turn that off, once all the training is over? How do you peel back the calloused layers when you enter civilian life? Want to know the essence of PTSD? It's not just a memory of some horrific shit you left behind in battle. Memories fade eventually. It's the war that rages inside your soul; the fear that you will never escape the monster that they have made out of you."

Dak stared down at the pine cone in his hand and aimed it at a dark hole in a nearby cypress stump. He let go with a flick of his wrist. A loud thump echoed through the swamp as the cone found its target with deadly precision. He turned back to Dan, his face a grim wash of color in the dim light. "We're cogs in a very large machine, with specific roles to play. Soldiers are trained to act out their orders with mindless loyalty. Civilians are trained to consume, inundated with thousands of advertisements every day, designed to fuel a desire to buy, buy, buy. Free will? It's a myth."

Dan thought to himself: *and some people are trained to unknowingly flush out famous hackers without being told the real reasons why.*

He had let another government bureaucrat play him for a fool. It was time to exact a little vigilante justice, get Hudlow off his back. Only then would he be free to find Rachel. He'd have to worry about the Horsemen later.

The two of them sat out on the deck for another hour, crafting a strategy, at which point he thought it wise to check in with Rudi. When he powered the phone up, the incessant pop-up window from earlier reappeared: "Identity reconfirmed."

Then a series of beeps brought up what appeared to be some kind of video game. Multicolored balls began to drop from the top of the screen. As they reached the bottom of the screen, they disintegrated with a loud popping sound. With each explosion, a large numeric counter labeled TIME TO DESTRUCTION ticked backward.

Fifty, forty-nine, forty-eight, forty-seven . . .

Dak hissed. "Failsafe! You need to solve that puzzle before it hits zero."

Dan stared in shock, unsure what to do. He touched one of the balls as it dropped, causing it to explode and disappear. As he tried to make sense of it, more colored balls dropped, some faster than others.

Thirty-one, thirty, twenty-nine, twenty-eight . . .

Something about the game triggered a memory, jolted him into action. The falling balls reminded him of the multicolored spiders that had dropped from the ceiling of Chemerra's virtual lair. He hastily began stabbing at the falling balls, each successful touch destroying them before they could reach the bottom. His muscle memory began to kick in and he stopped thinking, allowing himself to react instinctively, prioritizing certain colors that dropped faster than others. He took a nervous glance at the counter.

Eighteen, seventeen, sixteen . . .

He forced himself to relax and get into a rhythm.

The countdown slowed. Ten, nine . . .

Finally, the counter stopped altogether, as he continued to punch madly at the screen. The speed of the falling balls accelerated. A few errant colors slipped past as his aim faltered.

Six . . .

Suddenly, a loud jingle sounded and the melody from "Hail to the Chief" began to play.

Dan fell back into the chair, panting, as the cell phone's display changed. Several new pages of icons appeared.

Meeting Minutes, Latest Codes, Bitcoin Account, Minion, Horsemen Research, Lab Results—the list went on for several pages. As he swiped past the pages, an avatar of his likeness caught his eye. It was labeled with the text DAN CONFIDENTIAL.

He tapped it and a video began to play.

"Dan, if you're watching this, then something horrible has happened to me. It was inevitable that the Horsemen would flush out my identity eventually. And now, the future lies in your hands. Be assured that I have provided you with everything you need. I know this is not your wish or responsibility but I believe in you. If anyone recognizes the importance of balance of opposition, it would be you. If you have doubts, remember the words of Edmund Burke, 'The only thing necessary for the triumph of evil is for good men to do nothing.'"

Dan and Dakota stared at each other, trading incredulous looks.

"I'll be damned," Dan said. "She planned this all along. When I was inside the virtual simulation, she was teaching me the password for this phone. I had no clue."

Dakota grinned at him. "Welcome to the brotherhood. Isn't volunteering an involuntary bitch?"

23

AFTER A FITFUL night's sleep, Dan spent the next morning with Dak Pell on *Gillie*'s upper deck, polishing their strategy. First, they would have to return Pinky's boat, *Mossy Lynn*, along with his pride and joy, *Shyla*.

They agreed that Dakota Pell would pilot *Shyla*, with *Mossy Lynn* in tow behind the powerful boat, back to Pinky's Bait an' Beer. One detail of the plan left Dan particularly uncomfortable: he would have to hide inside *Mossy Lynn*'s coffin for the duration of the trip, just in case the feds were tracking their progress.

After a hearty breakfast of scrambled eggs and whole wheat pancakes, the two of them headed out to collect the boats, which sat abandoned near the ruins of Ada's cabin. The FBI had yet to process them. Dakota climbed into the Donzi 43 ZR and lashed his jon boat and *Mossy Lynn* to the stern.

Dan took a deep breath and climbed into the dark coffin. The idea of hiding inside the dark enclosure for over an hour seemed intolerable but there was really no alternative. He mustered all his courage, cycled through his relaxation routines, inhaled and exhaled rhythmically. Then, his heart pounding, he climbed inside the coffin and reluctantly closed the lid. In one last desperate move, he jammed a small pebble into the crack of the lid to allow light and fresh air to invade the blackened space. The thin sliver of light helped him relax a bit. Still, the morose nature of his situation triggered thoughts of Rachel's demise. The trip seemed to take forever, until finally, a thump and scrape signaled *Mossy Lynn*'s arrival at the dock of Pinky's Bait an' Beer.

Dan waited impatiently for the "all clear" signal from Dak and scrambled out of the claustrophobic space with a great sigh of relief.

They had docked in a small side harbor next to a warren of old buildings. Dak led the way toward a small utility shed.

Inside, Esrom Nesson sat quietly.

Pinky's Bait an' Beer was a perfect venue for a clandestine meeting. From a distance, the ramshackle buildings at the rear of Pinky's compound looked uninhabitable.

Dan pulled up a chair next to Esrom. "I suppose you've heard the news."

Esrom nodded. The feisty scientist Dan had known from Honduras a year earlier, now seemed like a shell of his former self. He was paler than usual, if that was even possible, his shoulders drooping, his hands trembling.

Dan introduced Dakota, then went straight into the main subject. "I was with Ada in her last moments. She said you two were working on several experimental projects. What were they?"

Esrom's voice wavered. "Ada was this . . . *Chemerra* person? The hacker? I don't believe it. She was a dedicated worker, loyal to the cause of helping others. Why would she steal the Devil's Paradox? She *knew* the dangers."

"She says she *didn't* steal it, that it had to be one of the security men from TaurusSec."

"What?" Esrom seemed shocked. "Why? For what purpose?"

"According to her, there is another organization that's experimenting with something called 'pharming.' They want the organism for its gene splicing abilities, to alter the genome of plants."

Esrom stared, an incredulous look on his face. "But that's *crazy*. As Ada and I had discovered, the Devil's Paradox could not be tamed. It's a powerful DNA vector, true, but we were never able to find and eliminate the genes responsible for its unpredictable behavior." He glanced nervously at Dakota. "Can we . . ."

Dan nodded at Dak and said: "Can we have some privacy?"

"No problem," Dak replied. "I'm off to take care of phase two." He turned and left.

Dan placed an encouraging hand on Esrom's arm. "Go on."

Esrom leaned back, took a deep breath, wrung his hands. "Um, where to start. One of the projects that we hoped to use the organism's power for was a gene therapy program to regrow amputated limbs. There's a billion-dollar industry out there to treat military veterans,

to reverse their amputations." Esrom reacted to Dan's dubious expression. "Before you laugh, the idea of regrowing limbs is not that
far-fetched. Human beings already possess the genetic ability. Children, until the age of nine, are fully capable of regrowing a missing
finger, up to the first joint. During puberty, we lose that capability
but the genes are still there. We just need to reactivate them, through
methylation."

Dan wrinkled his brow. "English, please."

Esrom paused, gathering his thoughts. "Let me put it into programming terms. The DNA molecule is like computer software, genetic code capable of many different functions. Methylation is how we
activate certain computer functions, much like an execution command.
Genes sit and wait for a command to activate their programming. That's
how a complete human being grows from a single cell. Specific genes
are activated at certain times during embryonic development, causing
certain cells to become muscles, while other cells become bones, liga-
ments, skin, etc. Yet each of these cells in the body still possess the
entire genome. But there's even more to the story. Ever heard of junk
DNA? It's not really junk. It's obsolete code that we have retired during
our evolution from amphibians to mammals to primates. If we can
reactivate old legacy code left over from our amphibious ancestors, we
can reactivate our ability to fully regrow severed limbs. To do that, we
use methylation. It's like a switch."

Dan squirmed in his seat. "And you tried to do that with the Devil's Paradox?"

"Exactly," Esrom replied. "For single genes, we'd typically use a
precise genetic enzyme like CRISPR CAS-9 to alter or activate a target
gene. But limb regeneration requires the activation of several different
genes that are scattered throughout the genome. That's the specialty
of the Devil's Paradox, to activate multiple genes simultaneously. Do
you remember in Honduras, how it could glue multiple organisms
together to create a completely new life form?"

"Yeah," Dan said. "And it was a nightmare. Whatever possessed
you to think you could tame that beast?"

"Well, we spent a lot of time stripping out its dangerous genes,
crippling it, so that it could only affect the genes we wanted. And it
worked." Esrom smiled grimly. "In the lab at least. We had several mice
completely regrowing entire legs. It was a miracle!"

"I sense that there is a 'but' in there somewhere," Dan said.

Esrom rubbed his temples. "Unfortunately, yes, something unforeseen. You see, there was a veteran on TaurusSec's payroll, Victor Moody. He had lost both his hands in Afghanistan while trying to defuse an IED. He saw the tremendous success of the experiment and decided to steal the vector one night." Esrom leaned forward, whispering. "He tried it on *himself*. We found out a week later. If the FDA had learned about the breach of security, we'd all have been arrested."

"So what happened?" Dan said, his interest tweaked.

"Well, it worked on him too," Esrom answered. "Within weeks, both of Victor's hands began to regrow. His actions were foolish and illegal frankly, but Ada and I were thrilled to see the success of the Devil's Paradox on a human subject, that is until . . ." Esrom wrung his hands and leaned back in his chair, a look of devastation clouding his face.

Esrom wavered a minute longer, then continued. "If you remember back in Honduras, the Devil's Paradox was triggered by a certain stimulus, a survival strategy. Large amounts of ultraviolet light can kill any single-celled organism. When exposed to UV light, the Devil's Paradox would activate its gene splicing abilities."

Dan nodded, remembering that strange behavior.

"Anyway, back here in the lab," Esrom continued, "Ada and I thought we had neutralized the organism's splicing capability, at least in our laboratory sample. But that infernal creature managed somehow to rebuild its survival genes, we think, from Victor Moody's own junk DNA. It not only activated Victor's limb regrowth genes but began to activate other genes in Victor's DNA, genes that had remained dormant through millions of years of evolution."

"I don't understand. Why didn't you notice that side effect in the lab mice?"

Esrom's glanced down at the floor. "Because all the lab mice were raised and tested indoors, under artificial light. Without UV light to trigger the vector's survival instinct, the experiment succeeded just as we expected. But Victor Moody left the lab and went out into the sunlight . . ."

". . . and the Devil's Paradox was reactivated." Dan fell back in his chair. He let that thought sink in for a minute. "So, you think Victor Moody is the one who stole the pristine sample of the Devil's Paradox?"

"If it wasn't Ada, I can't think of anyone else except Victor," Esrom said. "The week after he confessed to taking the treatment, we started noticing distinct changes in Victor's behavior and physiology. While his hands regrew, Victor himself began to change, growing more distraught and high-strung. Welts appeared on his skin, he suffered from repeated seizures, he couldn't sleep. Ada and I tried to treat him, doped him up on antianxiety medications. Then his hair fell out, all of it, every last follicle. We were working on another treatment when one day, he simply vanished. He could have taken the pristine sample of the Devil's Paradox at that time, because we had already archived it."

"So, you think he stole it to do what? Find a cure elsewhere?"

"Don't know," Esrom said. "But if he wanted alternative treatment, he'd need a sample of the primary vector. Perhaps this other shadow group promised him medical aid in exchange for the microbe?"

"That would be my guess," Dan said.

"But if they try to use it for genetic engineering, for pharming, the nightmare from last year could return . . . It could unleash another hell on Earth."

The air in the room seemed to grow thin. Both men sat silently, contemplating the future. Dan dreaded the next part of the conversation.

Even in Honduras, Esrom Nesson had known Rachel well, having served as her biology professor in college. Their reunion had been a shock at the time, yet Dan had no knowledge of just how much Esrom might know about Rachel's genetic legacy. He clung to a faint hope that Esrom might have some solution. What had Ada told him again?

Go to Esrom. That's where you will find your truth.

Dan began haltingly, struggling to find the right entrance into a conversation he dreaded. "I know you and Rachel were close in college. She was a prized student of yours back then, right? How much did she share with you about her family legacy?"

Esrom seemed shocked by Dan's sudden change of subject. He stared blankly, hesitant to speak. "What do you mean exactly? We talked about her family on occasion, yes."

"Did Rachel ever confide in you about her genetic heritage? A family curse?"

Esrom's eyes darted back and forth. He seemed unsure how to

respond to Dan's blunt question. "Rachel shared some intimate information about her family with me, yes." Esrom stopped talking and stared expectantly.

He knew, Dan realized. "Then you know of Rachel's father? That he died of Huntington's?"

Esrom simply nodded.

"What you don't know"—Dan paused to swallow a large lump that had formed in his throat—"is that she recently took the test. It came back positive . . ." His voice cracked.

Esrom's expression softened, his eyes drooping. "Dan, I'm so sorry. Where is she now?"

"I don't know, she disappeared. You know her. She's not going to take that kind of news passively. I suspect she's off planning her demise."

"Again, I can't tell you how sorry I am . . ." Esrom's voice trailed off.

"But there's more to it than that, isn't there?" Dan persisted. "Something you're not telling me, something Ada hinted at. She told me to find you, that only then would I find my truth."

Esrom's brow wrinkled. "I don't know . . ." Then a flash of recognition and momentary excitement flitted across his face. "Ada must be referring to an old experimental therapy that's been long abandoned."

"What, exactly?"

"When I first came to GenTropics last year, I wanted to invest my energy in saving lives, instead of studying pathogens. I wanted to focus on cures. When I got here, I went through all of GenTropic's past studies and experimental trials. There was one on Huntington's." He paused, looked at the ceiling, struggled to remember details. "It was an old gene therapy study. Back in the early days of the new millennia, viruses were the gene therapy vector of choice. Retroviruses could invade a cell and replace faulty genes in the genome with correct copies that had been spliced onto the virus. Back then we used a common cold virus, an adenovirus, to insert the working genes. It was primitive technology, a blunt tool, far more imprecise than our current CRISPR-based splicing tools. The technique showed promise, that is, until a subject of one study died during treatment. This one unexplained death shuttered all the other experimental trials that were being run at the time. Everything was mothballed."

Dan felt a sudden surge of hope. "So, does this Huntington's treatment still exist?"

Esrom looked at him with sympathetic eyes. "I know what you're thinking but forget it. First of all, I have no idea if the treatment was successful. It was shelved during phase one trials, the earliest stage of experimentation. Second, it would be highly illegal for me to test the treatment on another human being. Rachel could die."

"She's going to die anyway!" Dan shouted. "If there's even a slight possibility of success . . ."

"I'm sorry, Dan, I can't risk it. It could ruin my career. I could go to jail."

Dan's mood turned white hot. To have yet another reprieve ripped from his grasp . . . it was too intolerable to bear. He seethed at Esrom. "You mean a career that is already being threatened by the unauthorized treatment of a helpless victim, who is now suffering from your lack of security? A career that permitted the theft of an organism capable of triggering a worldwide pandemic? That career? What would happen if the authorities learned the truth?"

Esrom's face turned pale. "I confessed all that to you in confidence. It was a series of horrible mistakes. You wouldn't dare . . ."

"You have no idea what I would dare do," Dan hissed, "if there was even a slim chance of saving Rachel's life."

ONCE DAKOTA PELL left the two eggheads to talk out their differences, he headed off on his own mission, feeling a righteous jolt of adrenaline at being back in the game. Once an adrenaline junkie, always a junkie. He smiled.

Dan's friend Rudi needed to be updated, but how? Both the feds and the Horsemen were probably staking out his room. No incoming phone call would go unnoticed, even if made from a black phone, since Rudi's end would be a conventional connection. The room was probably bugged. Any attempt to access the hotel room physically would draw an instant response.

Dak wasn't sure why Rudi was so damn important but Clifford had insisted, so he decided to try something simple and easy. Before jumping into Pinky's pickup, he grabbed his go bag from the Donzi and double-checked its contents. In it, right where he'd left them were three items: his Nightforce NXS sniper scope, a folding walking cane, and a green laser pointer.

EVERY PERSON WHO worked on Savannah's River Street knew Pinky's distinctive 1958 Green Dodge Power Wagon, with its 480 hp Chevy LS3 and black knobby tires jacked up six inches, so Dakota wheeled it into the parking lot at Joe's Crab Shack and headed for the far corner. He slipped out of the pickup as quietly as possible and scurried a few rows over, turned right, and calmly walked toward the restaurant.

It was still early in the morning, barely past sunrise, so the area was mainly deserted and the restaurant closed, which was probably for the better. The seafood chain wasn't his favorite for local fare and besides, they didn't serve breakfast. Still, the building would provide the necessary cover and height. He approached the rear entrance and used a bump key to quickly pop the rear door.

Slipping inside, he found the keypad for the security alarm and used a black light to identify the buttons with the greatest accumulation of body oil. Thankfully, the security code was short: four digits. Using human psychology as a guide, Dak guessed the proper sequence of the four numbers on the third try. The security light switched from red to green and he wasted no time scrambling up the stairway toward the building's roof.

Once outside, Dakota padded quietly across the roof toward the eastern parapet wall, where he began to set up. He removed the rubber cap from the end of the walking stick and slid the green laser directly into the end of the tube. He had chosen this particular brand of laser for its dimensions, having used this technique once before, long ago.

Next came the Nightforce scope. He mounted it through a couple of holes that had been precisely drilled in the walking cane near its handle. Once assembled, Dakota rested the cane on the parapet wall and aimed it toward the other side of the Savannah River.

The Westin Hotel rose above the flat landscape, its windows starting to catch dim reflections from the early morning light to the east. He figured he had about another thirty minutes before the rising sun would make his task far more complicated.

He checked his hand for the room number Clifford had given him and did the math. He carefully counted his way up the floors to the fifth, then counted right.

Target confirmed.

The man Clifford had described as Rudi Plimpton was still in bed slumbering soundly. The hacker appeared to be a night owl and might require some rousing. Dakota reached down toward the end of the walking stick and flipped on the green laser. He reacquired the target and watched calmly as he moved the glowing green dot across the hotel window toward the target.

This green laser was powerful enough to blind a man in the right circumstances, so Dak moved cautiously to position the round circle, about the width of a marker pen, right at the edge of Rudi Plimpton's closed eyelid. He carefully wiggled the light a few times.

At first nothing. He wiggled again and got a reaction, an absent swipe, like one would do to shoo away a fly.

Another wiggle and swipe, then on the third try, a more significant reaction.

Rudi popped up in bed, rubbed his eyes, and glanced around the room, confused.

Dakota moved the wiggling green dot past Rudi's eyes to the wall, exaggerating the movement to attract Rudi's attention. Still groggy from sleep, Rudi was slow to perceive the dancing line of green light.

When his gaze finally moved to the wall, Dakota began writing in script, like a graffiti artist with a can of spray paint. The green laser had enough latency for the eye to track its path and soon, Rudi showed signs of recognition.

Spelling the word was tricky. The hotel's wall was a good three hundred yards away from his position. At that distance, even the smallest movement was amplified. Erratic movement would render his writing unrecognizable. Dakota took in a long, relaxed breath and exhaled slowly, using gentle movements to keep the path of the laser true. It taxed his skills as a sniper, since in this case he needed to constantly move his aim, rather than settling on a steady target. He enjoyed the challenge.

Slowly and steadily, the green dot began to spell out an emergency code word that Dan Clifford had given him. Supposedly, this was an alert word the two of them had arranged ahead of time, on the off chance that they would need to communicate surreptitiously in the future. Now was that time.

Dakota suppressed a chuckle over the choice of code word: dagnabbit.

He supposed either person could work that word into a conversation without arousing suspicion, if needed. Dakota felt a grudging respect for the programmer's skill at obfuscation.

After repeating the word three times, Dakota watched as Rudi Plimpton jumped out of bed and rushed to his laptop. He began typing furiously, stopping only when a message, too faint to read at this distance, popped up on the screen from an anonymous messaging service.

Dakota already knew the contents of the curt message:

warehouse at noon, u r being followed.

His task completed, Dakota dismantled the walking stick contraption, headed down the stairs, and reactivated the restaurant's security system. Then he quietly left the building and headed down River Street, in search of brunch.

DAN ARRIVED AT Stoker's warehouse a little past noon.

His meeting with Esrom Nesson had gone longer than expected, having covered a lot of ground and now, he was eager to see the results of his Minion Call.

During the early dawn hours of that morning, Dan had used Chemerra's phone, with a little help from Dakota, to issue a call through its Minion app. He had set the Minion Call to its highest level of access, designed to alert the upper echelon of the Firemen command.

Entering through a side door, Dan scanned the dark expanse and spotted a collection of individuals huddled around a computer monitor at the far end of the warehouse. As he covered the broad expanse, his gaze focused on Rudi Plimpton, sitting at the edge of the group, typing furiously on his laptop.

Dakota Pell had obviously succeeded in transmitting his secret code and since no federal authorities appeared to be hanging around, Dan assumed Rudi had managed to successfully evade any surveillance assigned to him. It had always amazed him that despite Rudi's childlike demeanor and naiveté, his hacker friend possessed an acute ability to outmaneuver anyone who attempted to monitor his activities.

Deep in the shadows, Dakota Pell stood to one side, maintaining a comfortable distance from the rest of the group. The former Marine seemed to prefer a certain level of distance from others.

Dan reached the group, his focus centered on Stoker, who stared back at him with an expression that he found hard to read. At the end of their last encounter in Echidna, Stoker had been less than supportive, kicking him out of the warehouse.

Now? He seemed conciliatory.

The rest of the Firemen's command structure seemed to be in profound shock, their attention glued to a website displayed on the large computer monitor.

"They're blaming *us* for Chemerra's murder?" Generic YouGene blurted, his rotund face shaking in disbelief. "Whoever posted this article, I want his skin on a pole! Who would believe this crap? Why would we kill our own leader?"

Psue Dominus stared sternly at the screen, her emotive blouse pulsating brightly, its tint reinforced by a blush of rage coloring her face. "It's the ultimate insult, designed to undermine our loyalty."

"Calm down, people," Stoker urged. "It's a classic diversion tactic, a 'false flag.' The Horsemen learned it from Sicilian pirates way back in 67 B.C. The pirates would disguise their guilt by flying the flags of their enemies. The guy who runs this site? Mike "the Word" Notten? He's a local conspiracy theorist, a Horseman shill. He's been promoting their misinformation campaigns for years." Stoker shifted in his chair. "This will cause us some difficulties, I'm sure, but we've handled worse."

"Really? Like what?" someone interjected.

The article that had captured everyone's attention screamed back at them in huge letters from a website called the Aquila Bearer. Its logo consisted of another variation of a stylized eagle's crest. The bird's talons clung to several sheaves of paper. Dan slid into a nearby chair and began reading the article:

Terrorist Group Executes
Local Pharmaceutical Employee

The nihilist terror group known as the Firemen unleashed an attack on our sacred institutions Friday night, right here in Savannah. It started with a demonstration meant to disrupt the medical research being done at GenTropics Pharmaceuticals, one of the nation's most innovative drug companies. During the demonstration last week, the

Firemen's disregard for law and order resulted in at least one innocent bystander being killed. But that was not enough for this depraved organization. Their insatiable desire for chaos led to more violence Friday evening when they targeted one of GenTropics' premier researchers, Ms. Ada Kurz. During the waning hours of daylight, a band of crazed hackers slithered through the deep woods of Savannah's pristine estuary and attacked Ada's home. According to nearby residents, the sound of semiautomatic gunfire could be heard echoing through the night near Moon River. It's estimated that no less than a dozen fighters converged on the area, firing hundreds of rounds from AR-15 rifles into Ada's home, killing her and the two federal agents who had been assigned to protect her.

Who are the Firemen? The staff here at the Aquila Bearer has been tracking them for several months. What we have learned is that this shadowy group of hackers deals in an obscure form of worship known as nihilistic Satanism. Their aims are to destroy the social fabric of America and replace it with their depraved Satanic principles. Recent traffic on social media indicates that the Firemen have a plan to release yet another pandemic, this one bioengineered to produce maximum pain and suffering on any unprotected American. It will make Covid-19 look like a common cold. From the ashes of this terrible chaos, the Firemen hope to build their Satanic empire.

The Department of Homeland Security and the FBI are currently on the hunt to capture the Firemen executioners, but be forewarned: this is no ordinary terrorist group. We urge our followers to keep their eyes peeled for any suspicious activity. Our vigilance is needed to vanquish this evil band of Satan's minions. Get involved now!

Email us with observations of any suspicious activity. We will be following up on this story in the upcoming weeks. With the patriotic devotion of our esteemed followers, we feel confident that this evil can be defeated.

Bob Sidian, the owner of Ant Mother, was in the crowd, which was good, since Dan had plans for the man's ant-sized motherboard.

Bob growled, "What a dimwit! The wingnut on this site thinks we're Satanists now? Who believes this stuff?"

"Don't underestimate the power of suggestion," Stoker said. "Even if people don't buy into the specifics, their negative opinions will grow.

They hear enough bad stuff and suddenly we're subhuman. Our rights don't matter. We'll have to be careful. People with a bias will be watching us."

The group stared at one another, unsure exactly how to proceed. "So, if Chemerra is dead . . ." said one member, "who called this meeting?"

There were several questioning glances around the room.

"I did," Dan finally said. "Ada Kurz gave me her phone. So, whether I like it or not, I'm the new Chemerra . . . for now."

"How . . . What?" The group stared at him, confused.

He spent the next hour recounting the events of the previous night, along with the circumstances of Chemerra's murder. And he called it that . . . "murder" . . . because that's what it was.

"Stoker's right; I've encountered people like this before," Dan finally said. "That conspiracy theorist may sound like an idiot but the opposite is true. Think about it. He knows *exactly* what happened. By focusing guilt on us, he's diverted attention away from the Horsemen. It's defense by offense. Once the public has someone to blame, it's hard to redirect that guilt back to the *true* guilty party."

"So what do we do about it?" someone said. "How do we defend ourselves?"

"By being smarter than they are." Dan explained the plan he and Dakota had cooked up. "If we want to take the heat off ourselves, we'll need to spread a blowtorch around. Focus the authorities on the *real* culprits. It's time to give these assholes a taste of their own medicine."

By EARLY AFTERNOON, the team had put the finishing touches on their plan and began dispersing to take care of their responsibilities. That left Dan and Stoker alone at the warehouse. The two of them stared at each other.

"I'm beginning to see what Ada saw in you," Stoker said. "You're a worthy addition to our crew."

"Thanks, I think," Dan replied. "But to be honest, I've got more pressing concerns than the Firemen right now and I can't have the feds or the Horsemen tailing me."

"Don't sell yourself short, Dan. Heroism comes in many forms." Stoker slapped his legs and stood up. "Let's get to it." He headed to his office to make some calls.

Dan pulled out Chemerra's black phone and dialed the contact number for Barrett Hudlow. Hudlow's smarmy voice came on the line quickly.

"Who's this?" Barrett asked.

"Dan Clifford."

There was a long pause. "You've got some nerve, I'll give you that. Why are you calling me?"

"Because, I want my life back."

"I don't know what you're talking about."

"Sure you do. I was there, remember? When your henchmen tried to blackmail Ada Kurz into giving them her codebreaking software? By the way, you know damn well I had nothing to do with her death, or your agents. You just made me a convenient scapegoat for your own corrupt intentions. What do you think will happen if I give Vince Peretti the codebreaking software you so desperately wanted and tell him what your plans were?"

Another pregnant pause. "You've got the software?"

Dan burst out laughing. "Ah, so now you know what I'm talking about! Let's cut to the chase, shall we? You want this software and I could care less. I want my freedom and reputation back. I want to be absolved of all blame. So, a trade? Chemerra's software and you exonerate me of all guilt."

"How am I supposed to do that? I don't even know what happened there."

"You told Vince you were listening in when your men died. Remember?"

"Oh, that. Well, that's inconvenient. Since we're talking frankly here, how am I supposed to walk back that statement without implicating myself?"

"You'll think of something, if you want this software. But just so you know, there's a much bigger problem out there. Ask yourself this question: who killed Chemerra with a hundred rounds of ammo? 'Cause it sure wasn't me."

"So, who was it then?" Barrett's voice sounded pinched.

"Do you care?"

"Of course!" Hudlow said, sounding insulted at the question.

"Then use your new codebreaking software to research Martin Orcus and the shadow company that took ownership of my former employer, NeuroSys. You might actually find the real criminals. Do we have a deal?"

"Spell it out," Hudlow said. There was a tremor in his voice, which Dan took as both nervousness and excitement.

"Meet me at the following address, this afternoon. Alone. If I see any of your henchmen, I bolt. Understand? You exonerate me in real-time, on the phone, and you get the software. Otherwise, I mail it to Vince with a full explanation of your involvement."

Dan gave Hudlow the time and location, then hung up before the man had a chance to negotiate or change the deal. He walked back to Stoker's office and poked his head in the door. "We're on."

Stoker let out a *whoop*. "Well, let's get crackin' then!"

24

THE ATTENDANCE AT the Atlanta Air Show had swelled on the weekend, providing Rachel Sullivan with a formidable crowd to witness her final act. She wasn't sure how she felt about that. If things went south it would be a traumatic event for the onlookers, but then she wouldn't be around to worry about it. She shrugged her shoulders. Can't be helped. The crowd was milling about, buying refreshments, touring the vintage airplanes on the tarmac that ran the gamut from early biplanes to modern fighter jets, with a healthy dose of vintage WWII fighters thrown in. Regardless of how the day turned out, the audience would have a heart-pounding adventure to talk about.

Her penultimate stunt was the opening act of the day.

Her mood had settled into a strange mixture of jitters, excitement, and melancholy. It did her no good to dwell on loss so she worked to force the melancholy to the bottom of the stack. She wanted to relish her memories of Dan and enjoy the adrenaline rush that came with confronting death.

She allowed herself one last moment of reflection over the last year, then just as quickly, pushed emotions aside, fearing a loss of courage. Instead, Rachel focused her attention on the Bücker Jungmann, her granda's legacy. The old biplane had never looked more formidable. Its red and white stripes and swept-back wings gave it a birdlike appearance, more so than most other box-wing biplanes. Resting on its small tail wheel, the fuselage angled skyward with noble intent.

The shiny new turboprop engine reinforced the look. Unlike the plane's original stubby radial engine, the turboprop was long and sleek. Its lighter weight also required it to be mounted farther forward on the fuselage to preserve the plane's center of balance.

The effect gave the Bücker a raptor's beak. Rachel grinned. Her granda would have laughed at the bizarre hybrid of past and present but she felt no remorse over the remodeling job. She would need a little extra modern oomph for this challenging stunt.

As she circled the vehicle, Rachel ran through a series of checklists long since committed to memory.

Moving the control surfaces, she verified the corresponding movement of the stick and rudder pedals inside the cockpit. The cabling had been rewired with virtually no play. During this stunt, the plane would have to become an extension of her body, so that her intentions would be translated instantly.

There would be no margin for error.

She checked the fuel tanks and drained condensation. Oil levels were good; tires fully inflated. Everything seemed ready to go. She worried whether the new cabling would be sufficient to withstand the tremendous g-forces generated by the outside loop. Planes were designed to withstand the downward tug of gravity, not a g-force aimed in the opposite direction. That made outside loops notoriously difficult: the stresses on the plane's structure were reversed, defying the classical assumptions of aircraft design and aerodynamics. The cockpit lay outside of the loop, resulting in centrifugal forces that tried to jerk the pilot out of the seat. In essence, the plane would be plummeting toward an endless downward arc.

Rachel would have to trust that her friends at Maule had taken all factors into consideration in their rerigging but when she had described her stunt to them, their expressions had turned from confidence to trepidation.

And then she added an upside-down ribbon cutting stunt to the formula, flying ten feet above the ground.

She visualized the movements in her head, mentally rehearsing each step that would ultimately determine her destiny. Granda had taught her well and she knew her skills. But this? Even she had her doubts. Did her granda have doubts at his moment of truth? When he chose to steal the Bücker from the Germans and attempt an escape? In that one critical moment, Finnegan Sullivan had tempted fate and placed everything on the line for family, God, and country. He survived. Why not her? If she managed to survive the stunt, she had another option for her final act, a flight to the Atlantic, never to return.

Rachel wanted to make her Granda proud. This would be it; her decision moment, a legacy she'd leave for others.

Her tribute to Dan Clifford.

As she labored to keep her emotions under control, the three Martins arrived. John Martin Senior, Junior, and his son, the Third, approached, then stopped a respectful distance away from the Bücker, to give her space to finish her final checklist. Her calculations were a guess, since she had never tested the stunt. No time.

This would be her "one off."

Do or die.

No second chances, no do-overs. One and done, like Finnegan, with his lurch toward freedom on his fateful summer day.

Her thoughts settled on the moment of truth, the axis of decision. She wondered what had gone through Finnegan's mind at that critical moment when he chose to challenge the odds . . . was he confident?

Was she?

Rachel approached the Martin family, hugging them all in turn. "I'm so glad you guys showed up."

"We wouldn't miss this for the world," John Martin Senior said from his wheelchair. "I only wish I could join you, one last time." He winked.

"Hey, there's always the rear cockpit." Rachel grinned.

"Don't tempt me," John Senior said. "It would be a fitting end to a fruitful life."

Rachel struggled to hold back tears. *Yes, it would.*

The four of them hugged again, awkwardly. Rachel was about to turn back toward the Bücker when two men in dark suits approached.

One of the suited men stepped in front of Rachel: "Are you Rachel Sullivan?"

Rachel hesitated for a moment. "Yes?"

The suited man smiled grimly and held out his identification badge, "I work for the Department of Homeland Security. Do you know the whereabouts of Dan Clifford?"

Rachel studied the man's ID and handed it back. "I have no idea where Dan is and you'll have to excuse me. I've got an aerial stunt to perform." She turned to head toward the Bücker, when a hand grasped her shoulder.

"Ms. Sullivan, you're not going anywhere until we find Mr. Clifford."

"Excuse me?" she said.

"We need to find Dan Clifford and you're going to help us," the man said.

"As I said," Rachel continued, "I haven't seen or spoken to Dan Clifford in days, so if you will excuse me . . ." She continued toward the Bücker.

"Stop!" the man demanded. "You're not going anywhere until you answer our questions."

John Martin, Jr. stepped forward. "You gentlemen need to relax. Ms. Sullivan has a stunt to perform. Chill out until she's done."

"Keep out of this," the suited man said. "This is a Homeland Security issue."

"No, it's not," Rachel said. "As I have said several times, I can't help you." She continued toward her plane.

"Rachel Sullivan! Put your hands in the air!" The suited man began reaching for his sidearm.

At that moment, John Martin the Third reached out and grasped the suited man by the arm. "There's no need for that. What cause do you have to stop her?"

"Get your hands off me or I'll arrest you too!"

Rachel wasn't about to wait around for this standoff to resolve. She started jogging toward the Bücker, determined to get her stunt underway.

The second man gave chase but barely made it two feet before he promptly fell to the ground with a yelp.

As Rachel raced toward the Bücker, she looked over her shoulder to see the second man's foot entangled in Big John Senior's walking cane. The ninety-year-old man was yelling from his wheelchair, "Young man! This lady has rights!"

Rachel grinned and climbed into the cockpit. Her fingers found the ignition switch and the McDonnell Douglas turboprop roared to life. She goosed the throttle and felt the torque of the massive turbine as it twisted the plane's airframe. Not waiting for any bureaucrat to interfere with her stunt, she released the brakes and let the prop-wash lurch the plane forward. Within seconds, the Bücker was airborne, virtually pulled into the air. Constructed of wood, enameled fabric, and steel cables, the Bücker Jungmann was a mere leaf, blown skyward by the overwhelming power of the turboprop. The ground receded quickly and soon, Rachel was sailing through the air like an eagle on the hunt.

She took the plane ballistic, relying on the power of the engine to pull the craft upward.

She was free!

The ground fell away and she glanced back over her shoulder at the runway below. The Martins were still arguing with the feds and a crowd was beginning to form. She tuned in to the airshow's radio frequency and listened as the announcer described her stunt to the audience.

The radio squawked: "Ladies and gentlemen, focus your eyes on the sky. Stunt-pilot Rachel Sullivan will attempt, for the first time in aviation history, to combine two of aviation's most difficult stunts, the outside loop and the upside-down ribbon cutting trick."

Rachel responded to the announcer's monologue, twisting the Bücker through several corkscrew maneuvers just to focus the audience's attention. The scene below seemed almost cartoonish, flattened into two dimensions by the high perspective. She lined the plane up with the grassy area alongside the runway, where crews had assembled her "ribbon," a long, paper banner that now stretched between the two wooden posts. She turned on the plane's smoke generator, whipped through a couple more corkscrews for good measure, and then pulled up into a hammerhead stall to whet the audience's appetites.

At the top of the stall, the Bücker began to fall backward and Rachel used the rearward momentum to turn the plane back toward the runway. Then she dropped the Bücker to a hundred-foot altitude and aimed directly at the banner.

She took a deep breath. *This is it,* she thought. *A rich life distilled down to five fatal minutes.* With one deft twist of the stick, the Bücker flipped upside down and she stared at the blurry green strip of grass racing past, a hundred feet below her head. The banner approached quickly and she'd need to fly just a few feet above it to enter the beginning of her loop. The next time she arrived at this point, she'd be coming out of the outside loop and flying quite a bit lower.

A split second after the banner passed directly beneath her head, Rachel pushed the throttle handle "balls to the wall" and jammed the plane's stick forward. The engine roared and the plane arced steeply downward, only in her inverted position, downward was up, taking her directly into the bottom arc of the loop.

She glanced up, which was down. Above her head, or below, depending on how you thought of it, the ground fell away quickly, replaced by a blur of bodies in the nearby stands and then the blue of the sky. She was no longer "flying by the seat of her pants," as the saying goes. Instead, the centrifugal force of the outside loop pressed her away from the seat and into her shoulder harness, the only thing keeping her in the cockpit. She could feel the straps digging into her collarbones.

The turboprop continued to growl. The wings shuddered and cables rattled. At this point, Rachel could see nothing but blue sky and a few wisps of clouds, leaving her disoriented. How circular was her loop? She had no way of knowing but her mind drifted to Granda and visions of dogfighting that had danced in her head as a child. A fleeting image of Dan crossed her mind and she suddenly felt an overwhelming flood of peace and contentment.

The end was near, or maybe it was the blood rushing to her head.

A flash of green and Rachel realized she was on the downward arc of the loop again, on the other side. Suddenly, she was staring directly at the ground that was racing up to meet her, then another blur of bodies in the stands.

The ground was coming up too fast. She needed more arc but the stick was already glued to the firewall. Instinctively, she backed off the throttle, as gravity had added its momentum to the arc. Slowly, painfully, the ground seemed to arch away. She pulled back more on the throttle, letting the Bücker drift into the bottom of the arc. The ground raced up and she caught a glimpse of the banner a few hundred feet ahead at the far end of her vision.

She wasn't going to make it.

She had miscalculated the downward half of the loop and her speed had grown too fast. Within seconds, she would meet the ground. It's true what they say, she mused, as her entire life played across her mind's eye in an instant.

Then, instinctively, she remembered an old trick Granda had taught her: in a dogfight, he'd go into a steep turn, then drop the flaps on the wings. The extra drag would drastically slow the plane, sending any pursuer flying by, right into Granda's gunsights.

Rachel jerked back on the flaps and the Bücker groaned and bucked against the added drag. It shuddered and slowed. She could see individual strands of grass rushing by now, then a *thump!* The Bücker's tail was dragging along the ground. Rachel's head was only a few inches above the grass and she choked on a mouthful of dried straw and detritus.

The plane was at the bottom of the arc and had slowed drastically. She added some throttle back in and the turboprop responded by pulling her back up and away from the ground. The banner appeared directly in front of her and the spinning props ripped through the paper. She spit out a mouthful of shreds and looked back over her shoulder.

The ground was receding again. She had made it! A complete outside loop! Judging from the taste of dried paper, she'd obliterated the banner as well.

A sudden rush of adrenaline and triumph rushed through her body as Rachel flipped the plane back upright and stared down at the incredulous scene. She could see excited observers clapping and cheering and an almost perfect smoke trail written into the air in the shape of a circle, with one drooping section near the ground, where she had almost planted her face.

The thrill of victory overwhelmed her. That had to be the biggest rush of her life! Then a sudden stab of disappointment. Despite her best efforts, she was still alive, still cursed with Huntington's. Her pride and need to complete the stunt had overwhelmed her wish to end things quickly.

It's not that she hadn't considered this possibility. She was, after all, a damn good stunt pilot. That meant she'd have to revert to plan B. She would move to the far end of the field and go through a few more stunts, just to titillate the crowd. Then she'd fly off into the sunrise and the Atlantic, and then it would all be over.

The announcer's voice reverberated breathlessly through her headphones. "Ladies and gentlemen, that was incredible! One of the most amazing feats of aerial prowess ever seen at the Atlanta Air Show! Give it up for the incredible, unflappable, *Raaaaachel Sullivan!*"

Rachel groaned. She almost hated to ruin her reputation with a sudden disappearance. Then, a vision of Dan Clifford flashed through her mind. It was her first opportunity to think about the two feds, who still stood on the tarmac waiting for her to return. Why were they trying to find Dan?

Dan Clifford, what have you gotten yourself into this time?

Rachel sighed. Dan was going to ruin a perfect day and her perfect end. She cursed several times, turned the plane south, and headed toward Savannah.

25

DAKOTA PELL DROPPED Dan off at the Sentient Bean, a vegan cafe in Savannah's Historic District near Forsyth Park, then headed to his strategic position. Dan walked into the rustic cafe and scanned the room. It was small and simple, decorated in a seventies-era motif, with numerous paintings covering the walls. About thirty circular tables with chairs filled the intimate setting. It wasn't hard to assess the clientele. Most of them looked like locals or SCAD students, all chatting quietly among themselves. There were only two tables with single occupants. Both of them were middle-aged men with closely cropped hair, wearing plain jeans and shirts. Both were reading newspapers and making an effort to look occupied.

Their appearance screamed federal agent. True to form, Hudlow had lied through his teeth. Dan turned away, grinning subtly. He walked up to the counter and ordered a large cappuccino, paid the bill, and walked out the rear entrance to an outside garden where he sat down at a corner table. Struggling to remain calm, he caught his foot twitching nervously, stopped it, and took a few deep breaths to relax. Then he inserted a pair of Bluetooth earphones, pulled out his black phone, and proceeded to stare at it. To anyone else, he was just a typical guy listening to music but the calm voice of Dakota Pell soon filled his ears.

"In position," Dak stated. "I've made at least seven agents scattered across the park and outer perimeter, dispersed at critical choke points. Timing will have to be spot-on."

Dan had to hope that his minions were as efficient as they seemed during the tactical meeting. Otherwise, he'd be spending his time in a federal prison, wondering where Rachel had gone to live out her final days. He sipped on his cappuccino and checked his watch.

It was time.

BARRETT HUDLOW LOOKED both ways, checked his earpiece one last time, and began a stroll down Park Avenue. To his left, the large green expanse of Forsyth Park brimmed with a crowd of people enjoying a warm summer day under the shade of moss-covered trees.

Hudlow clicked his mike: "Teams, check in. What's going on here? Why so many people?"

A number of random voices echoed through his earpiece.

"Alpha team in position."

"Bravo team, check."

"Charlie, check. Sir, it appears there are two events in the park," came the voice from his perimeter team. "A farmers market of sorts, near the fountain. The other looks like an art contest. SCAD students drawing in chalk on the sidewalks. Makes the logistics more complex."

"Should I call in more operatives?" Hudlow asked.

"We're it, sir. Unless you want the FBI guys involved."

"No, no!" Hudlow said. "Definitely not. Do *not* communicate with the G-men under any circumstances. Understood?"

All three teams responded. Hudlow paused in the middle of the park and cursed under his breath. He just wanted this over, with Dan Clifford out of his way. "Alpha team, have you got Clifford's location?"

A whispered voice. "Sir, he's out back of the cafe, far table."

"Roger," Hudlow said and walked straight through the Sentient Bean, toward the back. He had no time or appetite for coffee. Instead, he dreamed about the codebreaker software and the doors it would open. In the halls of Washington, power was all about *who* you knew and *what* you knew about them. The codebreaker would be his skeleton key, assuming Clifford came through on his promise.

Only, Hudlow didn't trust the man, not at all. Once a terrorist, always a terrorist.

As he approached the back door of the cafe, he could see Dan Clifford seated in the far corner, staring at his cell phone like a million other young people do nowadays. Never time for real life anymore.

Clifford was wearing a black baseball cap with a red *G* on the front pulled down low over his eyes. He was wearing a bright red jersey with the number 21 on the chest. The distinctive clothing would certainly make the takedown a lot easier, Hudlow thought with a quiet chuckle. This idiot might as well be wearing a sign, CATCH ME IF YOU CAN.

Clifford waved his hand. Hudlow approached and pulled up a chair.

"WELL, MR. CLIFFORD," Hudlow said with a deprecating smile. "It appears you have me at a disadvantage. Lots of activity around here."

Dan grinned. Hudlow looked particularly uncomfortable. He wasn't sure which one of them was more uptight. "Forsyth Park's a popular venue in Savannah on a sunny weekend. A little insurance, just to make sure things go smoothly."

"Do you have the software with you?"

"Not on my person." Dan smiled again. "I'm not *that* stupid. But it's nearby, don't worry. You'll need to call Vince Peretti first."

"Then how will I be sure you'll fulfill your end of the bargain?"

Dan shrugged. "What choice do I have? Besides, your possession of the codebreaker software is my insurance. If you double-cross me, arrest me, I can tell Vince about your corruption. Honor among thieves, right?" He smiled broadly. Judging from Hudlow's expression, the man didn't like being reminded of his own malfeasance. *Typical hypocritical bureaucrat,* Dan thought to himself.

Hudlow frowned, tilted his head to one side. "I don't trust you, Mr. Clifford. How do I know you won't betray me anyway?"

"Look, it's simple," Dan said. "Your freedom depends on your ability to maintain secrecy about the codebreaking software. Conversely, *my* freedom depends on me honoring that secrecy. You arrest me, we're both screwed. I betray you, *I'm* screwed. It's a simple transaction with a balance of mutual risk."

Hudlow didn't seem happy but he nodded almost imperceptibly. "Okay, how do we proceed?"

"Simple. You call Vince Peretti right now on your phone, put it on speaker, and tell him how you've exonerated me. Then you get your codebreaker."

Hudlow smiled weakly, his expression registering a kind of hesitant admiration at Dan's logic. He paused, looked down at his phone, and dialed a number. Vince Peretti's voice came on the speaker. "Hudlow? What's up?"

Hudlow's eyes focused on Dan as he spoke. "It appears I was mistaken about Dan Clifford."

Long pause. "What do you mean?"

"Well, as I told you earlier, I was communicating with my men, at Ada Kurz's residence, when I heard the voice of Dan Clifford threatening my men and the next thing I heard was a series of rapid-fire gunshots. I naturally assumed Mr. Clifford had fired at them but now I'm not so sure."

"Hmm, how so?" Vince said.

"Well, it just doesn't make sense." Hudlow stared fiercely at Dan as he spoke. "You know I don't trust the man. I thought he had sided with the hacker. But then, I got to thinking, why would the hacker plant the false APB, which resulted in Clifford's arrest? Besides, my men continue to hear chatter online indicating that Dan Clifford is persona non grata with the Firemen. I assume he was there to confront the hacker, just as my own men showed up. I also assume he's still on the run to avoid the wrath of the Firemen."

The conversation between Hudlow and Vince went silent for a long time, so much so that Dan began to feel his heart sink.

Finally, after what seemed like an eternity, Vince replied. "Well, that's good you cleared that up. We wouldn't want to falsely accuse one of our own. You might want to know, the forensics came back from the crime scene. We found remnants of over three hundred rounds of ammunition, looks like 5.56 mm, fired at the cabin from the direction of the river, based on trajectory. I was curious as to how you were going to explain Dan Clifford firing off that many rounds . . ."

"What?" Hudlow seemed genuinely shocked by the news. He closed his eyes, opened them but now they were focused into the distance. "Well, I guess we all make mistakes. But then, that means we have multiple killers, practically an army. I don't understand . . ."

"Have you been monitoring the web?" Vince said. "There's a conspiracy website claiming that a band of Firemen attacked Ada's home. I wouldn't normally put credence on conspiracy theorists but that accusation matches the evidence much more closely than Dan Clifford being involved. It appears he was a victim, rather than a perpetrator."

Hudlow's face wrinkled up into a ball of confusion. "But if Ada was . . ." He caught himself. "Well, I concur, then." Hudlow's focus began vacillating between Dan and the far wall. "So we'll talk later, okay?"

"Right."

Hudlow hung up, stared down at the table.

Dan could see Hudlow's mind struggling to process this new information. "That worked," he said. "Sounds like Vince had already seen through your lies. You're lucky I'm here to cover your ass."

Hudlow's confusion was palpable. "This doesn't make sense. Why would the Firemen kill one of their own?"

Dan felt a surge of triumph. "That's what I've been trying to tell everyone and I'll tell you too. The Firemen are not your enemy. That story about them firing on Ada's cabin is bullshit. You've got your focus so far up their ass you can't see the real threat. Think outside the box. The Firemen wouldn't kill one of their own but a bigger enemy would. One with far more influence and resources available to them. Like an armed drone, for instance, that could fire from the river with devastating effect. Maybe you should be checking out that security firm, TaurusSec."

Hudlow scowled. "Don't presume to tell me my job. Where's the codebreaker software you promised?"

Dan stood up and leaned over the table, until his face was inches away from Hudlow's. "Oh, you'll get your codebreaker software, right now. Just give me a minute. In the meantime, remember this. The most obvious answer can often be sitting right under your nose . . . so close it could bite you, if it were a snake. Think of *that*, while you're trying to decipher this whole mess."

BARRETT HUDLOW LEANED back, surprised by Dan Clifford's sudden aggression but before he could react, Clifford disappeared around the corner in a blur of red and black. Hudlow clicked his mike: "All teams! Clifford is on the move! Hold back until he has the software in his possession, understand? *Do not* engage until he has retrieved the prize, then take him down."

Hudlow leaned back in his chair, boiling with confusion and fear. Who were these other operatives Clifford was talking about? And what was he going to do with Clifford? He couldn't just let the man walk. Too dangerous. Too unpredictable.

Hudlow realized that he couldn't just capture a man that he had absolved of blame, and then return him to custody. If Vince Peretti and Dan Clifford put their heads together . . .

He stared down at the table where Clifford's half-consumed cappuccino sat alone in the middle of the table. Hudlow had half a mind to drink the rest while he waited . . . what was Clifford's last statement about?

The most obvious answer can be sitting right under your nose, so close it could bite you, if it were a snake.

The cup of cappuccino seemed to wink back at him like a demonic Cyclops.

Hudlow lunged forward, picked the cup up, and shook it. Liquid spilled out but he felt something rattling inside. He quickly held the cup over the ground and poured out the remaining liquid.

At the bottom of the cup sat a wrinkled glob of plastic wrap. He dropped it onto the table and noticed a glint of metal shining through. Hudlow tore open the shrink wrap. Inside, he saw the familiar shape of a USB plug protruding out of a plastic figure . . .

A figure molded into the shape and color of a coiled rattlesnake.

He screamed into his mike. "Take Clifford down, now! I've got the package! Repeat, I've got the package!"

Hudlow slumped back in his chair. It had been there all along. Fool! He could have kept his admission to Peretti to himself, if only . . . Hudlow's anger boiled over. At that moment he decided that Dan Clifford would fall victim to some nefarious accident on the way back to the joint task force's operations center.

MILES STERN, LEADER of Bravo team, watched carefully from a distance as Dan Clifford, wearing a bright red outfit, rounded the corner of the Sentient Bean's courtyard and walked briskly into the main crowd of Forsyth Park. Hudlow had ordered Stern to hold back, until Clifford had the opportunity to retrieve the prize that Hudlow wanted so badly. But now, Hudlow was screaming incoherently in his ear to capture Clifford immediately. Stern moved forward cautiously, unsure how to proceed. He was accustomed to commanders who knew their tactics and could communicate them succinctly but Hudlow's behavior seemed indecisive, changing his orders on a whim.

As Clifford melted farther into the crowd, Stern was finally forced to commit. He picked up his pace to intersect Clifford's path. As he approached, the perp's gait increased, prompting Stern to bull-rush him before he could break into a run.

Lunging forward, Stern grabbed Clifford by the shoulder and shouted: "Dan Clifford! Stop right there . . ."

The next few seconds seemed to transpire in a blur. Rather than the resistance he expected from Clifford, Stern felt his hand being grabbed and his forward motion accelerated in an arc. He was being spun into a tight circle, his center of balance pulled far forward of his feet. Then, just as suddenly, his direction was reversed, his wrist bent back painfully and twisted. Screaming in pain, he followed the trajectory of his wrist and arm backward into the ground, the wrist and elbow twisted further to the edge of agony as he torqued facedown into the dirt.

"Keep your hands off of me, you pervert!" screamed Clifford.

Stern struggled to twist his head around. Only, the target wasn't Clifford at all but a slightly built Asian woman glaring down at him malevolently. She held his awkwardly bent wrist in one hand, contorted in such a way that he had no leverage at all and was helpless to use his strength to twist out of the pretzel-like hold. In her other hand, she held her smartphone, taking his picture.

"Let go!" he sputtered. "Federal agent, Homeland Security. Assault of an officer."

"If so," the woman said, "you failed to announce your authority. Show me your ID then, or I'm calling the cops! I know my rights."

An inquisitive crowd began forming around them.

"My . . . jacket, inner pocket," he sputtered.

Psue Dominus relaxed her grip on his wrist slightly and leaned over, riffling through his jacket. "You look like a pervert to me," she said while staring at the badge.

Suddenly, Stern's arm was free and he sat up, spitting out sandy dirt and attempting to brush grass stains off his jacket. He stared up at the diminutive woman and a crowd of red-and-black T-shirted individuals who had formed a tight circle around him.

"Where's Dan Clifford?" Stern demanded. "Why are you wearing his clothes?"

"What, these?" The Asian woman pointed toward herself. "Since when do federal agents accost individuals wearing their colors? I'm a Georgia Bulldog fan. It's game day."

Stern stared blankly. Much of the surrounding crowd wore the same outfits, complete with black cap.

Stern clicked his collar mike and spoke to Hudlow. "Sir, we've got a problem."

"Is Clifford in custody?" Hudlow squawked back.

"Uh, no, sir. Suspect is in the wind."

"What! How?"

Stern winced. "Sir, I suggest you come outside, see for yourself."

DAN STRUGGLED TO ignore the action taking place a few feet away from him but it was difficult. Psue Dominus had just put a federal agent on his ass with a fancy Aikido move that happened in a blur, drawing several admiring gasps from the crowd.

He looked away, pulling the hood of his gray sweatshirt forward to hide his face.

The wardrobe change had taken a split second, as he was rounding the rear corner of the Sentient Bean. Two waiting Firemen approached from either side and grabbed his jersey, pulling it and his baseball cap off in one swift motion. A second later, he'd pulled the hood of the underlying sweatshirt over his head and the transformation was complete.

While the crowd's attention was focused on Psue, Dan strolled slowly along the perimeter of the park, head down, demeanor relaxed. Every particle of his body screamed, "Run!" but he forced himself to maintain his plodding rate of speed.

"Angle right," Dak's calm voice urged over Dan's Bluetooth earphones. "Agent at nine o'clock."

Dan abruptly turned right and walked across a large expanse of grass that bordered the tennis courts at the edge of the park.

"Sit down and rest," Dak's voice continued. "Look small, don't move. Let the action pass you by."

Dan sat on a small bench alongside the tennis courts. From his peripheral vision, he could see several men, presumably federal agents, converging on the action at the center of the park, revealing their purpose and motive through their rapid gaits.

BARRETT HUDLOW RACED across the street into Forsyth Park, where a group of young people had converged. Beyond the tight circle, SCAD students worked on their sidewalk art, strolled through the farmers market, or appeared to be enjoying the day, seemingly oblivious to the action at the center of the storm. Hudlow elbowed his way through the crowd to the circle's epicenter, where Miles Stern was questioning a young Asian girl.

"I could arrest you for aiding and abetting!" Stern yelled at the woman.

She stood her ground and took a confident step forward. "For what? Wearing school colors? Minding my own business when some pervert puts his hands on me?"

"What do you call this?" Stern shouted, pointing at the crowd.

To Hudlow's horror, a wall of Dan Clifford faces stared back at him accusingly, all identically dressed in red jerseys, black hats, and paper masks.

"What's going on?" Hudlow shouted at the crowd. "Why are you all wearing Dan Clifford masks?"

One chubby young person stepped forward. "We're fans," he said. "We're out here celebrating the anniversary of the Weatherman virus, when Dan Clifford exposed the corrupt Senator Becker to the world and saved the country. Dan Clifford is our hero."

The crowd chimed in, raising their arms in unison, screaming: *"Hail, Dan Clifford! True Patriot! Death to bureaucrats!"*

Hudlow felt his face flush. He clicked his collar mike: "Alpha, Bravo, Charlie teams! Converge on the crowd, find and apprehend Dan Clifford. I don't care if you have to unmask every person in this park." He broke out of the circle and headed toward the far end of the park where he spotted the captain of Bravo team.

"De-mask all these people," he ordered. "One of them has to be the real Dan Clifford."

"Boss," the man said, a ragged look on his face. "We can't just go around assaulting all these people. De-mask everyone? To what end? They can wear Clifford masks if they want. Plus, do you want to draw that much attention? What are you going to tell your FBI cohorts?"

Hudlow hadn't thought of that. He'd just exonerated Clifford on the phone with Special Agent Peretti. "I don't care how you do it," Hudlow said, his voice trembling. "I want this asshole found, before he escapes. He's still a fugitive."

"Move now," Dak said. "Follow the green dot."

Dan stood up as innocuously as possible. A quivering green dot appeared on the grass a few feet in front of him. It bounced and jerked across the grass toward the edge of the park, directly away from Hudlow's position. Dan kept his head down, afraid to look back.

The green laser beam danced its way across Drayton Street toward a line of restored antebellum houses packed together tightly, separated by thin passageways.

The green fairy danced its way down the street for a few more yards, then stopped suddenly.

"Turn right, then down," Dak said.

Dan fought his way through a cluster of rhododendron bushes and found himself at the top of a set of stairs, hidden behind the overgrowth. Bob Sidian was waiting patiently at the bottom.

"Ready?" Bob said and ushered Dan toward a small hole in the ground.

Dan stopped and stared into the void. This was the part of the plan he had objected to but now he had little choice. After a moment's hesitation, he scurried down a rusty ladder into a small dim room. A dank smell assaulted his nostrils. His foot slipped on the wet floor and he almost fell, not wanting to catch himself on the slimy walls. Bob Sidian followed, dropping beside him in the tight quarters.

A familiar tightness began drifting up from Dan's gut, threatening to encircle his lungs, strangle his breath, but to his shock and delight, he managed to quell the panic attack. His virtual experience spent in the dark tunnels of Echidna had functioned like a cathartic type of desensitization therapy.

Bob Sidian swung the bright screen of his phone in wide arcs, illuminating the dim shadows. "Pretty creepy, huh?" He giggled.

The wavering beam of light defined a small, bricked-in enclosure with a dark tunnel leading off into the abyss. The walls were covered with dark splotches of mold . . . and spiders. Hundreds of them. Large brown recluses, that scampered about on long spindly legs.

Dan shivered.

Bob aimed the light down the tunnel. "Just follow the blue arrows. Otherwise, you'll get lost down here. These tunnels wander all over downtown Savannah. We've been mapping them, connecting them. They reach all the way to River Street."

"These look ancient," Dan said.

"Oh, they are," Bob said. "Pre–Civil War. Out at River Street they were used to smuggle in slaves for the cotton fields . . . and for crimping."

"Crimping?"

"You know, kidnapping. Shanghaiing unsuspecting citizens. They'd ply the men with grog at the local bars until they passed out, then smuggle them to the docks through these tunnels. Next morning, the poor bastards would wake up on some spice scow sailing toward the Orient."

"I'm headed to River Street?"

"No, not from this tunnel." It was Bob Sidian's turn to shiver. "This one connects to the old Candler Hospital at the end of Forsyth Park. This tunnel was used for something far worse."

Dan rolled his eyes. "Pray tell."

Bob lowered his eyes, spoke in a whisper. "Back in 1876, yellow fever swamped Savannah in a horrible epidemic. Thousands died in agony, vomiting up their insides. No one knew what caused it back then. There was no cure and the city didn't want citizens to know how bad the epidemic was, so they hid the bodies down here in the tunnels, sort of like the underreporting on Covid-19 deaths."

"I guess misinformation has been around awhile, huh?"

Bob nodded. "Be careful that you don't trip over the rusty bars that poke out of the walls. They were used to stack the bodies."

"Gee, thanks," Dan said and pulled out Chemerra's black phone to use as a light.

"Like I said, follow the blue arrows and you'll be fine. When you get to the old Candler building, stick to the stairs. SCAD owns the building now. Avoid contact with anyone until you reach the roof."

"Got it," Dan said. Only, he wasn't really so sure about his new comrades in arms. He turned back to Bob. "I'm curious about one thing. If the Firemen are an international group, why are there so many here? In this small town?"

Bob looked surprised. "Chemerra didn't tell you? Savannah is where our enemies, the Horsemen, got their start in America. They were heavily invested in the Dutch East India Company, the world's first international corporation. They monopolized the Spice Islands, put an entire region under their thumb, stole their spices, and sold them throughout the world to finance their operations. Savannah was a primary port of entry, until General Sherman arrived."

"I see." Dan realized how little he actually knew about the Firemen's history and now he had become the de facto leader of a group he barely understood. Staring down the dank tunnel with its mold and spiders and fetid puddles, Dan took a deep breath and ventured forward. "See you on the other side."

"Yes, sir," Bob Sidian said, saluting.

He moved forward, taking care to avoid the walls, where hordes of brown recluse spiders scampered about. After about fifty feet, the tunnel split and he followed the blue arrow that had been dutifully spray-painted on the wall. Every twenty feet or so he could see a pair of rusty steel brackets that hinged out from the wall. Presumably, they would hold the wooden slats containing the dead bodies of yellow fever victims, all stacked like cordwood beneath the streets of Savannah, unbeknownst to the uninformed populace above.

He picked up the pace.

After several twists and turns, another ancient brick room materialized from the darkness. Another rusty ladder led to the world above. He pushed against the ceiling and a recently installed secret door clicked open.

At the top of the stairs, a small opening led into the Old Candler Hospital building. It had been dutifully restored and Dan could see evidence of modern styling in the hallways beyond the fire exit but following Bob's advice, he stuck to the stairs and headed toward the roof.

Stepping out onto its flat surface, Dan triggered his Bluetooth earbuds. "I'm on-site."

"Roger," Dak's voice replied. "Sending the package."

A few minutes later, the buzz of a drone approached overhead. It hovered seven feet above the roof, allowing Dan to grab a bundle dangling from a rope.

Inside was a change of clothes and one of Generic YouGene's silicone masterpieces.

Dan took a spray can of spirit gum and coated the inner surface thoroughly, counting to thirty to give the liquid time to dry. Then he carefully positioned it.

Five minutes later, the face of Generic YouGene appeared on the street at the bottom of Candler Hospital.

Scanning Forsyth Park, he could see Hudlow's men still working their way through the crowd, stopping every few minutes to demand some random person wearing a cheap paper "Dan Clifford" mask to remove it for full identification.

His mask was different, 3-D printed from silicone and custom fitted to the unique shape of Dan's face. He tested the quality of the mask by boldly walking past an unsuspecting federal agent nearby. The agent registered no hint of recognition.

Anonymity through ubiquity, Dan chuckled to himself as his ride pulled up to the curb. He smiled subtly, so as to not stretch the mask too far, waved at the federal agent, then climbed into the car.

His ride pulled away from the curb and headed back toward Stoker's warehouse.

BY THE TIME Barret Hudlow returned to the Circle, he was fuming. Dan Clifford had somehow managed to elude his grasp, embarrass his staff, and expose his agents to public scrutiny. Worse still, Clifford had planted seeds of doubt about the TaurusSec operatives. With limited manpower in Savannah, he had been forced to cover the logistics of Clifford's capture by hiring TaurusSec guards to fill in the gaps. No way could he chance the FBI getting wind of the codebreaker, so hiring an outside security firm was the only way.

And now, Clifford was claiming that TaurusSec was responsible for the deaths of his own men. Had he been that foolish, or was it just a ploy by Clifford to throw him off the scent? His expensive mercenaries had failed miserably at capturing the perp, even in a highly monitored environment. Was that intentional? It appeared he had underestimated his adversaries and possibly exposed his plans to an outside group. Not good. Now, he had to hope that Clifford would keep everything secret, for his own sake.

Forced honor among thieves, a familiar concept in Washington.

Hudlow reminded himself to look at the positives. At least he possessed the prize: Chemerra's magical codebreaking software. With it, he had the keys to the kingdom. One of the first systems he'd hack would be the TaurusSec server to see if he'd been betrayed.

Mentally regrouping, Hudlow headed down the hall, in search of his most trusted security analyst, Micah Strong. He found the man typing away in one of the Circle's many high-security offices.

Hudlow held out his prize. "Ignore the stupid decoration and be very careful with this package. It came from a bunch of hackers so it could contain some serious viruses. You need to take the utmost security precautions."

Micah took the memory stick and stared at it with a condescending expression. "Wow, not so subtle insult, huh? Don't worry, boss, this isn't my first rodeo. These Firemen are rank amateurs. We're safe."

"How can you be so damn sure?" Hudlow asked.

"Look," Micah said, opening his palms to the air as if talking to a child. "First off, this is a secure room, no internet access, and I'm gonna examine this stick with an air-gapped computer. It's fresh off the shelf."

Hudlow blinked his eyes, trying to decipher his head geek's cryptic language. "Uh, can you explain the air-gapped part?"

"Sure," Micah said, giving Hudlow a deprecating smile with a hint of derision underneath. "Think of an air-gapped computer as an internet virgin, sort of like a condom for the web." He grinned. "This laptop has never been connected to the internet, I've disabled its Wi-Fi processor and Bluetooth; it can't contact the outside world in any way. If there's a virus on this stick, it ain't going anywhere but down my rat hole." Micah grinned triumphantly.

"Fine, fine," Hudlow said. "Get on with it, then."

Micah booted up the laptop and inserted the memory stick. He browsed the contents. There were several cryptic files but one directory caught his attention immediately: *weekly_pwcodes*.

Micah clicked on the directory and got a listing. The folder contained a long series of small text files, each with a unique name.

Hudlow heard the gasp of surprise from Micah and leaned in excitedly, placing both his hands on the technician's shoulders. Hudlow stared at the files with wide eyes.

Cdc.txt
Fbi.txt
Hs.txt
Fbi_peretti.txt
Cbo.txt
Hs_hudlow.txt
Potus_ss.txt
Potus_priv.txt

As the files kept scrolling by, Hudlow's excitement escalated. He giggled excitedly. "Potus? We've got the president's personal login?" Hudlow pointed excitedly. "Click on hs_hudlow."

Micah clicked on the text file. Two solitary lines popped up on the screen. Line one contained a login name, the second line, a password.

Hudlow gasped. "This is legit. That's my private login, *damn*. The Firemen have been tracking me all along. But this is a gold mine! *Potus?* I've got my enemies by the balls! This is *incredible*. We'll screw those cocksuckers up one side and down the other. And fbi_peretti? Let's see what that asshole's been saying about us. Click on that file."

Micah closed Hudlow's file and scrolled down to click on fbi_peretti, when an alert popped up on the screen:

Camera protocol detected.
Wi-Fi detected
Virus detected

"What?" Micah's fingers scrambled madly over the laptop's keyboard. "This can't be right," he exclaimed. "My virus detection software says there's a Wi-Fi . . . a camera . . . that can't be, this is *airgapped*!"

Hudlow stood erect, alarmed by Micah's reaction. "What do you mean, a Wi-Fi? You mean a network? I thought you said this laptop was quarantined?"

"It *was*," Micah sputtered. "*Is*, I mean. It has to be!" A few flurries of frantic typing later, Micah fell back in his chair, a look of defeat and grotesque admiration clouding his face. He grew silent.

"What?" Hudlow protested. "What the *hell's* going on?"

Micah stared down at the laptop, his eyes locking on the plastic snake, coiled and ready to strike. "I'm afraid we've been snake bit. That damn USB thumb drive has a Wi-Fi transmitter embedded in it. An autorun virus activated the laptop's camera and it's been filming us, transmitting it, to some server, somewhere."

"*What?*" Hudlow could feel the blood pulsing in his neck, his face turning beet red. "I thought you said this laptop was isolated? What did you say? Air-gapped? Like a condom? How can it be transmitting?"

Micah's face grew pale. A conciliatory grin raised the edges of his lips. *"Touché,"* he mumbled to himself. Hudlow shook his shoulder violently.

"What?" he screamed. "Tell me!"

"Somewhere out there," Micah said, "is a portable server picking up signals from this friggin' Wi-Fi transmitter, because there's nothing in this room that is connected to the web . . ."

Hudlow barely understood what Micah was saying but he knew it was bad. The air in the room grew deathly still.

Hudlow finally spoke. "What's that sound? Do you hear it?"

Micah cocked his head. "Yeah, I do."

Hudlow raced to the window and jerked the blinds open. He stared, horrified, at a drone hovering outside the building's window. Below the drone's camera hung a box with a lone antenna poking out of the front like a middle finger.

"Son-of-a-bitch!" Hudlow screamed.

IN THE DARKENED corner of Stoker's warehouse, the Firemen hovered a few feet from the large monitor, tracking the activities of Barrett Hudlow through the camera of his air-gapped laptop. When Hudlow pulled back the curtain of the building's window, the crowd erupted into cheers.

"Gotcha, you asshole!" someone yelled.

Dan grinned, feeling a sense of triumph that he hadn't experienced since leaving Atlanta and Rachel behind. *Hoorah for small victories.*

He turned to Bob Sidian. "Did all that make it to the Aquila Bearer?"

Bob was sporting a victorious grin. "Oh yeah. It was a cinch to hack. For a conspiracy website, they sure don't keep up with their security updates. I posted the article and video." He turned his laptop around to show off his handiwork. Plastered across the top of the website in large block letters was the title:

Homeland Security Behind Plot
to Hack Federal Government Offices

Below the title was a player containing Barrett Hudlow's video, a performance that had been better than Dan's wildest dreams.

"Good job," he said, patting Bob on the shoulder.

"Thanks," Bob replied. "Oh, and I spread the video around on social media, just in case their guys delete it, which I doubt, since it's super-juicy *not-so-fake* news. It's better than their crap."

Dan pulled out Chemerra's black phone, dialed Vince Peretti's private number, and texted a link to the Aquila Bearer article. He hung up and smiled, as the rest of group continued to cheer, gyrate, and celebrate their victory. He realized the Firemen needed this victory just as much as he did.

Only a matter of time now.

Hudlow stared at the inexplicable vehicle hovering outside his window, struggling to comprehend what had just happened. Suddenly, he broke free and turned to Micah, who had buried his head in his hands.

"Destroy the laptop!" Hudlow screeched.

Micah sat up.

"And the memory stick!" Hudlow jerked the USB plug out of the laptop, threw it to the ground, and stomped on the plastic snake until the device was flattened.

"The laptop!" he repeated.

Micah hesitated for a moment, then followed suit, slamming the laptop against the corner of the steel table. The motherboard and screen sparked momentarily and broke apart. He continued to slam the broken device onto the table until it shattered into several ragged pieces.

"Let's get out of here," Hudlow said.

"Right behind you, boss," Micah replied.

Hudlow reached for the door just as a loud pounding echoed from the other side.

"Barrett Hudlow!" came the muffled voice of Vince Peretti. "FBI. Come out now, or we will breach the room! You're under arrest for espionage."

Hudlow sank to the floor, mumbling to himself, his hands gripping his head.

Although they couldn't hear the events that transpired after Hudlow destroyed the laptop, the team watched with glee from the drone's camera as Barrett Hudlow was handcuffed and led away by Vince Peretti. It didn't matter that Hudlow had destroyed the evidence. The video of his guilt had been transmitted around the world and would be impossible to erase.

Bob Sidian's Ant Motherboard had been the key to the whole plan. Small enough to fit in the memory stick's housing, the thumbnail unit contained its own Wi-Fi circuitry, powerful enough to communicate with a device fifty feet away. The challenge had been positioning a Wi-Fi repeater close enough to capture the signal through the window of Hudlow's safe room. The team had decided on the drone.

Dan felt smug satisfaction in the fact that Hudlow didn't even possess what he imagined. Of course, there was no real codebreaker software. That was an illusion that Dan had perpetuated. Ada's true codebreaker had been destroyed in the fire at her cabin. But thanks to Hudlow's greed, it was an easy con to make. As far as Dan knew, the passwords he had passed on from Ada's black phone were legitimate, which would only make Hudlow's guilt more inescapable.

Faced with a challenge from a superior adversary, the Firemen had proven to be a resilient force. Dan was beginning to establish a rapport and trust with these eclectic fighters. Warriors come in many guises, he mused, and in this age, the Firemen seemed to fit the mold.

For most of his life, Dan had struggled to fit in with the establishment, to change things from the inside but he was beginning to doubt the efficacy of change through traditional means. It seemed traditions were all controlled by the gatekeepers. Perhaps the status quo needed a shake-up, the ordinary evolving into the extraordinary, comfort giving way to disruption. Perhaps these socially challenged kids were the true path.

And now, Chemerra had bonded him to their cause. He had little choice but to follow the path she had laid out for him. To do that, he'd need more freedom to move and that meant getting the FBI off his back. Despite Hudlow's begrudging vindication on the phone with Vince, Dan was still considered a person of interest in Ada Kurz's death. He'd need to direct the FBI's attention elsewhere for a while.

He turned back toward the small group of elite members and garnered their attention. "Enough celebration for one day. We now need to move on to phase two."

26

Home.

Bradley Gruber settled back into the plush leather seat of his Learjet 75 Liberty as it lined up for approach into Hunter Army Airfield. It wasn't quite the streets of Washington but at least he was back in the States, miles away from the Honduras chip factory.

It was a start and the place he needed to be, for now.

The Pater had given him a difficult assignment, one that would require his sharpest skills and acumen. But he was stateside, so he was excited. Bradley's right thumb rubbed over the face of his watch, noting its presence as a sign of good luck. Considered one of the finest examples of horological artistry, his Patek Philippe was a bespoke original built by some of the most skilled watchmakers in Europe.

He loved its supreme and understated craftsmanship. He had always felt the watch reflected his own unique talents: nuanced, precise, complete. Since its purchase two years ago, the Sky Moon Celestial had already appreciated tenfold. Sophisticated tastes for fine watches were on the rise.

As the wheels of the Learjet touched down on the tarmac, Bradley returned his attention to the task at hand. He needed to harvest two individuals, both of whom would be difficult to acquire alone, much less as a pair.

The Learjet taxied to the far end of the airbase, next to a large, nondescript metal building emblazoned with TaurusSec's familiar logo. Two men rolled a set of stairs up to the Lear's hatch and Bradley Gruber stepped out into the humid dusk air of Savannah. He quickly spotted a strange man standing outside the building's side entrance, waiting passively. The man's appearance was off-putting and Gruber recognized him by description.

He approached and held out a hand. "Good evening. I'm Bradley Gruber. I assume you are Victor Moody?"

The man nodded silently but refused to offer his hand in greeting. "The Pater says you're here to help me. How?"

"Well, that remains to be seen," Gruber said. He had been given sparse information about the man, that he was an operative, highly motivated. Someone who could benefit from their genetic engineering efforts. "As I understand it," Gruber continued, "I'm to use your residence during my stay. I'll need your assistance on occasion."

"I'll do whatever I can," the man said. "But my condition is rapidly deteriorating."

"Yes, I can see that," Gruber said. Only he didn't really *see*; not completely. The man was extremely nervous, his frame shaking uncontrollably. Every few minutes his body was racked by a series of nervous tics.

But why?

To Gruber, the man seemed to be a human time bomb, ready to explode. His face was strangely youthful, almost prepubescent and his eyebrows seemed fake, painted on. Victor Moody wore a baseball cap pulled far down on his skull, the brim casting a dark shadow over dim features. Moody kept his hands buried in the pockets of his jeans, his shoulders hunched.

"Let's go inside and plan out the next few days, shall we?" Gruber signaled toward the hangar, turned, and led Victor Moody inside.

FIVE HUNDRED YARDS north, Dan Clifford, Bob Sidian, and Psue Dominus crept quietly along the fence that bordered Hunter Army Airfield. They had made it past the main runway to the far end of the base. The section they had entered was sparsely populated, made up mainly of large paved parking areas available for army vehicles whenever a deployment was needed from Fort Stewart. Beyond the parking lots lay an outcropping of other commercial buildings attached to but not part of the base, proper.

Dan stared at the distant area, hoping to find the evidence he needed to hold the Horsemen accountable for their crimes. If he did, it could buy him some time. Still, he felt exposed.

The three of them had dressed for stealth in the dusk-light. Bob was wearing his ever-present gothic outfit, black pants and shirt, accompanied by a pair of clunky black boots. Psue had notably left behind her expressive clothing, opting instead for a set of black tights and a hoodie that resembled a ninja costume. Dan had put on his darkest pants and borrowed a shirt from one of the crew at Stoker's warehouse but he was definitely the most visible of the three, so he tried to keep to the shadows in the waning light.

Straight ahead at the far reaches of the base, the fence took a sharp turn left. Through the chain links, Dan could see a stark white Learjet parked on the tarmac, next to an open hangar door.

Inside the opening, a wash of yellow sodium light exposed the nose cone of a much smaller and darker plane, most of its details obscured by the Lear. To get a better view, they would have to enter the grounds beyond the fence and circle around to the side of the building.

The southern end of the airfield was bordered by an estuary and the drone of crickets and tree frogs grew louder as they approached. Thankfully, the constant din served to mask the sound of their movements and they reached the corner of the fence undetected. The three of them hid behind the massive trunk of an old live oak and formed a huddle.

Bob Sidian said, "This place looks as good as any." He placed his backpack in the center of the group and pulled out a large battery-powered bolt cutter.

Psue silently held up a fist, signaling a halt, then lithely pranced over to the fence and ran her hands slowly up and down its dimensions, holding her palms a few inches away from the links.

To Dan, it looked like she was casting a spell. "What the hell's she doing?"

Bob grinned. "Psue's using one of her special powers. She's been body-hacking for years, got magnets embedded in her fingertips. She's searching for electrical fields." Bob nodded in her direction and whispered, "See?"

Psue retraced her steps. "Fence is not electrified, or monitored with sensors, far as I can tell. Didn't see any cameras either. Should be safe, at least until we reach the cover of the buildings. I see one camera on the far corner of the hangar, so we must keep right and in the shadows."

"Got it."

With a nod from Dan, Bob took the lead, far less elegantly than Psue, crawling along the ground like a wounded crab. He reached the fence and attacked it with the bolt cutter, the whine of its motor barely audible above the night sounds. In less than a minute, Bob had carved a hole large enough to walk through. On the last cut, Dan and Psue grabbed the loose piece of fence and quietly laid it to one side.

There was a large expanse of grass between them and the hangar, most of it cast in shadow. Dan checked the settings on his digital camera. He wanted to get in and out quickly, grab a few pictures of the drone, and be gone. He made sure the exposure was set and the camera in focus. Settings checked, he motioned for Bob and Psue to hold back.

There was no sense in endangering them all, he decided. Glancing both ways, he sprinted across the open expanse toward a shadowed area left of the hangar and knelt to catch his breath.

After a few minutes he eased forward.

Around the corner of the building, a trapezoidal aircraft material-ized, its wings constructed from multiple angled surfaces, designed to reflect and dissipate radar signals. It had to be the drone, since there was no cockpit. With no human pilot, the futuristic jet aircraft was compact, less than a third the size of its larger cousins.

It took Dan only seconds to notice the two most prominent features of the plane's airframe: the faceted wings each had a barrel projecting from their leading edges, the instruments of Ada's death.

He felt a vibration in his core as he depressed the camera's shutter. Several faint electronic clicks signaled the firing of his own rapid-fire weapon, exposing the evidence of Ada's murder with every click. Once emailed to Vince at the FBI, the Horsemen would be exposed.

The staccato clicks were soon interrupted by the sound of a low, throaty growl.

Dan glanced over his shoulder at a man in a camo-uniform, holding back the tensed body of a German shepherd, its teeth bared and gleam-ing in the sparse light. Another quick glance registered Bob and Psue slinking quietly out of the hole in the fence. For the better, he thought.

"Well, what do we have here?" the uniformed man said calmly as a burst of white light hit Dan in the face, obliterating his night vision.

"CRAP," BOB HISSED.

"Shh." Psue jerked him backward, tightening her grip on his collar, cutting off his breath. She held her finger to her lips, leaned over, and whispered in his ear. "Nothing we can do now. Gotta head back."

". . . We can't just *leave* him!"

". . . And we can't save him." Psue jerked violently against Bob's collar and he grew silent. Maintaining her grip, she silently led him back along the way they came, keeping low and making as little noise as possible.

DAN SPOKE LOUDLY, hoping to focus the guard's attention in his direction and away from Bob and Psue. "Are you the asshole who murdered my friend and two federal officials? If so, you're in a shit pile of trouble . . ."

The shadow at the other end of the flashlight replied, "I'm not the one in trouble here, pal. Keep your hands where I can see them and follow my directions."

"And if I don't?"

"Then you can register your complaints with my undertaker, here." The man twitched the dog's leash and the German shepherd let loose a vicious series of barks and growls.

As Psue and Bob disappeared into the night, Dan found himself truly alone.

THE TAURUSSEC GUARD led Dan into a large hangar and bound his hands to the frame of a folding chair. He then walked away. Dan had been bound before, in Honduras, by sailors who knew a knot or two and this one was professionally done. Not bothering to struggle, he spent his time studying the surroundings. This hangar was at least equal in size to the one next door that housed the drone but it was filled with military equipment, vehicles, and personal effects.

Through a small window on the main wall, Dan could still see the profile of the drone resting on its tripod wheels like a stink bug, its dark faceted profile in stark contrast to the sleek white Lear parked in front.

Suddenly, a door on the wall swung open and three men entered the hangar. The first was the security guard, the second, a strange-looking man Dan had never met, but the third one was instantly recognizable as he walked into view.

"You!" Dan said. "I should have guessed."

Bradley Gruber grinned. "Mr. Clifford, what a pleasure to meet you again. Your fortuitous arrival saved me a significant amount of time and effort looking for you."

Dan felt a sudden flush of rage and he jerked against the bindings, finding them tight and unmoving. "I guess you've found some other asshole to service, now that Martin Orcus is dead." He thought back to his untimely meeting with Gruber in Washington ages ago. Gruber had tried to persuade him to lie about an international conspiracy between Orcus and a US senator. Dan had refused, chaos had ensued, and Gruber vanished, only to reappear now, in this place.

"Ah yes, Martin Orcus," Gruber said, tilting his head to one side. "I remember. The man simply refused to listen to my advice. In a strange way, you did me a favor."

Dan chuckled derisively at Gruber's attempt at rationalization. "And yet, here you are, working for yet another rich asshole."

"Whatever," Gruber said, waving away Dan's observation like an irritating fly. He paced back and forth across the open warehouse, clearly enjoying his position of dominance. "You're a lucky man, Clifford. My new boss wants to meet you in person, for reasons I cannot fathom. I've warned him of the danger you pose." He shrugged and smiled sardonically. "There's only so much I can do."

Dan glared back at Gruber and scanned the room. The strange man standing in the shadows, clearly uncomfortable, was shaking visibly, his movements interrupted often by violent body tics.

Dan decided to speak directly to him. "You must be Victor Moody."

The man shuffled his feet but remained silent.

"That's what I thought," Dan said. "Did you know these men *killed* Ada Kurz? Even while she worked tirelessly to find a cure for your affliction? You were her friend once, weren't you?"

A hint of doubt crossed Moody's face as he struggled to maintain control. "Who told you . . ." An uncontrollable spasm interrupted his question. After he regained control, Moody turned to Gruber, another tic reverberating through his body. "Is . . . thaat . . . true?"

Gruber shrugged off the question. "Victor, I don't know anything about that. I just got here, remember? But I do know my boss is concerned for your welfare. I'm here to find answers and I suspect that Mr. Clifford here"—Gruber nodded in Dan's direction—"has the answers."

"Yeah, I do," Dan said. "The answers were in Ada Kurz's private laboratory, which thanks to your companions, burned to the ground."

Moody stared at Gruber. "Is he right? Ada's dead?"

Gruber sighed, stared at the ceiling momentarily. "From what I understand, yes. But we had nothing to do with it. Check the news yourself, Victor. Apparently, Clifford's Firemen friends were the cause."

Moody's eyes, filled with confusion, returned to Dan. "Is that true?"

Dan's focus shifted to Gruber. "Ah, so *you're* the one who planted that false flag article. How else could you have known about the Firemen being implicated?" He turned back to Moody. "Victor, don't believe these assholes. That drone outside murdered Ada in cold blood." Dan flicked his head toward the window. "They tracked me to her house, killed her. I know . . . I was there. It's a miracle I survived."

Moody's gaze vacillated back and forth between Gruber and Dan, interrupted periodically with more jerks and twitches. He reached in a pocket and withdrew a bottle of pills and swallowed several. "Why kill Ada? What was the point? I need all the help I can get!"

"Look, Moody," Gruber said in his silkiest voice. "I don't know the whole story behind your ailment. I apologize for that but remember who caused your problems in the first place. Kurz and Esrom Nesson. It was their experiment that made you sick. Did they have your best interests at heart? My boss is working on your behalf. He needs all their technology to formulate a cure. That's why I'm here. You can come along, be there to receive the cure." Gruber stood straight, his arms by his side, palms pointed outward, pleading.

"What a practiced *liar,*" Dan hissed. "Don't believe him, Victor. You know the truth. You stole the cure for your severed hands. Esrom told me the problems started when you exposed yourself to the sun, to its UV radiation. It was an unexpected side effect, an accident."

Gruber stared at Dan, a thin smile of respect clouding his expression. He turned back toward Victor Moody. "Victor, you can ask the boss directly about this. We'll return to Honduras together."

Two more twitching spasms racked Moody's body and he held up a hand. "Let's just get going."

Gruber smiled. "Fine. But before we can leave, there's one final task. You can help me . . ."

Gruber's conversation was suddenly interrupted by the whine of jet engines. He glanced over his shoulder, toward the guard. "What's going on?"

The man pulled out a walkie-talkie and spoke rapidly. "I don't know, sir."

The whine of the engines increased in pitch.

All heads turned in the direction of the hangar door. The guard raced forward and hit a switch. The door protested, squealing as it rose inexorably to reveal an inexplicable scene unfolding outside. The drone's engines whined loudly as it turned and drifted slowly toward Gruber's Learjet.

Gruber stared out the opening, a blank look of confusion and concern distorting his features. "Where's it going?"

The guard continued to shout into the radio as the dark vehicle rotated on its axis and suddenly let loose a barrage of machine gun fire. The roar of chain guns echoed through the still night air, ripping a ragged line of holes across the side of the Learjet. A shower of sparks erupted into a plume of flames that consumed the Learjet's fuselage.

"What the hell?" Gruber screamed, rushing out of the hangar, arms flailing. "My jet! My Lear! What have you done?"

A rolling ball of flames drifted across the tarmac and drove Gruber to his knees. He held his hands over his face for protection.

Dan turned his head away from the searing heat wave. An instant later, the crunch of twisting metal drowned out the night sounds as the two aircraft intersected, resulting in another huge ball of fire that rose into the night sky like a flaming mushroom cloud. The Lear's fuselage split in half. Men dressed in camouflage uniforms scrambled out of nearby buildings like ants from a disturbed nest.

Still anchored to the chair, Dan could do little but lean over and attempt to shield his face from the heat. The side door of the hangar suddenly burst open and Psue Dominus raced across the expanse, a large serrated knife in her hand.

She quickly sawed through Dan's bindings and grabbed his shirt. "Hurry! Follow me."

As they rushed toward the side door, Dan paused for one last look. Bradley Gruber was still kneeling, his frustrated screams filling the night. It appeared as if Gruber's cool demeanor had finally found its limits.

"My jet! My Lear!" He screamed repeatedly, his fists pounding on the tarmac.

Out in the cool night air, Dan and Psue retraced their steps back toward the opening in the fence. No one intercepted them. The TaurusSec personnel were all focused on the conflagration that was rapidly threatening the nearby buildings.

"How did you do that?" Dan shouted.

"Not now," Psue said and kept moving. They ducked through the opening and raced up the fence line toward the road. Minutes later, they reached the car they had parked behind a bush and stopped to catch their breath. A wail of sirens from the first wave of fire trucks could be heard in the distance.

Bob paced restlessly next to the driver's side of the SUV. "It's about time!" he sputtered. "Let's go!"

Psue jumped into the front passenger seat and Dan piled into the back seat, immediately stunned by the face of the person sitting next to him.

Rachel Sullivan.

She smiled as Dan embraced her.

"I thought I'd lost you!" he blurted, squeezing her tightly. He could sense her hesitance to reciprocate but stubbornly maintained his embrace. "What . . . how did you get here?"

Rachel allowed herself a fleeting smile of triumph. "I learned you were in trouble and came to bail you out, as usual. When I got here, I checked with Esrom and he told me of your plan to come here. I bumped into your friends and we hatched a plan. I found the drone's control room and decided to dust off my simulator skills. Piloting that plane was an adrenaline rush." She grinned. "That fireball should attract some attention."

"It already has," Psue said, pointing in the direction of the main road leading into the airbase. A long line of fire trucks roared onto the base and headed toward the flames.

Bob started the engine, took a sharp turn left, and drove away, just as another line of fire trucks passed them in the opposite lane, sirens wailing.

BACK AT STOKER'S warehouse, a crowd had gathered to watch the action on the big screen. Dan shared their victories with embraces, high fives, and handshakes. He introduced Rachel to the other members of the Firemen as they cheered and partied as reporters began to unravel the truth about TaurusSec's drone and its involvement in the death of Ada Kurz.

Through the celebration, Dan kept a close eye on Rachel, as she reluctantly participated. Finally, he pulled her aside. "Listen, I know about . . ."

Rachel interrupted him, placing her fingers against his lips. "Dan, I'm not staying. I can't. This was just a last attempt to save you from yourself."

"Your Huntington's . . . I know!"

"Then you should know why I can't stay . . ." she said, her eyes glistening. "Please allow me the dignity to face this alone."

"And if there's an alternative? You have to trust me, as your partner. We go through life together, suffer together, celebrate together. What else is there, if we can't share our joys and heartaches?"

Tears rolled down Rachel's cheeks. A sob caught in her throat. "I don't want you to see me like that."

"I won't!" he said and grabbed her, even as she fought against his embrace. "Never give up, until the end. There's always hope, no matter how dark the future."

"Not for this!" she screamed. "Be realistic. We can't fight against reality."

"You talked with Esrom, right? Did he tell you about the trial?"

"What?"

"His Huntington's trial."

Rachel's face went blank.

"He has an experimental treatment for your condition," Dan said. "Worth a try; better than resigning yourself to a certain fate. Share your gamble with me. We're in this together, win or lose. Don't rob me of this chance out of some false pride or fear. I can take it, win or lose."

Rachel's eyes stared back at him, brimming with tears. "Dan Clifford, why are you so damn stubborn?"

He laughed. "I have no choice. Being with you requires it. I can no more abandon you than I can stop breathing. Let's travel this adventure together. The journey will be worth it, regardless of the outcome."

For the first time since they had met, Rachel's stubborn resolve crumpled. She grew limp, giving in to his embrace, her sobs racking her body. She leaned into him for support and whispered in his ear. "Okay, I trust you. If there's a chance, no matter how slight, I'll gamble . . . with you."

After a long embrace, Dan explained the nature of Esrom's gene therapy treatment. Then they returned to the celebration. The inexplicable collision of two aircraft on the tarmac at Hunter Army Airfield was dominating the evening news. None of the TaurusSec employees were willing to talk on camera but the appearance of the FBI at the accident scene clarified a number of conspiracy theories.

After watching for another hour, Dan wandered off to call Vince Peretti. "Are we square?" he said into his black phone.

Vince laughed. "Dan, I don't know what you did and I don't *want* to know. We've confiscated the burned remains of the drone and will be testing the ballistics against the rounds recovered at Ada Kurz's cabin. We've collected enough pristine rounds for a clear match."

"Of that, I'm sure," Dan said. "So, am I off the hook with the FBI?"

"Not totally," Vince said. "You still need to answer for your disappearance and role in the destruction at TaurusSec headquarters."

"Sorry," Dan said. "I've got other priorities. You're just going to have to trust me when I tell you, I'm totally innocent. I was tied to a chair when that plane exploded."

"I'm not doubting that," Vince replied. "But we still need an interview. Protocol. Besides," he continued, "we still don't understand why TaurusSec wanted to murder a researcher at the very institute they had been hired to protect."

"Follow the trail to TaurusSec's employer, in Honduras," Dan said. "That's all I can say. Meanwhile, I'm taking a hiatus. Don't try to track me, okay? I have a personal issue that needs to be addressed."

Vince paused on the line. "Well, I can't stop you but my official position is that you're still a person of interest."

"Understood," Dan said. "Give me some space and you'll get your interview . . . eventually."

With that, he hung up and searched for Rachel. He found her lounging at the warehouse's beer bar.

27

BRADLEY GRUBER CONTINUED to fume inside Victor Moody's small apartment. Never in his professional career had he lost control the way he had when his Learjet went up in flames. He was accustomed to working in the shadows, moving pieces on a huge chessboard.

Not participating in the game, firsthand.

Maintaining a certain emotional distance, what he liked to call intellectual neutrality, gave him the perspective to notice the subtle complexities of a situation. But today, his anger had boiled to the surface for the first time since . . . when?

Of course, since his last encounter with Dan Clifford.

Gruber held out his hand, mystified by the tremor that had embedded itself there. What was it about Clifford that managed to destroy his confidence? He knew. The man was chaos personified, impossible to predict and that was a terrifying prospect. Gruber had built his reputation on understanding the emotional pulse of the common populace.

The common populace.

He hated their complacent lethargy. The vast majority of common folk wasted their time on petty and useless activities, concerned with television, sports, what their neighbors thought, or what social media thought about their useless and uneventful lives.

And yet, their gullibility provided his bread and butter. Mental couch potatoes made his job easier. What child's play it was to manipulate the thoughts and desires of people whose greatest ambitions were scoring tickets to the next pro-football game, or, if truly ambitious, to be elected to political office. Current-day politicians and voters were cast from the same mold. Voters loved to elect mirror images of themselves to lofty government offices, as if their own petty values and experience were somehow worthy of managing the world's most powerful nation.

Thankfully, he worked for the *true* stewards of order.

That realization forced Gruber back into present reality. Clifford had placed his mission in danger of failure, something he could not tolerate.

Fortunately, the TaurusSec soldiers had whisked him away from the conflagration before the authorities arrived. He would survive, undetected. His Lear was registered in Burundi, where ownership would be obscure at best. It was unlikely to implicate him. There would also be nothing onboard to link him to the plane. But that also meant he was forced to call up his backup Lear, the one he kept safely ensconced in the Maldives. Its ownership was more traceable but only slightly.

Regardless, it had to be done.

Unfortunately, Gruber couldn't risk checking into a hotel under his real name, exposing his presence in Savannah, so he had been forced to shack up with Victor Moody, the hyperactive bundle of nerves who had the personality of an urchin.

He'd been offered a lumpy living room couch as bedding and it was atrocious, with errant springs scheming to hook and poke him during the night.

Thankfully, Victor Moody's kitchen was well equipped.

Gruber strolled into Moody's bedroom and found the man swallowing a collection of pills large enough to choke a horse. "So, exactly what is your malady?' he asked innocently.

Victor turned, startled by Gruber's presence. "Can't I have some privacy here?"

"Difficult in this minuscule apartment." he replied. "Besides, my boss wants an update on your condition. He's truly concerned for your welfare." Gruber conjured his best empathetic smile. "That handful of antipsychotics and painkillers you just took would put most men into a stupor, yet you're still shaking. What's going on?"

Victor Moody leaned on the counter for support, his body still trembling. He was clearly upset by Gruber's invasion of his privacy, yet Gruber could tell the man felt isolated and embarrassed. People in that condition typically want to share their troubles, if nudged properly.

"I'm so sorry to invade your privacy but I can't help you without knowledge of the details," Gruber continued. "That's why I'm here . . . not only to learn the particulars but to bring back the necessary components for your cure. Know this, the Pater appreciates your sacrifice, so let me help you."

Victor Moody stood resolute, a man who had been engaged in a long and harrowing battle. But also a man near the end of his endurance. His stature slumped as his resolve melted away.

"It's my fault, I know," he choked. "Esrom and Ada were making great progress with their regrowth research. I was there, every day, as a security officer, watching those mice regrow their legs and feet and I kept asking myself, 'Why not me?'"

Moody released an involuntary sob. "Every day I went there, aware of my amputated stubs, all because of an instant of bad judgment in Afghanistan. My two hooks were pathetic substitutes for the real thing. I couldn't even pour myself a cup of coffee!" Moody slammed his young hands onto the table. "Then, seeing the progress of those mice, prancing around their pens with fully regrown limbs, I wanted my own hands back." Moody held them out, shaking them in protest. They were fully regrown but imperfect. The fingers were slender and youthful, lacking the texture of age.

The absence of fingernails highlighted the imperfect reconstruction. Moody had deftly applied false fingernails to disguise the malady but the result was poor, obvious to any astute observer.

"But that's not all, is it?" Gruber prodded.

"No," Moody replied, leaning against the cabinet for support. "I stole the vector and had a friend inject me. When Esrom found out, he was worried about his career but grew excited as the treatment began to work." Moody stroked the palms of his hand reverently. "We were all ecstatic at first. You know, people are more willing to ignore the rules when the results are positive. But then . . ." Moody's voice cracked. "The side effects kicked in. Esrom told me it was because of the sun, the UV rays."

Gruber tilted his head to one side, a thought slipping in and finding residence. "The sun? How so?"

Moody's face grew pale, apologetic. "He said their vector, the one I stole for your boss, is sensitive to UV rays. They trigger a survival response that creates runaway genetic mutations. That's how Esrom described it to me." Moody wiped his brow, paused, and decided to take another couple of Xanax. He shook them out of the bottle and downed them with a swig of beer. "Esrom explained it this way: they used segments of DNA from cuttlefish to stimulate appendage regrowth. They isolated the regrowth genes and that's why the mouse trials were so successful. But then, when I tried the treatment on myself and went out in the sunlight—something the mice had never done—I triggered some survival response in the vector. It started reactivating dormant genes in my DNA. Genes from my far distant ancestors. In essence, the vector was trying to turn me back into some ancient cuttlefish-like monster." Moody's voice cracked. "I'm a genetic freak, a nervous wreck. My body doesn't know what to do! If I don't dope up on multiple drugs every day, I can't control my actions. I'm desperate. I need the Pater to find a cure!"

"And he will," Gruber said with all the sincerity he could imitate.

"Tell me the truth," Moody pleaded. "Did the Pater really murder Ada? She was working to fix my problems. If he really cared about me, why would he murder the one person working on my behalf?"

Gruber stared at Moody, willing his eyes to pool up. "I can see the pain you've endured, Victor. Let's go to Honduras and you can get your answers directly from the man himself, okay?"

Moody nodded and lowered his head.

Gruber slapped his legs. "Great! But first I have one remaining task that I must complete. What's that old adage? *You catch more flies with honey than vinegar*? I need to use your kitchen."

After a trip to the local grocery store, Gruber set up his operation in Moody's kitchen. He searched around in the cabinets and found a large sauté pan and thermometer. Unlike his encounter with Clifford at the airbase, this would be a far more subtle operation, one that would verify their latest progress.

Moody sat in his bedroom, shivering and quaking. That gave Gruber the space he needed to finish his recipe. He melted his butter, brown sugar, and evaporated milk in a large pan, over medium heat.

Once the mixture began to boil, Gruber carefully added the special sugary ingredient he had brought along with him from Honduras. The thick clear solution snaked out of the bottle in a long, thin line, pouring into the boiling liquid that Gruber had previously prepared. When the entire mixture began to foam, he added another generous pat of butter and let the entire pot boil for several minutes.

He checked the mixture fastidiously until the temperature peaked at 235 degrees Fahrenheit. Then he removed the brown elixir from the stove and stirred in a generous quantity of locally grown pecans and vanilla extract. He continued to stir the mixture until it began to thicken, then spooned out generous mounds onto a sheet of wax paper.

THE NEXT MORNING, Dan woke up, surprised and encouraged to find Rachel's warm body still snuggled next to his. He could feel her back pressing into his chest with each rising breath.

They had spent the night at Stoker's warehouse, in one of his many upper-level apartments. After introducing Rachel to several of the Firemen, he could tell she was intrigued enough to hang around, her curiosity getting the better of her. Still, he had slept restlessly, worried that she might leave during the night.

He rolled over and ordered a ride on Ada's black phone, which he was beginning to realize was *his* black phone now, willed to him by Ada herself. Slipping quietly out of bed, he put on his clothes, deciding to give Rachel a few extra minutes of sleep, one of her passions in life. He looked down at her, peaceful and innocent in slumber.

Today would be a cathartic day.

On his way downstairs he decided to call Rudi on his black phone. Since their last meeting, before Hudlow's demise, Rudi had been embraced into the Firemen collective and had been given his own black phone. For the first time since arriving in Savannah, Dan felt safe to conduct private conversations without the risk of eavesdropping. It was a bizarre testament to the current state of life in America. One needs a black phone to achieve any modicum of privacy. He was beginning to understand the pervasive paranoia of his cohorts.

After five rings, Rudi's groggy voice answered. "Yeah, what?"

"It's Dan. You awake?"

"I am now." The sound of shuffling rattled the phone's speakers.

"Here's the deal," Dan said, once he had Rudi's attention. "Rachel and I will be gone for a week, out of touch. In the meantime, do as much research as you can on the Horsemen. Check with Stoker if you need more information on their activities. When Rachel and I get back, we'll figure out our next move. Be careful and lay low. You might get a visit from Vince. Oh, and watch out for Horsemen themselves. I'm sure they're looking for me."

Rudi laughed. "You mean, like, avoid getting hacked by their script-kiddies? Don't worry, I'm armored to the teeth . . . oh, and this black phone protocol is killer. I couldn't have done much better myself. Whoever the programmer was, my hat's off to him, or her. *Killer*."

"Good, I'm glad you approve," Dan said. "Just be careful. These guys are serious and deadly. Don't underestimate them."

"What, me worry?" Rudi laughed again.

"I'm serious," Dan insisted. "These guys almost killed me."

"Yeah, okay . . . gotcha."

28

DUSK APPROACHED AS Dan and Rachel crossed the border into North Carolina. Rachel's Bücker Jungmann hummed and whined behind its new jet-powered turboprop. Stuffed into the rear cockpit, Dan struggled to track the landmarks he needed to find his way. He had never traveled to this area by plane before and only once by car. But he'd hiked through the Nantahala National Forest on the Appalachian Trail and knew the lay of the land near the Yellow Creek Mountains. Steep and unforgiving, that portion of the AT was one of the toughest hikes he had experienced near the southern terminus of the trail. Their destination would be hard to reach.

Dan figured that Ada's murderers, the Horsemen, or whoever they were, would still be tracking him, especially after the scene at Hunter Army Airfield. The memory brought a smile. At the least, Bradley Gruber would probably pay a pretty penny for his head on a spike.

He wasn't going to let that happen.

They needed a safe shelter for Rachel's treatment, one that might incapacitate her for days, according to Esrom. It had to be somewhere beyond the ability of the FBI or the Horsemen to track them.

He knew of only one place that fit the requirements: his friend Ben's compound. If there was anyone on the planet whom Dan trusted to keep them incognito, it would be Ben Proudfoot. And he had visited Ben's cabin before and knew how remote and unreachable it was. If only he could find it again, nestled deep in the Nantahala Forest.

Ben Proudfoot was a traditional Cherokee, a member of the Snowbird clan, the only Cherokees never forced from their ancestral lands. They were the first true guerrilla fighters. As Ben told the story, several hundred Cherokees refused to assemble for the march west, known as the Trail of Tears, where thousands of Native Americans perished. Instead, the Snowbird Cherokees hid in the Smoky Mountains, relying on their knowledge of the land to evade the white settlers who entered the area when gold was discovered in the 1830s during America's first gold rush.

Ben was an enigmatic old man, Dan's confidant and rock climbing mentor. He also held a doctorate from the Santa Fe Institute in complexity science. It was a natural fit for a culture steeped in the intricacies and interrelationships of man and nature. The two had met when Dan took a course at the institute many years prior, taught by Ben himself.

Their mutual love for rock climbing had resulted in a quick and long-lasting friendship. Ben could still shame climbers a third his age but he was also maddeningly private, with an acerbic wit. Try as he might, Dan could never get a straight answer from the man without some ordeal, riddle challenge, or long story.

He worried initially if Ben would reject his sudden appearance but soon dismissed the concern. For someone so isolated, Ben had an uncanny knowledge of current events. It was a paradox Dan had struggled to figure out for years.

He looked forward to seeing the old man. He needed Ben's Socratic wisdom to help him figure things out. A week ago, he had been contemplating an engagement and now, he was a fugitive traveling with his suicidal girlfriend and a razor-thin chance for his own survival.

He needed to clear his head, focus on the crux factors, *think globally.* The quiet woods of North Carolina would be as good a place as any.

"There," he shouted over the whine of the Bücker's engine. He pointed toward a small pasture alongside a narrow highway.

With barely a pause, Rachel cut the engine and the dusky air grew quiet, leaving only the whoosh of wind streaming by the plane's fabric fuselage. She glanced in all directions, searching for traffic on the lightly used highway below. In this heavily wooded part of the country, highways presented the only viable option for a landing spot. Seeing no traffic, Rachel settled the biplane into a quiet, steady glide. As the asphalt rushed up to meet the plane, she dropped the wing flaps. The Bücker hovered on the sudden lift for a long time before settling gently onto the paved surface. She aimed the plane toward a small clearing alongside the road and stopped.

Dan hopped out. "This is the place. Hurry! Aim for the old logging road just up there."

The two of them struggled to push the plane forward through

the underbrush to a turnoff on the old abandoned trail. When they reached the turn, they were sweating profusely and rushed to hide the brightly colored plane behind a large tangle of mountain laurel. Then they covered the fuselage with laurel branches and pine boughs, until both were satisfied that the plane was invisible from the road.

A scant minute later, a car roared past, the driver completely unaware that a vintage biplane sat parked just a few feet away in the thicket. Virtually anywhere else in the country, the Bücker would be found by some passerby within a week but the Nantahala and Cherokee Forests were some of the nation's most sparsely populated areas, unusual for a region this close to the Eastern Seaboard. This, thanks to the Cherokee's staunch protection of the sacred area.

"Don't forget the package," Dan said.

Rachel pulled out the small flask containing Esrom's gene therapy specimens and stared at him. "I may literally be holding my life in my hands. You really think I'd forget?"

"Just checking." Dan turned and headed up the fading tracks of the old road. "We've got a couple of hours' hike over rough terrain, in the dark."

"Just wonderful," Rachel muttered. "And me, wearing shorts. You sure this guy isn't going to mistake us for a bear and shoot first, ask questions later?"

Dan laughed. "I doubt you'd see Ben needlessly shooting any bear unless he intended to eat it. Besides, I suspect we'll advertise our presence soon enough. On the other hand, we should be keeping an eye out for bears."

"Oh great!" Rachel said, whispering loudly. "Yo, bear! Yo, bear."

Dan probed the thick foliage ahead with his flashlight. "I really don't think that's necessary. Black bears are typically more afraid of you than the other way around."

"Yo, bear."

An hour into their hike, Dan was beginning to worry if he had lost his way, when the gurgling of a nearby stream gave him the point of reference he needed. Suddenly, the forest opened up and several time-worn trails appeared to converge alongside a babbling brook. "We can follow this stream the rest of the way," he said cheerfully. "These trails have been traveled for centuries by the Cherokee. They're virtual footpath highways."

"Yo, bear!" Rachel muttered from behind.

As the light continued to wane, the creatures of the dark forest began their nightly symphony. The air grew still and moist as the scent of loam and humus drifted up from every footstep pressed into the forgiving moss and leaf litter. A northern saw-whet owl joined the chorus, questioning them with its long, lonely cries. Dan suddenly understood Ben's reverence for this ancient place. He could almost feel the ancestral spirits of the old forest, stone and peat sinking into his bones.

The sudden transition from chaotic city life to the deep woods seemed to cleanse away his doubts and worries. Dan stopped to take in several deep breaths, feeling the stress drain out of him like a bloodletting. Rachel shuffled to a stop behind him, her heavy breathing mingling with the concert of sounds. They stood a few moments in reverent silence before moving on.

After another hour of hiking they finally reached Ben's cabin.

It was a modest wooden shelter nestled underneath a rocky niche that looked as if it had been carved out of the mountainside by some giant whittler. Underneath a porch overhang, two windows spilled yellow light across their footpath. The trail to the porch had been worn slick through the beating of innumerable footsteps.

Wearily, Dan approached the front door and tapped lightly, hoping that he wouldn't startle the occupant. A few minutes later, the door swung open and the weathered face of Ben Proudfoot appeared.

"*Osiyo,* I am here," Dan said in a traditional greeting.

"And so you are," Ben replied. "How was the journey?" He turned and left the door open behind him as if he had been expecting them for hours. "I've made you both a hot bowl of ramp soup, some chestnut bread, and two cups of sassafras tea."

Dan and Rachel dropped their bags at the foot of Ben's doorway and entered the modest room.

Just as Ben had said, there were two steaming pottery bowls resting on a huge table in the center of the room. Sawed from a single slab of wood, the table had been taken from the heart of an ancient and twisted tree trunk, its surface polished smooth through years of use.

"Ben, how the hell did you know we were coming?" Dan said. "You're impossible to reach on a good day."

Ben Proudfoot cackled as he poured himself a cup of tea. "My friend, your nickname betrays you. *Mouse,* you are not. You two stomped and stumbled your way through the forest. Bear and coyote both complained of your disturbance. Owl's eyes were crossed when he finally announced your arrival."

Rachel chuckled awkwardly at Ben's flowery language and Dan realized that in all the time he'd known her, she had never met Ben Proudfoot personally.

They both sat down at the long table and Dan reached for her hand. "Don't worry, you'll get used to Ben's Tonto shtick soon enough. He does it as a subtle insult to the white man."

Ben stared at the two of them, his face stricken, hand over heart. "Dan, you wound me with your insults. Tonto was a Mohawk, born in Ontario, Canada. Went by the stage name of Jay Silverheels, if I remember correctly, though his real name was simply Jay Smith."

Ben still moved lithely for an old man, kept fit by endless scrambling over Blue Ridge granite. He ladled himself a generous portion of ramp soup, grabbed it and his tea, and silently slid into his usual spot at the far end of the long table. "Jay was a good lacrosse player though. Just don't get me started on Johnny Depp's version."

That was the way it had always been with the old man. Riddles and twisted humor. Dan grinned and took a sip of ramp soup. It had a strong but mellow tone of wild onions, somewhere between the flavor of leeks and garlic. The soup's complexity was hard to describe, with hints of herbal spice, musky notes of mushroom, and a meaty, nutty overtone. Beads of fat hovered on its surface like jewels.

Rachel relished her bowl, taking in generous spoonfuls. Dan considered that a huge compliment to Ben, considering Rachel's Italian roots. She considered herself somewhat of a connoisseur.

"Ben, this soup is incredible," she said with another slurp. "What is in this?"

"Just what nature deigned to provide," Ben said. "Bounty from the yard and stream below."

"Well, like what?" Rachel probed. "I see the ramps, incredible flavor, like leeks on steroids, and I see some watercress for spice, and mushrooms, but the broth, mmm, such a musky flavor. And what are the small white pieces of meat?"

Dan watched with amusement as a familiar quixotic expression formed on Ben's face. It was one he had seen many times before as a recipient.

Ben's face went completely still. "Does the fawn ask the doe where the milk comes from? Or does it suckle gratefully at the teat?"

Rachel stared blankly, unsure exactly how to respond. She gave Dan a quick, desperate glance, to which he simply shrugged and smiled. *This one's on you,* he thought.

She grinned sheepishly and apparently decided to hold her ground. "Yeah, this fawn would like to know, if that's okay."

Ben smiled. "Well you are right about the herbs. Also a little juniper and orange sumac for spice. The white meat is tail of crawdaddy, pulled from the stream this morning."

"Wow crawfish; it's really good, Ben," she said as she examined the contents as if to decipher a hidden code. "I can't place the broth or the little brown nuggets, though."

Ben ladled another generous portion of soup into Rachel's bowl, filling it to the brim. "I'm glad you like it. The thin white slices are swamp potato. The broth comes from possum, a little heavy for most people but the grease makes a fine base in small quantities. Provides mouth feel, wouldn't you agree? Oh, and those brown nuggets are sautéed yellow jacket grubs. I found a large nest at the bottom of the trail this morning. Better to nourish our souls than to torment our skin." Ben smiled and sat back in his chair, watching as Rachel hesitantly raised another spoonful to her mouth.

She stared at it for a moment, closed her eyes, and swallowed.

An awkward silence fell over the room. Ben appeared to relish the discomfort of his young guest. Dan held back a chuckle, remembering the many awkward lessons he had learned from his mentor in the past.

Meanwhile, he sipped the sassafras tea, relishing the tart and tingly flavor. It was pungent but not sweet, unlike its oversaturated commercial abomination, that most people knew as root beer.

AFTER EVERYONE HAD had their fill, Ben collected the bowls and washed them in the sink. Once dried, he put them away in cabinets, each item with its own specific place to occupy.

Meanwhile, Dan signaled to Rachel to sit quietly, to take in the moment.

When Ben was done, he sat back down at the long table and studied his two guests. After a long pause he spoke. "So tell me, how long will your treatment take?"

Dan and Rachel stared at each other. "You mean Rachel's treatment?"

Ben expressed a subtle and knowing smile. "Mouse, unless you have some other treatment which coyote has failed to tell me about."

"It's true," Dan said. "Rachel has a treatment that may endanger her life but may also save it. We need up to a week to find out."

Ben nodded so subtly that Dan was unsure if the movement was intended.

"Then my house is yours," Ben said. "I have already prepared the room next to mine for your visit. You must forgive the accommodations. It is my library. I don't receive many visitors here."

Rachel interjected, "Anything is fine. Your hospitality is appreciated."

"And Fawn, I wish you the best outcome," Ben said, with a faint smile.

Another awkward silence permeated the room and Dan decided it was time to end the evening. He stood and said flatly, "Show us to our room."

Ben stood up and directed them toward one of only two doors in the cabin, which led to a small space, the walls covered with shelves and books and a makeshift bed placed in its center. Ben directed them into the cramped room. "Mouse, I'm afraid you will have to use the floor, as this space only has room for a single bed. During Fawn's illness, you may sleep in the main room."

Dan nodded and Ben left. "Let me get our things," he said. He retrieved their knapsacks and Rachel's therapy, placing them carefully in one corner of the room.

"Tomorrow," Dan said.

"Tomorrow." Rachel nodded. "Can you squeeze into this bed with me tonight? I don't want to be alone."

Dan smiled a Ben-like smile and saying nothing, slipped silently onto the platform that had been woven from a number of young maple saplings. He snuggled up to Rachel's backside and spooned her for the rest of the night.

For the first time in a week, Dan slept deeply.

THE NEXT MORNING, Dan was awakened by the clang of pots and pans and the faint smell of burning wood. The room was faintly lit by the predawn light. He and Rachel were entangled on the tiny bed and when he attempted to pull away, Rachel stirred and turned to face him.

She tucked her head under his chin. "Good morning."

"How did you sleep?" he said.

"Fitfully, at first," she replied. "But once you warmed me up, I fell into a sleep coma. I dreamed we were sailing the Greek isles together and diving on old wrecks."

Dan decided not to share his own dreams with her. He had dreamed that Rachel had slipped out during the night and disappeared. It had disturbed him so much that he woke up, only to find her body spooned tightly against his. He had dropped back to sleep almost immediately. Now, he pulled her close and squeezed, thankful that she had chosen to stick around.

They both reluctantly struggled out of bed, dressed, and entered the main room. Ben was stirring a large pot of something on the vintage wood stove.

Rachel approached and peered over Ben's shoulder as he stirred the mix. The pot was filled with a large mass of corn kernels suspended in what looked like dirty water. Ben continued to stir the mixture patiently.

"Ooh, what is that?" Rachel asked, her nose wrinkling at the smoky smell. "It looks like corn boiling in mud."

Ben ignored Rachel's curiosity. Dan watched from a distance, struggling to hold back a grin. Apparently, Rachel had not learned her lesson yet. Another Ben Proudfoot "learning moment" appeared to be imminent.

Without a word, Ben dipped out a spoonful of the dark, smoky liquid, offering it up to Rachel to taste. Her curiosity getting the best of her, she slurped a mouthful of liquid and immediately regretted it. She rushed to the door and forcibly spit the concoction out into the yard. "Yuck! What *was* that? It tastes like ashes from a fire!"

"Good guess, Fawn," Ben said without taking his attention away from the mixture. "I rinsed the ashes from the stove this morning to make this mixture."

"What?" Rachel's expression changed from surprise to disgust. "That's basically lye. My mouth is burning."

"Good," Ben said, a faint smile barely present on his face. "That means the strength is proper."

"Yeah but lye is poisonous!"

"Ah, and so is water," Ben replied. "If one drinks too much, and yet, in the proper proportion, it is essential to life."

Rachel returned to the door and spit again, trying to extricate the remaining harsh liquid from her mouth. "I don't get it. Why would you cook corn in that mess?"

Ben remained silent, his only acknowledgment of her question being a faint smile and a barely perceptible hum of music. Finally, he said, "We use wood ash to strip away the pericarp from the kernel."

"Why don't you just grind it?"

"Because . . ." Ben continued to stir the mixture. "The corn needs the nutritive value of nixtamalization."

"*Nicks* what?" Rachel was clearly becoming irritated by Ben's obtuse references.

Ben turned to look at Dan with an innocent expression. "I assumed your friend Rachel was conversant with biological terms. Nixtamalization is the unfolding of protein molecules by the use of a strong base solution."

Dan simply smiled and shrugged his shoulders, casting an amused glance Rachel's way.

Rachel did a double take and shook her head. "Say what?"

Ben finally turned and looked directly at Rachel, his expression indecipherable. "Rachel, as you probably know, corn lacks gluten, the protein that allows wheat to form an elastic dough. When we treat corn with an alkaline like wood ash, we break down the cellulose in the hull, emulsify the corn oil, and make the proteins bioavailable. Only then can we make a dough for bean bread. You know, nixtamalization."

"Well, I'm a microbiologist, not a nutritionist."

"Shall I give you the Cherokee explanation?" Ben continued stirring. "What is wood ash but the soul of a tree? The tree? A child of the soil. Like the corn plant. Nature provides us with all that we need to live and prosper. The wood ash also removes toxins from the corn, important here in the mountains where corn rust is common. Alas, the white man never learned to appreciate the language of nature. White settlers ignored the Cherokee tradition of treating the corn properly, relying instead on their old habits of crushing the raw corn with their grinding stones, leaving the meal in an infant state and poisoned with mycotoxins. Their vastly inferior product led to outbreaks of pellagra, a horrible disease of malnutrition."

Ben finally stopped stirring and removed the pot from the flames. "Cherokees never suffered from pellagra, because we understood the corn. That is, until the white man forced his stone-ground garbage on us. Only then did our culture begin to suffer health problems and obesity. That's why I prefer the old ways, because our ancestors *listened* to the corn."

Ben picked up the pot and moved toward the door. He nodded at Rachel, who opened the door for him. "I'll return, once the maize has been properly rinsed."

Once Ben had left, Rachel turned to Dan. "Your friend is starting to get on my nerves. Just because I'm a marine biologist doesn't mean I know nutritional biology. Who uses wood ashes to cook with, anyway? Is he a man of the past or the present?"

"I'd say both," Dan replied. "Ben is a traditionalist but he also has two doctorates in math and complexity. My advice is to follow his lead and just *listen*. I promise, you'll learn a lot."

Rachel stared at him silently, finally raising her hands. "Okay. Fine. Consider me properly dressed down. I'll keep my mouth shut."

"Not necessary. Just listen and keep an open mind. Ben will be insulted if you refuse to interact."

"Whatever." Rachel crossed her arms and dropped onto Ben's simple couch, made of gnarly logs and thatched with rushes.

After Ben returned from the stream, he took the drained maize and mashed it into a paste in his ancient mortar and pestle. He mixed the paste with cooked bean curd and flattened the dough into what he called broadswords. Then, he wrapped the patties in leaves and boiled them in a pot.

The resulting dumplings had a mild, nutty taste that went well with a stew of smoked rabbit that Ben had also prepared. After the meal, Ben said to Rachel: "Fawn, keep these dumplings by your bed during your treatment. They are easy to digest and will give you vital nutrition for your recovery."

Rachel accepted the basket of wrapped dumplings and said, "Thanks, Ben." She glanced tentatively at Dan. "I really do appreciate your hospitality, and the dumplings and stew were great, despite the wood ashes." She grinned coquettishly.

Ben smiled back. "Bean bread is like a wart. Not pretty but it grows on you."

They all laughed.

After several cups of sassafras tea, Dan looked at Rachel. "You ready?"

She shrugged. "As I'll ever be."

The two of them headed toward the bedroom.

"Good luck!" Ben said.

DAN PULLED OUT the flask and placed it on a wooden table alongside the bed. Inside, Esrom's potential cure loomed like a weapon. Dan pulled out the copious notes he had taken on his phone during his meeting with Esrom and read through them carefully. The experimental gene therapy treatment had never been tested on humans. It consisted of two biological agents:

The first agent was a powerful endocrine disrupter designed to shut down Rachel's immune system to prevent it from interfering with the second agent, the infectious one, an adenovirus genetically altered to reprogram Rachel's body.

Dan removed the first syringe from the cooler and cradled it reverently, glancing at an expectant Rachel. "Esrom said to inject this four hours in advance of the second treatment, which will be much worse. You'll feel like you've contracted the flu from hell. It will take several days for you to recover. Are you sure you're ready?"

She nodded and rolled up her sleeve.

Dan removed the guard from the end of the needle and held it forward. He hesitated for a moment before quickly injecting the solution into Rachel's arm.

She leaned back on the bed, awaiting some transformational event that never happened. There was no immediate effect, no drastic result. Only a subtle and gradual change inside her body as the suppressant disabled her immune cells, preparing the gene therapy for a devastating and total infection.

The air in the room grew stale. The two of them stared at each other in anticipation. Dan took Rachel's hand and squeezed.

The next few hours crept by slowly. They talked about the past and their adventures together. They discussed the many possible futures that might lie ahead for them if the cure worked. They discussed

Rachel's dream of sailing the Greek isles together. They joked and reminisced.

Finally, the one looming subject that had been avoided became too forceful to avoid.

"You must promise me this," Rachel said, gripping his hand more tightly than ever. "If this doesn't work, you must let me deal with the alternative in my own way. That means alone. Okay?"

Dan stared at her, a wave of sorrow and desire flooding over him. He felt an unbearable desire to be at her side, no matter what, but he also realized she would not tolerate his presence if she experienced a loss of mental control.

Reluctantly, he nodded. "So, how are we going to know for sure if the cure worked?"

"I'll just have to get retested."

"Do we even know if a standard Huntington's test will be accurate, after your genes have been altered?"

That thought had never occurred to her and she shrugged her shoulders.

"Then, you must promise *me* something," Dan replied. "You won't do anything rash or sudden until we know your diagnosis for certain. That means real physical evidence, agreed?"

Rachel stared out the window for a time, then back to him. "Okay, definitive proof."

The final hour crawled by at an agonizingly slow pace.

Finally, the time had come. Dan pulled out the active pathogen and stared at it, struggling to recall Esrom Nesson's description of the cure. Presumably, inside the innocent-looking syringe was an adenovirus, similar to a common cold, that had been altered, not only to inject a new strand of DNA but to cut an existing one.

The Huntington's gene consisted of several repeated DNA structures known as a trinucleotide repeat, which in turn made the "huntingtin" protein, essential to normal health. If the chain of repeats grew too long, the resulting protein that it produced would be defective and cause progressive dementia.

Rachel inherited her defective repeating gene from her father and it was her agonizing experience caring for him that had hardened her resolve against anyone going through the same progressive dementia on her behalf.

In order to work, the adenovirus had to infect the majority of Rachel's cells, slicing her long DNA repeats into more normal lengths, thereby allowing the production of normal huntingtin protein. But to do that, her immune system had to be turned off, by the suppressant. Until its effect wore off after a few days, Rachel would be vulnerable to even the slightest infection. She would need isolation and that would be the most difficult adjustment for Dan to make.

Dan hesitated, his hand shaking.

"Here, let me," Rachel said. She grabbed the syringe from his hand and thrust the needle nonchalantly into her arm. "I want this to be over with . . ."

RUDI PLIMPTON WAS down to his last bag of junk food when a knock came at the door of his hotel room. He had been deep diving into background on the security firm TaurusSec and getting to know the other members of the Firemen group, who had welcomed him into the fold. He'd even reverse engineered his new private black phone, just to understand how it worked and was quite impressed.

He had always been a loner. There just weren't very many other geeks who could appreciate his old-world approach to programming.

But these "phone phreaks" in the Firemen group were different. They were just as offbeat as he was, and seemed excited by his low-level assembler programming abilities. After all, phones were power hungry. A few well-placed assembler routines could pump up performance a lot. Some of the phreaks in the group had even managed to impress him with their "leet skillz," especially in the mobile arena, which was hard to do. Rudi wasn't often impressed.

He finished downloading an employee roster from the TaurusSec corporate server, which had been mildly challenging to breach, and then got up to answer the door. There was a fancy cloth-covered cart like the ones the hotel used for room service.

Only, he hadn't ordered any room service.

Rudi glanced down the hallway in both directions but saw no one. Must have been a mistaken delivery or the person got tired of waiting. Curious to see what some neighbor had ordered, Rudi lifted the circular cover off the tray to take a look. There was a fancy cellophane-wrapped plate of cookies or some such, and a card attached to a holder.

He picked it up and read it.

With our compliments, please accept these Savannah specialties, Pecan Praline Surprise.

Yours truly: the hotel and staff.

Perfect timing. He was starting to get peckish.

Rudi grabbed the plate and left the cart and serving tray outside by the door. He unwrapped the package and bit into one of the heavenly smelling pralines. They were soft, rich, with a deep caramel flavor that melted in his mouth. In other words, fantastic.

He scarfed down the first one, felt his stomach growl, and went for seconds. For reasons he could only imagine, he'd always been able to eat incredible amounts of junk food without gaining much weight, probably due to his high metabolism.

It wasn't Rudi's nature to feel any guilt with these things, so a few minutes later, he bit into praline number three, amazed at the strangely addictive flavor.

29

Dan found himself at a loss, not sure how to proceed. Rachel was in Ben's back room, isolated, suffering the effects of Esrom's gene therapy and there was nothing he could do about it. He could hear the occasional moan and wretch of dry heaves, and yet Esrom had advised him to have minimal contact with her during the initial phases, when her immune system was at its weakest. Even a harmless cold or infection combined with the adenovirus that was currently ravaging her body could prove fatal. He had to fight an almost irresistible urge to be by her side.

Worse still, he wasn't quite sure what to do about the Horsemen. After their adventure at Hunter Army Airfield, he was quite sure Bradley Gruber would be reporting to his bosses, whoever they were.

He had recounted the entire story behind the Firemen and Horsemen to Ben over the past two days, in hopes of gaining some insight or advice but Ben had simply smiled and listened, seeming to be barely surprised by any of his revelations.

He already knew what lengths these powerful men would stoop to, against a perceived enemy.

And the FBI? He had to assume that the pressure was off there.

But what now? He felt isolated, disconnected from the world. That was the downside of Ben's obscure compound, the isolation cut both ways. There was no internet, no TV, no Wi-Fi, phone, or other means of communication. He had no way to check in with Rudi, or Stoker, or Vince.

And yet, Ben always seemed to have a bizarre ability to keep up with current events. When asked about it, Ben would claim an owl or thunderbird had whispered messages in his ear. Dan had always tolerated Ben's Cherokee myths, thinking them harmless but now he was in a bad situation that required accurate facts and intel.

He needed answers.

Dan had a suspicion about Ben's secret thunderbird. That morning, while sleeping on the living room floor, he had been in that strange purgatory between fitful sleep and wakefulness, when he thought he'd heard Ben talking to someone in the unique rhythmical tongue of native Cherokee. There was only one phrase he recognized: *do-na-da-go-hvi,* which meant *till we meet again,* since the Cherokee had no real word for the concept of goodbye.

But who was Ben talking to, and how? The rest of the conversation was just a singsong pattern of meaningless phrases. Not many people in the world besides the Snowbird clan still spoke native, old-world Cherokee. They might as well be speaking in code, much like the Navajo code talkers in World War Two, who used their unique language to communicate between American troops in the Pacific. The Japanese never managed to decode the language due to its strange syntax and obscurity.

Despite his isolation, Ben Proudfoot was connected, somehow.

It was the only thing that made sense, unless he wanted to believe in myths and little people, the *Nunnehi,* or leprechauns.

Dan struggled out of the bed and rose precariously. His first instinct was to crack the door to Rachel's room and check on her. What he saw was a tangled bundle of bedsheets, the scribblings of a restless night. But he could see her chest rising and falling rhythmically.

Rachel was still alive.

Hearing Dan's stirring, Ben appeared at the door to his room and moved into the living room and to the old woodstove, to stoke the fire.

Dan quietly closed the door to Rachel's room and joined Ben, who had shoved several split logs into the firebox of the old iron antique. Despite the heat of summer, the deep woods of the Snowbird Mountains still offered chilly mornings and the warmth of the fire radiating from the stove felt welcome and calming.

"So, how is the fawn this morning?" Ben asked. "Is she weathering the storm?"

"I don't know," Dan said. "She's sleeping."

Almost on cue, they heard the sound of retching from Rachel's room, along with a string of curse words.

Dan headed back to the door, cracked it open. "You okay?"

"No!" She retched again, her head hanging over an antique basket that one of Ben's ancestors probably wove a hundred years ago. Thankfully, it had been lined with a garbage bag. "I'm sick of being sick," she said between heaves. "Just kill me now and get it *over* with!"

Dan instinctively moved into the room.

"*Don't* come in," she said, retching again, accompanied by a long moan. "I don't want you to see me this way . . ."

"Okay, I understand," he said and backed slowly out of the room. "Esrom did say to maintain a quarantine but *please*, let me know if things get serious."

"Why?" she said, wiping her mouth with a tissue. She struggled up from the basket and collapsed on the bed, turning her back to him.

Dan rejoined Ben in the living room. He was in the midst of preparing fried bean bread and oats for breakfast.

"The little fawn has lost her way?" Ben asked while whipping up a batter of bread, fortified with a generous slurry of mashed beans.

"She's suffering," he said. "I'm worried. She seems to be getting worse, not better."

"After breakfast," Ben said, "you will join me on a journey to find a remedy."

Dan shook his head. "No, I need to stay here."

Ben's brow furrowed. "And do what?"

"I don't know, support her, help her?"

"How can you help?"

"What if she gets worse?" Dan replied.

"Yes," Ben said. "What would you do? We're in the middle of the wilderness."

"I can't just leave her here alone."

"Why not?" Ben stirred his batter of bean bread. "Are you staying for her, or yourself? What can you do? We are miles from the nearest hospital. What sickness would you describe to a doctor? Go with me instead, to find something to truly help her."

He knew Ben was right. He needed to detach his emotions and think logically. "What are we looking for?"

"An old Cherokee remedy," Ben said. "It should help."

After breakfast, the two of them left the cabin and ventured out onto the ancient trails formed by Cherokee footfalls over thousands of years. They walked slowly but deliberately, the crunch of dried leaves and twigs coming mostly from Dan's boots. Somehow Ben managed to maneuver silently over the very same detritus.

Every few minutes, Ben would stop, smell the air, bend down, and pick some strange herb or mushroom, which he would then place in a small woven basket.

The huge stands of Fraser fir, oak, hemlock, chestnut, and pine had a primeval quality, their towering branches strangling the light like an insidious net. The forest remained in an eternal dusk. Ben had once described the Cherokee word "Nantahala" to mean "land of the noonday sun," since that was the only time when the sun's rays would reach the forest floor.

Suddenly, Ben stopped, raised his head to sniff the air. "Smell that? Cucumber. The *Nunnehi* are near and so is our target."

Dan shook his head and grinned. "So your Cherokee leprechauns are guiding us now?" He never knew quite when to take Ben seriously.

"Don't call them that," Ben whispered. "You'll scare them away. They would be insulted by such a comparison."

Dan sniffed the air. He did sense a faint, plantlike smell, more like watermelon than cucumber but sloughed it off as simply the power of suggestion.

Ben approached a large spruce tree, its branches turning brown at the tip. "This is it." He smiled.

A huge round fungus gall hung from the branches. Dan would have mistaken it as a hornet's nest due to its size and shape.

"What the heck is that?"

"We call them tree biscuits, an old medicine used to treat small-pox and many other illnesses." Ben pulled out a knife and sliced off a large portion from the bottom of the oval mass, stuffing it into his basket. "The formal name is agarikon or *fomitopsis officinalis*. It is a parasite, much like your nemesis the Horsemen. It steals the hard-earned nourishment from the fir tree, gives nothing back, and causes this spruce to eventually wither and die." Ben patted the trunk of the tree affectionately. "We exact our revenge on the tree biscuit by harvesting it to maintain our health. Even parasites have a function in nature, so long as their power is limited." Satisfied, Ben turned and headed back down the trail, padding quietly while Dan rushed noisily to catch up.

Back in the cabin, Ben began carefully mixing the herbs and tree biscuits together in a pot to steep, then he poured a dark brown liquid into a mug and handed it to Dan. "Give this to Rachel and make sure she drinks it all. It will not be pleasant."

Dan waved a whiff of steam into his nose. It smelled musky, like the earth. "Great. Can we cool it off a bit?" Ben poured a bit of cold water into the mix and Dan headed to Rachel's room, tapping lightly on the door.

A weak voice filtered out. "Yeah, I'm awake."

He walked in and was immediately taken aback by her appearance. She was pale, with dark rings under her eyes and sweating profusely. She pulled the sheets up defensively and shuddered with chills.

She saw the look on his face and turned away. "This sucks. I *hate* being sick."

"Are you okay?" he said.

"Nope. Feel like crap. I keep going back and forth between the chills and the sweats. My stomach feels a little better though."

"Good, because Ben cooked up a potion for you that he warns isn't the best tasting in the world."

She rolled away from him. "Not interested. Just let me grind it out."

"You sure you'll make it? Ben insists this will help and it looks like you need all the help you can get."

Rachel rolled back over, sighed. "Well, if it will shut you up . . ." She held out a trembling hand.

"Sit up first," he said in the most comforting tone he could manage. She did as he asked and Dan handed her the mug. "Might want to down it pretty fast."

She stared at the brown liquid and crinkled her nose. "You sure this is safe?"

Dan couldn't help but chuckle. "Compared to what you're going through, does it really matter?"

"Good point," she said and downed the cup in one long swig. Her face rolled up into a ball of wrinkles. "God, that's bitter!" She shook her head in disgust. "That makes me wanna puke."

"Try to resist, if you can. I'd hate to have to make another mug of this stuff."

Rachel rolled back over and pulled the sheets tight around her and let out a low moan. "I'll try."

He left her alone and returned to the living room, where Ben was sitting calmly.

"How's the patient?" he said.

"I'm worried, Ben. Frankly, she looks terrible. Maybe this wasn't a good idea."

"As opposed to what?" Ben said. "A slow and painful death?"

Dan collapsed into a chair, a rush of exhaustion taking over his body.

They both sat quietly for a long time, listening to the sounds of the forest outside and the occasional cough or moan that would filter out of Rachel's room.

FACED WITH NOTHING to do but wait, Dan's mind grew restless and pensive. Ben wasn't one for small talk and Dan wasn't quite sure what to talk about anyway.

He was trapped in the middle of nowhere, feeling helpless and insignificant. He *hoped* that Ben's elixir would help Rachel. He *hoped* she could weather the biological storm raging inside her body. He *hoped* he would forge a plan to handle the Horsemen and his newfound status with the Firemen. He *hoped* there would be a future with Rachel.

Hope. He hated it, preferring certainty or anger and the false sense of control it offered. Anything but this shallow feeling of victimization that came with passivity. He wanted to scream, yell, beat someone up, exact revenge for his suffering.

He wanted to be back in control.

And then he looked over at Ben, so calm and self-assured, a man who had spent his life bearing the lost hopes and dreams of his entire culture on his shoulders. Ben didn't complain, pout, or lose control.

Dan stared at the old Cherokee, who returned his gaze with liquid eyes, cool and calm and reassuring. It seemed as if Ben Proudfoot could peer through the veil of chaos obscuring the world and find the real truth.

"How do you do it?" Dan asked bluntly.

"Do what?" Ben said.

"Remain so calm? Stay informed when you're isolated out here?"

Ben's expression took on a quixotic air. He appeared to be struggling to suppress a smile. "The answers are all around you, if you look closely."

Dan shook his head. "Please, can we dispense with the Socratic Cherokee shtick for once? I need answers, not mysteries."

"Listen to me carefully." Ben leaned forward, his eyes drilling into him. "Do you think I possess all the answers to your problems? That I'm some magical shaman whose wisdom you can tap at your convenience? Wisdom is earned, not donated."

Dan returned Ben's gaze, the old Cherokee and visionary professor, the man who had inspired him in his youth. Ben suddenly seemed foreign and aloof, an alien he didn't recognize.

"Look, I'm sorry. I just want a chance to live my life, like anyone else. Embrace the time I have on this earth and share it with the woman I love. Is that too much to ask?"

"No, it's not," Ben replied. "But that's a journey you must travel yourself. There are no shortcuts."

Dan sank into his chair and considered the situation. A mysterious and powerful cabal of people pursued him, people with revenge on their minds.

"How do I become invisible in this modern digital world? Surely you have advice on that."

"First, pay attention," Ben said, his expression softening. "Become hypersensitive to your surroundings. Avoid all digital devices." Ben waved his arm around the room. "It's still possible to stay informed with analog electronics, because they receive but cannot transmit. Digital devices are programmable, capable of remote control. With a two-way system, there is no guarantee of safety."

Ben stood up and walked into his bedroom, prompting Dan to follow. He picked up a small carved ornament from his nightstand and placed it against the frame of a bookshelf. An almost imperceptible click prompted a movement of the shelf. Ben swung it out on hinges, revealing a niche six feet deep. Inside was a shortwave radio and an old tube television, festooned with rabbit ears that had crumpled wads of aluminum foil hanging from their tips.

"Meet my thunderbird," Ben said flatly.

Dan stared at the tangle of electronics and black wires, hooked up to a bank of lithium batteries. "So, you *were* talking to someone this morning."

"Have I said anything to the contrary?"

Dan laughed. "No, I guess not." He entered the small niche and ran his hands across the controls of the radio. "How long have you had a ham operator's license?"

"I've had the Extra Class License since 2000. One of the great American laws that have languished in obscurity. Shortwave radio still remains one of the great communication protocols. I can reach friends globally and it's secure, as long as the language is encrypted."

"Right," Dan said, grinning. "Cherokee, obscure for most listeners."

"There are subtle advantages to our historical culture." Ben ushered Dan out of the niche and closed the hidden door, directing Dan back into the main room. "Let's discuss your future." Ben settled back into his carved wooden chair. "How do you plan to protect yourself against these Horsemen?"

Dan thought for a moment. "I don't know. According to the Firemen, the Horsemen are rich and powerful, with access to social media, cell phone communications, digital tracking. If a person has a normal digital footprint, their movements, location, and current activities are known. I must assume the same applies to us, once we leave this safe haven."

"And so, how to become invisible?" Ben asked.

Dan paused again. "I don't know. Change names? My black phone gives me some anonymity but it still requires Wi-Fi to be functional, so I can't travel far from civilization."

"We can solve that problem temporarily," Ben replied. "What else?"

Dan was at a loss. "How can any ordinary person defend himself from such power?"

Ben stared back with that expectant look, one that demanded answers from the student. "Why do you think the indigenous peoples of Turtle Island fell so easily to the white man after surviving for generations?"

Dan knew many details, having learned them over the years from Ben and others. The Clovis people had migrated to their so-called "Turtle Island" over thirty thousand years ago. That made the indigenous peoples of the Americas one of the oldest continuous and peaceful cultures on Earth. Meanwhile, tribes of Neanderthals and humans battled it out across the European continent, trading one surviving culture for another.

"Well?" Ben continued to stare blankly.

Dan suspected it was a trick question but he gave it a stab. "Of course smallpox had a lot to do with it. An invasive illness for which Amerindians had no natural immunity. It killed over ninety percent of the population."

Ben's patient solemnity told him it was the wrong answer.

"Then, there was the Mediterranean advantage," he continued. "Eurasians had the benefit of a huge coastal area with abundant wildlife and domesticated beasts of burden. Amerindians had no horses, pigs, cattle, or other domesticated livestock to make life and survival easier. They lacked sufficient free time for discourse, study, arts, and science."

Again, Ben frowned at his failure to see the obvious. "Those facts are only partly true, *and* the white man was in a foreign land with few resources against a much larger, mature force that knew the land."

"So what else is there?" Dan hated the look of disappointment Ben could wield so effectively.

Ben paused, the silence deafening. "Think of your complexity training," he finally said with a sigh.

Dan thought through the seven fundamental tenets of Syncrenomics, Ben's doctoral thesis. Feedback Loops, the Butterfly Effect, the Fractal Universe, the Interconnected Hive, the Unexpected Trickster, Truth Radiates from the Center, *Balance of Opposition*.

"The white invaders' behavior was unconstrained," Dan finally blurted.

Ben smiled. "Good guess, Mouse. Balance is lost when feedback loops are unconstrained."

Dan didn't quite get it. "I don't see how that weakens your strength against the white man."

"Think slowly," Ben said. "Amerindians lived in peace with Mother Earth. Our customs, sacred beliefs, and the lessons of our ancestors had allowed us to thrive for thirty thousand years in balance with nature. Then, the white man arrived with no loyalty to these sacred lands, no centuries of tradition and culture to protect, no sacred values to cherish from their ancestors. The white man was free to behave without honor or principle in this foreign land. Even the constraints of their own God could be ignored, since the white man considered us savages, exempt from the protection of Christian values. Meanwhile, the Cherokees honored their sacred ancestral values by sticking to their word, attempting treaties with the white man to protect the land.

Meanwhile, white soldiers betrayed the treaties, killed our women and children, poisoned our villages with smallpox-laced blankets, razed our sacred forests, poisoned our streams. The white culture is a parasite race, stealing generations of wisdom from other cultures and re-purposing them for their own use."

"Imagine two pugilists," Ben continued, his eyes afire. "One boxer is a gentleman of European society, constrained by the Marquess of Queensberry Rules. The other is a common street fighter. Which one has the advantage?"

"Obviously the street fighter," Dan said.

"Why?"

Dan finally understood. It hit him like a stick upside the head. "Because the street fighter is not constrained by the rules and traditions of orderly society. He has no loyalty to that orderly society, so he's free to use more diverse and creative tactics."

Ben's look of satisfaction told Dan he was on the right track, yet it posed another question, the typical result of most of Ben's riddles. "So what the hell does that have to do with the Horsemen?"

"Think, Mouse. What one thing must the Horsemen protect at all costs?"

Dan thought for a moment. "Their power and influence? Wealth and assets? Strategic knowledge? Secrecy?"

"All of those. When the Horsemen come after you—and they will—they will threaten your most precious possessions. You must be willing to act with unconstrained fierceness, against their most valued assets. You must be the street fighter, or you will lose."

BEFORE DAYBREAK, AN owl's screech awakened Dan from an early morning dream. He moved slowly in the chilly air of the Nantahala morning, as the forest awakened to the stirrings of life. His night had been restless, filled with chaotic imagery, memories of Rachel, pushing fate to the edge, of Ada Kurz, her life ebbing before him, flames engulfing the arrogance of Bradley Gruber and his ilk.

He jerked up in bed, startled by a sudden presence in the room. Backlit by dawn-light, he saw Rachel's profile glowing like an apparition in the corner of the room.

"Are you okay?" Dan blurted. "You startled me."

For the first time since their reunion, Rachel's expression seemed relaxed and familiar. "Yeah. I feel pretty damn good, actually. Seems like Ben's pukey elixir worked." She grinned mischievously.

Wiping the sleep from his eyes, Dan struggled out of his bedroll and moved to her side. He grabbed her in a solid embrace, one she returned without hesitation. He squeezed tightly. "I knew you'd make it, you stubborn girl."

"Hey, there's no guarantee it worked," she said. "Only that I survived the treatment."

"Until we know," he said, "let's assume it worked."

"Fine. I'm famished."

Another shadow crossed the room. Ben Proudfoot stood at the doorway of his bedroom, staring at the two of them expectantly. "Crisis averted, I assume?" He grinned. "Fawn, it seems your spots are fading."

Rachel attempted a rough curtsy. "Why thank you, medicine man. I can't say much about the flavor of your elixir but it seemed to work."

"Medicine is not meant to be enjoyed," Ben said with a twinkle in his eye. "It is Mother Nature's reminder to live a more wholesome life."

Rachel rolled her eyes and grinned. "Well, then tell Momma Nature to quit giving me such crappy genes in the first place."

"Point taken," Ben said. "Breakfast?" He moved to the kitchen and stoked the fire in the old stove. Minutes later, a smoky aroma permeated the room as Ben began to prepare a proper Cherokee breakfast, complete with bean bread, eggs, and fried venison. As he worked, the old man hummed a rhythmic tune, steeped in centuries of tradition.

Dan's attention was focused primarily on Rachel. She moved tentatively across the room, testing her energy and strength. Her gait was weak and uncertain but determined. He moved behind her and wrapped his arms around her waist. "How do you feel?"

"A little weak," she conceded. "But compared to how I felt yesterday?" She grinned. "I feel incredible!"

He squeezed tighter and she let herself lean back, relying on his body for support. "Thank you for believing in me," she whispered.

"Always," he said.

After a hearty breakfast, the three of them sat in the living room and considered their options.

Dan went first. "Unlike Chemerra, the Horsemen know my identity. If they are as vindictive as we believe, then I'm a marked man."

He stared at Rachel. "It worries me that you will get caught up in this intrigue. I'm wondering if you should go out on your own, distance yourself from me, at least until we know where I stand against these thugs."

Rachel frowned. "Really? You don't think these assholes know about me and our relationship? If you think I can escape your sphere of influence, you're wrong. We're in this together, whether you like it or not. We fight together."

Ben spoke: "Fawn is right. These men will look for any way to access your vulnerability. That includes threatening the ones you love. Your bond with each other has become inseparable from the threat against you."

Dan had to admit, they were both right. But before they could proceed, he needed the lay of the land and that was impossible while isolated in the wilderness. "I need to touch base with Rudi and Vince. We can't stumble into a situation blind."

"I agree," Ben said. "For that, you will need to travel to a friend's house. There is no digital access in these deep woods but I can send you somewhere to connect to Wi-Fi via your black phone. Go and sniff the air. Get the lay of the land, then we can form a plan."

By midmorning, Dan had ventured out into the deep forest, following Ben's directions carefully. He traveled along ancient game trails laid down centuries ago. It was tough going at times, the trail often obscured by the inevitable march of time and undergrowth. He found himself lost on several occasions, having to rely on Chemerra's black phone for GPS positioning. It was a reality of the future that one was never truly isolated anymore, with the existence of satellites. But since there was no two-way communication, there was no way to track the receiving device.

After several route adjustments Dan found himself at a small clearing behind a modern house, one of Ben's neighbors. Caught between two cultures, the Snowbirds straddled both the modern world and their ancestral heritage. Dan chose not to disturb the family, hovering in the woods within range of the home's Wi-Fi. He used the password Ben had given him to connect.

The Wi-Fi icon on the black phone lit up. He first checked the local news. A GBI and FBI investigation was underway to investigate a mysterious armed drone connected to the murders of Ada Kurz and two federal agents. The TaurusSec staff had refused to cooperate, citing client privilege. Several of them had been arrested while the FBI tracked the origins of the prototype plane. No one admitted responsibility, although the drone's manufacturer resided outside the jurisdiction of the United States.

The manufacturer listed in the news article? NeuroSys Robotics in La Ceiba, Honduras, Dan's old company. He felt a rush of anger knowing that his neural net technology had been misappropriated to build a killing machine.

The very drone that had ended Ada's life.

He slumped against the trunk of an old sycamore tree and struggled to process the information. Ada had warned him that he had crossed paths with the Horsemen already.

Now he had verification. According to Ada, Martin Orcus, the former investor in the NeuroSys plant was a member of the Horsemen. Ironically, Orcus had died due to horrific effects of the Devil's Paradox, the same bug his cohorts had stolen.

Perhaps they were ignorant of the threat they faced. Maybe they would die from the same affliction as Orcus, Dan thought perversely. But no, the risk of another new and terrible pandemic would be the end result, so he banished that thought from his mind.

If anything, the Horsemen should be thanking him for cleaning up their previous mess and saving their asses. Instead, they wanted to kill or capture him. They killed Ada, obviously ignorant of her research into a universal flu vaccine. A vaccine that might have saved the Horsemen from themselves. The thought of all their uncaring stupidity left the taste of sour bile in his throat. If Ben Proudfoot was right, the Horsemen would try to get to him through his friends and loved ones. Dan hurriedly dialed Rudi's burner phone.

The voice that answered was not Rudi's but someone hauntingly familiar.

"WHO AM I speaking with?" the voice on the phone answered.

"Where's Rudi?" Dan growled, having recognized the smarmy, irreverent tone on the other end of the line.

"Ahh, Mr. Clifford," Bradley Gruber said in his silky salesman's voice.

Dan noted a rougher edge to the man's voice and the hum of jet engines in the background.

"You owe me a Learjet," Gruber continued. "It was my favorite. I had to call in my backup, a much older hunk of junk."

"And you owe me three lives and a ruined reputation, you son-of-a-bitch! Where's Rudi?"

Gruber laughed derisively. "I must say, Dan, despite being a major pain in my ass, you are quite an entertaining fellow. I had nothing to do with those deaths."

"Your boss did," Dan said. "What's the difference?"

There was a long pause.

"Where's Rudi?" Dan repeated. "I want to talk with him."

"Why, of course," Gruber said, his voice dripping with condescension "He's right here."

"Dan?" Rudi said.

"Rudi, what the hell's going on?"

"Your friend Bradley needs our help," Rudi said. "I'm gonna help him fix our software, to save the children."

"What children?"

"You know, the sick ones," Rudi drawled. "We gotta help the children, right? Bradley said you wouldn't mind. I wanna help the children. Hey! Guess what? Bradley says we can have our jobs back . . . at NeuroSys. Isn't that cool?"

Dan paused. He couldn't believe what he was hearing. The typical acerbic edge of Rudi's voice had mellowed. In its place was the lethargic delivery of an altered mind.

"Rudi, listen to me!" Dan screamed into the phone. "Don't trust Bradly Gruber, he's a liar! He's dangerous! Run away, get away from him, first chance you get, you hear me?"

"Why *Dan* . . . such insults." Gruber's voice returned to the phone. "Rudi is so much more polite."

"Give the phone back to Rudi!"

Another long pause. "Nah . . . I don't think so. Besides . . ." Gruber chuckled. "Rudi's chewing a mouthful of pecan pralines at the moment."

"Dammit, Gruber!" Dan stuttered. "If you harm him in any way, I swear, I'll hunt you down and . . ."

"And do what?" Gruber said. "We're headed to Honduras, to the NeuroSys chip factory. What are you going to do exactly?"

Dan held Chemerra's phone at arm's length, staring at the device like some incarnation of evil. He was speechless. For ten years, he had fought to quell his anger, fear, and frustration, to live within a measured world, one of reason, logic, and fairness.

But this was something else. A world gone mad.

Rage consumed him, a feral desire to wrap his hands around Bradley Gruber's neck and squeeze the life out of this evil man. He wanted to yell, scream, exact pain and suffering. Yet the sounds of his anger seemed to stick in his throat, stifled by a brief moment of clarity.

The disembodied voice of Bradley Gruber squeaked from the phone. "Dan?"

"What?" he finally said.

Gruber chuckled again. "I thought I'd lost you. Why not join us in Honduras? My boss is keen to meet you in person, despite my warnings to the contrary." He sighed. "Alas, the man ignores my best advice."

"What? You think I'm a fool?" Dan hissed.

"Actually, no," Gruber said. "In fact, I think you're extremely dangerous. Yet, my boss thinks his wisdom trumps your unpredictability. Pity him. Still, I'm quite certain you'll find your way to us, eventually. After all, persuasiveness is my specialty. I'm betting you won't be able to stop yourself."

Dan felt a remoteness, a sense of existing outside his body, viewing a man screaming uncontrollably, tossing a phone into the soft layer of rotting leaf litter that carpeted the primeval forest floor.

"I DON'T THINK that's wise," Ben said. "What can you possibly gain by placing yourself directly in harm's way?"

Dan was a bundle of nerves, adrenaline-fueled. After his return, he had told Ben and Rachel about the details of his conversation with Bradley Gruber. The three of them sat restlessly in Ben's cabin, trying to come to terms with the latest news.

Rachel's complexion had warmed considerably over the past few hours. She looked completely different from the day before, when she was in the full throes of the viral infection. She seemed almost normal.

"Rudi seemed out of it, drugged," Dan continued. "Not like himself at all. Chemerra had warned me the Horsemen were experimenting with mind-altering drugs, to build compliance among the masses.

Rudi is the most independent, paranoid individual I know. The fact that he was so trusting and compliant with Gruber's wishes, tells me he was drugged."

"Maybe so," Ben said. "But a neutral observer could say that Rudi volunteered to help. How would you prove he was manipulated? It is a common and effective tactic, forcing compliance through other means. White men kidnapped the children of Cherokees, sending them to schools where they learned the white men's ways, separated from their families and traditions. When interviewed later, what would the Cherokee children say about their identity? Their legacy? Were they Cherokee as before, or different, through indoctrination? Either way, they were free, on the surface, to do as they wished."

Dan slumped in his chair, processing Ben's invincible logic. Rudi had made a choice to accompany Gruber to Honduras, whether he was in full control of his faculties, or not.

Who would care?

After his call with Gruber, Dan had contacted Vince Peretti and explained the situation to him. Vince pointed out the obvious. Rudi Plimpton had traveled of his own volition. The FBI had no jurisdiction in Honduras. There was no way, legally, to save Rudi.

"What am I supposed to do?" Dan pleaded to Ben and Rachel. "I can't just leave Rudi down there."

Ben Proudfoot stared at Dan through sad eyes that seemed to reflect the suffering of centuries. "I honestly don't know, Mouse. You must decide whether your actions can succeed or are doomed to failure. Then you must accept the truth. Attempting a fool's mission will help no one."

"I can't," Dan said, shaking his head. "I can't abandon Rudi. I've got to try something."

"Then accept the reality of your fate," Ben said, his face stoic and hard. "You may fail. You may lose."

Ben was right. He would be alone with no support from his own country, Vince, or anyone else.

With no bargaining power . . . what could he offer?

Nothing.

It was a logical impossibility and yet his emotions kept overruling his logic. Chemerra was right. The Horsemen could manipulate reason through emotions. Bradley Gruber was controlling him like a puppet master, tugging at his heartstrings, forcing him into an action doomed to fail.

Still, his dedication to Rudi left him no alternative.

"I need an edge," he pleaded to Ben. "Some way to win. How can I overcome their strategic advantage?" He stared at the old man, the wrinkles of his face deepening with every question.

Ben stared back at him, his eyes liquid. "I can't offer much, except this. You must be unpredictable. Become the trickster, the skin walker, coyote. Find what is valuable to your enemy and *become it*. Only then can you take control of their desires."

"How do I get to Honduras? I'm still on the FBI watch list. That eliminates cars, trains, ships, and jets. I can't wait till I'm vindicated. It will be too late."

"I know a way to get us there," Rachel said, her eyes sharp and alert for the first time in days. "But you'll have to figure out the rest."

"I don't know," Dan said. "You're just recovering . . . besides, this is my fight."

"*No*," she said. "This is *our* fight. Isn't that what you keep telling me? We're a team?" She smiled. "Quit trying to protect me and let's defeat these assholes together, just like the last time."

Dan gripped her hand and squeezed. "Together, then."

"Yes, together," she said.

30

THROUGH BLEARY EYES, Rachel sensed a slight brightness in the sky, powered by a thin sliver of sunlight creeping over the horizon to her backside. After twelve long hours of flying, mostly in the dark and over open ocean, her adrenaline was beginning to run low. The exhilaration of surviving Esrom's gene therapy "flu" could only carry her so far. She didn't even know if had worked. But the challenge of traveling to Honduras incognito had given her the welcome distraction she needed to keep her mind off it. And now, she had almost reached her goal.

When she had shared her idea for circumventing America's border security, Dan had stared at her as if the virus had affected her brain. The memory made her grin. She knew something Dan didn't: she'd done this before, or at least something similar. It had been fun to revisit a childhood memory.

At age ten, her granda had decided to teach her a new skill in the Bücker: "Flying by the nap of the earth." This was the technique he had used to escape the Germans in Italy in his stolen Bücker. The trick required flying a few feet above the ground for hundreds of miles, following the rolling terrain of Italian farmland and then across the Mediterranean to Malta, all without detection. The technique also had the advantage of saving fuel, thanks to physics.

When Granda challenged her, she had balked, scared by the danger of flying so close to the ground. One wrong move and—she had been a nervous wreck.

Granda upped the challenge further by taking her to the Gulf, where he forced her to fly above the chaotic contours of the ocean waves. That's where he had introduced her to the secret of ground effect. At a height of one half the wingspan of the plane, in the case of the Bücker, eleven feet, lift from the ground or ocean's surface was magnified, creating a cushion of air. She was delighted to discover that a light touch on the stick would allow the Bücker to glide above the waves, not nearly as difficult as it seemed.

She had spent days of practice surfing the waves, letting the chaotic contours guide her altitude. The wings were so efficient at lift that fuel lasted almost twice as long.

Now, she had reawakened the old skill to literally "fly under the radar" of America's coastal security envelope. The trick had only required some minor modifications.

That morning, after leaving Ben's compound, the two of them had hiked back to the Bücker and headed south, making a quick detour to Moultrie, where she had her friends at Maule attach two additional fuel tanks, sandwiched between the Bücker's dual wings.

Then they had flown to Naples, Florida, for a final refueling stop, before heading out into the Gulf of Mexico. The first few miles had been harrowing, as she had to hug the ocean's surface, hiding among the random chaos of the waves. To the US radar umbrella, they would simply appear as a speedboat darting across the ocean or random signal clutter. About thirty miles offshore, she was able to gain some extra speed and altitude, which made the task less harrowing. From there, they had continued on, across the Gulf of Mexico, past the far corner of Cuba and Guantanamo Bay.

No jets had been scrambled to their location, no Cuban speedboats, nothing. They were an insignificant fly darting along the edges of human perception.

And now, she was thrilled to see the bumpy outline of the Bay Islands to the west, poking out of the smooth horizon, their mountains turned golden by the early morning sun. Not a moment too soon, as the Bücker's fancy turboprop engine was running on fumes.

She wondered how Dan had fared during the long midnight trip. The Bücker had no communication system and the wind noise made talking almost impossible. As the plane rose and fell along with the undulations of the ocean, she had felt some seasickness and noticed Dan hanging his head over the rear cockpit a few times, leaving an unsightly stain that trailed backward across the Bücker's bright red-and-white-striped fuselage.

She'd have to clean that up tomorrow.

Dan's plan seemed even crazier than hers and she worried about it. Back in Ben's cabin, they had all agreed that traveling to the Honduras chip factory was a fool's mission. They had nothing to bargain with, no support from authorities, no rule of law.

Only the audacity of the unexpected.

Yet somehow, Dan felt that it would be enough, or at least he had convinced himself of the lie.

Barely clinging to the hope of a tenuous new life, Rachel knew she would be risking the loss of both of them to a hopeless cause. There would be no talking Dan out of his foolish loyalty. It was both his strength and his weakness.

Swallowing hard, she dug into her resolve. At least they'd face the end together, just like their last time here, when they had ventured into the hopeless abyss together.

A sudden pooling of moisture at the corner of her eye was quickly swept away by the relentless wind.

THE BÜCKER'S SUDDEN bank to the right woke Dan up from a fitful nap. He looked down to see the familiar unoccupied end of Guanaja, a location far away from the island's premier diving resort, Palacio del Sol. This area was considered haunted by most of the locals, which made it the ideal location for Duff McAlister's remote hideaway. Dan and Rachel had consummated their relationship in Duff's private cabin here, during their last visit to the Bay Islands.

The Bücker leveled, aiming for a small stretch of black sand nestled between two tall spires of dark volcanic rock. Standing nearby was Duff McAlister, proprietor of the diving resort. Alongside him were four jerry cans of aviation fuel, lined up in a row. Duff looked the same as always, tall and dark, muscular for a man in his sixties, wearing an irreverent grin that reached from ear to ear. He was wearing his trademark paddy cap, Hawaiian shirt, and sandals.

The landing spot was small, forcing Rachel to use the surf as part of her landing approach. She backed off the throttle and held the plane's speed barely above stall as she coasted across the water, aiming her touchdown point for dry ground. The Bücker bounced a couple of times and came to a stop, close enough to Duff to prompt a nervous step backward by the old Irishman.

"Whoa! Miss Sullivan, when you said you'd be flying a vintage bird," he exclaimed, "I had no idea she'd be, well, so *sporting*! Love the bright paint job." Duff moved forward and embraced her with a mighty hug. "Welcome back, lassie," he said with a slight crack in his voice.

Dan struggled out of the rear cockpit, dropped to the ground, and walked haltingly across the black sand, trying to regain his land legs. He held out his hand to shake Duff's but the tall man engulfed him in another bear hug.

"Dan Clifford, as I live and breathe," Duff roared in his thick brogue. "I wondered if I would ever see you two lovebirds again and then your sudden call caught me off guard. Let's get your brightly feathered bird refueled and secured. Then we'll head up to my cabin. I've got several pints of Guinness waiting, with your names on them!"

AFTER REFUELING AND tying down the Bücker, the three of them headed up the steep, winding trail that led to Duff's cabin. The locals avoided the area, gifting Duff with a uniquely private getaway. It also made for the perfect war room, far away from prying eyes and visitors.

The grueling climb gave Dan plenty of time to run through a host of memories from his last visit here. He and Rachel had developed a relationship, shared tears and joy . . . and schemed to expose an illegal conspiracy taking place at the NeuroSys chip factory in La Ceiba, his old employer.

And now, he was back . . . *to do what, exactly?*

That sobering thought had nagged at him during the entire night flight. His plan, what little of it existed, would require the help of both Rachel and Duff and the thought of placing both of them in danger wasn't sitting well.

Each step up the trail pulled him further into the old memories.

It seemed like a lifetime had passed since they had confronted their own pandemic threat, not Covid-19 but one that had come out of nowhere. Prior to Covid, the Honduras epidemic had caused real suffering and death for the residents of the small coastal fishing village of La Ceiba, only a few miles across the sea from Guanaja. Luckily, most Americans remained oblivious to the threat, since he, Rachel, and a crack team of epidemiologists had contained the epidemic's spread, eventually conquering the pathogen.

The US government should have learned its lesson but politicians had convenient amnesia. Soon, stockpiles of personal protection equipment and other medical supplies became depleted. It was as if the American government wanted to ignore reality, rather than deal with an uncertain future. Then Covid hit and reached the shores of America. The suffering had been exacerbated by American's willful ignorance and laziness when it came to unimaginable black swan events like a pandemic. Spoiled by the benefits of modern medicine, Americans began to believe that nature "owed" them comfort and security.

The painful truth is that reality owes us nothing.

The hike soon had him huffing and puffing. Duff McAlister was a good fifty feet ahead of them, bounding up the trail on his long legs. But then, Duff had a lot of practice negotiating this trail.

In the distance, hiding among the coconut palms, hibiscus, orchids, and loroco vines, the brown siding of the cabin suddenly became visible, contrasting with the monotonous green of the jungle.

Dan and Rachel arrived minutes later, collapsing on the deck, out of breath. Duff had already entered the cabin and stood in the doorway with an expectant look, grasping two pints of Guinness, one in each hand. "What's with you Yanks?" he said, a bemused grin spreading across his face. "Don't you ever get any real exercise?"

Unable to respond, Dan grabbed one of the beers and slipped into the dark interior, followed close behind by Rachel. The three of them plopped down on the old lumpy couch and sipped on their drinks quietly for a few minutes.

The modest wooden structure looked the same as he remembered, with a simple kitchen and wooden bar facing the den. The niches in the walls were crammed with even more bric-a-brac than ever, from Duff's many years as a deep-sea diver in the northern oil fields of Alaska. Faded pictures from past dive trips hung askew from virtually every surface of the mahogany paneling. Dan spotted a couple of newer photos from his own dives, when he had visited the island on a scuba vacation, young, naive, and oblivious to the events to come. It seemed like a century ago.

The three of them spent the next hour catching up on personal news, from Dan's adventures in Savannah, Rachel's battle with Huntington's, and Duff's struggles to rebuild his scuba resort in the aftermath of the Honduras pandemic. They consumed several pints of Guinness, so tart and fresh, that Dan wondered how Duff could obtain kegs of such young beer at this remote location.

They had been fully engaged in conversation, when Rachel began to withdraw, her eyes fluttering from exhaustion. "Guys," she said sleepily, "I've been up for, what? Thirty hours?" She yawned. "I'm beat."

"By all means," Dan said. "Get some sleep. I can't believe you lasted this long. You need time to recover."

Rachel smiled weakly, struggled from her seat, and pecked Dan on the cheek. "Thanks, doc. Wake me if anything exciting happens."

"Absolutely," Dan said.

"Lassie," Duff interjected. "Feel free to use my bedroom for . . ."

She waved them off, stumbling into the back room. "I know where it is . . ."

"Pardon the mess, I . . ." Duff grew quiet as Rachel slammed the door shut. He turned back to face Dan. "Is she . . . ?"

"All right?" Dan huffed. "Who knows? There's no real way to tell until she gets another test but I haven't noticed any changes, except for her mood. She's definitely more reserved, tentative."

"Humph," Duff said. "That sure doesn't sound like the redheaded fireball I remember."

"I like to think I've domesticated her wildness a bit."

Duff frowned. "Where's the fun in that?" He squirmed in his seat, got up, and headed back to the kitchen. "Another pint of plain?"

"Nah, I'm ruined enough already. Besides I'm exhausted too. Lots to plan out."

Duff returned to the couch and handed him another pint, having ignored his request. "So, what's with this crazy plan of yours? Sounds like madness to me."

Dan chuckled ruefully. "Me too, I guess. Still trying to figure it out. What can you tell me about the NeuroSys factory?"

"You already know my thoughts on that flying saucer abomination. They've expanded a lot since you were here last. Built more housing for the employees, developed the fallow farmland surrounding the dome. They've put in crops and grazing cattle presumably to feed the workers."

"So what are they doing inside the plant? Certainly not building my advanced weather forecasting network. From what I've heard, that contract with NOAA is officially dead."

"Robots, that's what." Duff replied with a disgusted frown. "From what I hear, they've got government contracts to create automated war machines, tanks, cargo haulers, stuff like that. They're the coming apocalypse, I tell you. *Terminator* stuff. Why the hell did you ever work for that company, Dan? That's not you!"

And automated drones, Dan thought to himself. "When Rudi and I worked at NeuroSys, we were using the company's multilayer neural chip to develop autonomous underwater vehicles. You know, small submarines that could dive the oceans, return to the surface, and recharge through solar, while mapping underwater currents and temperature gradients. We wanted to build the world's most accurate global climate prediction system from the data." He said it almost apologetically. "Obviously, the new owners have no interest in saving the planet. Unfortunately, the autonomous logic that allows a sub to navigate the ocean, works just as well for a drone flying through the air."

"Aye," Duff grumbled. "Some of the locals have seen those monstrosities flying around La Ceiba."

A flood of guilt overwhelmed him as the image of Ada Kurz haunted his memories, killed by a technology he had helped empower. "This is all my fault," he said, his voice breaking. "I screwed this all up; now I've got to fix it somehow."

"Laddie," Duff said. "You can'na take this all on your shoulders. What these *gombeens* are doing with your work is no longer your concern."

"Yeah, but now they've kidnapped Rudi, for some purpose I don't understand. I have a sinking feeling they have a new project, one that requires Rudi's expertise."

Duff seemed confused. "Your quirky friend? Why would they need him? Couldn't they just hire some other programmer?"

"Duff, you don't appreciate Rudi's genius. He wrote all the low-level routines for the NeuroChip. There are few people in the world who can do what he does."

Duff grew quiet, sipped on his Guinness, barely mindful of the caramel mustache adorning his lips. "The idea of you walking right into the lion's den sounds crazy to me."

"What other choice do I have?" Dan said.

Duff shrugged his shoulders. "Well, as my father used to say, 'If it's drowning you're after, don't torment yourself with shallow water.' The idea just might be crazy enough to work."

"Is there anything else you can tell me about the chip factory? Something that might even the odds?"

"There is one other thing," Duff continued. "A lot of construction equipment has been lingering around the old saucer for a year now but for the life of me, I can'na see any progress being made—no new buildings or other structures. Trucks come and go, taking away stuff, bringing in even more, but nothing seems to change, on the outside, at least. So what's going on inside?"

Dan struggled to fit the pieces of the puzzle together, and then, it suddenly hit him.

The Horsemen were building their own underground lair.

He suddenly had a plan, one that birthed in his mind in full form, causing him to bolt upright off the couch. "Thanks, Duff. Now, I gotta get some sleep. Big day tomorrow."

Duff grinned and gave Dan a knowing wink. "Somehow I have faith in you, Dan. But as my mother used to say, 'You'll never plow a field by turning it over in your mind.' Join your lassie and hold her close. See you in the morning."

"That I will," Dan said and made a beeline to Duff's bedroom.

THE NEXT MORNING, Dan and Rachel woke together, tangled in bedsheets. He hugged her close and she turned to face him, giving him a peck on the lips. Her cheeks were pink and the sparkle had returned to her eyes. She seemed like the Rachel he had always known.

She grinned. "Together then."

"Yes, together." Their long embrace was interrupted by the clang of plates and utensils. They rose quickly, dressed, and entered the den.

Duff had laid out a full Irish breakfast on the table. "Come," he said. "Wars are won on full stomachs."

"Mmm," Rachel exclaimed. "That smells heavenly."

The three plates were brimming with fried eggs, sausage and ham, fried tomato, and a generous mound of "bubble and squeak," a traditional Irish hash made from leftover potatoes, carrots, peas, and cabbage.

All three of them sat down at the tiny table and attacked the meal, barely speaking. When his plate was scraped clean, Dan turned to Duff. "You have a map of the coast?"

"Sure, laddie." He rose and rummaged through a pile of papers stacked on a bookshelf. Once Rachel had cleared the table, he unfurled the paper map, marked prodigiously with old diving sites.

"What's the most obscure route to the plant from here? One with the least number of eyeballs?"

Duff thought for minute. "That'd likely be from the south. It's mostly jungle beyond the plant. There's a long line of trees acting as a windbreak between the road and the fields alongside the dome. Leads right up to the main gate."

"Great," Dan said, then proceeded to describe his entire plan to both of them. When he was through, Rachel was grinning and Duff looked appalled.

"That's mighty gutsy," he said. "Aren't you making a lot of assumptions?"

Dan shrugged. "Let's call them educated guesses. Besides, what other choice do we have? You have a better plan?"

Duff thought for a minute. "No, can't say as I do. I have some contacts in the plant. Let me make some calls, see if I can verify some of your thoughts."

"That would be helpful."

AN HOUR LATER, Dan and Rachel had made the hike down the trail to the fully fueled Bücker, leaving Duff back in the cabin. Rachel used the short stretch of beach and the turboprop's power to muscle the plane into the air. She set a bearing toward the coast and rose to an altitude of three thousand feet. From that perspective, they could see the tiny port town of La Ceiba, the port's quay bustling with activity. Tiny, ant-like people wandered back and forth between the large shipping vessels at the far end. A flotilla of shrimp junks packed the docks farther north, their nets and poles swaying in the early morning breeze. There were several empty berths as boats headed out to sea.

Far in the distance, beyond the streets and markets of the central town, the NeuroSys plant's circular dome poked out of the forest like a blister on the land.

Rachel suddenly banked the biplane to the left and headed farther south, beyond the town's border. She arced back to the right and crossed over the threshold between sea and land. Throttling back on the Bücker's turboprop, she banked right again and began a long, gen-

tle glide over impenetrable jungle. There were no houses or roads below, no signs of civilization, just a blur of green velvet.

The NeuroSys plant was on the edge of town, leading Dan to suspect that the investment group now owning the former American
company had bought most of the surrounding acreage for future development. As their altitude steadily dropped, the plant soon disappeared over the horizon. Rachel held the plane on a steady bearing,
leveling out a few feet above the treetops.

An occasional ambitious limb would brush against the lower fuselage but by this time, Dan had grown accustomed to flying "by the
nap of the earth." The turboprop engine's rpms had dropped to an
inaudible level, barely discernible above the rush of wind. Suddenly,
the cover of the jungle peeled away. Rachel reacted quickly, dropping
to within ten feet of the ground. She aimed for a primitive dirt road
that flanked a hedgerow of trees and bushes and followed its path.

Through the gaps between trees, Dan could see the dome of the
NeuroSys plant looming. The last time he had visited this place, the
surrounding farmland had been fallow but now, there were several
pastures filled with longhorn cattle grazing. Adjacent to the pastures,
several fields had been planted with juvenile corn about a yard tall.

Rachel suddenly cut the engine and the air grew quiet. She flared
slightly and touched down on the grass ten yards from the hedgerow.
When the plane rolled to a stop, they both jumped out and pushed it
as close to the hedges as they could. Their vantage gave them total
obscurity from the factory's security tower.

After throwing some chocks under the wheels, Rachel grabbed
Dan and gave him a long, passionate kiss. "Good luck."

"You too," he replied, giving her an additional peck on the cheek.

He turned and walked in the direction of the NeuroSys plant and
to his fate.

31

CONFIDENT THAT RACHEL'S plane was obscured from view, Dan started the long walk toward his destiny. Near the end of the hedgerow he could see the security entrance to the NeuroSys plant coming into view. This was not the time for hesitation or reason. His plan had to be the craziest and most unlikely thing he had ever devised but as Ben Proudfoot had reminded him: "Audacity is the trickster's domain. No one bothers with a strategy for the unimaginable, so act accordingly."

He was pretty sure no one would anticipate his next move.

Strolling up to the security gate, Dan waved his arms and yelled. "Buenos días! I'm here to see Señor Bradley Gruber."

His sudden appearance startled the two security men inside the building. They stared out through the security glass, searching for a vehicle that could have deposited this stranger at their door.

One guard's expression suddenly changed to one of recognition. "Señor Clifford? How did you get here?"

What great luck. Apparently the guard had been employed during Dan's last visit to the plant, when he had been the company's director of business development and soon after, a local hero, having brought in a team of American doctors to treat victims of the local pandemic.

"I was out for a stroll," Dan said, standing directly in front of the gate. "I had the taxi driver drop me off a ways back. Is Bradley Gruber here?"

The gate rolled open and one of the guards bounded out excitedly. "Señor Clifford, it is truly a pleasure to see you again! How have you been?"

To Dan's surprise, the man embraced him in a strong bear hug. "Fine, fine. And you?"

"My family is doing well, thanks to you! Come in." He motioned

Dan inside the cramped gatehouse where he introduced him to the second guard.

Dan tried to maintain small talk with the two of them for as long as he could, finally asking again, "Is Señor Gruber here?"

"*Sí*, Señor Clifford. I alerted him on your arrival," the first guard said. "He should be waiting for you at the entrance."

"Gracias, I'll just stroll up the path then."

"*Sí, sí!*" The first guard nodded.

During their conversation, Dan had managed to learn both of the guards' names, Chucho and Rodrigo, in the hope that it might come in handy later. The two men seemed eager to share local news, telling him that some bigwig had arrived in town a few weeks prior, causing a stir inside the plant.

After several handshakes and goodbyes, Dan began the walk up the path toward the grand entrance to the NeuroSys dome. With every step forward, Dan could feel his heart pounding faster, the sudden reality of the moment hitting him. This ill-conceived plan was real and very, very stupid.

Too late to back out now.

Just as his terror and angst seemed unbearable, when he felt like sprinting for the fences, a sudden sense of relief overcame his fear, replaced by an old friend and companion:

Anger.

On the steps leading up to the dome, Bradley Gruber leaned nonchalantly against a concrete column, his expression bearing a look of satisfaction.

A shot of adrenaline washed any remnants of fear away in a flood of rage. Dan clenched his fists and calmly continued forward, vowing to maintain control.

"Hello, Dan," Gruber said. "What took you so long?" He grinned and extended a hand.

Dan ignored the gesture, focusing instead on Gruber's eyes so intensely that the man looked away.

"Where's Rudi?" he said.

"Oh, don't worry, Dan. He's doing just fine, a great addition to our team, I must say."

"I don't believe you," Dan said. "Take me to him."

Gruber's look of amusement evaporated, replaced by a subtle hint of irritation. "In due time, Mr. Clifford. Meanwhile, my boss wants to meet you. Why, I cannot fathom. I've warned him of your unpredictable nature, that you are very dangerous, a loose cannon, chaotic shrapnel ricocheting in an orderly world. Alas, he doesn't listen to me."

Dan huffed. "You call your world orderly?"

Gruber's eyebrows shot up. "Why, of course, don't you? The chaos happens when unpredictable assholes like you get involved."

Dan said nothing and simply grinned.

Bradley sighed. "Let's get this over with, shall we?" He walked up to the entrance and held the door open.

Dan felt a clash of memories as he entered the building. The lobby seemed the same as he remembered but with an unfamiliar face staring back at him from the reception desk. Straight ahead he could see the massive glass wall separating the exterior perimeter of the dome from its interior space: the largest class-1 clean-room in existence.

"Before we go up," he muttered, "mind if I use the men's room?"

Gruber grinned. "Of course, it's down that the hall on your—"

"I know where it is." He walked down the hall, struggling to maintain a relaxed gait, then pushed through the door into a row of urinals. He leaned against the countertop to steady himself and took several long, deep breaths, imagining a warm, grassy field, the sun shining, a peaceful breeze . . . then he went to the window, thrust it open, and took in several more breaths.

The land outside the dome had been developed since his last visit, to include rows of tenement houses, cattle pastures, and farmland. He scanned the yard, watched the activity outside for a few minutes, then took another deep breath before heading back outside to meet his fate.

Gruber led him up the large spiral staircase to the upper level ramp, where a ring of offices were suspended from the dome's walls, designed to give the occupants a bird's-eye view of the activities taking place below in the clean-room. Dan watched as a line of workers toiled below on an assembly line, wearing their white bunny suits designed to maintain the ultra-clean atmosphere inside the dome. Cleanliness was essential for the fabrication of NeuroChips, the brains behind the company's artificial intelligence.

Gruber turned left toward the executive offices. Dan paused for a moment to study the tall gangway that still led from the upper ramp to a metal tower sticking up inside the dome. It had once housed a powerful camera that could photograph intricate drawings of the NeuroChip from the floor of the assembly room, reducing the image thousands of times to a minuscule flake of silicon no larger than a thumbnail.

Modern technology had mothballed the old chip camera, having replaced it with digital lasers that carved out the complex wiring directly, at a fraction of the cost. The tower itself stood resolute, an antique vestige to old technology. The gangway to it still appeared operational.

Scattered below, among workers in white bunny suits, were the occasional smattering of orange-suited security guards, moving to and fro like drones in a hive, keeping tabs on the white worker bees. Everyone was anonymous inside their bunny suits, faceless blobs of cloth, plastic and human, fulfilling their obligations to the hive.

When he had last viewed this factory floor, the army of white-suited workers had been assembling his AUVs. His dream was to use them to collect a gigantic dataset of temperature data, large enough to predict climate with extraordinary precision.

No more. That dream was dead. Now, the assembly line was dominated by the muddy grays and greens of military machines.

"Is that where the drone was built that murdered Ada Kurz?" Dan asked.

Gruber glanced back over his shoulder, wearing a subtle smile. "I'm really not privy to all that. My skills are in the art of persuasion. I leave the mechanical details to the experts."

Dan huffed. "Sounds like a convenient tactic for avoiding responsibility. This plant used to make things to improve the world, now it just makes machines that kill."

Gruber habitually rubbed the thin watch on his wrist as they walked. "I would think you'd have a better appreciation of the military industrial complex. The world runs on consumables. What better consumable than a machine designed to destroy and be destroyed? It's the consumption engine that feeds the world, wouldn't you say?"

Before Dan could reply, they reached the cluster of executive offices. In the distant past, he could remember being one of those anonymous worker bees outfitted in his white bunny suit, fighting to uncover the intentions of Martin Orcus, the original investor in NeuroSys. Orcus was now dead, a victim of his own narcissism.

This time, he would have the opportunity to confront his enemy face-to-face.

Bradley Gruber stopped at the entrance to one office and with a sweep of his hand, invited Dan inside.

The person standing behind the desk caught Dan totally by surprise. "I know you," he said haltingly.

STANDING ACROSS THE room from Dan was a man he recognized as Lucas Henshaw, from his many television appearances. Henshaw was a popular Hollywood producer and media mogul, an icon in the entertainment industry but also an enigmatic figure who seemed to be perpetually embroiled in controversy. Somehow, none of the accusations against him had ever managed to stick. Henshaw's company, Medax Studios, had become an entertainment empire, involved with movies, gaming, books, social media, and streaming. The company's latest venture had been a foray into live action role-playing games. At first, Henshaw's connection to the Horsemen didn't seem to make sense but as Dan thought about it, Ada Kurz's words echoed in his mind: *The Horsemen are masters of bread and circus, architects of perception, manipulators of opinion.*

Lucas Henshaw's power and wealth flowed directly from his ability to entertain and captivate the public.

Looking at the actual person face-to-face, Dan found it hard to imagine Henshaw as the leader of a secret cabal of ancient Roman soldiers. His wealth certainly fit the premise but there was nothing Romanesque about the man.

Henshaw was short and rotund, with a round, sun-etched face and long gray hair that had been combed backward and frozen in place with copious amounts of hair gel. He had to be in his eighties and examined Dan with a pair of piercing blue eyes, the man's one distinctive feature.

"Well," Henshaw said, a pensive look forming on his face, "Bradley portrayed you as some sort of genius, an engineer of chaos, but to me, you just seem, well . . . *ordinary.* So I'm curious, how did you manage to cause so much havoc within our organization? How did you commandeer our drone, destroy Bradley's jet?"

Dan stared back, jaw set, trying to gauge this conundrum of a man. *I'm ordinary? What about you?* He knew perception and reality could be very different things, with one serving to fulfill the mind's expectations and the other acknowledging the truth. With Lucas Henshaw, Dan doubted his ability to discern the difference.

His long moment of silence prompted Henshaw to speak again. "What's the matter, Mr. Clifford, don't you have anything to say?"

"Sure," Dan said, mustering his self-control. "I want you to bring me Rudi Plimpton, right now, and I might decide to leave you and your organization in peace."

"What?" Henshaw took a halting step backward, momentarily rendered mute by Dan's boldness. A faint smile soon drifted across his face. "I don't think you understand the situation here. You're in *our* domain. Surely you know better."

Dan shrugged. "Maybe Gruber's right. I'm an engineer of chaos."

A slight hesitation clouded Henshaw's face, then he laughed heartily. "You're certainly entertaining, I'll grant you that. Look, Dan, may I call you Dan?"

"I'd prefer Mr. Clifford."

"As you wish, Mr. Clifford. You must realize the fool's game you are playing. You have no bargaining power and yet you risked everything to come here. *Why?* For some senseless loyalty to a friend? You've let your emotions betray you, Mr. Clifford. I can see the anger in your eyes."

"Hell, yeah, I'm angry! You killed Ada Kurz, a brilliant scientist who only wanted to help people. Then you kidnapped my friend!" Dan glanced over to see Victor Moody enter the room and join Bradley Gruber, who stood to one side watching the meeting with great interest. Victor Moody looked more distressed than ever, staring back and forth intensely between Dan and Henshaw. He suffered through several spasms and tics before managing to regain control of himself.

Henshaw's brows were raised when Dan looked back in his direction. There seemed to be a hint of consternation brewing underneath the man's cool demeanor.

Henshaw slowly clapped his hands together three times. "You've obviously got moxie and some balls, to be so brash. Frankly, that's the kind of self-confidence we value in our organization. I'm beginning to understand what Gruber sees in you. We can make your life so much more rewarding, if you simply work with *us*, rather than your doomed friends."

"You mean the Firemen?"

"Ah, yes, the *Firemen*," Henshaw said. "Descendants of traitors, a betrayal that dates back two thousand years. What is it that they call us?"

"The Horsemen."

Henshaw laughed. "Oh right, the *Horsemen*. Not quite sure how they settled on that moniker. They would have been better off to call us the *Cattlemen*. Your friends, the Firemen, are nothing more than anarchists, hoodlums, who sow doubt and discontent wherever and whenever they can. Meanwhile, we fight to maintain an orderly and productive society. We've battled the Firemen's insolence for a long time. But *now*, I think, we've finally got them on the ropes, thanks to *you*. You led us right to their leader's door."

Henshaw's reference to his unwitting role in Ada's death cut deeply. Dan felt a stab of remorse and guilt at having been so naive, to have been manipulated so easily.

He suddenly felt like a fool, but an angry fool.

Looking down at this ordinary man, so short in stature, yet so influential, Dan wondered how he had allowed himself to be so easily hornswoggled. Was his lizard brain really so powerful that it could lull his intellectual brain to sleep? Suddenly, Dan's allegiance to reason and moral fortitude seemed like a waste of time against this depraved manipulator. What good was all his training in prediction science when a simple emotional instinct could short-circuit the truth?

In a moment of lucid epiphany, Dan saw Henshaw for what he truly was: a privileged laggard with a huge ego, someone who felt entitled to power beyond his ability to earn it. Henshaw relied on that power, yet he *needed* the mindless dedication of hopeful sycophants to achieve his goals.

Henshaw was a *parasite*, feeding on the dreams of others.

Dan needed to create a schism between the man's false promises and the desires of his cohorts, so he clapped his own hands together slowly, three times. "*Bravo*. Yes, you managed to fool me in a moment of trust and naiveté. But what about now? Once burned, twice shy. Why should I trust anything you say to me now? And why should anyone else in this room trust you?"

Henshaw smiled knowingly and moved to the far wall, drawing a curtain away from a large picture window. "Look out there," he said. "What do you see?"

Dan moved forward cautiously and peered out the window. Beyond the dome's wall of glass, he could see the pastures below, filled with longhorn cattle. "A bunch of cows. So?"

"Those cattle, like most social animals, are herd motivated," Henshaw continued. "They have no cares in the world beyond their immediate comfort and happiness. As long as they have cud to chew and the instinct to procreate, they are happy. They lack the capacity to imagine a future and will blindly follow the whims of the bell cow, right off the side of a cliff, if we let them."

Henshaw picked up a small computer chip from the shelf beneath the window and held it aloft. "We embed these RFID chips into every cow's ear. It provides us with data on their every movement, how much they've eaten, where they travel, when they're hungry and when they're horny. Then we provide for their every need, treat their illnesses, fulfill their sexual desires, provide pure, mindless happiness. We write them a fairy-tale story of bovine existence, until their final destiny is rendered. When their time has come, they feed our workers. Thus, the circle of life continues. It's a better life than they could possibly hope for in the wild."

Dan stared down at the field of cattle, all shambling about in their daily routines, grazing, totally unaware of the illicit drama taking place in the office above their domain. "That's a compelling story but I'm still not sure I see your point."

"Aren't you a prediction scientist?" Henshaw said. "Don't you try to imagine the future? It takes ruthless pragmatism, a certain distance above the fray, to see all the moves on the board, does it not?"

"Again, I'm not sure what that has to do with the current situation."

Henshaw pointed out the window again, for emphasis. "Can't you see the resemblance? Human workers are herd animals too, slightly more sophisticated than their bovine cousins, perhaps. But they live their lives in much the same way: consuming, playing, socializing, obsessed with pleasure and family, slaves to their own instinctual emotions. The unwashed masses are unwilling to accept responsibility for their own actions. They would rather fantasize about a world where they are free to do whatever they want with no recompense, while the invisible shadow of control manages their every movement. Humans just want a simple, happy story, a choice between good and evil, black and white. No complexity, no randomness. A planned life, fulfilled by destiny, where dedication and absolute faith is always rewarded. Such is their desperate desire, that they'll ignore the truth and accept even the most ludicrous premise, just as long as it satisfies their need for order. Humans don't want to use their intellect. It's a needless waste of mental energy. They would much rather rely on us to do the thinking for them, so long as they *believe* that it was their own idea. That's the secret. Give them that excitement of ownership and their lust for wonder will feed the story we have given them. Such is the power of persuasion. Perception truly is reality."

Henshaw turned to face Dan, his blue eyes ablaze. "That is our domain, the domain of *gods*. We forge reality from the biases of the human mind. In return, the masses pay us handsomely for the privilege of existing in the world we create for them."

Henshaw took a deep breath, calmed himself, and placed a hand onto Dan's shoulder. He leaned in, speaking in low, measured tones. "If we left the world to the mindless masses, they would destroy it all. We're their overseers. We've been directing the herd for two thousand years, feeding them their fantasies while managing their institutions, traditions, laws, and religions. They gladly reward us with their loyalty until the final rendering. Join us, Dan, in the rarefied air of nobility. Lift yourself above the herd and you too can control the moves on the board from a lofty height."

Dan realized the truth in Henshaw's flowery speech. "Yes, I can imagine that you see yourself as some godlike being."

Henshaw stared back with great intensity. "Would you prefer to wander around with the plebes, instead? That would be a complete waste of your unique talents. We can offer you so much more: the opportunity to make *real* decisions, to alter the future. The alternative is to battle forces you cannot hope to defeat." Henshaw paused, letting his words sink in.

The man made a compelling argument, Dan thought. So compelling, in fact, that Henshaw must believe in his own fairy tale. "So tell me, why did you kidnap Rudi? What's his purpose in your grand scheme?"

"We didn't kidnap him," Henshaw replied. "He made a choice to work with us, on programming that he, himself wrote, for the computer chip that he and *you* helped design. A chip that has so much to offer the world. We want to expand your NeuroChip into the realm of real-time DNA analysis. With it, we can decode the genomes of entire populations, build a database that will conquer disease, enrich health, increase life span, allow us to reach full human potential."

Dan hesitated for a moment, unsure exactly how to respond to Henshaw's eloquent story. What had Ben told him? *Find out what your enemy values and become it.* These men were deluded but not idiots. If he appeared too gullible, then everything he had to say would be distrusted.

"Really?" Dan penetrated Henshaw's eyes with a disparaging look. "You want me to join your organization? And yet you lie to me with a straight face? Why would you want to bring *poor ol' dumbass me* into your organization? That's what you'd be doing if you thought I swallowed that bullshit you just fed me. We both know you drugged Rudi with some substance, that you killed Ada Kurz with one of your automated drones made right here in this factory with my NeuroChip and that you are lying to me *right this minute*."

He cast a quick glance at Gruber and Victor Moody. Gruber's expression was one of bemused wonder and grudging respect. Moody, however, was standing awkwardly, struggling to control his tics that seemed to grow worse with every moment. The look of distress on his face was palpable.

"Frankly, I don't understand why you chose to kill Ada Kurz in the first place," Dan continued in a derisive tone. "No one had mastered the art of DNA engineering better than she had. She understood the true nature of the Devil's Paradox, you know, the organism you stole from your own pharmaceutical company. I assume that organism is at the heart of your aspirations and the one slowly destroying Mr. Moody's body, here." He pointed in Moody's direction, deciding right then and there to up the ante. *Might as well join in the lies* . . . "Did you know that Ada had already discovered a cure for Victor's malady? She was concerned for him. But then your drone destroyed her lab and all the work she had accomplished. Who's going to cure Victor now? Wouldn't it have been far better to sway her to your side? After all, you own the moral high ground . . . right?"

Henshaw's expression transformed into an unreadable tangle of confusion, vacillating between admiration and anger. Dan knew he had achieved his goal. He held fast, forcing himself to remain still, studying the faces of the three men in the room while they processed his comments.

"Is . . . that true?" came the shaky voice of Victor Moody. The man was trembling severely, his eyes drilling into Henshaw. "Did you kill Ada? Destroy her lab?"

"Good grief, Moody!" Henshaw blurted. "She's the one who made you sick in the first place."

"But *did* you?" Moody persisted.

"Did I what?" Henshaw's anger at being interrupted began to show.

"*Kill* Ada Kurz?" Moody asked again. "I'm *dying* here. If she had a cure . . ."

After an awkward pause, Henshaw suddenly shrugged. "Ada Kurz was an insolent bitch and Clifford's trying to pull your chain. Don't be such a fool, we'll talk about this later."

Henshaw turned his attention back to Dan, the silkiness returning to his voice. "I see you're not afraid to express your opinion, Mr. Clifford. That could be useful to our organization but only if you direct it in the right way. For instance, you could help by alleviating the concerns of your cohort, Mr. Plimpton."

"In what way, exactly?" Dan said.

"Well, since his arrival, Mr. Plimpton has grown more, let's say . . . *intractable,* questioning things."

Good for you, Rudi, Dan thought.

Henshaw moved forward again and leaned in near Dan's ear, whispering with quiet intensity. "Let me make this clear. We've been doing this a long time. If you think you can manipulate the situation, you should reconsider. This is *my* domain. I have the high ground. Pledge your fealty to our cause and you might survive the day. Betray me"— Henshaw poked Dan in the chest for effect—"and I'll send you and your friends to the slaughterhouse, along with the other mindless cattle."

Henshaw's threat had the commensurate effect. Dan could feel the heat of the exchange on his face and experienced a brief moment of panic.

A moment that was suddenly interrupted by a bloodcurdling scream.

32

A SLIGHT BREEZE brushed Dan's face as Victor Moody raced past in a blur. The man moved with inhuman speed and agility, screaming maniacally at the top of his lungs. Dan blinked reflexively and saw Moody lay into Lucas Henshaw with unfettered ferocity.

Henshaw responded with a whimpering wail of pain as Moody tore into his face with his false fingernails. Dan took two steps back to avoid the spray of blood that seemed to emanate from the flurry of violence like a fog. He backed into Bradley Gruber, who screeched, ran from the room, and bounded down the hallway at a rapid clip.

The two guards standing outside the office were shocked into action by the inhuman screams. They rushed past Dan and attempted to subdue Victor Moody but the man seemed to possess catlike speed. He managed to slither away from the guards' grasp and continued his relentless assault on Henshaw, who had slumped to the floor and rolled up into a fetal ball.

Unnerved by Moody's sudden animalistic rage, Dan backed out of the room and headed down the gangway that circumscribed the inner dome of the factory.

He'd only covered about ten feet when a thunderous boom rattled the glass wall that separated the ultra-clean-room below from the upper executive offices. A cloud of gray smoke rose from the center of the facility below, triggering a wail of alarms.

Good job, Rachel, Dan thought and he paused for an instant to examine the damage below. The cloud billowed upward and began to spread out in a plume across the ceiling of the dome. On cue, crowds of white-suited workers fanned out in all directions from the explosion, like bees from a disturbed nest. Lights began flashing above the exits. He knew what that meant.

Due to the toxic chemicals used in chip manufacture, the factory's stringent safety systems would be engaged automatically. All the doors would be unlocked, the evacuation lights activated. Which was good, since his destination lay straight ahead: the access ramp to the mothballed chip camera.

He could see a contingent of security personnel racing up the spiral staircase to intercept his position. Dan broke into a sprint toward the ramp access door directly across from the spiral staircase. He had to reach there before the guards, who were only a few feet away but huffing and puffing as they struggled up the stairs.

They all reached the same spot at the same time.

Dan pointed down the gangway, toward the executive offices. "They're attacking Lucas Henshaw! It's horrible! Help him, please!" The guards followed his finger down the hall toward Henshaw's office and the screams that still echoed from there.

Dan used their momentary confusion and planted his right foot onto the ramp, bolting suddenly to the left and through the unlocked door onto the elevated ramp. It swung precariously, suspended from the dome's ceiling, a hundred feet above the maelstrom of bunny suits still milling about chaotically below. He bounded across the shaky ramp toward the tower that housed the decommissioned chip camera.

A quick glance behind him revealed two security guards who had chosen to follow in close pursuit. He reached the ramp's end and flung himself over the side of the camera tower, grabbing hold of the jumbled steel framework and scrambling down the beams with agility born from years of rock climbing with Ben Proudfoot. Above him, both guards stopped at the guardrail, unable to muster the courage to follow.

Dan grinned. He was in his element, a steady stream of adrenaline fueling his movements as he descended rapidly, hand over hand. He dropped to the smooth white floor below and looked up. The two security guards had retreated, presumably to pursue him from ground level.

He had no time to waste.

The workers had begun to create a ragged line near the rear exits directed by orange-suited security personnel. In his street clothes and alone in the abandoned center, Dan stuck out like a sore thumb. He quickly headed to a side building for cover. Before long, he'd be caught in a pincer movement from the orange suits near the rear of the factory floor and the security guards who would soon be entering the front entrances at ground level.

He squeezed down a narrow hallway and turned the corner past the room where all the mayhem had started. It was a chip fabrication room, housing a number of highly toxic chemicals. Several containers had been upended and mixed into a toxic flaming brew. Overhead nozzles sprayed fire suppression foam on the flames but the initial blaze had done the job of clearing out the building.

Dan continued down the narrow hallway, trying to stay hidden, when suddenly, an orange-suited guard grabbed him by the collar and jerked him into a side office. Caught off-balance, Dan sprawled across the floor. Before he could regain his footing, the security guard jerked him upright and tapped on the clear visor of the orange suit.

On the other side, Rachel grinned at him, yelling, her voice muffled by the visor. "This way!" From a box in the corner of the room, she pulled out another orange suit and thrust it into his hands. "Hurry!" she yelled.

Dan struggled into the unwieldy jumpsuit, expecting someone to burst through the office doors at any minute.

But no one did.

Suddenly, he was transformed from a fugitive into an anonymous threat. The white-suited workers were trained to accept the full authority of orange-suited security personnel. No one would question their movements. The two of them had essentially become invisible.

They checked themselves out for flaws in their disguise and gave each other an OK sign.

"Great job with the security suits!" Dan yelled loud enough to be heard through the visor. "Did you find an elevator shaft anywhere?"

Rachel's muffled voice replied: "I think so, follow me."

They glanced both ways out the doorway, then forced themselves to walk calmly but swiftly out into the open hallway of the dome between two large assembly lines. Rachel led Dan toward a new structure that had been built since his last visit. The tall square tower dominated the center of the hallway.

She stopped at the center of the tower alongside a pair of elevator doors. Straight ahead, a long tunnel extended from the tower to the rear exits, presumably to conceal anyone coming up from below while also preventing them from breaching the dome's stringent clean-room requirements on the assembly floor.

A clean-room that Rachel had contaminated with her well-placed fire.

The ding of a bell signaled the arrival of the elevator car. They moved toward the parting doors, hoping their disguises would hold up.

A large crowd of lab-coated workers paused expectantly, as if waiting for a command. Dan pointed in the direction of the rear exits and the group obediently followed his lead.

Rachel turned toward Dan and grinned. "Well, that was easy. I like this new authority designation."

"Let's hope we don't meet up with any other orange suits. They might question us."

They entered the elevator and pressed the lone button on the wall labeled BASEMENT. The downward journey seemed to take an unbearably long time. Dan pulled off his hood and helped Rachel remove hers.

"Good job!" Dan said. "How did it go?"

Rachel grinned. "Like clockwork. While you distracted the guards at the front gate, I snuck past and followed the hedgerow down to the building and waited for you to open the window. From there, it was a simple stroll down the hall to the dressing room. I found the orange suits and the rest was copacetic."

"Did you use the bump key to get in?"

"Nope," Rachel said. "You were right. No one had ever bothered to invalidate your old security account, back when you worked for NeuroSys. I guess they never expected to see you here again. I just punched in your code and walked right through the front door, easy-peasy. So much for their high-tech security."

Dan laughed, amazed at their good fortune and the Horsemen's incompetence.

The elevator began to slow, prompting them to replace their hoods. The doors opened to another crowd of scientists, their concerned faces reflecting an eagerness to escape the imposed threat of the sirens.

Dan and Rachel moved forward and the crowd parted like the Red Sea, respectful of their orange suits. They waited to one side as the group stuffed into the elevator. Once the doors closed, they continued forward down a dimly lit tunnel, lights flickering. After a few feet, the tunnel split at a three-way junction.

"You go right, I'll go left," Dan said. "Meet back here in five minutes and whatever you do, don't get lost."

Dan marveled at the sheer size of the facility, which seemed to go on forever. Every few feet, side tunnels would lead off in other directions. There was something hauntingly familiar about this convoluted space. He continued for five minutes, then turned back and carefully retraced his steps. He and Rachel met back up at the center tunnel.

"You see anyone else?" Dan asked.

"Nope," Rachel said. "Appears everyone has cleared out."

"How is that possible? This place is huge. Where are all the other workers? And where's Rudi? I didn't see him in either group of lab coats."

"Maybe they left before the alarm." Rachel shrugged, her concern visible through her mask. "What now? Where do we go from here? If we head down the wrong corridor, we'll never find our way back out."

Dan hesitated. He couldn't quite explain it, but felt confident in the general direction to take. "Let's continue straight down the main tunnel."

They walked on for another hundred yards or so, until the main tunnel ended abruptly. Dan stared at a heavily fortified security door, labeled with a sign saying: AUTHORIZED PERSONNEL ONLY. There was no doorknob or latch, just a small card reader anchored to the left side of the door. *Why does this feel so familiar?* Then it hit him.

He had been here before, in another life.

Chemerra's lair. Dan slapped the side of his head and laughed. Ada Kurz had understood the nature of black swan events, unlikely outcomes, defeat, and reconciliation. She had prepared him for the unimaginable. "Good job, Ada," he said aloud, staring upward toward an imagined sky hundreds of feet above their current location.

Turning to Rachel, he said, "You remember me telling you about Ada Kurz and her avatar's lair? Well, this is it, or a rough facsimile, at least. At some point while hacking the Horsemen's systems, she must have found blueprints for this facility and used it to design her own virtual-reality space. She knew I'd end up here eventually . . . I already know my way around."

He stared back at the door, half-expecting multicolored spiders to drop out of the ceiling but nothing happened. He said to Rachel: "Is there a security card in your suit?"

She fumbled around in her pockets and came up with an ID badge. "Is this what you're looking for?"

"Maybe." He stared down at the card. A newly designed NeuroSys logo had been printed on one side consisting of three interlocking circles colored cyan, green, and orange. He held it up to the flat plate and heard a welcoming click.

THE DOOR SWUNG open and the tunnel continued. Flanking both sides were numbered, nondescript doors. Dan stopped several times to test the locks and found a few unlocked. Most of the rooms were administrative offices furnished with desks and filing cabinets. Other doors were locked. He couldn't make sense of their purpose. If they had more time, he could examine the files for clues but he suspected their time was growing shorter. They had to find Rudi before the toxic spill was cleaned up.

On the right, a few feet farther down the tunnel, he encountered an ornate archway covered with mythological carvings that seemed distinctively out of place in the sterile, high-tech facility.

Dan was still staring when Rachel finally tugged on his arm. "We don't have time for that, *come on*."

"No, there's something . . . important here," he muttered. "It's the Minotaur's lair. We gotta check it out." He opened the door.

Inside the entrance, the narrow corridor was dimly lit by flickering LEDs designed to look like ancient candles. On both sides of the hallway ran a row of hard marble benches, the walls behind them rough-hewn and unfinished. It looked like the tunnel had been carved right out of the bedrock.

As they moved farther into the space, Rachel drew close and squeezed Dan's arm. "There's something about this place that gives me the creeps."

At the far end, the tunnel opened up into a cave containing a circular apse. Against its back wall was mounted an exquisite stone carving, ancient by appearance. The center of the carving was dominated by a muscular bull, deep in the throes of death. Astride his back sat a man wearing a cape and an oddly draped hat, pulling the bull's head back and thrusting a short sword into the bull's shoulder. A dog hungrily licked blood from the mortal wound. Beneath the wound, blood dripping from the bull's shoulder landed on the floor as a cluster of grapes, where a snake had been carved, curling around it. At the rear of the sculpture, a large scorpion grasped the bull's genitals, while the bull's tail swung in an arc, its tip carved into the likeness of a sheaf of wheat. Overlooking the entire scene, a raven sat perched on an arch populated with astrological symbols.

Dan struggled to decipher the meaning. "What the hell?"

"I know this carving," Rachel said. "From trips to my grandmother's hometown in Capua, Italy. They were everywhere, popular tourist merchandise." She approached the carving, running her hand across the relief, studying it carefully. "This one looks ancient. It's called the Tauroctony, I think, part of an old Roman religion called Mithraism." She glanced around the room, nodding in recognition. "Their temples were always underground, like this one. Nobody knows their exact theology because the priests never left any written records. You'll find their underground temples scattered all around Italy, Britain, and Europe." She frowned. "It was a male-only cult, mostly military soldiers and Roman leaders."

Another relief caught Dan's eye and he approached it. There were seven images, with seven names carved alongside them into the natural stone, aligned in a hierarchy. He stared at the strange words. "Any idea what this says?" he asked Rachel.

"Well, my Latin's a bit rusty . . ." She stared at the carving, reading from the bottom up. "But if I'm not mistaken, it reads, 'Corax the Raven, Nymphus the Bride, Miles the Soldier, Leo the lion, Perses the Persian, Heliodromus Courier of the Sun, and Pater the Father.'"

"You think this is some kind of rite of passage, or rank?"

Rachel shrugged. "Could be." She did another circle of the room. "Whatever they're worshiping here, it involves a lot of astrology."

"Humph," Dan said dismissively. "Guess these self-described 'gods' need their own gods to worship." He felt a shiver down his spine, as if he'd witnessed some forbidden truth. "Let's get out of here." He turned his back on the room and headed out, stopping momentarily at an alcove in the wall containing several rows of small ceramic idols. On a whim, he slipped one of the figurines into his pocket as a souvenir. When he picked it up, he could feel a liquid sloshing inside.

———

THEY REENTERED THE central hallway and continued on, until they reached a second heavily fortified entranceway. Dan signaled for the security pass card. After several unsuccessful swipes, it became clear that this level of the basement was off-limits to ordinary security personnel.

He wasn't quite sure what to do next when a distinctive sound echoed behind them. Far back up the tunnel, at the elevators, the doors slid open, disgorging a team of men dressed in full assault gear, weapons at the ready. There were no orange bunny suits. The team leader barked an order and they moved forward at a rapid pace.

Dan and Rachel were standing in full view, in the distant shadows, decked out in their orange suits, which probably saved their lives. The team leader shouted in their direction but Dan pretended not to hear. He pushed Rachel down a corridor to the right, out of the line of fire. He figured they had about three minutes before the assault team put the pieces together.

"Go, go, *go!*" He hissed.

Another shout came, along with the echo of boots on concrete.

Dan stopped for an instant, visualizing the layout of Chemerra's lair, remembering a similar chase. Only this time, real bullets were involved.

The sounds of pursuit grew louder.

He worked to remember the twists and turns of Echidna's cave. Then he grabbed Rachel's hand and took off at a full run, slipping and sliding on the slick floor as he took several sharp twisting turns toward his destination. After a few minutes, Dan felt confident he had lost the assault team and slowed his gait, hoping to make less noise, so as not to give away their position.

He was growing more familiar with the mazelike layout of the basement. Even though Chemerra's lair had been fake, the emotions he had experienced there felt real enough to clarify his memories.

Dan took another turn, reaching the spot where Ariadne had greeted him in the cave. Instead of a glowing ball of yarn, he found a brightly lit sign overhead with an arrow pointing right, its illuminated letters spelling out **UTILITIES ROOM**.

Shouts down the corridor urged him forward and he broke into another run, dragging Rachel behind him until he reached the utility entrance. He swiped the passkey and held his breath. A satisfying click popped the door open. They eased inside and quietly closed the door.

The room on the other side was more of a chamber, huge in size, a chaotic maze. Two long rows of commercial air conditioners receded into the distance, their ducting spreading out in all directions like tentacles. What activity would need this much cooling underground? The incessant drone of all those BTUs was deafening and made it hard to concentrate.

The Minotaur's labyrinth indeed, he thought.

He began removing his orange jumpsuit. "Our disguises are useless now," he shouted over the din. Rachel joined him. They stuffed the suits into a nearby bucket and covered it over with a mop.

"Now what?" Rachel said.

He held up a finger, closed his eyes, and tried to reconstruct the path he had traversed inside the virtual labyrinth, using Ariadne's glowing thread. He stepped through every turn, mistake, and backtrack, using the memory of the thread to build a mental path through his mind's eye.

Finally, he grabbed Rachel's hand and moved forward, careful to count his steps. A few minutes later, he spotted flashlight beams raking across the pipes and corridors. The security team had caught up. The only advantage they had was the thundering drone of the machines masking the sounds of their movement.

Dan paused, then headed down a narrow path between two rows of pipes that reminded him of a familiar narrow passageway in the cave. He picked up speed as his confidence grew, turning left and right instinctively, finally stopping at a far corner where two side walls converged.

This was it.

One last air-conditioning unit droned in the corner. A ventilation shaft larger than the others poked out of the top of the unit, took a hard left, and disappeared into the wall. Dan hopped up on an electrical switch box and removed an access panel from the side of the vent. "Up you go," he said, forming a stirrup with his hands. "Climb in and I'll hand you this panel, then you'll need to give me a hand up."

"You're climbing into *that*? With your, uh . . . what is it again?"

"Taphephobia," Dan said. The look of incredulity on Rachel's face prompted a burst of nervous laughter. "I've done this before, *sort of.* Hurry, before I change my mind."

She shrugged and placed her foot into Dan's hands, allowing him to boost her up. He followed with the access panel.

Then, with some help from Rachel, Dan lifted himself into the vent. The space was cramped, forcing Rachel to back up until her butt nearly touched the unit's roaring fan blades. Dan struggled to fit the access panel back in place, just as two members of the assault team panned their lights around the area. Dan held the panel tightly to the vent and grew still, staring down at the two men through louvered slits.

"End of the line," one of them shouted. "Asshole must have taken a different route." One man aimed his flashlight directly into the vent. The intense beam hit Dan right in the eyes and he struggled not to flinch. After a brief moment, the light passed and the men headed down the far wall, the squawk of their radios growing fainter.

"That was close," he whispered.

Rachel gave his leg a reassuring squeeze. "Get me out of here. My rear end is about to become hamburger on this fan."

Dan finished securing the panel and turned to face the black void ahead. He half-expected a familiar hot snake of panic to wrap itself around his chest. In anticipation, he took a long, deep breath, exhaling slowly.

To his surprise and delight, the panic attack faded, leaving only a flutter of discomfort. *Damn!* Chemerra's virtual-reality experience had desensitized him. Grinning, he crawled forward with newfound confidence, until the light faded. As the tunnel grew darker, Dan had to feel his way along blindly, until fingers of panic began tickling his phobia again. Then, the path dead-ended and forced him into a claus-trophobic 90-degree turn. He struggled around the corner, felt his shirt catch on a sharp piece of metal. His panic increased. He grunted, made one final push, and broke free.

In the far distance, sweet, exquisite fingers of light streamed in through an opening in the shaft. Sighing with relief, he scrambled for-ward, happily drinking in the sudden connection to open space. He reached the vent and peered through a louver into a vast space filled with twinkling lights. Pulling the vent loose, he checked both di-rections. The space seemed unoccupied, so he quietly dropped to the floor and helped Rachel down behind him. He half expected to see the mythological form of the many-eyed creature Argus Panoptes bearing down on him.

But instead, he found a large expanse occupied by something far more upsetting.

33

DAN'S JAW SAGGED. Argus's cave, the space so hungry for cooling, was filled with servers.

NeuroSys servers. *His* servers. *Thousands* of servers.

Rows and rows of status lights blinked back at him accusingly. *Where have you been*, they seemed to say.

Dan began to tremble with rage. When he joined the NeuroSys Robotics Corporation years ago, his network of servers had been designed to process vast stores of climate data from around the world: wind, temperature, ocean currents, and oxygen levels. The NeuroChip's 3-D design was ideally suited for the singular task of predicting climate change.

That dream died with Martin Orcus.

Now, NeuroSys was being directed by a new consortium, members of the Horsemen. His servers had been repurposed: row after incomprehensible row of processing power, crunching data with incredible speed and insight, predicting something important.

But what?

It took only a split-second to realize the answer. Chemerra had warned him of the Horsemen's penchant for assembling data on every man, woman, and child on the planet, through their numerous corporate connections and ownership of a South American cell phone service.

These servers were tracking *human-change*.

Like the tagged cattle outside, every movement was being quantified and analyzed, every prurient desire registered. Dan's mind raced through the possibilities. With sufficiently accurate predictions, the Horsemen could control the opinions of a naive public, pinpoint their fears and expectations, fulfill their social fantasies and biases. The herd would be none the wiser, content to be told what to think in exchange for a fantasy of individuality and freedom.

Armed with that power, the Horsemen would be free to render human aspirations into the tallow of their own wealth and greed.

With *his* servers. And they would need Rudi's expertise to do it, since he had written the operating system for the chip.

"Are you okay?" Rachel whispered, giving his arm a concerned stroke.

His trance momentarily broken, Dan turned to her and saw the concern written across her face.

"You look, well . . . *monstrous*," she stammered.

Rachel had never seen the true depths of his rage before, he realized, a rage he had spent a lifetime burying beneath the surface. Its raw fury had leaked out onto his face, frightening her. Rachel's look of fear was unfamiliar and unsettling to him.

"Follow me. We've got to find Rudi before we run out of time." Dan headed toward the exit, moving boldly forward, without fear of a surprise appearance from the mythical Argus Panoptes. In the real world, the creature with a thousand eyes had taken residence inside his own servers and within the ambitions of the Horsemen.

DAN WOVE HIS way through the maze of servers, his adrenaline at a high pitch. Near the exit, he stopped to allow the two of them to catch their breath. The door seemed to have no security on the server side but through the door they could still hear the muffled sounds of the alarms.

"What if Rudi left with everyone else?" Rachel said.

"He's got to be here. There's no other option."

"But wouldn't they make him leave with all the others?"

Rachel was right. He'd been so focused on breaching the Horsemen's lair that he hadn't thought that far ahead. Back in Echidna's virtual world, this was about the point when he had been thrown out of the simulation.

He hesitated, his hand on the doorknob. No way to see the future. *Oh well, what the hell?* He pushed the door open and stepped into another world, one filled with glass-lined offices, laboratories filled with equipment similar to the ones in Ada's Kurz's cabin.

And *crops*. Several enclosed rooms glowed with hydroponic lighting, filled with rows of plants growing out of PVC pipes and Styrofoam rafts.

The warren of cubicles each had their own ventilation ducts attached to a sealed ceiling. The ducts led back toward the utilities room and the HVAC systems they had just left. There was much more going on here than just maintaining a server farm.

As he wandered down the central hall, Dan's heart sank. Where was Rudi? Had he followed everyone to the surface? Would he still be under Gruber's spell? Would he even recognize the two of them? How would they find their way out? Where was the security team? The enormity of the challenge became clear. He had known all along that this was an impossible mission, a tiny David against a multi-tentacled Goliath.

Then he spotted the profile of a lone man, hunched over a computer terminal, his long black hair draped over his shoulders, earbuds dangling like nerd jewelry.

He'd recognize that posture of indifference anywhere.

Rudi.

He started banging on the glass wall. Rudi was immersed in his music and ignored them at first. He headed around the corner of the cubicle to Rudi's frame of view and tried again, finally eliciting a response.

Rudi grinned and opened the door. "Welcome, guys. It's about time."

"Rudi!" Dan hugged him instinctively, something he'd rarely done in their years working together. "Are you okay?"

Rudi backed away, caught off guard by Dan's affectionate gesture. "Right as rain. Took you two long enough."

"You knew we were here?" Dan said.

"Of course." Rudi shot Dan one of his classic expressions of disdain. "I knew you'd come eventually, so I've been monitoring your digital footprint. I set up a back door into their server system. You guys fell off the radar a couple of days ago but when I saw your log-in to the security system, I knew you'd made it. I had a hell of a time convincing the other programmers to leave me behind."

Dan wasn't quite sure how to broach the next subject but Rudi seemed his usual self, so he opted for the blunt option. "So, are you okay? Are you still on drugs? What about Bradley Gruber?"

Rudi laughed heartily. "Nah, I know what you're gettin' at. *Chill*, man. That ass-wipe Gruber fed me magical pralines that turned me into some kind of sucker for bullshit. It was weird. I felt normal-like but just, I don't know . . . *agreeable* somehow." Rudi seemed to shiver at the thought. "Next thing I knew, I was kissin' his ass and doing anything he asked. It was bonkers . . . I sort of wanted to . . . and then those pralines." Rudi licked his lips. "They were the *bomb*. I still dream about 'em, late at night, when I get the munchies."

"But you're not eating them now, right?" Dan studied Rudi's face. His eyes seemed clear and bright, not the dull, lifeless eyes he had noticed on Molly, back at Stoker's warehouse.

"Oh no." Rudi waggled his head. "All fun and dandy makes Rudi a dull boy. I was here a couple of days and Gruber kept giving me pralines and jobs to do and I wanted to do them, don't get me wrong but . . . well, I just didn't know *how*. It was like all my creativity went out the window. All I wanted to do was wipe the guy's ass but for the life of me, I couldn't muster an original thought. Gruber realized his mistake by the end of the second day and weaned me off his grovel-candy." He licked his lips again. "Truth is, I'd chow down on those damn pralines right now if they were around. If we could market the taste without the aftereffects, we'd make a million."

"What exactly did he want you to do?"

"Aw, his naught-noggin programmers had made a mess of my code, screwed everything up. For one thing, they wanted me to genericize the prediction engine, so they could write custom routines for it without me having to babysit their every move. They wanted to use it for a ton of stuff. It's pretty scary, man. They're designing this DNA chip that can read an entire human genome in less than a minute, so they can profile everybody on the planet, that is, if I would fix the operating system." Rudi laughed. "Fat chance. They also want to predict the likely effects of genetic changes to their plants, so they can achieve some specific goal, like refining their grovel-candy. Gruber told me he made the pralines with high-fructose corn syrup but that the formula wasn't exactly right. He wanted me to alter the routines so they could engineer cooperation and gullibility into their grovel-candy, without the lethargy. I don't think that's possible, frankly. When I wanted to satisfy his expectations, I couldn't think outside the box, be creative. I just did what he told me to do. No arguments. But of course, what he wanted me to do was *stupid,* so nothing happened. I guess one needs to be an asshole to innovate, at least when self-righteous pricks want you to do things their stupid way." Rudi grinned. "So I finally did what they wanted, but with a twist."

"What do you mean?"

"Well, I guess you saw the server farm in the other room," Rudi said, his brow suddenly lined with concern. "That guy, Henshaw? The big boss? Everybody around here calls him the *Pater*. Anyway, he comes down here and tells me he wants those servers tracking everybody on the planet, then to use that info to predict world events, stock markets, social trends, economics, shit that's simply impossible, *you* know that. Complexity is chaos. There are limits to accuracy, especially in the long term, which is what he wanted, next week's stock price, for instance." Rudi giggled. "So I set up a virtual simulation, one that looked legit and guessed better than random but only barely. If they try it out for near-future predictions, it'll look good but when they project out past a week, the results will bankrupt their accounts. All I need is to trip the dead man's switch."

"So, you've got a back door into their system," Dan said.

Rudi laughed. "You kidding me? My operating system *is* the back door, and the front door too. They can't lock me out of my own OS."

"Good, let them think everything is fine, until we decide it's not." Dan began to feel back in control but needed help solving the next piece of the puzzle. "Rudi, how the hell do we get out of this place?"

"Huh?" Rudi stared at him with his trademark look of incredulity. "You just walk down that hall there." He pointed down the aisle they had just traversed. "There's an elevator about twenty yards down that way."

"What?" Dan laughed. *Ada, you sent me around my elbow to get to my nose.* The circuitous route he had followed to get here had diverted him through the server room and sent the assault team on a wild-goose chase.

He had no idea how long their position would remain a mystery. "Let's get the hell out of here. Are there any lab coats or garb we can put on to disguise ourselves? Long enough to sneak out of the building?"

"Sure," Rudi said. "Lockers down the hall, with lab coats, masks, face guards . . . the lab guys were always wearing that shit. Lots of scientists, experimenting."

They started toward the locker room when Dan remembered something. "You said Gruber cooked those pecan pralines using modified high-fructose corn syrup. Where'd he get that?"

"Oh, from *there*," Rudi said, pointing. Across the hall was a lab crisscrossed with white PVC pipes. Mature corn stalks brown with age, poked out of holes along the pipe every eight inches.

Rudi continued, "According to Gruber, they engineered those corn plants to make the ingredients of his high-fructose grovel-juice. Gruber was real proud of those plants, said the details were in the devil."

"What?" Dan stopped in his tracks. "He said that, exactly?"

"Yep," Rudi said. "He seemed to like the play on words. '*The details are in the devil.*'"

"Like the Devil's Paradox?" Dan stuttered.

Rudi grew pensive, stared at the ceiling. "Yeah, as a matter of fact, I've heard that term a couple of times. What does it mean?"

"The Devil's Paradox is the new name Esrom Nesson chose for the organism we found in Honduras. He thought it was a more apt description."

"What?" Rudi stared at him, his impudence dissolving. "You mean they've been fucking around with that monster to make his praline shit?"

"Exactly." Dan stared at the exhausted stalks of brown corn, their ears long since harvested. "It's called biopharming, with a *p*. A da Kurz says this group has been experimenting with using crops to manufacture drugs."

Rudi stared blankly, his mind churning.

Up until now, Rachel had been mostly silent, content to provide Dan with support but now she moved to the glass wall between them and the lab. She placed her hands against the glass, staring at the depleted stalks of corn. "Rudi, this was a large crop in here. Is this where the high-fructose corn sugar came from? The stuff in your pralines?"

Rudi shrugged. "I, uh, assume so. Once Gruber got me here, he didn't seem so careful about bragging on their accomplishments. Guess he thought I was just some clueless dweeb."

"Is this the only crop?" Rachel said.

"Yeah, I guess so . . . *Wait!* No, that *Pater* guy, Henshaw, was all excited at the result. Told Gruber to plant their field of dreams."

"Plant where?" Rachel said.

Rudi shrugged.

Rachel and Dan stared at each other.

"That field of young corn, the ones we saw flying in, you think?"

"Yes," Rachel said, her eyes aflame. "You remember what happens when the devil sees the light of day?"

Rachel pointed to the exhausted crop in the lab. "That corn was all grown hydroponically, under artificial light, LEDs. What do they lack? They don't emit ultraviolet light. Only the sun does that. If the crop up *there*"—she pointed toward the surface—"contains genes from the Devil's Paradox, then its mutation instincts will be triggered and there's no telling what genetic adaptations those plants will construct. Same thing happened to that guy, Victor Moody."

"My god," Dan stammered, suddenly remembering Victor's violent outburst in Henshaw's office. "These idiots have no idea what they've unleashed."

The three of them stood silently, staring at one another in shock.

"We've got to destroy that crop," Rachel said. "No matter what it takes. If those corn plants mature and mutate, put out pollen, it'll blow away in the wind, affect other crops. The devil will be out of his prison and there's no telling what will happen!"

Visions flashed through Dan's mind, memories from the waters off Honduras, where he and Rachel had faced a similar challenge. Could they pull it off again? Avoid the horror of the unknown?

"How?" he said. "How can we destroy acres of corn plants? Just the three of us, with Henshaw's men chasing behind? How do we make sure we get them all?"

"Don't know," she replied. "But we've got to try."

Dan's mind was racing at full speed. "Rudi, you've got to make sure to destroy what's left of that crop down here, any seed banks, research notes, etc. Can you do that?"

"The research is easy." Rudi grinned. "It's all on the servers. I got a lot of pent-up frustration to release. I can think of something for the lab itself, like another fire. This place has mondo ventilation."

"Good! Get it done. We get to the elevator that way?" Dan pointed down the hall.

"Yep. Go to the end and turn right. It's right there."

"When you're done down here, put on a lab disguise, head up the elevator, and look for an old-fashioned airplane. Hide in the shadows until you see a chance to meet us, okay?"

Rudi tilted his head to one side. "Old-fashioned airplane?"

"You'll know. Just *get* there." Dan looked in Rachel's direction but she was already halfway down the hall.

"Come on!" she shouted over her shoulder.

Before passing through the one-way security door, they stopped in the locker room long enough to don protective gear: Tyvek suits, hoods, protective masks, and splash guards—personal protective equipment typical for genetic scientists and common in the age of Covid. No one would think twice about their outfits, which should buy them some time. Outfitted, they passed through security and entered the elevator, checking first for any signs of the assault team.

"Looks like our pursuers still think we're down below," Dan said, as the elevator doors opened on the surface. The chip factory was empty, except for a handful of orange suits working on the toxic spill. Far down the hall, outside the plant, he could see a crowd of bunny-suited workers milling about randomly on the rear loading docks.

"How are we gonna do this?" he said. "We have no way to destroy an entire corn crop."

"I've got an idea," Rachel replied. "We just need to put the Horsemen's mindless servants to work." Then she explained.

Dan rolled his eyes at the absurdity and brilliance of Rachel's idea, but agreed.

It was the only way.

"Together then," he said.

"Yes, together," Rachel replied.

34

WEARING THEIR LAB disguises, Dan and Rachel walked briskly down the long enclosed hallway that separated them from the surrounding clean-room. The tunnel ended at the loading docks.

They stepped out into the bright sunlight. To the right, down the sloping hillside and level with the loading docks, was a small parking lot, presumably for the laboratory workers who manned the hidden depths of the Horsemen's lair. Straight ahead and to the left, the land behind the plant had been carved out of a large hillside, its soil held back by a vertical stone retaining wall, one that Dan remembered vividly from his last visit.

A random mixture of clean-room employees and lab technicians milled about aimlessly, waiting to be told what to do, or for the alarms to quit sounding. Most were still dressed in their bunny suits and lab coats, stubbornly unwilling to violate protocol. Other workers had removed their hoods and were pacing impatiently, sweating in the hot noonday sun. Dan spotted several orange-suited security guards weaving their way through the crowd in an orderly fashion.

Looking for the two of them.

"Time to act," Dan said.

Rachel nodded, peeling off to the right and heading around the dome's circumference.

Dan broke left and dissolved into the crowd of lab coats, keeping distance from the orange suits. He made his way to the outer perimeter of the crowd, struggling to maintain a relaxed gait, as if he were just another worker. A long line of delivery vans were backed up to the loading docks, blocked by a pair of fire trucks, which had arrived to fight the fire Rachel had started earlier.

He turned left and slipped down the narrow pathway between the delivery vans and the tall retaining wall. Straight ahead, twenty feet up the sheer stone, he could see the longhorn cattle languidly grazing on the pasture above.

A shout echoed down the narrow pathway from two orange suits a hundred yards back. They gave chase, prompting Dan to pick up his pace. He broke into a full run, aiming for the corner, where two stone walls converged. During his last visit to this facility, he had descended this wall to hide inside one of the shipping vans.

Now, he would need to *ascend* that same vertical wall before the guards managed to catch up with him. It would challenge his rock climbing skills in the best of circumstances.

Not this time.

He opted for a shortcut, using a climbing technique known as "stemming" to ascend the 90-degree corner. With full momentum, he leapt up the wall as far as he could reach, wedging his feet against the two perpendicular surfaces. He scrambled crab-like up the corner, fueled by adrenaline and the thrill of the chase. It was amazing how fast he could travel up a featureless wall when properly motivated.

At that moment, his motivation was high and the shouts from behind grew ever closer. Using alternating foot thrusts and wall palming, he had almost reached the top when the guards arrived at his position. One man yelled an unintelligible warning. Dan was reaching for the top ledge when he heard a familiar popping sound coming from below.

His heart fluttered. *Sticky-stunners.*

He remembered the cursed devices from his last visit to the factory floor, air-propelled cartridges containing a battery-powered Taser device. The sticky-stunners could subdue a fugitive from a far distance without the risk of bullets damaging the ultra-clean environment inside the chip plant.

If a sticky-stunner hit him now, he'd fall twenty feet to the concrete pavement below. Luckily, the stunners were not very accurate and the first one bounced harmlessly off the stone wall about a foot from his right arm.

He wasn't going to wait around for another shot. Dan took a mighty thrust, propelling himself upward another several feet. He managed to roll over the top of the retaining wall just as a second stunner tagged the right cheek of his butt and held on. He rolled to a stop on the dirt above, every muscle in his body seizing from the electric pulses.

He was locked in a catatonic embrace with the electric device and

wondered how long the charge on the battery would last. The electronics were designed to alternate through release and stun cycles. Every
time he'd reach to pull the stunner away, another terrific jolt of high
voltage would render him helpless. He was stuck.

A cow walked over and nudged him with its wet nose, curious about
the gyrating human wallowing in the grass, helpless.

ONCE SHE AND Dan had split up, Rachel rounded the curvature of
the dome and disappeared from the sight of the crowd. She broke into
a full sprint, aiming for the guard tower at the entrance. She followed
the hedge line bordering the sidewalk, picking up speed, mustering all
her energy and stamina, honed from years of running.

Risking a glance back at the dome, she saw a tranquil building,
ordinary, the only hint of trouble coming from a wisp of dark smoke
rising from its rear and spiraling upward into the wind that circled the
dome's apex.

It was a sight strange enough to attract the attention of the two
guards, who were standing outside their guard tower staring back in her
direction. One guard was attempting to raise someone on his walkie-
talkie.

Even from this distance, Rachel could see the confusion on the two
guards' faces. Unsure how to get past them without getting shot, she
finally decided to leverage the current circumstances and her latest
disguise: a white lab coat, splash visor, and N-95 mask.

As she approached their position, both guards tensed, ready for
action. She slammed to a stop right in front of them, hands on knees,
gasping for breath.

"Who are you?" one of the guards demanded. "What's going on
back there?"

Rachel sucked in a couple of extra breaths and yelled at the top of
her lungs. "Chemical release!" she gasped. "The cloud's headed your
way. Lethal hydrofluoric acid! Run for your lives!"

She didn't wait for a response and took off in the direction of the
security gate, hoping her helpful suggestion and their confusion would
buy her enough time to escape.

It worked, sort of.

She heard one of the guards yelling at her. "Wait! Miss! You can't . . ."

She kept running at full tilt, hoping she could make the cover of the large hedges at the entrance to the factory before the guards recaptured their wits. The run seemed to last forever, her legs burning but as she rounded the hedge, she glanced over her shoulder.

The ruse had worked. Both men were still standing at the security gate, one of them shouting into his radio.

Straight ahead, the welcome shape of the red and white Bücker Jungmann greeted her. She'd never been so happy to see the venerable old plane.

Reaching the cockpit, she scrambled over the side, tearing off the visor and face mask and replacing them with her granda's old vintage goggles and silk scarf, the ones she always wore for luck whenever flying the Bücker.

She flipped on the ignition and waited for the familiar throaty whine of the turboprop engine. It roared to life and she pushed the throttle's balls to the wall, feeling the familiar acceleration of the plane lurching forward as the rpms reached maximum rotation.

The Bücker went airborne almost immediately. Over the nose, she spotted one of the guards rounding the corner of the hedges, gun out.

She could imagine his shock at finding a WWII biplane roaring down at him at full speed. Rachel kept the trajectory low, long enough to drive the guard into the ground, gun flailing out of his hand.

Then she pulled the stick back into her crotch and the Bücker roared up and away.

She was free!

A rush of adrenaline coursed through her body, eliciting a yell of sheer glee at being back in control of her granda's legacy. The Bücker went ballistic, rising skyward under the sheer power of the powerful turboprop engine. She rolled the plane upside down and took in the scene below, the vista spread out before her like inverted heaven.

Above her head, the factory's white dome hovered like a giant moon, its orbit filled with verdant green fields, ant-like four-legged cattle, white termite workers in their bunny suits milling about and orderly rows of young corn plants poking out of brown soil, like lances from the devil's handiwork.

No telling what genetic horrors were brewing down there in the light of day, she thought.

Before she could roll back over, Rachel spotted a lone white figure lying on the grass next to the chip factory's rear structure. Two orange-suited termites raced along the lower edge of a stone retaining wall separating the tiny figure from the loading dock at the rear end of the dome.

That must be Dan, she realized. But why was he just lying there? Had he been shot? She could see movement from the body and felt a flood of relief, remembering Dan's warning about the guards and their nonlethal weapons.

The two orange suits were rapidly approaching a staircase leading up to the level where Dan's body was located.

Rachel whipped the plane back upright and arced over the top of the dome, clearing its apex by a few feet. Then she banked left, toward the staircase and the two orange suits ascending it. The best she could do would be to buy time for Dan to recover.

She dipped the Bücker down almost level with the ground and aimed the plane for the head of the stairs.

The Bücker crossed the threshold just as the two guards reached the apex.

The sudden appearance of a three-bladed prop whirling at head height caused an instinctive reaction in both men. They fell backward to avoid the spinning blades of death and tumbled down the stairs.

Rachel glanced backward over the right fuselage to see bodies tumbling like bowling pins down the stairway. Both men landed at the bottom of the stairs, writhing in pain.

The Bücker gained five hundred feet of altitude in the few seconds it had taken her to observe the scene below. Dan would have to fend for himself. She had to place herself into a position to fulfill her part of the plan—that is, assuming Dan could recover.

THE ELECTRICAL JOLT from the sticky-stunner seemed to linger forever. Every time Dan thought he had respite from the debilitating charge, it would fill his body with paralyzing voltage, seizing his muscles and thwarting any attempts to control his own motions. He didn't know how much longer he could last.

The sticky-stunner was effective. The tiny, battery-powered device had left him helpless, pulsing with debilitating voltage. At any moment, he expected the orange suits to arrive and carry him away.

But they didn't. He continued to suffer alone in the throes of seizure.

Finally, imperceptibly at first, the time between stunning charges lengthened. The stunner projectile was small, its battery limited in power.

And that battery was beginning to lose its charge.

Between pulses, he mustered energy to take control of his muscles. He began timing the cycles, attempting to make an organized movement between them. Each cycle grew longer and weaker, until he finally managed to jerk the stunner's prongs out of his butt and throw them into the grass.

He shuddered with relief and struggled to stand, his muscles quivering from the high-voltage shocks. Stumbling forward across the field, he glanced again over his shoulder at the distant stairway, expecting an orange suit to appear at any moment . . . but no one came. He headed toward a large metal gate separating the cattle pen from the adjacent cornfield when the throaty growl of Rachel's Bücker passed overhead.

He stopped and stared at the sky.

Rachel's red-and-white Bücker Jungmann was circling overhead, its free flight urging him forward. He let out a yell of triumph and attempted an awkward wave and was rewarded with a waggle of the Bücker's wings.

The gate's padlocked chain came into view, barring his way to the other side. Dan reached into his pocket and retrieved the collection of bump keys Rachel had returned to him in the Horsemen's lair.

He fumbled through the collection, looking for one that would fit the profile of the padlock. After several tries, he found one that slid in with no resistance. Placing a small amount of pressure against the key, he tapped it several times with a rock. Amazingly, the lock responded with a grateful turn of the shaft. He released the chain and swung the gate wide open.

Circling above, Rachel responded by plunging the Bücker into a diving arc, directly toward the herd of cattle massed at the far end of the pasture.

The sudden appearance of the Bücker startled the bovines into action. They raced across the field toward the open gate. Dan ran in the opposite direction, content to let Rachel herd the cattle from the air.

The herd streamed through the opening into the adjacent cornfield, still fresh from plowing, the young shoots of the plants barely into their adolescence, their stalks about two feet tall.

Scattering ahead of the Bücker, the cattle trampled through the field. Rachel suddenly angled the Bücker skyward and the herd relaxed, settling in to their new world. Soon, they began to do what mindless cattle do.

They began to eat.

They munched relentlessly on the young corn plants and stomped others into the ground. With luck, Henshaw's cattle might destroy the entire crop.

It was time to move toward a prearranged rendezvous point the three of them had agreed to beforehand. Dan paused long enough to reach down and pluck a young corn shoot from the soil, wrapping it in a torn piece of lab coat and slipping it into his pocket. If the Horsemen were foolish enough to continue experimenting with the Devil's Paradox, then he needed a sample for Esrom, so some countermeasure could be engineered.

He circled to the far right of the herd and continued across the field, searching for Rudi, who should be arriving from the basement by now. Risking a glance behind him, he noticed a strange scene that froze him in his tracks.

The cattle's normally docile behavior began to change.

BRADLEY GRUBER SAT in his office at the far end of the dome, staring out the plate glass window toward the frenzied activities still taking place in Henshaw's executive suite. It appeared the guards had finally managed to subdue Victor Moody after a long period of intense struggle and the addition of several more guards and medical personnel. The medics were now hovering over a motionless Henshaw as the guards struggled to carry away a handcuffed, maniacal, screaming banshee of a man, who had once been the quiet soldier, Victor Moody.

Moody's feral screams could be heard clearly echoing across the dome and they had Gruber totally unnerved. He held up a trembling hand and struggled to get his heartbeat under control, all the while obsessively stroking his Patek Philippe watch until the tip of his finger was raw.

He'd never seen anything like that and his panicked behavior had embarrassed him. Bradley Gruber was supposed to be the man in control, cool as a cucumber, the manipulator, not the *manipulated*. He choked back an involuntary sob, suddenly realizing that he wasn't cut out for the front lines. He'd always had loyal soldiers to do the "wet work." The vision of Victor Moody ripping at Henshaw's face and the bloody imagery that had escaped his natural censoring mechanism was burning a hole in his brain.

Come on, Gruber, you're better than this.

He closed his eyes, inhaled deeply, slowed the strokes on his watch, and tried to remember a childhood in Switzerland, filled with order, wonder, and promise.

After a few minutes, he sighed, felt his heartbeat slow, and decided to make a fateful call.

The voice on other end answered quickly. "Bradley Gruber? This is a surprise. What does Henshaw want now?"

"Good afternoon, Dromus," Gruber said with the silkiest and most reverential voice he could muster. "I'm just calling to congratulate you."

"Oh?" The voice rose in pitch and interest. "Congratulate me for what?"

"Why, on your pending promotion, of course. You know I keep my nose to the wind about these things and I strongly suspect that your movement to Pater is imminent. There have been, uh, let's say, some complications at the chip factory that may require a new, fresh leadership approach."

The voice on the other end paused. "What kind of complications? And why call me? I thought you were Henshaw's lackey."

"Such an unfortunate term, 'lackey,'" Gruber crooned. "Dromus, my loyalty is to the cause, not to any one man and right now, it is my firm belief that you are the man of the hour. Please allow me to provide you with a smooth transition and excellent advisory capacity."

"Humph," the voice said. "Why do I get the feeling you are playing me? Besides, you haven't even told me what's going on."

"I beg your patience for the rest of the day," Gruber crooned. "But, be assured that I will be back in touch with all the details when they fully reveal themselves."

Gruber said goodbye and hung up, suddenly feeling much better about things. He watched quietly as two medics wheeled a gurney containing Henshaw's body down the long, circular gangway that gave management their lofty oversight of the workers below.

Maybe he could get used to the backwoods of Honduras, if he only had a better executive suite.

FROM HER LOFTY perspective, Rachel watched the herd of cattle pour into the cornfield and trample the plants.

Their plan appeared to be working.

Predictably, the cattle dispersed across the field, relaxing into foraging activity. They began devouring the tender young seedlings. Rachel pumped her fist and released a defiant scream. She circled, far enough away to avoid panicking the cattle any further, while tracking Dan's path as he jogged across the field toward their rendezvous point.

At first, the herd munched away quietly, trampling over any plants not eaten in the first few minutes. But as Rachel continued to watch, a subtle change seemed to alter the cattle's behavior. Several steers in the herd became agitated, abandoning their meal to wrestle with one another. Soon, the entire herd was fighting amongst themselves, bucking, leaping, pawing the ground, their tails twirling wildly, their aggression directed at every other animal in the pasture.

Rachel stared at the inexplicable scene, soon realizing what had happened. The Horsemen's test crop of pharming chemicals had already gone awry. Whatever alterations the Horsemen had intended for this test crop, it had been usurped by the Devil's Paradox. Triggered by its own unique survival response to UV light, the organism's three-billion-year-old programming had created its own bizarre genetic mutation. Pharming chemicals were obviously still being produced but it definitely wasn't accomplishing the Horsemen's original goal of creating docile obedience. Instead, the herd was acting like feral creatures, brimming with ancient aggression. She wondered how long it would have taken their lab techs to realize their mistake. Probably not until the corn was harvested, after clouds of contaminated pollen would have blown away in the wind to poison nearby crops.

Rachel planned to bank the plane for another pass but her attention was interrupted by a dark gray form rolling out of the rear entrance of the chip factory. It headed across the long paved shipping area and picked up speed. Scattering suited workers in all directions, the mysterious vehicle turned and aimed toward the parking lot. A few feet from the end of the pavement, it lifted off the ground and shot into the sky at a steep angle. The vehicle's distinctive shape triggered a flash of recognition in Rachel's mind.

Powered by its twin jet engines, the unmanned drone gained altitude quickly, turned, and aimed directly for her.

DAN RAN THROUGH the melee of cattle, trying to avoid potholes and keeping to the far edge of the field. He was aiming for the fence that separated the cornfield from the hill leading down toward the rear parking area.

The sudden change in the mood of the cattle caused him to pick up his gait. A couple of the larger steers broke from the herd and focused their aggression toward him. They gave chase, closing the distance quickly.

Dan broke into a full sprint, heading straight toward the fence's perimeter. A loud bellow from behind prompted a glance back. One crazed steer had closed the distance to a few feet and was gaining. Dan reached the fence and launched himself over the barbed wire. He hit the ground on a roll and bounced right back up into an upright position on the other side.

He was astonished to watch the steer collide with the fence at full speed, snorting and huffing as it became entangled in several strands of barbed wire. It rolled to the ground and thrashed about madly until finally wrangling free from the barbs. With rivulets of blood streaming down its sides, the steer hesitated, wobbling in distress. Dan took off again, hoping to put distance between himself and the crazed creature. The steer snorted, kicked the ground with its hoof, and gave chase haltingly.

Noticing the gaping hole in the fence, the rest of the herd broke into a run and headed his way. Dan had become the bell cow, directing the herd down the hill toward the parking area: the very rendezvous point where Rachel would be attempting to land her plane.

Somehow he'd have to change direction and lead the stampeding herd away, but he was flanked on the right side by the retaining wall that dropped vertically to the shipping area. There, a crowd of workers had gathered to watch the bizarre activities taking place on the hill above. Dan searched the exit at the end of the shipping dock, hoping to see Rudi appear at any moment. A new stream of smoke had begun rising from vents along the dome's perimeter, signaling that Rudi had been successful at starting a fire deep underground.

The stampede was gaining on him and he was getting winded.

Before he could change direction a loud roar turned his attention back to the shipping area, just in time to see a NeuroSys drone roaring out the back of the dome and directly over his head. The searing exhaust of its twin engines sent him rolling into the grass.

The startling noise spooked the cows and the herd broke right, heading directly toward the retaining wall, where they promptly ran off the edge without a pause, falling fifteen feet to the concrete below. The lead animals hit the pavement with a splat, scattering workers in all directions and creating a writhing, bellowing mass of bloody beef. The cattle at the rear of the stampede were more fortunate, landing on the misshapen carcasses of their brethren below. Stunned and crazed, the survivors struggled up from the mound and took off in all directions, chasing desperate bunny-clad workers, colliding with plate glass doors and windows, slamming into trucks. Several distraught cows entered the former ultra-clean facility through a broken window, tracking mud and manure over the floors and knocking over assembly tables.

Mesmerized by the chaos below, Dan had to force himself to look up in search of the drone. Its trajectory was aimed directly toward Rachel's Bücker.

THE METALLIC RATTLE of a chain gun echoed through the air as bullets tore through the thin fabric of the biplane's rear fuselage. Stunned by the sudden act of aggression, Rachel faltered for a split second. She reacted instinctively, slamming the Bücker's control stick into her thigh, sensing the sudden torque of motion as the plane responded with compliant aggression.

The biplane flipped upside down and torqued away from the stream of bullets. She slammed the control stick in the opposite direction and the Bücker's fragile frame of wood and fabric shuddered under the g-forces, reversing again as a burst of hot exhaust scalded Rachel's face. The gray metal of the drone rushed past her, gaining altitude in the blue sky, twisting its frame and returning for another pass.

Its sudden appearance left her disoriented. Her mind went blank. She couldn't concentrate.

A strange sense of dread clouded her senses. What was she feeling, exactly?

Fear?

It was an emotion she had scant experience with, having spent most of her adult life secretly fantasizing about a quick and easy exit from this world, unencumbered by the long and difficult struggle assured by a Huntington's prognosis.

The fantasy of a painless escape had always kept her fear at bay.

But now, all she felt was *hope,* hope for a real life with Dan, of a normal existence, of peace and happiness into old age.

For the first time in her life, Rachel realized she feared death.

The realization left her paralyzed as the drone bore down once again.

Another stream of bullets wrote Rachel's epitaph across the sky.

Daughter, granddaughter, unexpected sibling, stunt-flyer, reluctant lover, adventurer.

It was true what they said: your life passes before you in its entirety, a sudden distillation compressed into a fractal life.

Another rain of lead pierced the plane's fragile fabric. Rachel felt the sting of penetration like a tearing of flesh into her granda's legacy. The Bücker had defined him, a fusion of man and machine greater than their component parts.

The legacy was hers now, the last vestige of her grandfather's heritage.

Rachel's basic instincts took hold. She banked the tattered Bücker to the right, struggling to maintain control with the damaged tail surfaces. Then she remembered Granda's old lesson: *agility beats power.*

Only this drone was powerful *and* nimble. Without a pilot to protect, or g-forces to concern itself with, this drone defied the natural limitations of most jets.

Rachel dipped and swerved the damaged biplane but couldn't seem to shake the drone. She tried every tortuous aerobatic maneuver she could think of, but a quick glance revealed the jet still on her tail, spraying bullets wildly across the fields, now strangely devoid of cows.

It was zeroing in . . .

She needed a flaw to exploit and remembered one from her brief time piloting the TaurusSec drone in Savannah. This drone's keyhole camera was aptly named, because its peripheral vision sucked.

Another spray of bullets tore more fabric from the rudder. Rachel banked left steeply, using the architecture of the dome to guide her trajectory.

DAN STARED UP at the sky, horrified at the mad scene playing out above. The metallic rattle of the drone's chain gun took him back to the chaos in Ada's cabin, the spray of bullets, blood, and splinters. Whoever piloted the drone seemed focused solely on Rachel's plane, oblivious to the clamoring crowd below and the wild spray of bullets.

Several cows in the shipping area dropped dead from the random fire. The shower of random bullets sent many of the suited workers back into the plant for cover, against the desperate shouts of security.

Dan's feet were frozen to the ground as he stared at the scene, wondering if he had saved Rachel's life only to watch her lose it in a moment of madness.

He was helpless, unable to do anything but find Rudi. He continued down the hill toward the parking area and the basement exit, hoping to at least reunite with the man he'd gone all this way to rescue. There, staring up at the sky, was Rudi, dressed in a lab coat and mask.

"Come on!" he shouted. "We've got to reach the open area of the lot."

Rudi stood like a mannequin, pointing skyward.

"Yes, I know!" He grabbed Rudi's arm and jerked him forward into a run, away from the crowd and toward the outer perimeter of the factory grounds. There would be just enough open field there for Rachel to land her plane.

If she survived.

THE BÜCKER'S TURBOPROP engine screamed at full throttle. Rachel kept the biplane's control stick anchored to her left thigh, drawing the craft into an ever-tightening, accelerated turn. The tenuous frame of wood and cabling protested, shuddering and twisting, shreds of fabric peeling off in the intense turbulence of the turn.

Having moved beyond the panic of her earlier shock, Rachel suddenly felt clearheaded, focused on every twitch and nuance of the vehicle she had grown up piloting. She remembered the old dogfighting trick that Granda had taught her as a child.

A last-chance maneuver for escaping an ace on your tail.

As the turn tightened into a corkscrew, the Bücker's speed and angle of bank increased, approaching the edge of an accelerated stall, at which point pilot and machine would simply lose lift and fall from the sky.

Unable to look behind her, Rachel had to hope the drone had followed her into the ever-tightening death spiral. Straight ahead, the creamy blank wall of the NeuroSys factory dome filled her vision. A thin line of concrete bits and shrapnel exploded across the blank dome to her right, verifying that the drone was indeed on her tail, its gunfire closing ever more tightly onto her position.

Right at the moment when the shuddering frame of the plane could take no more stress, she suddenly released the control stick, pulled back on the throttle, and jerked the plane's landing flaps into their bottom-most position.

The sudden introduction of the flaps had two effects: it vastly increased the lift of the wings and their drag. Slowing drastically, the Bücker fluttered upward like a leaf on the wind and seemed to hover motionless in the air, a few hundred feet above the dome.

Caught unawares by the sudden deceleration and lift of the Bücker, the jet-powered drone continued forward, its streamlined fuselage incapable of slowing so suddenly. It passed directly underneath the Bücker at full speed.

Chain guns still rattling, the drone collided midway up the side of the concrete dome, erupting into a flaming ball of jet fuel.

Rachel reengaged the throttle and banked the biplane to the right, gliding above the dome's curvature on a cushion of air a few feet above its surface. She stared out the left side of the cockpit at the conflagration below.

The drone had punched a hole into the side of the dome. Beyond the fireball, she could see debris scattered across an elevated platform suspended above the factory floor.

Allowing herself a fleeting sardonic smile at besting the modern weapon, Rachel made a U-turn and flew toward the far boundary of the factory. Two white-coated shapes were bounding across the open field toward their rendezvous point.

35

DAN WASN'T SURE what was more stressful: the chaotic events at the NeuroSys plant or the journey back to Duff McAlister's remote cabin, crammed into the rear cockpit of Rachel's ravaged plane, air billowing through gaping holes in the plane's fabric, with Rudi Plimpton sitting on his lap like a child having a tantrum. Dan could barely contain his frustration.

He'd had no idea Rudi had a fear of heights but the unstable journey back across the ocean had left his friend in a state of restless panic. The damage to the Bücker hadn't helped matters. Luckily, the plane's overpowered turboprop engine managed to compensate for any reduced lift from the plane's many bullet holes. By the time they reached Guanaja, Dan's knees were numb and he had been elbowed numerous times by Rudi's nervous gyrations.

They landed on the beach at sunset, the tranquil scene belying the mayhem they had endured that day. Dan spilled out onto the beach and struggled to recover some circulation in his legs.

Once on the ground, Rudi quickly returned to his typical irreverent personality. Meanwhile, Rachel, having been joined by Duff, rolled the damaged Bücker underneath a cover of trees.

That night, back in Duff's cabin, the four of them crowded around Duff's small table, dining on succulent fresh oysters, copious amounts of Guinness, and island salad.

Every few minutes, Rudi would jump up to check the internet for news updates.

"Holy crap!" he exclaimed. "The chip factory is all over the news but not a word about us."

"That doesn't surprise me," Dan said. "How can they mention our involvement without admitting to kidnapping charges? There's no evidence of our presence here." The day had been a dream, a fantasy of hope against the reality of insurmountable odds. And yet, they had survived, somehow. "What about Henshaw? The Pater?"

Rudi studied his laptop screen. "Not a word. Well, except one. There's an American news report that says, 'Lucas Henshaw, the famous American movie producer, has mysteriously vanished, supposedly lost in a private plane accident over Alaska.'" Rudi laughed. "Who's gonna believe that? I just saw the man yesterday."

"What else can they say?" Rachel said. "I'm sure Henshaw was visiting Honduras incognito, so they'd need some kind of cover story. As we all know, international air travel isn't quite as secure as the public is led to believe." She grinned mischievously. "Like, we're not even . . . here."

"Well, your plane's famous nonetheless." Rudi giggled. "Everybody's trying to figure out the identity of the mysterious biplane that caused so much mayhem. Hmm, no pictures though. How did we escape without a single cell phone pic? Amazing."

"Not surprising," Dan said. "No one working at the NeuroSys factory would be allowed to possess a cell phone during working hours. Too much of a security risk. That's the flip side of secrecy over truth." He took a generous gulp of Guinness from his glass. "Nevertheless, we'll need to keep the Bücker under wraps. There can't be too many vintage biplanes flying around the world."

"Yes, but we're still in the States, remember?" Rachel grinned. "Nobody's going to believe we snuck past American flight security."

"Maybe." Dan shrugged, grinned. "Let's not give them the chance to make the connection. We need to become visible stateside, as soon as possible." He groaned, thinking of the marathon trip home with Rudi Plimpton sitting on his lap.

THE NEXT MORNING, Duff arrived at the cabin with containers to refuel the Bücker's tanks. The decorative red-and-white decor of the plane was almost unrecognizable due to copious amounts of duct tape used to patch the numerous bullet holes. Rachel insisted the aerodynamics of the biplane would be fine.

Duff had built a wooden contraption consisting of bracing that could be mounted above the seat in the rear cockpit. Dan would switch places with Rudi, insisting that he sit in the original seat. Then the second seat would be placed above Rudi's lap and take the full weight of Dan's body. Hopefully, the two of them could endure the long trip crammed into the small space.

By the time the Bücker had been refueled, patched, and modified, the sun was beginning to dip in the western sky. The four of them convened one last time in the cabin for a farewell dinner of fish tacos and Spanish rice. They stuffed themselves, knowing it would be their last meal until reaching Spence Air Base. Rachel had already arranged for a new fabric makeover and paint job for the old Bücker.

After dinner, Dan led Rachel out to the cabin's deck to watch the sunset at the place where their relationship had begun. What more fitting time and venue for a move he'd postponed for far too long? He dug around in his pocket for his key chain and felt the familiar circular shape he'd nervously checked for, several times during the last several days.

The ring was still there and he let out a long sigh of relief. Rachel must have noticed his worried expression, because she backed up cautiously. Dan awkwardly turned away from her to remove the engagement ring from his key chain, then turned around, about to drop to one knee, when Rachel placed both hands on his shoulders.

"No, don't," she said, a thin smile drifting across her face. "I know what you're about to do, and I love you for it but . . ." She squeezed his shoulders and drew him closer. "Now's not the time. We don't know if the gene therapy worked but I promise to stay around until we know for sure. Just, please don't ask me to inject myself into your life until I know for sure . . ."

The look on his face had to be palpable, judging from Rachel's heartsick expression. Dan continued: "Look, we're going to die eventually. What difference does it make if it's tomorrow or fifty years from now? We still have each other . . . now. Let's make the most of it."

"I know," she said, looking away, unable to face him. "But protecting you from suffering is *my* gift to you. Accept it willingly. I'm still here. Patience," she said and hugged Dan tightly.

He let the ring fall silently back into his pocket. "Then promise me, you won't abandon our relationship without fair warning. No sneaking off in the dark of night. I'm your partner and we'll endure the news together, whatever it is. Then, if you must, you can handle the end your way. Deal?"

Rachel stared at him, her eyes pools of sadness and joy. "Okay, together."

"Yes, together." He grinned.

The two of them held each other in a long embrace as they listened to the sounds of the night creatures coming alive in the Honduran forest.

TWO WEEKS LATER

It was a hot and sultry day in Savannah when Dan stepped out of his car. Dressed in his new disguise of baseball cap, wide sunglasses, and a two-week growth of beard stubble, Dan stopped momentarily to take in a whiff of ocean air. The sun was bright and he could feel its warmth on his face. After a pause, he continued across the parking lot to the front door of Stoker's warehouse.

He knocked.

A young woman dressed in full goth attire opened the door. She showed a hint of disinterest and stepped back to allow him inside. The warehouse space seemed the same as he remembered, with the exception of several new machines that had been installed on the warehouse floor. Several makers, using the new machines, were hard at work on various projects.

Far ahead in the shadows, Stoker sat at his small bar.

Dan walked over.

Stoker grinned at him. "Welcome home."

"What do you mean?" Dan feigned surprise. "I never left."

"Right." Stoker smiled. "Beer?"

"If you've got a normal one, yes," he said. "No special brews."

Stoker waved his hand dismissively. "Only good for special occasions. I can offer you a plain old Guinness."

"Perfect." Dan sat down and placed a manila envelope on the bar.

Stoker eyed it ruefully. "You know, the Firemen would be thrilled to welcome you as their new leader."

Dan took a long pull from his Guinness and slid the envelope across the bar. "I want you to have this. It's Chemerra's black phone." Dan smiled. "I'm not cut out to be the leader of a secret society but *you* are." He tapped the envelope for effect. Stoker grinned demurely and accepted the package, sliding his own package forward. "We'll miss you."

"As will we," Dan replied. "I plan to keep in touch but I think Rachel and I need some time alone."

Stoker's right eyebrow twitched skyward. "You know the Horsemen will never stop looking for you. The damage you've done to their organization, their plans—they won't forget it."

"I know that," Dan said, staring down at Stoker's offering. "Is this everything?"

"Of course," Stoker said. "As you requested, new identities, officially 'Daniel and Rochelle Steadman.'"

Dan grinned. "Perfect." He had requested fictitious first names that were syntactically similar to their own, to help with recognition. But even he couldn't avoid a little subtle irony. If 'Dan and Rachel Clifford' couldn't be married in real life, then their fictional personas could be.

"Oh, and one other thing," Dan said. "When I was browsing through Chemerra's files, I came across this." He swiped through the black phone to an icon labeled BITCOIN ACCOUNT.

Stoker's eyes grew wide. "Is this real?"

"As real as any fiat currency can be," he said, grinning. "Apparently, Chemerra's DNA computer was good at more than breaking encryption cyphers." He scrolled through the Bitcoin menu. "It also made a damn good Bitcoin miner." The balance in the Bitcoin account exceeded eight figures, an incredible amount for a virtual bank balance.

"This should be plenty to finance the Firemen's activities," Dan said. "I hope you don't mind but as Chemerra's prime benefactor, I transferred a certain amount of the balance into our private account. Trying to stay incognito will be expensive. We'll need funds."

"I totally understand," Stoker said breathlessly. "Here. Take these." He pushed two phones forward. "If you ever need our help, call us on these black phones, totally untraceable, of course. You and Rachel can use them to communicate, without fear of monitoring."

Stoker completed the transaction with yet another envelope containing a complete historical record of Daniel and Rochelle Steadman, including childhood photos, high school portraits, a full employment history, and links to social media pages.

"Per your request," Stoker continued, "you have a degree in anthropology and Rochelle is a former professional diver."

Dan nodded. "Sounds good, and what about Rudi?"

"Oh, don't worry. We'll take care of him." Stoker sat back in his chair. "He's a perfect match for our organization. We can use his skills to fight the Horsemen, especially with his back doors into their data acquisition system."

"Can I reach him?" Dan asked. "On my new black phone?"

"Absolutely. He's already programmed into your contact list. Oh, and I took the liberty of setting your Minion app to colonel rank. If you ever need help, you'll be able to garner our services anywhere in the world."

"I guess that's about it," Dan said as he rose to leave.

"One more thing," Stoker said. "Generic YouGene has added your likeness and Rachel's to his inventory of masks. Very soon, Generic Dans and Generic Rachels will be triggering facial recognition algorithms worldwide."

"Anonymity through ubiquity, right?" Dan said.

"Right. Your persona as a hacker is well-known. It only makes sense that you and Rachel exist in the hacker realm as hero figures. You'll soon have cosplay personas imitating you two at gaming conventions."

Dan hesitated for a moment. "I'm not sure I like having our faces everywhere. How is that going to allow us to travel incognito? Our real faces will still trigger facial recognition systems whenever we go through security. What does it matter that hundreds of other people will be doing the same? We could still get caught."

Stoker winked and grinned. "Let's just say, you two have been given some digital plastic surgery."

"What does that mean?"

"You should know, YouGene is our resident magician. Tricks are all about directing the observer's focus where *you* want it to be. Haven't you noticed that his Generic YouGene masks look a little bit off? Not quite right?"

Dan thought about it for a minute. "It's pretty damn close, I just thought that was the limitations of his 3-D printer."

Stoker laughed. "Nope. He could make an exact replica of his face, down to the nose hairs, if he wanted."

"So? I don't get it."

"Humans really aren't that good at recognizing faces," Stoker said. "We cue on changeable things like hair style and color, eyebrow size, bridge of the nose, facial hair, and so on. Things we can easily alter. But facial recognition machines cue in on unchangeable values, ratios between eyes, nose, and mouth positions. Do you really think YouGene wants his face recognized any more than you do? His Generic YouGene masks were run through a 'Genericize AI' program, which altered the mask's facial recognition parameters, while remaining recognizable enough for humans to identify. YouGene's *real* face doesn't trigger any facial recognition, but his masks? Oh yeah."

"His face has got to trigger for somebody."

"Does it?" Stoker asked. "Generic YouGene doesn't exist. He's an avatar and the name of a mask. A mask that the *real* YouGene imitates."

"Then who is the real YouGene?"

"Hell if I know," Stoker said. "And he likes it that way."

Dan still felt lost. "Yeah but everybody knows Dan Clifford. How are a bunch of cosplay Dan Cliffords going to help our disguise?"

Stoker grinned. "How do facial recognition systems know Dan Clifford really exists?"

"Well, I have a birth certificate, driver's license. My fingerprints are on file. I've been on the news several times."

"No, 'Generic Dan Clifford' exists," Stoker replied. "His mask has been genericized just enough to differ from you to facial recognition machines but not to your admirers. *You* are Daniel Steadman. Next week, someone wearing a Generic Dan Clifford mask will register for a new driver's license and passport, for Dan Clifford. They will register their fingerprints. Every facial recognition machine in the world will be referring to your identification data that is currently on file in your passport and motor vehicle records, to identify Dan Clifford, who will only be triggered by a Generic Dan Clifford mask. As we speak, YouGene's Genericize AI routine is combing through all your and Rachel's old social media pictures and videos, running a subtle 'deep fake' routine to match the Generic Dan Clifford and Generic Rachel Sullivan masks. By next week, the old original Dan Clifford will cease to exist, at least to any digital machine on the planet. And I'll bet if you two work on your disguises, most human acquaintances will fail to recognize you as well."

Stoker grinned and shook Daniel Steadman's hand. "Welcome to your new life."

AFTERWORD

What is the difference between a magician and a con man? The magician announces his deception up front for the benefit and entertainment of the audience. The con man hides his deception from the audience behind a veil of false truth, for personal gain and profit.

In a sense, authors and scriptwriters are magicians. We weave our magical flights of fancy for our audience, but as professionals, we have an obligation to announce our deceptions up front by labeling our work as fiction, novels, techno-thrillers, or movies.

Ever since the human race could talk, stories have shaped our opinions and perceptions, whether told around the campfire in hushed tones, pressed into the pages of a book, or acted out on the stage or big screen. Stories offer lessons for life, precisely because they dramatize the challenges we all face, without the risk of personal harm or responsibility. Stories can either entertain or enlighten, and sometimes, they accomplish both.

But when fiction disguises itself as truth, it can become a very dangerous force, putting our lives and futures at risk. The "real world" lacks imagination. It doesn't care what humans believe, or that our "emotional instincts" can usurp our acceptance of the truth. When we, as a society, start believing that our perceptions and desires have become reality, nature will often remind us harshly of the stark truth that our imaginations are *not* in control. Just ask any survivor of war, pestilence, flood, drought, riots, mass shootings, or a pandemic like Covid.

Con men learned long ago of these human emotional vulnerabilities. Ever since, they have used deception and fear to gain wealth and power from a gullible audience. Americans seem to be particularly vulnerable "marks for the con," perhaps because we consume so much fiction in the form of books, movies, games, and television. We truly have become the "United States of Entertainment." It behooves us as a nation to be more discerning and careful when determining fact from fiction.

But even fictional stories benefit from embedded facts. They add verisimilitude.

Therefore, it is useful for this author to point out to you, dear reader, what parts of this story are based on fact and which parts are fictional. Of course, all the events and characters in this story are fictional (with a few notable exceptions) and any resemblance to real persons is purely coincidental.

Flying ace Finnegan Sullivan, Rachel's grandfather, is fictional, as is his Bücker Jungmann, although the two-seater training biplanes do exist. Finnegan himself is loosely based on an amalgam of Irish aces who chose to forego their country's neutrality in World War II and fly for England in the Battle of Britain, saving the country from defeat by the Germans. These foreign fliers were known as "the Few," a moniker given to them by Winston Churchill in a famous speech in which he said, "Never was so much owed by so many to so few."

Likewise, Finnegan's friendship with the famous stunt pilot Bevo Howard is fictional. However, Bevo Howard himself is very real, along with his aerial acrobatics and flying prowess.

This author, as a young Air Force brat during the sixties, had the honor and excitement of watching Bevo Howard perform his upside-down ribbon stunt for President Eisenhower, who often stopped at Spence Air Base for refueling on his way to vacationing in Florida. Spence Air Base still exists in Moultrie, Georgia, where my father worked for Bevo Howard and Hawthorne Aviation. As a flight commander, my father helped many young pilots "earn their wings" before shipping out to fight in World War II and the Korean War.

As for Bevo Howard's infamous Bücker Jungmeister, it flew to America in the hold of the Hindenburg Zeppelin a year prior to its fateful crash on May 6, 1937. Bevo died in 1971 while performing his famous upside-down ribbon stunt but his plane was lovingly reconstructed and now resides inside the Smithsonian's Udvar-Hazy Center at Dulles Airport, hanging in its customary upside-down position.

Maule Aircraft exists. Its factory is still located at the far end of Spence Air Base. They continue to manufacture fabric-covered bush planes with incredibly short takeoff and landing capabilities. Maule bush planes are considered essential transportation in remote areas ranging from Australia to Alaska. I have no doubt that if asked, they would be capable of altering Rachel's fictional Bücker.

When I was a wide-eyed child, I would often sit on my father's knee and listen to his fanciful stories of flying adventure, never quite sure which parts were true and which were "embellished." This book and Rachel's flying adventures have been inspired and dedicated to that childhood experience and to my father.

The concept of a universal flu vaccine is real. There are several companies working to develop such a universal vaccine. The possibilities of gene therapy cures, the regrowth of limbs, the existence of amateur biohackers, and the profit motives of the pharmaceutical industry are with us today. Corporations are experimenting with "pharming" techniques to develop drugs via plants and animals.

The feline disease *Toxoplasma gondii* is real and may have already changed the emotional behavior of over 30 percent of the world's population, through its manipulation of the emotional centers of the brain. The drug scopolamine has been known to produce extreme compliance in victims of theft who have willingly helped the thieves load their booty into a getaway car. It is produced by the burundanga plant, also known as "Devil's Breath," an aptly named henchman for the Devil's Paradox.

Many of the locations in and around Savannah, Georgia, are real, although not all. GenTropics Pharmaceuticals is fictional, as is TaurusSec. The Nerdvana convention is not real either, although perhaps it should be. Obviously Ada Kurz's cabin does not exist but Moon River does. Palm Frites and Pinky's Bait an' Beer are fictional but the Sentient Bean is a real and wonderful coffee house located near Franklin Square. With some effort, one can find information on a network of underground tunnels near the former Candler Hospital that once housed victims of the nation's yellow fever epidemic that occurred in the 1820s.

And finally, most of the historical legacy from the fall of Rome is factual. Much of our modern legal system is derived from the Twelve Tables of the early republican era and the Corpus Juris Civilis, a collection of laws assembled by the emperor Justinian. Modern legal concepts such as habeas corpus, pro bono, affidavits, subpoenas, and the notion that one is innocent until proven guilty, all originated from these Roman documents. Classical architecture, most modern European languages, and the legal definition of a corporation can be traced directly back to the achievements and failures of that very real, one-thousand-year empire. The Praetorian Guard and the Vigiles Urbani were real and controlled much of Roman government during its heyday.

As for the continued existence of the Firemen and the Horsemen, who knows? Perhaps they are the magician's deception, or the con man's lie.

You be the judge.

Acknowledgments

Writing a sequel can often be more challenging than a first work. There is a certain level of expectation by readers and author that adds additional pressure to the mix. I would like to thank my agent, Russ Galen, for his continued support and inspiration, and for keeping me on my toes.

Thanks also goes out to my in-house editors, Bob Gleason and Robert Davis, for their excellent feedback, support, and critique, which resulted in a sequel that exceeds the standards set by *The Seventh Sun*, the logical prequel to *The Third Instinct*.

My kudos go to Esther S. Kim for a brilliant book jacket design. I'd also like to thank Jennifer McClelland-Smith, marketer; Ryan Jenkins, production editor; and Libby Collins, publicist; for their fantastic help and support. Many other members of the Tor/Forge team have undoubtedly contributed to the success of this project, so to them, I extend my heartfelt appreciation as well.

Creative writing is an inexact science and often proceeds forward in fits and starts. I am grateful to Tor/Forge for their eternal patience. The help and support of friends and family has also been invaluable. Thanks to Gary for his creative input into the character of Dak Pell. Finally, a very special and loving thank-you goes out to my wife, Penny, for her undying support and incredible patience.